Between the Cracks

One Woman's Journey from Sicily to America

(*a novel based on a true story*)

Carmela Cattuti

Three Towers Press

Milwaukee, Wisconsin

Published by
Three Towers Press
An imprint of HenschelHAUS Publishing, Inc.
6450 W. Forest Home Ave. Suite 102
Milwaukee, Wisconsin 53220
www.henschelHAUSbooks.com

ISBN: 978159598-239-1
E-ISBN: 978159598-240-7
LCCN: 2013938380

To my family,
who gave me the essence for the form.

Also by Carmela Cattuti:

The Ascent

Table of Contents

Prologue

Across from Italy's mainland sat the city of Messina like an indomitable fortress. Proud of its solid presence, Messina was the travelers' first encounter with the island of Sicily. The earthy colors of the buildings and landscape signaled to the visitor or returning Sicilian that Messina and its people belonged to the island, not to any outside political force or cultural tradition. The clang of the donkey-drawn carts and the voices calling out to customers to buy wares in the market added to the music of the city's sounds. Visitors marveled out loud at the cathedrals and ancient artwork throughout the city, but the locals walked and spoke softly, especially near the narrow slits between the buildings.

Visitors delighted in the snake-like movement of the streets. Most led directly to a famous church or street market but then would slowly veer off in a different direction. They seemed to be designed to intentionally confuse. The city offered no help in arriving at a specific destination.

Ancient buildings were so close together that air barely squeezed through. Residents believed that between the buildings old mysteries sat, holding the true essence of Messina. Townspeople walking close to the openings felt a whisper—not a sound you could hear with your physical ears but heard in your mind. The whisper seemed to convey a yearning that had been imprisoned for hundreds of years. When this happened, people scurried past, heads down.

Hopelessness was the disease that plagued the citizens of Messina during the early twentieth century. The city was so congested with ancient energy it felt like it could explode—and small eruptions did occur. Whenever some of the dark energy needed release, outbursts took place between the locals who were often surly with one another. Their interactions were always based on scarcity, and not just in terms of money. If a resident didn't show enough respect to a compatriot, there would be a confrontation. If someone had more stylish clothes than another, there would be jealousy over their lack of quality clothes. If a citizen had more leisure time than the next person, there would be

1

gossip about how the person with more time for pleasure was lazy and didn't deserve the extra time. Daydreaming was frowned upon. What was the point of daydreaming when it was just fantasy and would never come true?

The city's poor were especially vulnerable to the local mafia and thieves. Many of the men met an early death at the hands of murderers, accidents from factory jobs or shoveling coal, or disease. Women were left to raise children who would most likely not move above their family's social status. The lack of light between the buildings prevented transcendence or change. This cycle had repeated itself for hundreds of years.

The dark energy of Messina was relentless in its hunger for the human spirit. Feeding off people's dreams, it left them with doubt, fear, and misery. This shadowy energy prided itself on soul theft. Once the soul was stolen, an overwhelming amount of energy was required to retrieve it—and few in Sicily were familiar with the practice of soul retrieval.

The neighborhoods were filled with children running, playing, singing, and giggling. Youth were not affected by the dark energy. They nourished each other with joy and playfulness; qualities that the malevolent force could not penetrate. The children breathed deeply and dreamed blissful scenarios of the future, but when they returned to their homes, a grim reality met the physical eyes of many: parents yelling, often with a blow or two to a mother's face or stomach from a drunken father. Imperceptibly, like a slow death from a chronic debilitating disease, the children played less and gave up their bliss and dreams to the heavy energy between the buildings.

The cycle of poverty and abuse branched out through time like a spider unconsciously spinning its web. No police force protected the women or the poor, so the residents lived in fear of everything. Unconsciously, they feared the small spaces between the buildings. At times, a glimmer of light seeped into the locals' fear. This usually took place in their conversation around sunset, when many would gather in the town piazza.

There was talk of freedom and protection in America. The townspeople heard it was a country where anyone could become rich—but more than that, one could become happy. America equaled happiness. They didn't know what happiness felt like, but they were sure they could find it if only they could go to America. However, few had true hope of leaving Messina. The spark of light ignited by these conversations flickered but was extinguished at the last spoken word.

It wasn't that the townspeople couldn't find a way to get to the New World; there just wasn't enough determination or will. When the energy between the buildings took their will, the residents were left with despair. While the Black Plague of the Middle Ages had been cured by an awareness of sanitation techniques, the town's hopelessness could only be cured by cleansing Messina of the dark, heavy energy. This would require a belief that they could reclaim their stolen individuality, comprised of their dreams and hopes. In the end, it was easier to cure the Plague.

The shadowy energy became so thick at times that it took on form. It was a master shape-shifter that became stronger as it gathered human dreams. From the corners of their eyes, the residents would perceive a shape leaning against a building—but when they looked directly at the form, it would vanish. This energy frightened the residents into thinking that they had to stay in the city to remain safe.

The dark energy took whatever it could from the city's residents. But for 13-year-old Angela Lanza, neither her dreams nor her distinct presence could be stolen. Her awareness had never allowed it. Different from her contemporaries, as she entered adolescence, she was increasingly able to communicate with the unseen. She hadn't been afraid of the lurking, mysterious force between the buildings, as visions while she slept had instructed her how to oppose this force.

One night, during a dream, two beings appeared to her. Both had shoulder-length, wavy, light hair and faces glowing with a radiance that compelled her to look away at first. Angela realized she was dreaming and looked back at the faces of the beings, with light streaming toward her. These creatures explained that they were infusing her with light for protection against the dark power of the city. If she paid attention to their guidance, she would live to manifest her dreams and aspirations and use her will to do so.

When she awoke, she felt special. Whenever she was sad, alone, or ridiculed, Angela would think of the two friends from her dream and know everything would be all right. She maintained the integrity of her internal space and knew she could not be violated by the shadowy energy. She stayed away from certain buildings without really knowing why. At times, her body seemed to be guided by an unseen, gentle sensation or a distant voice inside her head. She sensed that her time in Messina would be short—that she wasn't supposed to stay here.

Angela no longer attended school, which was typical of girls of her age. The oldest of three children, it was her responsibility to help her mother. One day, she came home to learn her father who had been a silk trader was killed on the silk trade route and would not return. A few weeks later, a man moved into their house. Her mother explained that he would help with the rent. After a few months, Angela noticed her mother's belly protruding beneath her homemade, faded smock. Angela pretended she did not notice. She thought of her dream friends and felt less alone.

In December of 1908, the earth made a decision that would change the lives of Messina's inhabitants forever. The amount of pressure caused by the malevolent energy between the city's buildings seeped under the earth and into the surrounding area. It nestled itself under Mt. Etna, an active volcano.

After Mt. Etna erupted, causing an earthquake, the city moaned. Screams from the undead, buried under debris, echoed off the skeletons of structural remains. It was as if the earth released a scream that resounded through time, releasing a millennium of abuse and maltreatment.

The morning the earth exploded; Angela was awoken from her sleep. She and her younger brother, Antonio, jumped out of their second-floor window and ran to the edge of the city, where she blacked out and started to drift. She floated above the earth, peering down onto the city. She saw people running, buildings collapsing, and gaping holes in the earth.

Chapter 1
Palermo, 1908

Angela ran down the hot cobblestone street and fell, scrambled to her feet, and ran, then fell again. She threw herself on the street and screamed a long scream that echoed off the ruins of the ancient churches.

Her city, Messina, was a massive graveyard. She searched for her family—her mother, sister and brother. She yelled their names into the air, into demolished houses. She screamed at bodies crushed by fallen beams. Other bodies were caught between the open earth and the street. They were the souls in hell that she had seen in paintings—forever in agony, never at peace.

"Felicita, Felicita!" she shouted, pointing her face toward the sky so that her voice would ascend to heaven and God would hear her plea and have mercy. She lay down, her ear to the broiling ground, as she thought she'd heard the earth growl again—as if it was about to open up and swallow her.

It was a human moan. Looking up, she saw a man impaled by a beam near one of the destroyed houses. He let out another moan. She slowly got up and walked over to him. Blood trickled from his mouth and down his chin, and his eyes were open and fixed.

"Signore, have you seen a small girl?" asked Angela in between gasps and tears. "She is only eight years old with dark hair and eyes?"

The man stared, unable to answer her question. He blinked, and then his head fell to one side as if it were a brick that had been thrown. She felt hot liquid flow down her legs. It warmed her legs from the frigid air.

The earth began to tremble. The cobblestone street in front of the dead man separated, and bodies once buried and lost began to ascend to heaven. She had a vision of her mother rising to the heavens in a long, white dress—the dress in which she had been married many years ago.

"Mama, don't leave me! Mama! I'm scared!"

Angela heard her words echo off the ruins. She opened her mouth again to call after her mother, but no sound came. Every time she tried to yell, no sound came out—but her echoing voice became louder and louder.

She heard herself scream and woke up. Her legs were damp and stuck together with urine. She sat up in bed and squinted, trying to see the other beds in the large dormitory. She heard the rustling of nightclothes. A few of the girls stirred and rolled over.

Angela took a deep breath and dropped back in her bed. It had been three years since the eruption of Mt. Etna and the earthquake, yet she still had this nightmare. The same man always hung from a beam, and her mother always ascended to heaven. And every time, she called for her sister.

~ ~ ~ ~ ~

After the earthquake, a band of homeless children spent the following month roaming the city for loved ones and food until the Americans came with relief. She had been separated from her brother and hoped to find him. Angela smiled the day the Americans came. How happy all the children were! They would at last have food and shelter and be aided in locating their families.

Angela remembered the morning she was on the deck of one of the docked American relief ships and saw two boys walking along the shore. As they came closer to the ship, she recognized them as youths from her neighborhood. She shouted and waved her hands as she ran down the gangplank. Now she was certain she would find her sister and brother. If she were able to run into boys who had lived on her own street, then God would surely unite her with her sister and brother.

"Gino, what happened? Where have you been?" she asked one of the boys as they approached.

"Roaming the hills. A group of us stayed together and hunted for food and shelter. I can't find many people from our area of town."

"Have you seen my family? My little sister and brother are lost. They'll be terrified." Angela grabbed his arm.

"There's no one left of our neighborhood. I've seen no one."

"But you're not sure if my sister is dead. You are not sure? You didn't see her?" Angela kept shaking his arm as if it would trigger a memory about her family's fate.

"No, I'm not sure. I don't even know where my family is," Gino looked off into the distance. She realized he was as lost as she was.

Angela put her arm around Gino's thin shoulders and gave thanks to God that He had sent her someone familiar. They boarded the ship and found a little girl crying as she clung to one of the ship's rails.

"What's wrong?" asked Gino. "Is your family gone?"

"No...my sister lived, but a large stone fell on her legs and now she has no legs. The doctor took them off," cried the little girl.

"Where is your sister now?" asked Angela.

"She's in there," said the little girl, pointing to a door opposite them. "That's where they put all the sick people or all the people who will die."

Angela thought that maybe her sister or brother was beyond that door. Maybe they had been rescued after all. She turned and walked toward the door.

Rows of children lying in beds spread before her. Some cried quietly, and others stared silently at the ceiling. Angela walked along the foot of each bed and looked at the children, praying that one would be her sister. A doctor and a nurse hovered over one child, with the doctor saying they couldn't stop the bleeding from the stumps. Angela looked down at her own legs, wondering what that must feel like. She came to the end of the row, seeing that there was one empty bed. She wondered if the child in that bed had died.

A few weeks later, Angela's brother Antonio found his way to the American ship but was brought to the infirmary with a continuous, harsh cough that medicine could not seem to cure. It was decided that the children would be sent to Catholic convents until families could be found. Angela was sent to a convent in Palermo and Antonio was sent to live with priests in the same city.

Angela was permitted to see Antonio twice a week. Each week, less and less of her brother was left. His energy seemed to move farther and farther away. His presence slowly waned until one day the doctor told Angela that her brother had pneumonia and they could do little for him except make him comfortable.

"Antonio," said Angela, "I am sure you will get better." She held his hand. His skin was hot and brittle, like burned paper. She felt his forehead and kissed his eyelids.

"Stop worrying," said Antonio. He forced his chest to rise, attempting to take in more air.

"I want us to go home," said Angela. "I want us to be together so we can find Mama and Felicita."

"This is a nice place, Angela. You have food and you go to school."

"I want us to go home," said Angela with a whimper. His eyes became glassy and he struggled for air.

"He needs his rest now," said a nurse. "You can see him in a few days."

Angela kissed Antonio goodbye. They both said they would see each other soon.

Angela continued to pray to God and all the saints for Antonio's recovery. She asked her two unseen light beings to intercede for her. She implored them to explain to God that she was alone in the world apart from Antonio. When she could think of no one else to pray to, she pretended she had the power to heal her brother. She imagined that she had a magic wand, would run it over Antonio's body, and he would jump up out of bed ready to take on their situation. She felt frightened about that fantasy. The church strictly forbade any practice of magic, even if it was just in someone's daydreams. She knew time was running out and that the inevitability of death was not far behind.

The last time she saw her brother, he was unresponsive. His breathing was faint, his chest barely moving. He could no longer be there for her. That night, as Angela dreamed her recurring dream, Antonio quietly slipped away.

Angela now had to focus on the search for her sister. She would make it her lifetime quest. Whenever she began to brood or become despondent, she would elevate her thoughts by focusing on her quest. Through this simple choice, Angela learned the alchemy of thought.

As the sun streamed into the dormitory window of the convent, Angela knew that she had to let go of her nighttime thoughts and start another day.

Three Years Later

Angela sat on a bench in the courtyard among the olive trees. It was one of her favorite places in the convent, and she felt protected and happy among the olive trees. It was also a space where she felt comfortable thinking about her two unseen friends who continued to appear in her dreams. She was at peace with these thoughts in the courtyard. If she thought of her light-being friends inside the convent dormitories, she was afraid someone would read her thoughts and that there would be severe repercussions.

"Angela, Angela, why are you sitting here?" asked Patrizia Buttita, appearing behind her.

Patrizia was one of the girls who studied at the convent school but was not an orphan. She was accompanied by a young man.

"I'm waiting for the dinner bell to ring," answered Angela, rather than admitting she sat in the garden to feel safe.

"This is my older brother, Roberto. He's come to visit."

"Hello," said Angela. She remembered seeing Roberto at a distance some time ago.

"*Signorina*, it is a pleasure to meet you. Patrizia has told me how well you sew," said Roberto.

"Roberto is a poet," said Patrizia as she clung to her brother. "He's already quite famous."

Angela had heard Patrizia brag about Roberto. All the girls talked about how they disliked him because of his arrogance, but she knew they all secretly admired him.

Roberto took a deep breath and filled his chest, then extended his hand to Angela. She was amazed at how blue his eyes were—not at all common for a Sicilian.

Angela could see into a person's depth if they locked eyes for any length of time. She could uncover what was hidden. She had learned this from her unseen friends, who told her this skill could carry her through trying times. She could tell by the energy in Roberto's eyes that he kept secrets well.

"It's unusual that you have such blue eyes," said Angela nervously.

She heard Patrizia try to stifle a giggle.

"Sorry. I guess that was stupid to say."

"No, you are absolutely right," said Roberto. "You are an observant girl, Angela. That is what poets are—observers. Observers of character and detail."

Angela touched Roberto's hand and felt the arrogance, sincerity, and humor. She knew he wished her the best.

"Someone so bright should not be alone in the world," said the poet.

"But I am alone," said Angela. "The earthquake took my family. There is no one left. I've made up my mind to become a nun."

"Then the world will have lost someone of value," said Roberto.

"We need to catch our train to Bagheria," said Patrizia.

"We will see each other," said Roberto.

"We will see each other," repeated Angela.

Angela sat back on the bench, envying Patrizia and Roberto's closeness. It was true that Roberto was a little conceited, but he made her feel like she was part of the outer world. What difference would it make to anyone if she became a nun and never walked beyond the convent gates again?

The convent was run by the Sisters of Charity, and many prosperous Sicilian families sent their daughters there to be educated. The convent provided a solid foundation in Latin, mathematics, and the Holy Gospels, and students read the Catholic mystics. The Sisters of Charity was a French order, so French was spoken as well as Italian.

The convent was part of Piazza Butera and the building was donated by the Prince and Princess of Palermo. The order had accumulated religious paintings dating back two hundred or more years. These graced the corridors, the church, and every room of the convent. For Angela, it was as if her unseen friends had shined the light of fortune on her because without the convent, her education would have been truncated.

The sisters were known for the art of sewing and embroidery. In the modern world, sewing was becoming a lost art, but the sisters preserved the techniques. They passed down their knowledge and skill as a high art form. They preserved their creations as carefully as they did the paintings on their convent walls. All the girls learned the techniques and produced intricate works of art on tablecloths, bedspreads, and clothing.

Not only did Angela receive an education, she also connected with girls from other social classes. The horror of the earthquake was somewhat tempered by the creative and social opportunities provided by convent life. Families who were aspiring to rise in social standing were happy to pay the convent—not only to educate their daughters, but to improve the girls' marriage prospects through the culture and decorum of the school.

Angela often felt guilty about her good fortune to be part of the convent. The people of Messina had been uneducated and poor prior to the earthquake; those who survived were worse off now. Her situation had improved. She wished she could share her new life with her sister, and she still held out hope that her sister would one day find her. Angela imagined Felicita walking up the convent road with her arms outstretched, eager to embrace her.

Angela brought her focus back to the present and her dilemma. She needed to commit more fully to her Latin studies if she wanted to enter the convent as a novice.

~ ~ ~ ~ ~

One year later, Angela sat on a bench near a bustling thoroughfare in downtown Palermo. Angela had forgotten about the rhythm of city life: ladies hurrying to the market to buy dinner, the men sitting in cafes sipping wine or espresso. She was waiting for the Mother Superior and Filomina to come out of the cheese shop.

Out of the corner of her eye, Angela noticed a young man sitting in a café across the street. She thought she had seen him leaning against the city gates earlier. He is a foreigner, she thought. She noticed a gold watch shining on his left wrist and a red stone ring sparkling on his finger. He seemed to be a stranger, because Sicilian men still carried large pocket watches—yet there was something familiar about him. His clothing was Italian, his mustache European, and yet she sensed a foreign element. She felt that men in general were strange creatures anyway.

The Mother Superior and Filomina came out of the shop. The Mother Superior looked inside the shopping bag.

"Oh, I have forgotten something. Girls, wait here."

Angela felt the man across the street staring at them. She stood and started to pace.

"What's wrong with you?" asked Filomina, her hair tied back in a bun. Filomina's orange hair and blue eyes were the envy of all the girls at the convent. She also liked to read modern-day love stories about princes and princesses and castles. Angela felt that reading those novels was a waste of time. Everyone knew that fairy tales were false, and those things never happened. She encouraged Filomina to read St. Anthony's writings.

"Are you ready, girls?" asked the Mother Superior as she came out of the shop.

"Yes, Mother," said Angela.

"Please button your collar, Angela," said the Mother Superior.

"It was hot, and I thought..." Angela quickly buttoned her top collar.

"I know what you thought, but you must never forget modesty," said the Mother Superior as the three began the walk back to the convent.

~ ~ ~ ~ ~

In the room she shared with three other girls, Angela opened the chest of drawers and pulled out a long, white nightgown. She took down her hair, which had been coiled on her head, and unraveled her braid. Picking up a brush, she stroked the dark hair from her forehead to her waist.

"Why did you two get to go with Mother Superior today?" asked Maria, one of the older girls.

"Because Mother knows what hard workers we are," said Filomina.

"We all work hard," said another girl with pink cheeks. "It's not fair for only two to go on an outing."

"It was not an outing," said Angela. "We had to accompany Mother to town because she needed help with packages."

"What? She needed help with two packages?" said Maria, her hand on her hip. "I saw you coming back with only two packages. She didn't need any help."

"So she wanted us for company. And anyway, it is none of your business," replied Filomina.

"Some company," said the pink-cheeked girl.

The French doors swung open, and a tall nun with porcelain skin appeared. Sister Eveline was Mother Superior's secretary and made sure the Mother Superior's requests were carried out. The girls had dubbed her "The Scribe," because she always carried a writing pad under her arm.

"Girls, girls," Eveline clapped her hands, her veil shielding half her face. "Everyone in bed, please." She paused and searched the room until her eyes rested on Angela.

"Angela, Mother Superior would like to see you in her office before you go to class tomorrow morning."

All eyes turned toward Angela.

"About what, Sister?" Angela asked softly.

"I cannot speak for the Mother Superior," said the nun. "Go to bed."

She backed out of the room and closed the doors. The girls knelt beside their beds for prayer.

Angela wondered what the Mother Superior wanted. Maybe they had found some clue as to her sister's whereabouts. That must be it! The authorities had discovered someone who had seen her, or maybe an article of Felicita's clothing.

She looked around and saw the other girls blessing themselves and getting into their beds.

"Amen," said Angela loudly and got up to turn down her bed linen. As she drifted off to sleep, her sister's likeness formed and dissolved in her mind's eye. She tried to freeze one of the images to look deeper, but the picture kept morphing. She could no longer hold the images as she drifted off to sleep.

Angela floated in space over her city, Messina, and looked down at its ruins. It looked like the black and white photographs taken after the earthquake. With her intention, she slowly lowered herself down into the middle of the black and white world. It was still and deserted, and as she called her sister's name, there was no echo.

"I am here," Angela said.

Suddenly her unseen friends emerged from the ruins. They smiled and told Angela that Messina was a static world now and that she would not return.

"Where is my sister?"

Her unseen friends looked toward one of the ruins. Angela's eyes followed.

Felicita stepped out of the tumbled walls and broken beams and waved Angela toward her. She wore the same nightgown she had on the day of the earthquake. Angela frantically waved back.

"I am here, Felicita! Wait for me!"

Felicita ran into the shell of the building. Angela ran after her.

"Wait, Felicita! Where are you going?"

When Angela reached the building, there was no trace of her sister.

"Felicita!" called Angela. "Where are you? I have been searching for you."

She called out again. There was no response. Her unseen friends appeared, but they said nothing. Angela had the feeling that they wanted her to wake up. She awoke, dripping with sweat.

~ ~ ~ ~ ~

Angela tapped lightly on the Mother Superior's door.

"Come in, Angela," rasped the older woman's voice.

Angela slowly opened the door and walked up to the heavy oak desk. She put her right foot behind the left, grasped her skirt on either side, and curtsied.

"You wanted to see me, Mother?" asked Angela, her head still bowed. She noticed that the nun had her veil pinned back so her face was exposed. Angela tried to survey the nun's face without being obvious. She loved the nun's long hooked nose and high cheekbones, which gave her an air of dignity and strength that Angela admired and wanted for her own life.

"Yes, I have something very important to discuss with you," said the nun as she stood up. "A young man has come from America and has taken a liking to you."

13

Angela parted her lips to speak, but the nun held up her hand.

"Let me explain. Yesterday when you and Filomina went into the city with me, it was not because I needed help, but because this young man wanted to see two of the most eligible girls at the convent. He is Sicilian by birth, but he went to America when he was twelve years old. Now he would like to marry."

"But, Mother, ever since my family died in the earthquake, I have decided to become a nun," said Angela.

"I realize that. But you are seventeen now, and this will be a good test for you. I would like you to meet this man. He comes from a good family. His cousins still live outside of Palermo. I think you should meet him."

Angela raised her head and saw a firm seriousness in the nun's eyes. She thought about a delivery boy for whom she had once felt an attraction. She used to wait behind the garden wall for him to deliver milk and eggs to the convent. He would smile and nod at her when he came, and she would be happy for the rest of the day.

"Mother, I am sure I want to become a nun," said Angela.

"Angela, I want you to be clear about your decision to take vows. If you take your vows and decide that the spiritual life is not for you, then you would have to leave the convent immediately."

"Mother, but I would have no place to go."

"Yes, that is why I want you to meet this man. You must consider all your options. At any rate, Franco Bellini has traveled all the way from America. I am asking you to meet him. If you decide not to marry, then you can stay with us and become a nun."

Angela realized the Mother Superior really wanted to test her. If she should refuse this test, then the nun would always wonder whether she had made the right choice in admitting Angela to the order.

"I will see him, Mother," said Angela, "because you have gone to so much trouble."

"I am glad," said the nun. "This way you can make the best choice for your life."

The convent bell tolled.

"It is time to go to the sewing room. I will make the necessary arrangements for you to meet Mr. Bellini."

"All right, Mother," said Angela. She curtsied and left the office. Angela wondered why the nun was so adamant about her meeting this man. Did the

Mother Superior think that she was too weak to become a nun? Maybe she thought her inadequate in some way. Angela had seen several wealthy women admitted to the convent who brought beautiful possessions with them and donated their money to the convent. Angela had no money or worldly possessions to give. Maybe the Reverend Mother would see her as a burden if she became part of the order and not as an asset. Angela's thoughts swirled as she made her way down the stone-lined corridor.

~ ~ ~ ~ ~

The noise from the sewing machines seemed louder than usual, and Angela's shoulders ached from maintaining the same position for hours. She rubbed her shoulders and looked up from the sewing table to stare at the statue of the Blessed Virgin overseeing the work they were doing. She wondered what the Virgin thought of her intended meeting with a strange man. Did she think her weak? After all, she had promised herself to God. Angela prayed that she was still under the Virgin's protection.

"So, what did Reverend Mother want to talk to you about?" whispered Filomina.

"I can't say right now," said Angela.

"Oh, tell me now! I can't wait!"

"Shh! Girls, please maintain silence during work time," said Sister Ramona, the sewing teacher.

Angela wondered about the future, not only about her own but that of the other girls as well. What would happen to them?

"Angela, are you going to spend the afternoon daydreaming or sewing?" asked the nun.

"She's always daydreaming," said the girl sitting across from Angela.

"I'm sorry if I have not been working. I will try to pay attention to the work at hand."

Angela could feel everyone's eyes on her. She knew what they were all thinking: Angela is the privileged one. Her embroidered linens were always the ones chosen for the altar where the priest offered mass. They were always the most beautiful and the most original because she made up her own designs. The other girls were always jealous of her good fortune. Angela decided that she would not say anything to anyone, not even to Filomina, until she met with Franco Bellini.

~ ~ ~ ~ ~

It had been nine years since Franco had seen his homeland, and it was wonderful to see his cousins, aunts, and uncles again. He had a fondness for one cousin, Roberto, who had become a famous Sicilian poet. It was Roberto who suggested he visit the convent if he wanted to find a wife. He had guessed Franco's purpose for returning to Sicily before he said anything about it.

Roberto introduced Franco to some well-bred neighborhood girls who wanted to go to the United States because of the affluence of American life. Franco knew better. He wanted someone who knew how to work and was willing to build a home with him. He also wanted someone without family ties. He was only able to take care of one person, and that person would have to have a skill to make money. He found the Mother Superior had a sympathetic ear for his quest.

~ ~ ~ ~ ~

"Don't men in America wear cuff links?" asked the old nun as she focused on her embroidery. Franco sat across from her with his fedora in his lap. He was not able to see her face, just her gnarled fingers.

"I'm glad the Reverend Mother chose me to be the chaperone," said the nun. "I always like hearing about America."

"They're making shirts with buttons on the sleeves now, Sister," said Franco. He uncrossed his legs and settled back in his chair, wondering if she had noticed his hands. They were rough from working out-of-doors. Franco looked around at the heavy antique furniture in the second-floor visiting room of the convent. The old Roman grandfather clock ticked in the corner. When there was silence, the ticking was so loud it seemed to echo. He heard a light tap at the door. The nun continued to embroider. Another tap.

"Sister, there's someone at the door," said Franco cautiously.

"Well, then open it. It's for you," said the nun. Franco opened the door.

Angela's eyes and mouth opened wide when she saw Franco. "Where is Sister Regina?" asked Angela. "She is to be here."

"She's in the chair," said Franco, taking in Angela's face. "I'm afraid she doesn't hear very well."

The nun got up from her chair, grabbed her cane, and slowly limped over to the couple.

"I am here to make introductions," said the nun. The sides of her veil shielded her cheeks. "Angela Lanza, this is Franco Bellini, who has come from America to find a wife. Franco, this is Angela who has been under the good sisters' care since the earthquake in Messina four years ago. Please sit, the two of you."

Franco took a seat closest to the fireplace. The nun touched Angela's arm.

"I have no eyes to see nor ears to hear. Talk to your friend."

Angela touched the nun's hand. She had always liked Sister Regina. Of all the nuns, Angela felt she was the most perceptive, and she was glad Mother Superior had chosen her as the chaperone. Angela eased herself onto the chair across from Franco, and the old nun sat in the corner near the grandfather clock.

Angela felt there was something familiar about this man. She noticed his gold watch and looked at his mustache.

"You...you were the man outside the cheese shop the other day." Angela suddenly felt exposed. He had seen her while she was unaware. She had been on display.

"Yes, Reverend Mother wanted me to see two girls. I don't know why, but she did." Franco noticed the light blue veins standing out on the backs of Angela's finely boned hands. The skin on her face was smooth and clear—an olive color like the landscape.

"Things have changed since I lived here," said Franco.

"You have been away for a long time," said Angela. "You know the world, and I only know Sicily." Angela wondered if she still, in fact, did know Sicily. After all, she lived in a convent and did not venture out much.

Franco said, "There's no steady work here. People are brutal here sometimes. In America, I can work hard and keep all my money. No one tries to take it away. I live outside of New York City and work for nuns doing plumbing, gardening, and landscaping. People say I would make a good lawyer, except I don't have an education."

"But you can be educated in America," said Angela.

"I had to leave school when I was fifteen to support my mother, brother, and sister in America. They all live in the city at the moment, and I send them money."

Angela looked more closely at the ring on Franco's left hand. A dark red stone was mounted in a yellow-gold setting. She became uneasy when she thought it could be from a girl.

"I am staying in Bagheria with my cousin Roberto. He suggested I come to the convent and choose a girl."

"Roberto Mineo?" asked Angela.

"Yes, do you know him?"

"His sister studies here. She is a friend of mine." Angela was pleased with the connection. She felt a little less like a commodity.

"Well, he said there were many beautiful girls here to choose from."

Angela wondered if Roberto thought her beautiful.

"Your ring is lovely," said Angela.

"My father gave me this ring when I was a boy. He said it would protect me. Many of the old people were superstitious."

"Do you really think it's just superstition?" asked Angela, relieved that his father had given him the ring. "When I was a girl in Messina, there was this old beggar man who was said to be a fortune teller. A few days before the earthquake, he sat in the street and told everyone to leave the city because there was going to be a great disaster."

"There are many coincidences," said Franco.

Angela felt content with Franco's answers, as he seemed clear about himself and what he wanted. She could tell he used his head for reasoning. Unlike Franco, Angela always felt there was a cloud surrounding her at the convent that kept her from seeing things as they were. The cloud followed her throughout her day and permeated her daydreams.

"Why don't you live with your mother and family? Why live apart?" asked Angela.

"Because I like the country. City life is not for me. Besides, I do not want to work for a big boss. I like to work for myself. Eventually I will bring my mother and sister to the country."

"Mother Superior said you were hardworking and responsible, and I see that you are," said Angela. She twisted the handkerchief in her lap, looked over at the nun, and whispered, "If I had a family, I would take care of them the way you do." Angela wondered if she could be brave enough to be married and away from the nuns' protection.

Franco smiled.

"My family died in the earthquake," Angela continued. The nuns have been good to me here and have become my family. I am grateful for all they've done for me."

"Angela, time is up. We have to go to afternoon vespers," announced the old nun.

Angela and Franco stood up.

"You will have another meeting next week, so don't worry. You'll see each other again before Mr. Bellini goes back to America."

"Yes, I must go back to American and get back to work because Mother Superior said I have to have a certain amount saved before, if you consent, we get married. I have to wait a year before I return to Palermo," said Franco.

"Oh, I see," said Angela. She was relieved that she had more time to think but upset that she had more time to be confused.

"We'll see each other next week?" asked Franco.

"We will see each other," said Angela. He took her hand and held it for a second. It was the first time someone had touched her like that. It made her smile.

The old nun opened the oak door, and Franco waved as the door closed.

"Well, Angela, do you like him?" asked the old nun.

"Yes, Sister, I like him. He seems like a good man."

"Yes, he seems like a good one, all right," said the nun as she led Angela out of the room. "In my day, our parents chose our husbands. Fortunately, when my parents saw that I had a calling to be a nun, they did not hold me back."

Angela thought about the new feeling she'd just experienced. It was so pleasingly different from the atmosphere of the convent, where everyone seemed to walk around in a haze. At times it felt like she was floating, even with the nuns' strict discipline. If she felt that way about living here as a student, what would it feel like as a nun?

"Sister, can I ask you something?" asked Angela.

"Of course. I am so old that I no longer have secrets," replied the nun.

"What does it feel like being a nun?"

"Feel like? What do you mean?"

"I mean, do you feel like you are disconnected all the time, not being in the outside world?"

"Do you mean to ask if I miss the outside world?"

"No, not exactly, but have you come to know yourself living in the convent all these years? I do not think I'm asking the question properly. I guess I'm confused."

The nun looked up and past Angela, with her eyes tilting as if she drew information from the inside of her forehead. "I think I have come to know myself. After sixty years here, I'm sure I would certainly know if I had not."

"Yes, Sister," said Angela.

"Angela, you have to choose which life is more suited to you, and only you know that. Now make your way to vespers and pray to be guided."

"Yes, Sister."

Angela walked down the corridor to the chapel. She could feel the air change the closer she came to the chapel door. Before going in, she looked back toward where she had just come from. She felt a difference in her body, as if she had just crossed the border from her old life in Messina. She knew a choice had to be made.

~ ~ ~ ~ ~

Franco walked slowly down the stone stairs to the first floor of the convent. He came to a landing where a huge painting of the Virgin Mary hung. She appeared to be opening her arms to him with a sad face. He paused for a moment and looked at the Madonna's delicate, white hands and long, blond hair. He thought about how much Angela's physical appearance had appealed to him—her glowing skin, liquid brown eyes, and lovely dark hair.

It seemed that in America, everyone preferred fair hair. The men wanted blond hair on their women, and the women even bleached their hair to be more attractive. Even the women wanted their men to be blond. Franco had pretended that he liked blond hair for a time, but that did not last.

His mother had always told him that red-haired and blond women were untrue to their husbands. He did not know if that was true or not, but he knew he needed to find a partner—and he was not thrilled with the prospect of marrying an American woman. American women were nationalistic, but not as committed to hard work. Besides, most parents wanted their daughters to marry doctors and lawyers—not an immigrant laborer.

Franco walked down the front steps and went out into the late afternoon Sicilian sun. The sun's warmth penetrated his face and body, and Angela's face began to form in his mind. Oval brown eyes, a strongly defined nose. The collar of her blouse had been buttoned up, but he could see that she had a long and elegant neck. Her arms were full, and when she stood up, he saw her well-formed breasts and slim waist.

Angela had no family left, and Franco's only ties to Sicily were his cousins. There would be no reason to return if he and Angela were married. His spine tensed. He wondered if that was the best thing—to have no ties beyond a few relatives. In America, he had his mother, sister, and brother. Maybe he should marry someone more connected to a family and to Sicily.

He walked along the back streets of Palermo. Smells of freshly baked bread drifted from several basement bakeries. It was just after siesta, and the streets were beginning to fill with people on afternoon strolls. Adults and children were licking ice cream cones and walking, stopping occasionally to talk to a shopkeeper who was just reopening his store for the evening's business. A child ran ahead of his father, shouting and crying. The man quickly ran after his son. His arms gestured wildly in the air like cooked pasta. Franco smiled. Only a Sicilian could balance an ice cream cone and packages and still express himself with his arms and hands.

There is nothing like this in America, he said to himself. Life, it seemed, took place inside everyone's houses in America. He remembered when he was a boy and had once played on the streets of Palermo with other children. They were all from poor families, but that did not matter. They had each other. He thought about the old man who used to come out and play soccer with the boys in the late afternoon. The old man was as spry and agile as the youngsters with whom he played. He often amazed the boys with his ability to jump and leap like a frog. Franco remembered how they called the old man the "Toothless One," because he said that he had been born without teeth. He showed the boys his smooth pink gums— "the healthiest in the city," he would say, because they never had to suffer the disruption of teeth pushing through.

One day, when Franco and his friends waited for the "Toothless One" in the usual place, he never came. After a few days, a neighborhood priest told the boys that the old man had died alone and penniless in a hut on the outskirts of the city. It had saddened Franco—not because of his death, as he would certainly miss him, but the way the old man had died: alone and destitute.

Franco sauntered into the Botanical Gardens across from the Cathedral of Palermo. The Gardens had not been there when he was a boy. It would have been unheard of. Why would anyone put wild trees and plants in the middle of a city? Nature was not meant to be ordered like that. Nevertheless, he walked in. The air was wet and thick. The tropical atmosphere was life-giving to the plants, but not to humans. He decided to leave.

As he turned toward the entrance, he heard a plop coming from a small pond under a few palm trees. He heard it again and walked over to the small pond. Lily pads floated on the surface of the water, and the banks of the pond were covered with vegetation unfamiliar to Franco. He saw a small green frog sitting still on one of the lily pads. The frog stared at Franco as if to see what he would do next. Franco thought of the old man who had once leaped like one of these creatures. At least the frog had somewhere to leap to, thought Franco.

Franco walked toward the gate and heard another plop as he went out into the street.

~ ~ ~ ~ ~

Franco sat on the porch of his cousin's villa and smoked a cigar. He looked out over the Mediterranean Sea and watched the dome of the Cathedral of Palermo slowly fade as the sun set. The houseboy was picking up the last of the dinner dishes.

"Would you like more wine, sir?" asked the houseboy.

"No, no, thank you," said Franco. He wondered what his cousin thought of his coming from the Land of Plenty without a maid and living in a rooming house. Maybe his cousin thought him foolish.

"Well, Franco, tell me what you're contemplating, staring out over our sea," said Roberto as he came out with a newspaper under his arm. He often declared ownership of the Sicilian landscape, as if he had just paid God for his handiwork. He sat down in the recliner next to Franco.

"Damn Socialists, they're taking over Italy. They make me sick," said Roberto as he glanced at the paper. "My next book of poetry will denounce the bastards."

"The poetry you printed in the newspapers denounced the Socialists and the Mafia. Haven't you had any trouble from that?" asked Franco.

"I have had a few threatening letters, but nothing has happened. Besides, I never worry. They would never harm Sicily's rising national poet. Anyway, these types are not interested in words. They feel that words can do little. Blood is what makes people act and react in this country."

"I see you have great expectations for your words," said Franco, smiling.

"I say what I feel the Sicilian people feel and think, so why shouldn't I be commended for being the voice of my people?" The poet poured a glass of wine, and as he drank, he raised his little finger.

"All these problems are why my mother left here with her children," said Franco. "It's all misery and tears." He flicked the ashes off his cigar.

"Not completely. Sometimes people are happy—and when they are happy, it is a sight to behold," said the poet.

"Is that why you stay?" asked Franco.

"I stay for that and for many other reasons. The major one is that I am the speaker for the people here. They have no one else to give them voice."

Franco stepped on his cigar and turned toward his cousin.

"Roberto, how can you speak for the people? You have money. You have a big villa overlooking Palermo, a houseboy, and an apartment in town."

"They still feel that I speak for them, and I feel I do. Franco, remember when we didn't have money, years ago when we were boys here? We helped our families. I have never had an education. I am a self-made man—a poet. You, too—you're self-made. My father did well in the cheese and wine business and made some money, so there was no need to emigrate. I've decided to stay, and you have not."

Franco said nothing. If he had been of money, would he have left his country? He couldn't answer that. He would like to think he would have left anyway. There was always more opportunity in the New World, especially if you had money. Franco knew he hadn't done as well as his cousin, but he had plans.

"And now," said Roberto as he poured another glass of wine, "you've come back looking for a wife."

"I can't find the wife I want in America." Franco shifted in his chair. He wondered how well the New World had served him.

"How was your meeting with Angela today? I have met her. She's beautiful. She also speaks both Italian and Sicilian."

"I think she will make a good wife if she accepts my offer," said Franco.

"And when will you marry?" asked Roberto.

Franco thought about the humiliation he would suffer if Angela should decide not to marry him.

"I will marry when it's time."

"So my suggestion to go to the convent to find a wife has been beneficial?" asked the poet as he sipped his wine. "And you really never met a woman in America you wanted to marry?"

"Well, there was one woman I would have considered, but she was a cousin of ours and I didn't want to marry someone so closely related."

"Cousin? What cousin?"

"Bella. Bella Visconti. She had been living in America with her father, who died last year. She later had to come back to Sicily and settle his estate."

"Oh, yes," said Roberto. "A pretty woman with some money now, I hear. She wanted to marry you?"

Franco remembered the day Bella had held her hand out to him: it felt like the finest linen; soft and supple. She was in mourning for her father and dressed in black. They had sat out on her front porch and talked. He told her how his own father had been killed while working on the train tracks. An approaching train didn't sound its whistle, and his father couldn't hear the train because of construction noise. He told Bella how they had to sew parts of his body together for his wake. He had felt close to Bella and liked her, but they were cousins. The familial relationship was too close.

"We liked each other," said Franco as he lit a cigar. He sat next to Roberto.

"You are sly," laughed the poet. "You will dance around the edge of things. I admire that."

Franco refrained from telling his cousin what he had suspected. Bella couldn't stay in America without an American husband. She had been born in Sicily and was able to stay in America because her father had appropriate papers. Franco questioned her motives.

"I don't want to marry someone who is related to me. I've seen it too much here. What happens is not good."

"Ah, yes, Americans don't inter-marry. They're against it. In Sicily, you can marry your first cousin. It keeps land and possessions in one family. That's why Bella wanted to marry you. If she married a stranger, he could steal from her. Well, I think you've made a fine choice with Angela."

"I think I'll go to bed," said Franco as he stretched.

"Well, pleasant dreams, cousin. They say that when you sleep while in Sicily, your dreams become so vivid they seem like reality. I hope you enjoy them."

Franco heard Roberto's laughter resonate down the hallway as he walked to his room. Sometimes Franco couldn't understand his cousin's conversation. He didn't know why Roberto said certain things. Dreams are dreams, regardless of where you sleep. It's all one sky.

~ ~ ~ ~ ~

Franco took off his vest and loosened his tie. A wooden cross hung over the bed with several leaves from a palm tree attached to it. Franco was glad his room was in back, where he could hear nothing but the crickets. He sat on the edge of the bed and took off his shirt. He pushed his torso back toward the head of the bed and rested his head on the pillow. Franco watched his chest rise and fall with each inhale and exhale, and then he drifted off into a soft sleep, still imagining his first view of Angela.

~ ~ ~ ~ ~

Franco sat at a small round table at an outdoor café, and he watched two young women come out of the wine and cheese shop across the street. One had flaming red hair that seemed to burn with energy from the rays of the sun. The other had deep brown hair that glistened with reddish and chestnut highlights.

Franco wondered why he was sitting in the café. He looked down to glance at his gold watch, but it was gone. His starched, white linen shirt had been replaced with the typical wool jersey of a peasant. Suspenders clung to either side of his chest, holding up an old pair of cotton trousers. Franco pushed himself back from the table and gasped.

"Where are my clothes?" he shouted in English. He tried to speak Sicilian but was unable to pull the words together to utter a sentence. Only English came out.

"Can't someone help me?" he shouted as he stood up and addressed the other patrons. They all sat in silence and stared. Franco suddenly recognized Angela as one of the girls across the street. He ran over to her. As he drew closer, her features changed and she resembled his cousin Bella. He began to back away.

"Bella, tell me where Angela has gone," he said in English. Bella was silent and held out her arms to him. She put her finger to her lips to encourage him to be silent. He turned and looked at the patrons of the café. They all sat in silence.

Franco turned and began to run down a long, but familiar, street. He saw First Avenue written on one of the street signs. A woman's figure was at the end of the street. He approached her cautiously. He couldn't make out her features, as there was a heavy fog. As he came closer, her figure faded.

When he awoke, he was drenched in a cold sweat. He sat up and saw that he had never finished undressing. For the first time, he felt homesick for the United States. He looked out the window and saw that the sun was climbing between the buildings. Another six days and he'd be home. He would be glad to sleep in his own bed again, even though he lived in just one room. He had his freedom, which was all that mattered. Once Angela joined him, he would have his own home.

With a hint of morning coming through the window, Franco got out of bed and went to the kitchen. The housekeeper handed him coffee with steamed milk. He walked out onto the terrace, where he watched the sun come up over the Mediterranean. Franco had often thought of this body of water as the Sicilian Sea. When he was a boy, he couldn't imagine anyone but the Sicilians enjoying the water that was so much a part of their culture. He marveled at the view from his cousin's villa. There was neither a more beautiful view in the world nor one so deceiving. He knew that underneath all the beauty and serenity was a confused and despondent population.

It was strange, but he actually felt that Bella was the one who had originally put the idea in his head to come back to Sicily and marry. When he saw that Bella thought nothing of marrying her own cousin, he understood that the tradition of intermarriage did not dissolve when people left Sicily. He knew he wanted to marry someone from his own culture, so he decided to return to Sicily and marry a complete stranger. Then he met Angela, an orphan who could leave Sicily without the bonds of family. Angela owned no land or possessions, nor would she want to, after what the earth here had done to her family. All he had to do was take her to America to start a new life. They would both leave their connection to Sicily behind.

Franco left the terrace as the brilliant morning sun illuminated the sky.

~ ~ ~ ~ ~

Angela tossed and turned. Life had always seemed like a dream to her, and now more so than ever. Why did this man have to show himself to her, especially now? If he hadn't come, she would have taken her novice vows in a year and spent the rest of her life in the convent. She would have been safe inside the solid structure, rarely venturing out into the world. Her future would have been decided for her. Now she had to choose.

26

She rolled on her right side and listened. She heard slow, shallow breathing and an occasional rustle of sheets. Everyone else was asleep. Slowly, she sat up in bed and lifted her bed covers. She quietly put on her dressing gown and got down on the floor, crawling on all fours to the door. Cautiously, she turned the doorknob and eased out into the corridor. She stood and closed the door carefully behind her.

Old oil paintings, many painted by nuns hundreds of years ago, hung on the hallway walls. Other artwork had been collected by the convent. Angela had never noticed them much during the day, because the reflection of the sunlight made them difficult to see. But at night, the flickering gaslight enhanced their presence as she made her way down the hall. Some of the paintings made her uncomfortable, and the one she disliked the most was directly across from the door to the chapel. It portrayed disasters in Italian history and calamities in the Bible: the Great Flood, the crucifixion of Christ, and the destruction of Pompeii. The eruption of Mt. Vesuvius was depicted as well, which was not from the Bible and left Angela wondering why the nuns had included the painting in their collection. She turned away from the painting, opened the door to the chapel, and slipped inside.

A large statue of the Virgin Mary stood on a pedestal and overlooked the altar. Candles were placed on both sides of the statue; their flames cast a shadow on the figure's flowing gown. Her left arm was down by her side, and her right hand pointed to her chest, where a red heart sat with an arrow through it.

Angela slowly approached the figure. In times of confusion, she would always pray to the Blessed Virgin Mary for comfort. In the past, these were in times of need. This time, she needed guidance in choosing a life path. She also knew she needed practical advice, independent of the Catholic Church. Her light-being friends came to mind, but she was standing in front of the Christ's mother. Knowing this would be frowned upon, she dismissed thoughts of her dream friends and went up to the altar, looked around, and fell to her knees. Angela bent forward and put her face on the floor. She stretched her arms forward and laid her fingers out on the floor.

"Please, Mother. Tell me what to do," she whispered as if a throat infection had stripped her voice from its normal pitch. "How can I leave my home here at the convent and go with a stranger? If you want me to go, I will—but I need a sign that you want me to go. Please, Mother, help me."

Maybe God wanted her to marry and have children. Maybe that was her destiny in life and not the convent. How was she to know which was right for her?

For the next few days, she would have to watch and listen carefully for a sign. She was sure the Virgin would help her, but she knew she had to pay close attention so she wouldn't miss it. Angela made the sign of the cross, genuflected, and left the chapel.

She cautiously opened the dormitory door, closed it, and slipped in between the sheets. She felt content.

"Where have you been?" whispered Filomina.

"Why didn't you let me know you were awake!" gasped Angela. Her heart thumped.

"I didn't want to frighten you. I heard you go out. Where did you go?"

"To pray."

"At this hour? You went out to pray at this hour? What's going on?"

"I don't want to say just now," whispered Angela.

"Why not?"

"Filomina, I just don't. If you're truly my friend, you won't ask again."

"All right, but you're lucky you didn't get caught. Will you tell me soon?"

"Yes, as soon as I know."

"Know what?" asked Filomina in a normal tone.

"Shh! As soon as I know, I'll tell you. Now go to sleep."

~ ~ ~ ~ ~

Franco climbed the convent stairs and knocked on the sitting room door, carrying a bouquet of flowers and a box of chocolates he had bought in town. The old nun opened the door and motioned for him to take a seat. He had thought about what he would say if Angela had decided not to accept his offer, but something inside had reassured him that she would say yes. The knock came, and the old nun let Angela in. Franco stood up.

"What lovely flowers," said Angela. "I don't eat much candy, though."

"You could share the chocolates with the other girls," said Franco. "I'm sure they would enjoy them." He touched her hand as she accepted his gifts. She sat in a chair opposite him.

"I'm sorry if I seem a bit tired, but I got up extra early to finish some linen for the Princess of Palermo. She had seen my work on the priests' vestments and then asked me to do some embroidery and sewing for her."

"Wouldn't you like to have your own home to work in?" asked Franco. "And have your own dining room table to make linens for?"

"Yes, I would," said Angela.

"Then you accept my proposal?" asked Franco. He realized he was too abrupt, but it had slipped out of his mouth. He was surprised at his own question.

"I accept your offer," said Angela. "But Reverend Mother said we have to wait a year. If you feel the same at the end of this period, then you can return to Sicily and we can be married."

"Mother Superior told me that before we met," said Franco. "I also have to have a certain about of money saved. I accept these conditions. I may come back in between this time so we can get to know one another better." Franco had already saved quite a bit of money, anticipating that he would marry someday.

Franco looked over at the old nun. Her head was bowed, and she seemed to have dozed off. He reached over and touched Angela's cheek. She touched his wrist.

The old nun sat back in her chair and pulled out a pocket watch from underneath the panel in her habit.

"I am sorry to say, but you young people have only five minutes left." She snapped the watch shut, put it back underneath her habit, and bowed her head again.

"I thought she was asleep," said Franco. He kept his hand at Angela's cheek.

"One never knows with Sister Regina," said Angela.

"One never knows what?" asked Franco.

"Anything. She keeps to herself." Angela smiled.

He loved her smile. It warmed him. He grasped her fingers, and their hands fell to Angela's lap.

"You won't come back," she said. "This will be the last time I will see you."

"I'll come back." He squeezed her hand again.

~ ~ ~ ~ ~

Angela sat at the sewing table with several other girls. She cranked the wheel to the sewing machine and held the linen steady. Five months had passed since Franco left, and she could still see his well-shaped mustache and broad smile. She wondered if he would return to visit as he had promised. If he did, a whole new life would present itself and she would have to accept it—good or bad.

"Where are you today, Angela?" asked one of the girls.

"Yes, it seems that every day she picks a different spot on the wall to stare at," said another girl.

"She's thinking of her beloved. You know—the man from America. The one who looks so uncomfortable all the time. Like he doesn't know where he belongs," said the first girl.

"Do you really think he looks uncomfortable?" asked Angela.

"Well, I only saw him enter the building," she said. "Maybe it's because he'd been away for such a long time. You know, just because you grow up in a place doesn't mean that you'd be comfortable there again."

"We should be quiet," said Angela. "Sister will be back soon, and we should not be talking."

Angela pushed the linen under the needle and cut the thread. She thought about how uncomfortable she might be in New York, even with other Italians. Most of her life had been spent inside the convent with a French order of nuns—not out in the streets of Palermo or with its people.

The door to the sewing room swung open. Angela heard wooden rosary beads clicking and the rustling of material, as if sheets were blowing in the wind. She stood up as the Mother Superior entered the room.

"Good morning, Mother," said everyone as they curtsied.

"Please be seated," said the nun as the material to her habit settled around her.

Angela thought the Reverend Mother always seemed harried. She never seemed to stay in one place very long, as if there was always something else more pressing to take care of.

"Girls, I have an announcement to make. Since the convent has been in financial trouble for some time, we've received special permission from Rome to sell our linens and make a profit. I've already taken the liberty of asking some outside sources if they would like to buy some of our beautiful work."

"Who will buy our work, Mother?" asked one of the girls.

"I can't say right now, because I haven't received any replies. Sister Jessica will be in directly to oversee this session, as she will be handling some of the business aspects of our venture. I hope you will all take extra special care about the way you sew. I will see you all at vespers."

Everyone quickly stood up and curtsied.

"Isn't it exciting that we're going to be selling our fine work to the outside world?" asked Filomina.

"Oh, yes, I've heard that Mother has even written to wealthy people in America. The American dollar is worth so much more than the Italian lira," said another.

"Angela," said Filomina, "doesn't anything excite you these days? You're daydreaming all the time. It's as if you're not here."

"Well, soon I won't be." Angela had waited for the right time to tell everyone about the choice she had made. She had been carrying this secret, and it had been a burden.

"What?" asked Filomina.

"Mother Superior has consented for me to marry the man from America."

"The meetings you had?" asked another girl.

"Giuseppina, how do you know about my meetings?"

"Someone had to find out what was going on. He came to the convent twice."

Angela surveyed all the faces. She should have known better than to think anything could remain a secret in this group.

"When will you marry?" asked Filomina.

"In six or seven months. If we both feel the same then, things should go as planned."

"We'll help you with your hope chest. We'll make nightgowns and tablecloths and your wedding gown," said Giuseppina.

Sister Jessica opened the door. She was a younger nun who had just taken her final vows.

"Well, girls, I see you're all hard at work," said the nun.

"Oh, Sister, we're all so excited about Angela and her marriage," said Giuseppina.

"Can't you keep anything a secret?" hushed Filomina.

"Oh, it's no secret," said the nun. "I'm sure we all wish Angela good fortune. God will watch over her in her journey. Now let's everyone pay attention, as I have some new linen designs for the altar for Easter festivities."

Angela wished her future marriage had never been discussed. After all, it was some time away, and a lot could happen in seven months—especially since Franco lived in America. It was true she had said yes to him, but all her plans seemed far into the future. She liked the idea of taking a chance—a risk. But they were just words. What about the day, if that day ever came, she would have to leave?

The convent was the cultural cornerstone in her life. She had not known Italian until she came here. Only Sicilian was spoken where she grew up, and anyone who spoke Italian was held under suspicion. It was said that a truly educated person spoke both languages, and the convent had made her more than she would have been. Angela told herself that she would bring the knowledge she had accumulated to her new life in America. She would draw strength from what she had learned to face the challenges in the new world.

"Angela, Father Luci found the linens you designed for Christmas services last year very beautiful," said the nun, as she laid a white material on the table.

"Angela?"

Angela could hear the nun's words, but she was focused on the many questions in her life. She felt someone kick her foot.

"Excuse me, Sister, I was just thinking," said Angela.

"Well, I was just saying how Father Luci complimented you on your work. And also, the gown you made for the Princess of Palermo. She was so pleased that she would like you to do more work for her. Keep up the good work."

The twelve o'clock bell sounded in the courtyard. The girls rose and in single file walked to the refectory.

~ ~ ~ ~ ~

"Angela, I can't wait to start on your wedding gown," said Filomina, taking a forkful of pasta.

"It's a bit too early to be thinking of a gown," said Angela. "Maybe he won't come back."

"He'll come back," said Filomina. "Why would he have come here in the first place if he wasn't serious?"

Angela sipped her milk.

"You're sure brave marrying someone you don't know," said Giuseppina, "My cousin did that, and he used to beat her."

"Be quiet," said Filomina. "You're always full of positive news."

Angela knew that this was a possibility, but she had made a promise that if Franco kept his word, she would certainly keep hers. She would always have a home here at the convent anyway, although she wondered if they would take her back if her husband was mean to her. And yet she did like Franco—how hard he worked, his looks, his independence, and the way he liked her.

She also enjoyed the allure of America. She felt indebted to the Americans' kindness when they came to help Sicily after the earthquake. They all seemed to care so much. There was no reason for them to, but they did. She had never received that level of kindness from her own neighbors.

"Angela, you haven't eaten a thing," said Filomina.

"I'm not very hungry."

"Well, you had better eat something, because here comes Sister Tiziana to check that we aren't wasting food," said Giuseppina.

"A little less talking and a bit more eating would serve you well, girls," said the nun, "Angela, why haven't you eaten?"

"This is her second helping, Sister," said Filomina.

"You should never take more food if you can't eat it," said the nun.

"We're all going to take portions and finish it, Sister," said Filomina.

"Make sure it's all gone by the end of lunch." The nun went to the next table.

"I can't eat any more," said Giuseppina. "My poor stomach won't allow it. I have a delicate stomach and ..."

"Oh, be quiet. Angela, you have got to wake up. You'd better pay attention to what's going on."

"I'm sorry," said Angela, "I've just had a lot on my mind."

"Well, you've been taking chances lately that you shouldn't. Just be careful. Remember the Mother Superior gave you permission to go to America, and she can take it away."

"I'm sure it's just the excitement of the past few months," said Angela. "Soon I'll be back to normal."

~ ~ ~ ~ ~

Franco's letters were filled with news from America. Angela liked to hear about the work he was doing with the nuns and other customers and how proud he was of it. He had bought antique furniture and refinished the pieces himself, which would be for their home once they were married. He wanted to buy a house before he returned to Sicily.

In her letters, Angela would describe what went into her trousseau. She told Franco how hard all the girls worked on her bed linens and tablecloths. They also had to work hard to produce finished products for the convent's selling of goods for profit. The more she corresponded with Franco, the more she began to see that God had wanted her to take a chance and marry him.

Any letters received from Franco and sent to him from Angela had to be first read by the Mother Superior. One day, when Angela was on her knees washing the dormitory floor, the Mother Superior came in.

"Angela, I want to speak to you about the letter you wrote to Franco this morning," said the nun.

Angela got to a standing position as quickly as she could. The worst feeling was looking up at the Mother Superior while she was speaking.

"Yes, Mother?" The Reverend Mother always wanted to make a small change to her letters. Sometimes it was grammatical; sometimes it was a suggestion to include some uneventful daily activity at the convent. This seemed more urgent.

"I feel it is inappropriate to use the word nightgown in a letter to a gentleman."

"But, Mother, I was only describing what went into my trousseau."

"I'm sure it was done out of innocence, but it is inappropriate." said the nun. "I've crossed it out. Please rewrite the letter and bring it to me."

"Of course, Mother," said Angela. "I'm sorry. It won't happen again."

"I would also prefer that you do not mention convent business in your letters," said the nun. "I've let it go this time, but in the future, please do not mention it. We have permission from His Holiness, and it would not look proper to the outside world for a convent to be selling and profiting. It is for the glory of the church, but the outside world would not understand our mission."

"I was just telling Franco about our good fortune," said Angela. She knew it was not for the glory of the church. Angela was aware that the nun saw the talent at the convent, and she wanted the cultivation of that talent to be profitable. The Mother Superior was, above all else, a practical woman.

"I understand that. It is perfectly natural for you to talk about what you do, but don't mention convent business."

"Yes, Mother," said Angela and bowed her head.

"I'm glad you understand. Carry on with your work," said the nun.

Angela raised her eyes slightly to catch the shadow of the Mother Superior's habit leave the dormitory. She couldn't understand the Mother Superior's objection. After all, the nun looked to America's wealthy people to buy their fine linens. What difference would it make if Franco knew about it? Angela was sure he would only wish them luck. She wished she had never mentioned the convent's activities in her letters.

Angela wrapped the towel around the mop and pushed it along the marble floor. It had taken her all morning to wash and shine the floor, and it was so clean that the entire room was reflected in it. Soon she would have her own home to keep clean.

Chapter 2
A New Life, 1913

The girls worked long hours, as the convent had several customers in America and expected the demand to increase. Since they only had two manual sewing machines, most of the work had to be done by hand. The increased work meant less time for the girls to devote to their studies and more time to sewing. With the increased work, Angela developed a dislike for the work sent to America. All Americans seemed to have the same taste— tablecloths and armchair covers were all they seemed to want. Two designs sold well in America, one of them being off-white embroidered flowers arranged in a connected and ordered pattern.

The Princess of Palermo owned the building and land upon which the convent had been built, and she had become a patron of the convent's work. She made yearly contributions to the convent, and the convent reciprocated by sending girls to work at her villa. One day, the Reverend Mother invited her to the convent to look at some of the items the girls had created. The Princess was so impressed with some of the work that she asked whose it was.

"That is Angela Lanza's work," said the Mother Superior.

After Mass one Sunday, the Princess waited inside her carriage for the girls to come out the convent chapel. She saw the Mother Superior and waved.

"Reverend Mother, I wonder if you could point Angela out to me. I would like to meet her."

"Certainly, Madame, there she is." The nun pointed with her index finger, then waved Angela toward her as if she were a conducting a symphony.

Angela saw the nun waving her forward. She wondered who owned the large black carriage with gold trim. My God, she thought, these must be rich people. Maybe people from America who bought our work. She walked toward the carriage.

"Angela, this is the Princess of Palermo. The Princess has on several occasions admired your work."

Angela was taken aback by her beauty. She wore a large black hat with a purple feather on the side and a mesh veil that covered her eyes. Angela bent down to kiss the Princess's hand.

"My great pleasure to meet you, Princess."

"No need to do that, Angela, and please address me as Madame," said the Princess as she held Angela's hand. "I think the work you do is beautiful. I wanted to meet the girl who possessed such talent."

"Thank you, Madame," said Angela as she curtsied.

"Would you like to come around to my villa next Sunday?" The Princess turned to the Mother Superior and gave the nun a nod. "That is, if the Reverend Mother approves."

"Oh, of course, Madame. It would be an honor," said the nun.

Angela, surprised at the nun's quick response, turned toward the Mother Superior. Excursions outside the convent were discouraged on Sundays—plus all the girls sewed on Sundays because of the large demand. The nun's decisions were usually well thought out—certainly never spontaneous. Angela found it curious for a moment that the nun would agree to this meeting, but she was so shocked by the conversation that it didn't concern her for long.

"I will pick you up at the convent, Angela," said the Princess. "And please bring along some new linens you've created. I'm anxious to see them."

"I'll have Angela bring several of her buffet covers," said the Reverend Mother.

"It is almost dinnertime. I must be getting back. See you next Sunday." She tapped the carriage door with her walking stick, and a moment later, the carriage lurched forward.

Angela and the Mother Superior watched the carriage disappear out of the convent gates and into the distance.

"Angela, be sure to finish whatever you're working on by next Sunday. You'll want to have something special to show the Princess. If she recommends our work to her friends, then we will have more business."

Angela thought it strange that the Reverend Mother often referred to the products produced at the convent as "our work." She doubted the nun could even sew.

"But, Mother, it will take me a long time to finish my project. It's a bedspread. I wouldn't want to hurry it and not do a good job."

"Isn't that for your trousseau?"

"Yes, Mother."

"Well, put it aside for a week. Start on a pillow slipcover and make a new design. Something fit for the Princess and her friends."

They walked toward the convent. Angela wondered what would be fit for a princess. She was grateful for all the convent had done for her, but she never received one lira of the money brought in by her talent and hard work.

"On second thought," said the Mother Superior, stopping mid-stride and turning toward Angela, "why don't you bring along your bedspread, even if it isn't finished? Maybe the Princess would like to buy it. The girls could certainly help you make another one before you're married."

"My bedspread?" asked Angela. She was sure the Princess had more than enough bedspreads.

"Remember, Angela, the convent is in dire need of money. It is essential that we acquire as many paying customers as possible right now. It will not take you long to make another."

Angela saw no evidence that the convent was suffering financially. In fact, they had accepted several new paying students.

"Of course, Mother, I'm sorry to seem so selfish. I'll bring the bedspread along."

They entered the convent and paused in the large foyer. A painting of St. Anthony surrounded by birds, rabbits, and deer hung on the wall.

"You are a good girl, Angela. I am sure you will do well in your new life," said the nun as she turned to walk down the hall to her office.

~ ~ ~ ~ ~

Angela waited inside the convent door for the Princess. Along with her other work, she brought along the bedspread as she had promised the Mother Superior. She went over to a window and gazed at her reflection. There were only a few mirrors in the convent because the nuns had taken the vow of modesty and insisted the girls do the same. Some of the older nuns even felt that mirrors brought in the devil. One full-length mirror hung across from the Mother Superior's office, but very few would pause to view themselves for fear of the Mother catching them. Angela thought that the Reverend Mother had hung it there to catch anyone who committed the sin of vanity.

Angela peered at herself in the window, but she didn't have a clear vision of what she looked like. She remembered resembling her mother when she was small, but now she didn't know. Her former life felt like something she had read about long ago. She didn't have a photo of her mother, brother or sister, and her birth record had been destroyed in the earthquake. There was no evidence she had been born or even had a family. She was reborn when she came to live with the nuns, and the face reflected in the window had no history. Her present was her history.

Angela felt a vibration under her feet and then heard the thumping of horse hooves in the distance. She went out to greet the Princess's carriage. The gleaming horses trotted through the convent gates as they pulled the black carriage.

"Good afternoon, my dear," said the Princess through the door. She wore a wide-brimmed white hat with a multi-hued pink feather that protruded from the side.

"Good afternoon, Madame" said Angela. The Princess extended her hand. Angela wasn't sure what to do. The Princess gave Angela a firm handshake, so she reciprocated.

The Princess wore soft pink gloves that matched the pink in her feather. Angela had never seen such a combination on a lady. The Princess tapped the carriage door, and they sped toward the convent gate and onto the road.

"I'm so delighted you could come, Angela," said the Princess. "I've wanted to meet you for some time. You have a unique talent, you know."

"I sew like everyone else, Madame." Angela knew the Mother Superior did not want any of the girls singled out as more talented than the others—but she also knew that where money was concerned, the Reverend Mother would ignore the sin of vanity.

"No, not like everyone else. You are unique. Unique ladies need to become friends." The Princess took off her gloves and laid them in her lap.

The carriage pulled into a long driveway.

"Here we are. This is my home."

The carriage came to an abrupt stop, and Angela stepped out. She was faced with a huge white structure that seemed to radiate such light that Angela could not look directly at it. The image of the light beings in her dream formed in her mind. She sensed that they were with her.

The Princess had referred to her residence as a villa, but Angela was sure she was looking at a palazzo, or palace. She had heard about palazzo living, but few in the modern world actually lived that way. The two women entered a large courtyard with a fountain in the center. The sound of the cascading water, combined with a sense of calm, made the world stop for Angela. Complete silence always made her hold her breath, because it reminded her of the deep quiet after the earthquake. The atmosphere in the courtyard was soothing.

"Come, Angela, up the steps," said the Princess, bounding up the stairs.

Angela walked closer to the fountain. It had little angels with bows and arrows balancing on one leg. Their smiles suggested that some comedy or mischief had just taken place. A larger angel stood on the top with a trumpet to its lips. Water flowed from the trumpet and from the bows of the other angels.

"Angela, come up the stairs," called the Princess. "It's almost noon, and we want to be in a cool place. It will be very hot today."

"Yes, Madame. I'm coming." Angela thought she would be uncomfortable at the Princess's home, but the memory of her unseen friends put her at ease. She was supposed to be here.

The Princess opened large, white French doors, and they stepped inside. Angela had never seen such streamlined furniture before. The modern white couches and chairs glistened in the midday light, and electric lamps were made of chrome. The light bounced off the metal like sprinkles of crystals. The shade on one of the floor lamps reminded Angela of a hat the Princess would wear—it was white and very wide.

"Do you like my home, Angela?" The Princess threw her hat on the couch. "Would you like some tea and biscuits?"

"If it's not too much trouble, Madame."

"No trouble at all. I'll just go out to the kitchen and tell Maria to fix us a treat. I'll be back in a minute. Sit down, Angela."

This must be what American houses look like! Even people who aren't very rich probably have rooms like this one. Angela now found it strange that Franco had written her that he was refinishing antique furniture for their home. Maybe he thought that she wanted ornate antique furniture, since the convent was filled with it.

Everything in the Princess's palazzo was new and bright. There was lightness everywhere. Angela had never seen a room so bright during the daytime. The large bay windows welcomed the sunshine into the room and gave home to radiance. One could read here during the day and not have to turn on the electric light.

She looked out the window. There was a pond on the grounds surrounded by palm trees, and ducks and swans serenely swam on the still water. The hills could be seen for kilometers. The earth was many shades of brown. Sicilian earth seemed like dry, lifeless dust to Angela. But now, with the reflection of the light, she saw how alive the land really was.

The maid brought in the tea.

"Do you take cream and sugar?" asked the Princess.

"Just black is fine, Madame."

"A girl your age taking black tea?" The Princess smiled at Angela.

Angela tried to guess the Princess's age. She had light, unlined skin, and her hands were smooth with polished nails. She guessed that the Princess was around thirty. Angela was embarrassed about her own hands, which were lined and dry with brittle nails. There was no doubt that she had worked hard her whole, short life.

"We never have sugar at the convent, Madame, because it's expensive. Any cream we have we sell to local merchants." Angela knew that the Princess owned the convent's land. She did not want to give the impression that they were having trouble caring for it.

"Yes, Mother Superior was telling me that the convent is in great need of repair and the church in Rome can only offer a small sum." The Princess poured a cup of tea and handed it to Angela.

"Yes, Madame, but the girls are helping. We're selling our sewing to America. They need help in maintaining the orphanage itself—the buildings. The grounds are always cared for. Gardeners are cheap."

"You were orphaned in the earthquake of Messina?" asked the Princess as she sipped her tea.

"Yes, Madame. Many of the girls at the convent came from that disaster." Angela wondered why the Princess had singled her out. There were several girls who were just as talented as she was.

"Have you any family?" asked the Princess. She placed her cup on its saucer.

"No. Well, they have never found my sister. Maybe she's alive somewhere."

"Have you looked?"

"The Mother Superior sends out inquiries every so often, but nothing is ever found." Oh, thought Angela, that's why I'm here, sitting in front of the Princess. She is going to help me search for my sister! Angela felt a pang of guilt. Here she was enjoying tea with the Princess of Palermo while her sister may be begging on the street somewhere.

"If she were alive, I'm sure she would have been found by now," said the Princess.

Angela's heart fell to her feet.

"No one has proved that she died," said Angela in a soft voice. Her sister's unknown fate had weighed on her mind since she was brought to the convent. She kept her concerns and questions hidden, and she even tried to hide them from herself. Every time she thought of her sister, she would tell herself that God would watch over the younger girl—and then she immediately dismissed the thought. Now that the wedding was drawing near, her sister's voice kept invading her quiet moments—moments Angela wanted to spend thinking about her new life.

"I think it is always best to look toward the future. Your wedding day will soon be here, and I would like to participate in your wedding festivities, if you'll let me," said the Princess.

"Of course, Madame."

"I have plenty of space here at my villa for a wedding reception. Even if I'm abroad at the time or in the North on business, I would still like you to use my home for your party after the ceremony."

"Oh, Madame, that's so generous of you. I can't accept the offer unless I have the Mother Superior's permission."

"I'll speak to the Mother. Now, what do you have in the package?"

"Oh, the Mother told me to bring along a bedspread I have been working on to show you." Angela pulled it out of the bag and spread it on the back of the couch. A large seagull was the center image, flying over a blue ocean.

"It's to remind me of the sea here when I move to America," said Angela. She realized she shouldn't have said it was a personal item.

"Is it for your trousseau?"

"Well, the Mother thought you might like to see it, and if you liked it, maybe your friends would like to see it, you know." Angela knew what the Mother Superior had in mind. It wasn't enough that she had rich customers in America. She also wanted to make use of the Princess's wealthy friends. Angela looked away from her hostess and prayed for the moment to pass.

"I'm familiar with the Reverend Mother's approach to business matters," said the Princess, smiling. She got up and neatly folded the bedspread. "Angela, you should certainly take this lovely spread to America. I'm sure your husband will like it. It'll also remind him of the beauty of Sicily." The Princess glanced at her watch.

"Is it late, Madame?"

"Time for you to be getting back, I'm afraid. I hope you don't mind going back to the convent with just my driver. He'll take good care of you."

"No, Madame, I don't mind. It's a short distance."

"Then I'll see you soon at the convent," said the Princess. She hugged Angela and led her to the front door.

~ ~ ~ ~ ~

The horses galloped toward the convent, passing lemon and fig trees. Angela liked to see the world rushing by. She felt safe inside the carriage and wished that she could always be going toward something or going somewhere, yet never arriving at her destination. What about her sister? Could she leave Sicily without even looking for her? The Princess said she was most likely dead. Angela told herself that she needed to release any hope of finding her sister.

Angela turned her attention toward her wedding day. She imagined herself in a long, white, lace gown dancing at the Princess's home after the ceremony. She tried to imagine Franco's face, but it was blurry. Maybe he had also forgotten what she looked like. Angela thought it strange that she hadn't received a letter from Franco in two weeks. Since his departure from Sicily, he had written her every week. She told herself she would receive one tomorrow.

When she reached the convent, the girls were hard at work sewing. Angela went to the sewing room, sat in her usual seat next to Filomina, cleared her mind of the day's activity, and began to sew. A nun sat in a corner reading.

"Angela, Angela," whispered Filomina.

"Not now, Filomina. I'll tell you about it later," said Angela as she adjusted herself in her seat.

"No, it's not about that."

"What?"

"Ask to go to the lavatory. Meet me there."

Angela sat back in her chair and slowly raised her hand.

"Yes, what is it, Angela?" asked the nun.

"Sister, I'm sorry, but may I be excused to go to the lavatory?"

"You should have gone before coming to sew, but go ahead. Don't be too long." The nuns rarely refused the girls anything within reason, but they felt they needed to establish control before they gave permission.

Angela waited in a lavatory stall in case one of the nuns saw her loitering and questioned her. She heard the door open and squatted to see the person's shoes.

"Angela, are you here?" whispered Filomina.

"What is it that's so urgent?" asked Angela as she opened the stall door.

"Ah, don't scare me like that!" said Filomina loudly. "What's wrong with you?" Her voice echoed in the empty bathroom.

"Shh." Angela put her index finger to her lips. "Tell me. What is it?"

"Listen. Have you been receiving mail from Franco during the past few weeks?"

"No. No, I haven't. How did you know?" A ridiculous question, thought Angela. Filomina made it her business to know everything that went on in the convent.

"I've seen several letters from him, but addressed to the Mother Superior. When he wrote to you, were the envelopes addressed to you?"

"Yes. They had my name on them, but Mother would open them first."

"Well, these were addressed to Mother. You haven't received these letters or any others?"

"No. How do you know this?"

"I wait for Sister Anna to open the box when mail is delivered, and she looks through the letters for me. You know I have a cousin I write to in Rome. Anyway, for the past few weeks, I've seen Franco's letters. What do you suppose is going on? The Mother hasn't changed her mind, has she?"

"Not that I know of," said Angela. Her stomach turned.

"Maybe you should ask her what's going on?"

"No, I can't do that."

"Look, I just wanted you to know. We've got to get back to our sewing. Sister will come looking for us. You go first."

"Thank you, Filomina. Thank you."

Angela sat with her embroidery and began to sew. She remembered the Mother Superior's request concerning her correspondence with Franco. Why would she not want her to mention the convent selling goods to America? It had seemed strange then, and it seemed even stranger now. She sensed something was amiss when the letters stopped. Franco had been very consistent.

Angela held no illusions about Reverend Mother. She reminded Angela of a cat that had lived in her neighborhood in Messina. The cat lived nowhere in particular but was always well fed. Sometimes the cat slept with one family and then another, but it did have a favorite house. It was with the most well-off family. The neighborhood named this cat "The Specter."

"Sewing is over for the day, girls. Time for evening prayer," said the nun. "You all need to study your Latin for class tomorrow. The exam will be difficult."

~ ~ ~ ~ ~

Angela brushed her hair, twisted the thick strands together, and pulled it back in a bun. She had opened the window next to her bed and pulled up the Venetian blind so the sun could warm the room. Inspired by the Princess's light-filled house, she took every opportunity to let the brightness enter her environment.

"What are you doing up so early?" asked Filomina. "It's not yet 6:30."

"I couldn't sleep."

Angela decided to greet the mailman herself and see if there was a letter from Franco addressed to the Mother Superior. She recalled when she had collapsed on her knees in front of the statue of the Virgin Mary and begged for guidance. Mary and her unseen friends had guided her, and her new life was not to be taken away. Action on her part needed to happen.

Angela was the first one in the sewing room. By the time the other girls came at 7:30, she was halfway finished with an outline for a new design. She worked nonstop until she heard the twelve o'clock bell ring.

"Sister, may I be excused?" said Angela. "I've worked very hard this morning, and I would like to take a walk on the grounds to rejuvenate."

"I am so pleased with the work you've done, Angela. You really have encouraged everyone to work harder. You may go to lunch and then go straight to Latin class."

"Thank you, Sister."

Angela hurried to the mailbox. She saw Sister Angelica unlock the box and walk toward Mother Superior's office. Move! said a voice inside her head.

"Sister, Sister, may I see the mail? I'm expecting something," said Angela as her heart pounded. She tried to calm her heavy breathing.

"Now, Angela, you know the rules. All the mail goes to Mother before it's distributed."

"Oh, I know, Sister. All I want to do is look at the envelopes and see if anything is for me. I don't want to read it."

"Oh, I see. Your friend from America," said the nun with a grin.

Angela could see that Sister Angelica liked the thought of putting one over on the Mother Superior.

"Well, there's no harm in letting you look," said the nun.

"Thank you, Sister." Angela perused the envelopes, moving her lips as she read each address. Most of the mail was from Europe. Then she came upon an airmail envelope from America. It was from Franco Bellini in New York, and it was addressed to the Mother Superior. Angela felt the rush of blood spring from the middle of her chest to her shoulders and neck.

"Thank you, Sister Angelica." She calmly handed the letters back to the nun.

"Nothing for you? Oh, cheer up. I'm sure he'll write soon."

"Thank you, Sister," said Angela with a half smile.

Angela was sure the Mother Superior was trying to sell Franco the linen they were making at the convent. Franco was probably angry because he thought that Angela had something to do with it. Her choice in life was slipping away, and she had to do something about it. She ran to the second floor sewing room, took a piece of black chalk they used to mark white fabric, and went into the lavatory. She took a piece of toilet paper and used the waxed side to write a note:

Dear Franco,

I have often stayed awake at night wondering why you haven't written me. Today I think I know why. I did not encourage Mother Superior to sell you our linens. This thought has only come to me today. You have a right to be angry, but not at me. These past few months, I have looked forward to becoming your wife. I care for you. My conscience is clear. Please let me know how you feel.

With Affection, Angela

The next day, Angela waited for the postman in the vestibule of the convent. She heard the jingling of keys and saw him come toward the door.

"Good morning, sir," said Angela.

"Hello, Miss," said the postman as he searched for the correct key to the convent mailbox.

"Sir, I have a letter to go to America, but I have no money to mail it. I wonder if you would be so kind as to lend me a few lira so that my cousin will know I'm alive?"

"Your family doesn't know you're alive?" asked the postman as he looked up from sorting the envelopes.

"You see, I was in the earthquake years ago in Messina, and it's taken this much time to find them since they live in America. Please, sir, would you do me this kindness? I am poor." Angela hung her head for effect.

"But the nuns usually give me the mail to be posted." He obviously did not want to anger the nuns.

"You see, our good sisters are behind in reading the mail. They have to read everything that goes out. Unfortunately, mine would be on the bottom of the pile. You would be saving them the dull task of reading my ramble. Please, sir, just a few lira?"

"Well, I guess it's all right. But just this once."

"Oh, of course just this once. God will bless you for this. You'll see."

The postman shrugged his shoulders. "I had an aunt who was killed in that earthquake. We didn't learn of her death for over a year."

~ ~ ~ ~ ~

Franco took off his grease-stained shirt and tossed it on the wicker chair, went over to the sink, filled it with water, and lathered his face with soap. The mirror over the sink reflected the room he called home. His roommates' two beds were unmade, and their thermal underwear was randomly thrown over the beds. The thought of living with these two slobs for the next few years made Franco dismiss any thoughts of the future.

He had looked for a house with the anticipation of marriage and shared life. Now it seemed the marriage was off. How could she have tried to trick him into buying linens from the convent? Didn't Angela know that he would have provided her with all she needed, and that all she had to do was ask? Well, he was through. He didn't want to marry someone who was so sneaky.

Franco changed into a clean shirt and went down to the room below, put a key in the lock, and turned it. All the antique furniture he had planned to put in his new home stood, half-refinished, as if waiting for a corner to stand in or a wall to lean against.

Just a few weeks ago, when he had completed a plumbing job or was done painting a room at work, he would hurry home to this room and begin building his and his bride's future. He had the energy after working all day to do more work.

Franco glanced at his watch and hurried upstairs. He was on his way to New York City to visit his family, and he would have to tell them the marriage was off. His mother would say that he should marry one of the girls she knew who lived in the city. He had met these girls and felt that there was no one for him. They all seemed either too independent or would become too dependent.

Franco reached under his bed, pulled out a leather suitcase, and filled it with clothing he had laid out on his bed. He heard the door open at the bottom of the stairs. It was the mailman. He snapped the case shut and carried it down the stairs. He paused at the mailbox. Most of the letters were addressed to his roommates. The last one was for him. It was from Palermo, but there was no return address.

He opened the envelope and took out a crumbled piece of what looked like the wax paper he used for storing food. Carefully, he unfolded the paper with the tips of his fingers. It was from Angela! For a few moments he read in silence, then out loud. He had to hear it out loud. What a fool he had been for not seeing through the Mother Superior's letters.

A weight lifted from his chest. Franco took a deep breath and leaped up the stairs, skipping one, then two steps at a time. He grabbed a pen and airmail paper to write to Angela while he traveled to the city.

~ ~ ~ ~ ~

Franco came out of the post office on Fourth Street. He'd just posted his letter to Angela and felt his life was back on track. He turned the corner onto East Third Street and strolled past the factories and occasional shop. Passing a men's clothing store, tucked between two abandoned buildings, he stopped and gazed at the well-dressed mannequins on display. One mannequin wore a black tuxedo with a burgundy cummerbund. It was a European cut, and Franco thought that it would fit his small frame. The shop obviously served the worker community, so it would not be too expensive.

"Franco! Franco! I'm waiting for you at home. What are you doing?" shouted a large woman as she crossed the street and came toward him.

"Mama, I was on my way up to the apartment."

She embraced Franco and kissed him on both cheeks. Her enormous, firm belly pressed into his ribs.

"Go home. Your brother is waiting for you. I have to get some bread. I'll be right back."

Franco watched as his mother shifted her weight from one leg to the other, and then he crossed the street and walked a few blocks to Goerick Street. He went into a tenement, climbed the stairs, and knocked on a door. He stepped to the side to hide himself from view. A thin young man in his late teens opened the door.

"Who's there?" asked the young man as he stepped into the hall and turned away from Franco.

"It is I," said Franco from behind him. The young man quickly turned around, and Franco hugged him.

"Franco, you rascal, I should have known it was you."

"Alessio, you get taller and skinnier every time I see you. Don't you ever eat?"

"Mama feeds me, and I eat. I guess this is me."

"I met Mama in the street. She was going to the bakery."

"To get something to fatten me up, no doubt," said Alessio.

Franco put his arm around his brother, and they went into the apartment. A little girl with dark hair and eyes stood with a doll in her arms.

"Franco, Franco, you're home! You're home!"

"Speranza!" said Franco. "You grow prettier every day."

"So tell me," said Alessio, "when is the wedding? I can't wait to meet my sister-in-law." He sat at the kitchen table and took an apple from the fruit bowl. An ironing board stood in the middle of the kitchen with several shirts piled on top.

"Yes, tell me about her," Speranza said as she pulled at Franco's jacket. "Is she going to be my sister? Is she pretty?"

The little girl looked into her brother's eyes and blinked a few times. Franco noticed that Speranza did this when she wanted to know what the other person really thought. It was her way of uncovering the truth. No one could resist those eyes.

"I've told Angela all about you," said Franco. He squatted and gently held his sister's shoulders. "I said that I had such a beautiful little sister at home who is anxious to meet you. She's so excited about meeting you that I'm sure you'll be best friends."

"I hope she likes to play," said Speranza.

"Franco, what have you been doing to prepare for her arrival?" asked Alessio.

"I'm busy refinishing furniture and looking for a house. I saw a beautiful tuxedo in a store on Third Street."

"Oh, yeah. Castalano's. His clothes cost plenty." Alessio took a bite of the apple.

"I think it would suit me on my wedding day."

The apartment door flew open. The large woman came in, her arms filled with packages.

"Will someone please help me with these?"

"Mama, I thought you were just going for bread," said Franco. He took the bundles and put them on the table. Alessio brought his mother a wooden chair.

"Well, Bruno had a sale on his tomatoes and olive oil. I have to buy what's on sale." She lowered herself in the chair and attempted to catch her breath.

"Mama, if you need money I can give you some extra," said Franco.

"No. That husband of mine will bring home a check today. Thank God you give us money every month, Franco. We really need it for the extras."

When Franco got engaged, he had thought about that money every month and how he would need it for his bride and his new house. He always felt that his stepfather should provide better for his mother.

"Mama, Franco is going to buy a tuxedo for his wedding," said Alessio.

"Yes," said Speranza, clapping her hands. "He's gonna look so handsome, and Angela will look beautiful."

"Listen to her. Nine years old, and she thinks about beautiful clothes and fancy parties," said the large woman. "Franco, you should marry a girl from here so we could all attend the wedding. And besides, what kind of fortune can an orphan girl bring?" With a grunt, she got up and pulled out a pot from underneath the sink.

"I've made my choice. When we arrive in America, we'll have a party here, too."

"Sure," said Alessio, "we'll have a party here. Why not?"

His mother turned away from the stove and folded her arms across her ample breasts. Her arms met at the wrist. "And when will this wedding take place?" she asked.

"In a few months. I'm getting ready now. I have to have a certain amount of money saved," said Franco.

"Well, if you have to have a certain amount of money, why waste it on a new suit?" asked Franco's mother.

"Ma, there's nothing wrong with looking presentable on your wedding day," said Franco. He did not want to tell his mother he had more than enough money to meet the required amount. His family would need more, but any extra would go toward a new home.

"For a poor man, you have high ideas," she said. "Besides, you're not marrying royalty."

"Ma, he can't go to Sicily dressed like a pauper," said Alessio. "He's American now. People will expect him to dress like he has money."

"Ah, high ideas—that's what he has." The large woman moved her hand as if flicking away a fly.

"Ma, I know I'll never change your mind," said Franco, "so I won't even try. But please, when I bring Angela to America, please welcome her."

"Of course. She will be my daughter-in-law. What do you think I am, an animal?" She chopped up a tomato and dropped it into the pot.

Franco put his arm around her shoulders. His hand didn't quite reach to the other to the end of her shoulder.

"Mama, I'm sure Angela will like you," said Franco. "Besides I am buying a house in the country and you and Speranza will come and live with us."

"Stop talking and set the table." She pinched her son's cheek.

"Listen, I want to run out for a few minutes," said Franco. "I have something I want to do."

"Well, don't spend time hanging around. Dinner will be ready in an hour."

Franco put on his jacket and went out the apartment door, walked to East Third Street, and gazed at the tuxedo in the store window. Yes, it would look good on me, he thought, if I don't gain weight from now until the wedding. The suit was surely beyond his means. Most of the time he wore work clothes, and any suits he had were made by a friend of his mother's and were often too big. He looked around to make sure no one was watching and then slipped into the store.

"Excuse me, sir," said Franco to a salesman.

"Yes, can I help you?" asked a man in a dark brown suit and white shirt.

"Yes," said Franco, "I very much like that tuxedo in the window."

"An excellent choice," said the salesman. "Is it for a special occasion?"

"I'm getting married in a few months."

"Congratulations. You'll look as good as the bride in that tuxedo. The one in the window seems to be your size. Romano, please get the black tuxedo out of the window for the gentleman!"

Franco put on the tuxedo and studied himself in the full-length mirror. The jacket was a perfect fit, but the pant legs were too long. He found himself wondering if Angela would think he was putting on airs. There were two mirrors behind him, and it was the first time he had ever seen his back. When he was being fitted for a suit by his mother's friend, she would just use one mirror. Now he could see not just the front, but also the back and sides. He could see his entire form. He looked better than he thought.

"Your bride won't be able to resist you," said the salesman, as he bent down and folded cuffs on Franco's pants.

Franco hoped that would be true. He remembered last year when he had gone for sledding ride with a girl who had the reddest hair he'd ever seen. He couldn't look directly at her face, because the white snow reflected intense light off her hair. It was as if God had wrapped a halo around her head. He had showed his strength that day by carrying the sled up the hill, and she had laughed and hung on to his arm when she'd slip on the ice. He'd begun to feel more confident as the hours went by, and later he had the courage to try to kiss her. She had pulled back and said that they were just friends.

A few days later, he decided to make the trip to Sicily. The first time he saw Angela, he knew she was for him. He had almost lost her, but that would never happen again.

"How much?" asked Franco.

"Are you renting or buying?" asked the man.

"I need to buy. I'm getting married in Sicily, but I don't have much money."

"A wise choice to take a Sicilian bride. Since you are a paisan, I will make you a good deal."

"I appreciate any special price you can make."

The salesman quoted a price of $15. Franco thought he could pick up an extra painting job to pay for it, since an average job usually paid $10 a day, but he assumed the salesman never intended to sell the suit in the window. It was probably just for display.

"I can pay $10," Franco said.

The salesman paused for a moment, then said, "All right. Sold. A fine choice sir, a fine choice. We'll have it ready next week."

Before taking the suit off, Franco looked at his reflection again from back to front. He began to see more of his world and his possibilities. He imagined his image was frozen in time on this particular day in this specific shop in New York City.

~ ~ ~ ~ ~

Angela peered into the full-length mirror across from Mother Superior's office and straightened the sleeves on her blouse. She wished she could jump into the mirror and disappear into an unknown world. What if there were creatures in the mirrors who could see into the convent's world? Maybe that's why this was the only full-length mirror in the convent—to prevent demons from observing the comings and goings of Mother Superior's world. The mirror might be outside her office so the nun could observe their world and make sure they stayed on the other side. Angela thought the demons probably feared Mother Superior.

The Reverend Mother never did anything indiscriminately. She was sure the nun had found out about the letter she had written to Franco and wanted an explanation.

Before she could tap on the Mother Superior's door, two men stepped out.

"Thank you for the delivery," called the nun from behind them. "Angela, come in here. I have a large trunk for you."

"A trunk for me? But I'm not expecting anything." A large cedar trunk stood in the center of the room.

"Here's the card," said the nun as she handed it to Angela. The envelope was open.

Angela shrieked, "It's from Franco, and its postmark is Genoa! He's here already, Mother! But it's before the time! I'm not ready—it has only been eight months!" She bent down and touched the wood. As she brushed her hand over the wood, the aroma of cedar seeped into her skin. She brought her hand up to her face and took in the fresh, woody scent. It smelled like a new life, full of clarity and brightness. "It's beautiful—a beautiful cedar chest."

"And so it is," said the nun. "Would you like to open it? I have the key." She dangled the key from a string over Angela's head.

"Should I? Should I wait until Franco gets here?"

"I think if he had wanted you to wait, he wouldn't have sent it. He would have brought it with him." She held out the key to Angela.

"Mother, how will I get it to the dormitory?"

"Dormitory? You'll open it here. You're not married yet. Any letters or packages must be opened before they're distributed. You know that."

"Of course, Mother. I'm sorry." Angela would not miss the Reverend Mother's rules. Soon she would be a married woman living in America, and she would be free to open as many letters and packages as she wanted. She took the key from the nun and inserted it in the padlock. Click! The trunk lock opened.

The nun helped her lift the top of the trunk. When Angela investigated the trunk, she could see her future. She pulled out a tailored navy-blue jacket with white lace trim and held it up to herself.

"Look, Mother, he knew my size," said Angela. She reached into the trunk again and dragged out a matching straight skirt with a slit in the back. "A suit! It's a suit!"

Excitement was not something Angela had ever experienced, and she felt as light as her unseen friends. She kneeled so she could easily bend her upper body into the cedar chest. As she hung over the trunk, she again breathed in the scent of the fresh wood. It cleared her head. This must be what America smells like—new! Angela extended both her arms deep into her future and grasped an armful of garments: silk stockings, nightgowns, dresses, and a leather handbag and shoes.

"Mother, look!" she said, holding the items up to the nun. Angela had never had a wardrobe. She got up and showed the Mother Superior the garments.

"Well, you don't have to worry about not having your clothing ready for the trip," said the nun.

"No, Mother. It's all here. All I need is here!" Angela dropped a silk stocking. She quickly bent down to pick it up and stuffed it in between the other clothing. She felt the nun's stare as she put the items back into the chest and closed the lid.

"Franco Bellini is a good man," said the nun. "But he is young and bold to send such items to a convent. He really should have brought the clothing with him. I will keep the trunk here until you're married."

"Yes, Mother." Angela had hoped to show the contents of the trunk to the other girls. She wanted to share her excitement so all the girls could experience it. They had all worked so hard on her hope chest, making her wedding gown, nightgowns, and table linens.

"Oh, Angela, one moment." The nun cleared her throat. "Sister Priscilla would like to see you before the wedding. I hadn't planned to have you see her yet, because Franco wasn't scheduled to come for a few more months. It's important for you to see her because she has had experience being a wife—only briefly, though, poor thing. Her husband was killed a few days after the wedding. Then God called her here. She can give you some instruction on being a wife."

Sister Priscilla was the oldest nun at the convent. Angela not only couldn't imagine her married, she couldn't imagine her as a young woman. In fact, she was sure Sister Priscilla had been old since birth. When all the nuns had moved their sleeping quarters to the more modern wing, Sister Priscilla chose to stay in the old section. She said she had slept in the same room for fifty years and had no intention of changing.

"I know why Mother Superior sent you here," said Sister Priscilla. "I, myself, told the Mother that it is unwise to marry a girl off without proper instruction, especially an orphan girl. Since I am the most worldly of all our sisters, I urged the Reverend Mother to send you to me here."

"Yes, Sister," said Angela. The nun's room was little bigger than a confessional box. Whenever Sister Priscilla passed Angela in the hall or in church, there was always a musty odor that immediately followed. Now, sitting in the nun's room, the mustiness hung in the air like the rotting corpses after the earthquake. There was one small window above the nun's bed that looked as if it hadn't been opened since the building was erected. There was no choice but to breathe.

"I had been married when I was young for two wonderful days when God saw fit to take my husband so I could fulfill my destiny. Nevertheless, I have had experience being a wife, and that is why you are here. I would like to pass my wisdom on."

Angela wondered how Sister Priscilla could remember that far back. If she had only been married for two days, how much experience did she actually have being a wife?

"I know you want to do your duty properly as a wife. This is especially important since you have no family to protect you. In Sicily, you have the sisters—but once you are in America, there will be no one. Take care not to provoke anger in your mother-in-law and father-in-law. This is very important. They are your parents now and must be obeyed. Treat them as you would treat your own parents."

"But what about my husband?" asked Angela, hoping to receive wisdom about relating to her husband.

"Ah, once he sees your willingness to honor his family, he will know you are eager to be a good wife. Then your real duty will begin. You must cook and clean without complaint and bear healthy children."

From the tiny window, Angela could see the sun begin to set. A gray shadow was cast over the white walls of the room. The old nun seemed to fade as the sun descended into the hills; her voice seemed to come out of nowhere.

"Only give suggestions if he asks you for them," said the nun. "Then there is something else that a wife must perform as a duty to her husband. You must pay attention for when it is time to conceive a baby. You will know because God will tell you when it's time. You will feel an ache just below your stomach. This is God telling you it's time. When this happens, then you and your husband will come together and make the baby that God wants."

"We'll come together," repeated Angela. She saw the last bit of daylight disappear behind the hills. The nun's black habit dissolved into the darkness. She leaned forward to see the nun's face.

"Yes, Our Blessed Mother will guide you when it's time." The nun stood up. "Do you pray to the Virgin?"

"Yes, Sister, all the time. All my prayers are offered up to Our Blessed Mother." Angela knew that the Virgin was her guide, along with her unseen friends.

"Angela, may the Virgin bless you in your new life," said Sister Pricilla in a low, tired voice.

"Thank you, Sister." Angela curtsied.

Angela walked down the stairs, went into the dormitory, and sat on her bed. At least now she knew what was expected of her as a wife. Franco had told her about his family: his sister, brother, mother, and stepfather. He told her that his little sister, Speranza, hoped Franco would marry so she could have a sister. That sounded nice to Angela—a little sister.

"Hello, Angela, how did it go?" asked Filomina as Angela came into the dormitory.

"What are you doing here? You're supposed to be in class," said Angela.

"I received permission to come back and get my book. So, how did it go?"

"How did what go?"

"Your meeting with Sister Priscilla."

"Isn't there anything that goes on around here that you don't know about?" asked Angela.

"Life is dull if you don't pay attention to what goes on. Besides, I've worked hard on your hope chest, and I like to know the story that goes along with it." Angela was aware that Filomina delighted in the discussions of her marriage and that her travel to America gave Filomina hope. She moved closer to Angela. "Tell me what she said."

"All right, well, when you're married you should take care of your husband's family so that he can see you love him," she whispered. "And when God wants you to have children, you'll know when it's time to be with your husband." Angela hoped that what she just said made sense to Filomina so she could explain the whole business to her. Angela looked at Filomina in silence.

"You understand it, don't you?" asked Angela.

"Of course I understand it. But are you sure you didn't miss anything Sister said?"

"No, that's all she said." Angela tried to recreate the conversation in her mind. No, she hadn't missed any of the nun's words, but she did sense that something was missing. Angela looked at her friend again, as if she might find what was absent.

"Do you think it's true?" asked Angela as she swallowed to moisturize her dry mouth.

"I think it's true. It must be. Everyone knows Sister Priscilla was married once. True or not?"

"It's true."

"Then what she says about being a wife must be true. Right?"

"Right!" Angela said. "I never thought of it that way. I mean, there were married women I remember in Messina who I would never ask about being a wife. They weren't very happy."

"That's because nobody told them," said Filomina nodding her head.

"That's right! No one told them!"

Angela hugged Filomina. She pretended that Filomina was her sister and they had just finished one of the conversations they used to have before the earthquake. She was sure her sister would have helped her the same way, just by talking.

"When will Franco arrive?" Filomina asked.

"I don't know. The trunk he sent arrived two days ago, so he should be here soon." Angela put her hand to her mouth. She hadn't told anyone about the trunk because of Mother Superior's warning.

"Don't worry, I know about the trunk, too. Don't you know that if there is a secret to be found out, I'll find it?" laughed Filomina.

"And you never get caught! Why?"

"Because I open my eyes and pay attention. I saw the men delivering the trunk. Who else would get a package of that size? It had to be from a rich American."

~ ~ ~ ~ ~

Franco sauntered along the docks in Genoa, looking for an opening that led to the sea. He heard children giggle. It was a welcome sound. As he passed people on the streets of the seaside town, he would listen to their conversations. There was talk of war in Europe. The situation was becoming tense, and Franco did not want to be in Europe if war broke out.

He followed the laughter and came to an opening on the side of the dock, where several boys played by the water's edge. When the waves displayed their huge humps before breaking on land, the boys threw their tanned bodies into them. Franco walked closer to the water. He heard one boy yell to another that the tide was coming in and that the waves would get bigger. He saw the boy cartwheel across the water's edge as if celebrating the incoming waves.

Had he been that happy as a child? Franco couldn't remember. It consoled him that these children were too young to fight in a war, but then he thought that they might be left fatherless.

Church bells tolled, and the children ran to gather their clothing on shore. Franco looked at his watch. The boys would certainly be late for nine o'clock mass if that was their destination. Maybe they were going home to eat breakfast and bathe in a hot tub and attend a later service. After mass, they would go home and wait for the entire family to gather—aunts, uncles and cousins—and then sit down to a delicious meal prepared by their mothers and grandmothers. He envied the simplicity of such a life.

Franco knew that if he had stayed in Sicily, his life wouldn't have included a swim on Sunday mornings and long leisurely family dinners in the afternoon.

After a lot of hard work, he felt he was finally exercising the personal freedom he had gained by immigrating to America. Soon he would be married to a girl who was of his background and culture but did not have any family connections in Italy. There would be no reason to return or to look back to the past.

He planned a slow journey to Palermo, making stops in Venice, Florence, and Rome. He wanted to give Angela time to prepare for his arrival, since he had come four months before the scheduled date. However, the threat of war weighed in his mind like cement, so he was anxious to marry as soon as he could. He did not want to be caught in a middle of a war that would delay his return home.

Franco bent down, dusted off his trousers, and looked up at the sun. He held his arms out to the side and opened his chest, stretching his heart skyward and taking in the sun's rays. Tomorrow he would travel to Sicily.

~ ~ ~ ~ ~

"Franco, I'm so happy to see you," Roberto said as he embraced his cousin. "I wish you would come every year to get married. That way we would never become strangers."

"Our mothers are sisters," said Franco. "We could never become strangers."

"With Europe in such turmoil, who knows what will happen?" Roberto asked. "How was your trip? You're only three hours late. Not bad for an Italian train, eh?" He put his hand on Franco's shoulder as they walked out of the station. "When you wrote from Genoa, you said that it would take you at least a week to arrive in Palermo. I was surprised to receive your telegram to meet you this morning."

"As you say, Europe's situation is not good, and I don't want to be caught in a difficult situation if war breaks out," said Franco. "Even if Italy is not involved, there could still be problems with travel." He felt that it would be a while before Italy entered the war if there was one, but Franco was a cautious man.

"You're a wise man, Franco Bellini," said Roberto. "Wait here. I'll buy our tickets for the trolley."

Franco always expected to feel disconnected from Palermo when he returned, but the energy of the city's streets propelled his body and mind into the past and future. He envisioned what his life would have been like had he stayed in Sicily, even down to the slightest detail. When he had returned to America after meeting Angela, he described to his mother the house they had lived in when he was young. The connection was there, whether he wanted it or not.

They returned to Roberto's house for a dinner party. After the houseboy finished serving the pasta and pouring the wine, Roberto stood.

"I would like to make a toast to Franco," he said as he tapped his glass with a knife. "To Franco and his beautiful bride. To a long and happy life and many children. Salute!"

"Salute!" said the table of diners as they lifted their glasses.

"When will we meet Angela?" asked Giulietta, the poet's wife. "I would like to tell her about how Roberto and I met. You see I...."

"Franco, did I ever tell you how Giulietta and I met?" asked Roberto, dominating the conversation. "I was sitting in back of her on a train going from Messina to Palermo, and she was reading a volume of my poetry." The poet got up and stood behind his wife and pretended he was riding on a train. "I looked over her shoulder and said..." Roberto motioned to his wife, letting her know it was her turn to speak.

"He said, 'Do you like this poetry?' I said, 'Yes I do, very much.'" Giulietta looked up at her husband to make sure she should continue to speak. "Then he said, 'What about the poet? Do you think you could like him?' To which I responded, 'Yes, I like his ideas.'"

"And then I offered her my hand, like so," said Roberto, as he rested his arm on his wife's shoulder and touched her hand. "And said, 'I am he. Nice to meet you.'"

The poet bowed, and the diners applauded.

"An encounter you've told a million times," laughed Franco. He liked Giulietta and knew she was giving Roberto permission to treat her as a puppet. He also knew that the poet would hear about the infraction when the party was over.

"And then his mother didn't want us to marry," said Giulietta. "She didn't want her son to marry a 'stranger.'"

"You know how the old-timers are," Roberto said. "Because Giulietta comes from Messina, not Palermo, Mama didn't want me to marry her. Years ago, people married people who lived in the same village or city. But today, things are different."

"Yes, I know, my own mother didn't want me to come to Sicily to find a wife," Franco said. "She wanted me to marry someone she knew, from within the Italian community in New York."

"Every mother wants to pick out a wife for her son. That way, she still has a say in things," said Roberto. "It's only natural. Women need to be close to their children."

The poet lit a cigar. All the men took out their cigars and struck a match. Puffs of smoke twirled skyward.

"Yes, but she must accept Angela," said Franco.

"Once she gets to know Angela, things will change," said Giulietta. "They'll grow to love each other."

On his previous visit, Franco got the impression that Giulietta didn't like her mother-in-law, Roberto's mother. She apparently bossed Giulietta around and was not satisfied with her housekeeping. Giulietta also went to teacher's college and taught elementary school. Roberto's mother did not want Giulietta to outshine her because her daughter-in-law had an education.

"If you will all excuse me, I have an important day in front of me tomorrow," Franco said as he got up.

"Sleep well, cousin," said Roberto, blowing smoke rings.

~ ~ ~ ~ ~

Franco walked up the convent staircase. He had decided to give the convent several thousand lire for allowing him to marry Angela, and for the wedding ceremony. As he walked down the hallway, he saw a familiar old nun with a cane limping toward him. She was so far hunched over her cane that it was as if she would kiss the floor.

"Sister, Sister. Hello, it's Franco Bellini."

"Franco?" asked the nun as she searched his face like a map she couldn't read. "Oh, yes, Angela's boyfriend. You're back so soon. It seems like yesterday when I was your chaperone. Is the wedding soon?"

"I hope so, Sister. I'm a few months early, but I hope the Mother Superior will forgive my impatience."

"Oh, I'm sure she will. It will be so exciting to attend a happy wedding. The only time we have special services is at Easter Christmas, and a funeral mass when one of us dies." The nun shuffled closer to Franco and peered at him. "I'm glad to see you've kept your mustache. A man should have hair on his face. I'll be at the wedding." She patted his face as if giving a blessing.

Franco watched the old nun limp down the hallway. He shook his head and smiled. He felt more confident about his meeting with the Mother Superior. He made his way to her office.

"Well, Franco, you're here," said the Reverend Mother as she looked up from her ledger. "It's good to see you." She sat behind her large oak desk.

Franco sensed his early arrival was an inconvenience. He wondered when he would be asked to sit.

"I know I'm early, Mother, but I am anxious to get married. Europe is in such turmoil that I felt I should come before the agreed-upon time. I've saved more than the required amount of money." He glanced at the two chairs in front of the desk.

"That you have come early is not a problem. The girls have worked hard with Angela's hope chest, and most of the linens are finished. The finishing touches have to be put on her wedding gown, but that can be done in a few days. We have a priest who can perform the wedding, and the Princess of Palermo has offered her villa for the reception. She is not in residence, but we can use the villa at any time. So, you see, everything is arranged."

"I suppose the reception will take time to plan," said Franco.

"My concern is not with the festivities but with Angela's welfare. I'm talking about treatment. You must remember that she is an orphan alone in the world except for the sisters here. She will depend on your good graces once she is in America."

"Mother, I love Angela. I'll take care of her the right way," said Franco, as he shifted on his feet.

"Please sit down, Franco." She motioned to the chairs with her chin and closed her ledger. "I know you are hardworking and honest and that she will be provided for. I just want you to know that she always has a home here if something unexpected should happen," said the nun, with a smile.

Franco understood the nun's concern. Sicilian men were known to beat their wives. She didn't understand that he was American now—and that Americans treated their wives differently.

"Mother, I love and respect Angela. I would do nothing to harm her in any way," said Franco as he uncrossed his legs and sat up straight. "She will be my first concern."

"Good. If you respect someone, then things will go well. If not, then there will be turmoil," said the nun. "At any rate, we will correspond with her on a regular basis."

"Respect has always been important to me, Mother. Respect of personal rights." This he understood deeply. Everyone had a right to personal happiness and well-being—although he had never thought of it in terms of marriage.

The Mother Superior stood up.

"You must be anxious to see Angela. Wait in the front courtyard."

"Thank you, Mother."

~ ~ ~ ~ ~

Franco paced on the cobblestone walk with the pungent aroma of olive trees filling his nostrils. It was a scent he remembered from long ago. When he was a boy, he had played among olive trees on an estate where his father worked. He was happy hiding behind the trees and pretending that he owned the great estate. He looked down at the garnet ring he had inherited from his father and thought about how someday his own son would wear it. It would bring him the luck it brought to Franco in finding Angela.

The idea of individual happiness tugged at his mind. He was always so sure that Angela would be happy with him, but what if she changed her mind and later returned to Sicily? He knew the sisters would take her back without question. Wouldn't it be right for Angela to return to where she was most content if she wasn't happy? Although once she was in America, she would see how free people were to express opinions.

The convent door opened, Angela stepped out and walked toward him.

"I've come back," said Franco. He wasn't sure how to greet her. A kiss? A hug? He touched her hand.

"The trunk was beautiful, and all the lovely things—they're wonderful," said Angela.

He looked at her high cheekbones and smooth skin and realized he had seen that face and body often in the past several months: in store windows, in his dreams, and sitting in the chairs he refinished.

"I wanted you to know what life was going to be like once we were married. I wanted you to know you would not only have nice linens to dress up your home, but that you would wear fine things as well. I hope you didn't mind." Franco looked around and saw a nun sitting on a stone bench among the olive trees.

"You're here so soon," said Angela as she leaned toward Franco.

"I came early for many reasons." He looked over at the nun. She seemed to be out of earshot. "First, because I didn't want to lose you; and second, because the European situation is not good. If we are to marry, now is the time." He searched her face. "Is now the time?"

"Yes, Franco, I feel that now is the time." It was her time to leave. Her time in Sicily was destined to be short—her unseen friends had conveyed this to her a long time ago.

~ ~ ~ ~ ~

Angela studied the convent chapel for the last time through her wedding veil. She looked up at the painting of the Madonna that hung over the altar. She closed her eyes and tried to recreate the Madonna's face in her mind so she could summon it up whenever she needed it, similar to how she could summon her light beings whenever she needed comfort.

Franco's extended family attended the wedding. All of the girls who had helped work on her hope chest were in attendance. She wished she had some blood relative who could watch her get married; she yearned for someone in this world who shared her beginnings to participate in her transition to a new life.

"*Kyrie eleison*," said the priest.

"*Christi eleison*," responded the guests.

Angela watched the altar boy as he waved the gold incense holder in the air. A thin cloud of smoke filled the chapel, emitting the fragrance of orange blossoms. The veil of smoke made the scene feel distant in Angela's mind. When she tried to remember her life before the earthquake, she had the same distant feeling. It seemed unreal. What she did clearly remember was her dream about the two beings enveloped in light. That seemed more real than her waking life in Messina. Out of the corner of her eye, she saw the white rims of the nuns' veils as their black habits faded behind the light layer of smoke.

The priest and altar boy, carrying a silver tray, stood over Franco and Angela. Roberto stepped forward and gave the priest the wedding bands. The priest waved his hand over the rings and dangled the bands of gold, and the altar boy placed the tray under them.

Angela raised her eyes and saw the symbols of her future come hurtling down toward the tray in a straight line as if propelled by some magnetic force. When they hit the tray, the echo sounded throughout the chapel like a gong and vibrated the walls of the chapel.

~ ~ ~ ~ ~

Angela and Franco climbed into the horse-drawn carriage that would take them to their wedding reception at the Princess of Palermo's villa. Angela was very careful of her beautiful white lace gown and the long veil.

"This is a very beautiful carriage," said Franco. "I have never been in one."

"Don't you have carriages in New York?" Angela asked.

"We used to have horse-drawn trolley cars, but now the trolleys are electric. We also have automobiles. I will buy an automobile once we move out of the city."

"An automobile? That is very expensive," said Angela.

"I have prepared for certain expenses," said Franco. He put his arm around his bride.

This man is a mystery, thought Angela. She thought that he might think the same of her. They were riding in the Princess of Palermo's carriage to their wedding reception at her villa. This was probably not what he expected from an orphan girl raised by the Sister of Charity.

They pulled up to the villa, and the bride and groom descended.

As they made their way down the corridor to the main room, servers with platters of food lined the hallway. The Princess was not in residence, but she had left some servants behind to assist with the reception. The food had been provided by the convent but prepared by the Princess's staff.

As Franco and Angela entered the spacious main room, applause echoed off the walls. The girls from the convent surrounded Angela and wished her a safe journey into her new life. Most of the girls knew how precarious and unpredictable life could be, for they had come from unsafe conditions. Safety was imperative at the beginning of any endeavor.

As the girls finished their well-wishes, Franco's cousins, aunts, and uncles hugged and kissed the couple at length, wishing them a safe journey to the new world and the blessing of many children.

The tables were dressed in white tablecloths made by the girls, and the menu was simple. There was pasta with tomato and clam sauce, handmade sausage, salad, cannoli, and a small wedding cake. The Princess had hired a local band for dancing. Angela and Franco danced the first waltz while everyone applauded again, including the servants. The girls joined in and danced with each other.

After the first dance, the servants approached Angela and expressed their congratulations and their envy. They wished to have the same experience she was having. These girls desired a way out of their situation, as they would most likely spend the rest of their lives serving others. Angela's favorable circumstances seemed magical to them. They surrounded Angela and asked how she had come to meet and marry Franco.

Angela told them that she never longed to leave the convent; the opportunity had simply presented itself. If it had not been for the earthquake, she would also have been a servant girl. Her entire history had changed because of a natural disaster. I will never have to serve strangers, thought Angela. I will care for Franco and our children, sew, and make a new life.

For the next few hours, everyone danced and celebrated Angela and Franco's new life. She smiled and said all the right things, but in the back of Angela's mind loomed her sister's shadow, coloring everything she thought and felt. She would leave her sister behind, never to know if she was alive or dead.

Her unseen friends would come with her, since they had no form. They had been with her before the earthquake and remained with her to this day. She spoke to them about confusing situations, and answers would come in a day or so. Maybe it is time to give them up, thought Angela. She had Franco to talk to now. No, it was not necessary. She would keep them close to her heart, and no one needed to know. Knowing that she could call upon them at any time made her strong.

"Dance with me, Franco," said Filomina. "With your wife's permission, of course."

"Angela?" Franco asked.

"My parting gift to you," said Angela to Filomina.

As the band played a waltz, Angela watched as Franco and Filomina glided around the perimeter of the room. He winked at Angela with a triumphant grin as they flowed past where she was standing. He is happy, thought Angela. She had made the right choice.

~ ~ ~ ~ ~

Franco unlocked the door to the small cottage and pushed the door open. He hadn't really thought about the moment when he would be alone with Angela. The trip, the strain of dealing with family, and the wedding made him feel spent. He wondered what Angela expected.

"Do you like the cottage?" asked Franco as he helped Angela off with her jacket.

"Yes, I think it's lovely."

"It belongs to my cousin's friend. He's gone for a few days," said Franco. He thought of the two bedrooms upstairs and how they could sleep on their own for tonight. After all, they hadn't seen each other in nearly a year and had hardly touched. Besides, he had never been with a woman before——not completely, anyway. She would think he was a failure as a husband in bed. But then, how would she know what to expect, coming from a convent? He was too tired to pursue it.

"Angela, there are two bedrooms upstairs and if you want, I could sleep in one and you the other. If you become frightened, you could just call out."

"My own room? I've never had my own room, not even for one night." She looked at Franco and hesitated. "I would like to do that."

Franco felt relieved. They had to save their energy for the long journey home.

~ ~ ~ ~ ~

The next morning, Franco walked down the stairs and paused at the bottom to button his shirtsleeves. There was a knock at the door. The old nun who chaperoned their initial meeting stood at the entrance.

"Hello, Franco, good morning. I've come to speak with Angela," said the old nun, glancing at his shirt. "I see you're still wearing shirts without cufflinks."

"Oh, Sister. Well, come in."

"The Mother Superior has sent me to speak with Angela." She cleared her throat.

"Oh…all right. I'll call her." Franco now understood that Angela would always think of the convent as her home and the nuns as her family. Maybe he had married someone with a deep connection to Sicily. Perhaps she wasn't as free as he had thought. He wasn't sure if he should permit this meeting. She was his wife. His position as a husband should start now. Maybe he should never have given Angela a choice of bedrooms last night.

"Sister Regina," said Angela as she descended the stairs. "What are you doing here?"

"Franco, I'd like to speak with Angela for the last time alone. You understand, if Angela ever returns for a visit, I'll surely be dead," said the nun with a smile. She hobbled over to Franco and put her weathered hand on his shoulder. "We won't be long. I know you have a train to catch."

Franco remembered the old nun's presence when he first met Angela. She pretended she wasn't there so he could talk to Angela without feeling self-conscious.

"Angela, I'll finish packing," Franco said. "Thank you, Sister." He touched the nun's hand, feeling her large bones covered with loose skin, and went upstairs.

"Angela, Mother Superior has sent me to ask you if you are all right." Sister Regina had requested that she send another nun instead of herself, but the Reverend Mother insisted that she go since she had chaperoned the young couple. She had thought that Sister Priscilla might be a better choice, but she had been told that Sister Priscilla was too old to go outside the convent.

"All right? I'm perfectly fine," Angela said, wondering what all the fuss was about.

"Everything went well, then?" She shifted her cane back to her other hand.

"Everything went well…. Yes, the wedding was lovely. Franco and I are leaving for Rome today and then on to Genoa and then New York."

"And after the wedding and the reception, everything went well?" She hoped that soon Angela would understand what she meant, as she wasn't sure herself. Hadn't Sister Priscilla spoken to the young woman?

"Well, yes, I'm feeling…. Oh, I…Yes, I have no problem. I'm fine. There is no problem."

"Mother Superior will be glad to hear the news," said the nun as she patted Angela on the arm. "Well, I'll be off. Good luck with your journey and with your new life. God be with you. Remember, you always have a home with us. Always."

"Thank you, Sister," said Angela she as kissed the nun on both cheeks. "I know I always have a home at the convent." Angela opened the door and watched the nun limp toward a waiting carriage.

"Angela, are you ready?" asked Franco. He carried a large heavy suitcase as he came down the stairs. He stopped to straighten his tie.

Angela knew it was part of a wife's duty to help her husband. She went over to assist him with his tie. It was the first time she had ever held a male article of clothing, except for priest's vestments that needed to be mended.

She picked up his tie and untangled it, pretending to know what she was doing. He looked down at her hands and began to help her with the knot. Their hands intertwined; their fingers bumped into each other.

"What did Sister Regina want? Don't they think I'll treat you well?" Franco touched her hand and held it, never making eye contact. He looked up for a moment and brushed her cheek with the back of his hand. She smiled.

"Sister was just checking to see if we needed any help getting to the train station. I told her we were waiting for our carriage."

"Why couldn't she have asked me?"

A man shouted from outside.

"There's our carriage," said Franco.

"I'll go and get dressed," said Angela, and ran up the stairs.

Franco did not want to play second fiddle to nuns, nor did he want his wife to keep secrets from him. Wives should not keep secrets from their husbands. Even if a woman has a family and would like to visit them, she has to ask permission from her husband. That's the way things are. He would have to mention this to Angela during their overnight journey to Rome. He picked up the suitcase and walked out to the carriage.

~ ~ ~ ~ ~

Franco awoke with a jolt. He looked out the window of the moving train and saw darkness. The train began to slow down, and workmen with lanterns waved it forward. Franco could feel the train being loaded onto the boat to cross the Strait of Messina.

He had first crossed the broad expanse of water at the age of five, with his father. His father had woken him at dawn to go on deck to see the sun rise, and he remembered his first view of the Italian mainland as shimmering. It was in winter, just after a rain, and the hills sparkled like the Mediterranean Sea when the noonday sun reflected off the water.

"Angela, wake up."

"What?" mumbled Angela as she wiped her eyes.

"Wake up. Let's go upstairs and watch the dawn."

"What for? It's still dark outside."

"In about fifteen minutes, the sun will begin to rise. We can see Italy coming toward us, and we'll be going toward it."

"I don't want to see it," Angela said.

"Come on. I don't want to see it alone."

Angela reminded herself that she was married now. Her husband wanted to do something, and she should accompany him. She shouldn't let him go alone. She wanted to be a good wife.

"All right, Franco. Let me get dressed."

They opened the compartment door and went up on deck. The air was still and quiet, and the water seemed to breathe rhythmically, slowly guiding the boat toward its destination. The deck began to fill up with passengers to watch the ascending dawn. Franco knew many of these people had made the crossing before and didn't mind interrupting their sleep because they knew it was an extraordinary sight.

The dawning light was always different—the wind was sometimes soft, other times sweeping, and the water had a mind of its own as it slapped against the boat. The performance of the elements transfixed its audience. The passengers whispered to one another as if not to disturb the actors. The audience sat on the seats provided and patiently waited for the sun to make its appearance.

"What is everyone waiting for?" asked Angela. She closed her shawl around her chest.

"The sunrise," said Franco.

"But why? Haven't they ever seen the sun before? I've seen the dawn many times from my room at the convent."

"The sun has special meaning when you go from Sicily to Italy, especially as a Sicilian. It means the sun will warm you until you return."

"What's the difference? The sun is everywhere."

"Yes, but you've not seen it from Sicilian waters. It is said that the light is more intense and illuminating. Some say they have been healed from ailments just by the light reflected off the Mediterranean."

Not even in church had Angela ever seen a more reverent group as these Sicilians patiently waiting to see the sun. Franco had left Sicily when he was twelve, and it seemed he knew the people and the land far better than herself. It seemed that everyone was looking for the light radiating from the sun rather than the sun itself.

Every time she thought about her unseen friends, she also felt their light, which made her feel connected and safe. She wondered about the passengers' lives. Their dress and mannerisms were foreign to her. They spoke the Sicilian dialect of their villages and towns, which she could not understand very well. She still remembered her dialect from Messina, but the nuns had forbidden the girls to speak Sicilian in any form. At the convent, pure Italian was spoken at all times. If any girl were caught speaking a dialect, the nun would make her kiss the floor in repentance.

Franco put his arm around Angela's shoulders, and together, they looked up at the sun that began to show its golden lights from behind a mountain. They watched the brightest star in the heavens slowly emit its rays and shower warmth on all who stood on deck. The sun displayed its entire circular form and spread a warm, protective, white light over the passengers.

In her imagination, Angela saw her unseen friends smile and send her extra light. Within their light was wisdom and clarity. That's why she was on deck: to receive the gifts her dream friends wanted to give her. She gazed into the distance and saw brilliant, variegated colors reflected on the sea. A shimmering gold surrounded the purples, yellows, and reds. Families exchanged greetings and wished each other health and a long life.

"Do you see what I mean?" asked Franco.

"The light is beautiful." Angela felt it was a sign from God that her future was to be bright and bathed in light. She thought of her unseen friends and their light and how she took them with her everywhere. Angela prayed that the light would warm and guide her sister, wherever she was.

~ ~ ~ ~ ~

Angela yawned and opened the wooden shutters. Piazza Navona began to fill with tourists. The ancient fountains took on a different spirit in the morning light; they thrived and pulsated. In the evening, they receded from the crowd and became more statuesque.

It was their third day in Rome, and they had visited museums and seen many paintings—but Angela's favorite works of art were the sculptures. She loved the sense of movement and form. The stone and marble took on human characteristics for her. Whenever she passed a small fountain with a sculpture in the middle, she imagined the statue turning and watching her walk down the street or a garden path. She liked the feeling of someone or something watching over her. The forms confirmed that she was guided in all her choices.

She remembered an ancient fountain in Messina upon which she and her sister would play, located on a deserted street where most of the buildings were abandoned. There they would mimic the women who gathered around the major fountains in the larger piazzas to fill their water jugs. The women gossiped about the high price of vegetables and their unfaithful husbands. Angela recalled Signora Millani, who complained about her husband sleeping with the neighborhood whore.

"My Giuseppe," the signora would say, "he treats me like I am his donkey. He goes with his whore without shame. He parades her in front of his children. What am I to do? I am a woman completely helpless in a grave situation." After her speech, she would fill her jug and with one swoop of her massive arms, balance it on her head. Her neck was long, and the muscles stood out like the Sicilian hills. All the women would nod in sympathy when Signora Millani told her sad tale. Inevitably, the following day, her husband would be seen hurrying to work with his face buried in his coat collar to hide a black eye. He would say his donkey kicked him.

When Angela was feeling down, her sister would entertain her with her imitation of the wronged woman at the ancient fountain.

"Oh, my God, you women don't know the grief I bear," her sister would shout, her hands clutching at her breast. "My husband is no better than his ass. I am a helpless woman, so this time I will have to blacken both his eyes to show him how helpless I am."

The two girls hung onto each other and laughed and laughed. She couldn't imagine sharing that moment with anyone else. It was the closest she had ever felt to anyone.

A few days after the sisters' last visit to the hidden fountain, the earthquake came and she was gone. Now Angela was leaving her sister behind.

"Are you enjoying Rome, Angela?" asked Franco as they walked through the Borghese Gardens.

"I think the artwork is beautiful," said Angela. "I'm glad we're here for the Easter festivities." She took a deep breath and looked at her surroundings. "I've never seen flowers in so many different colors. In Sicily, I only saw the wildflowers that were a pale yellow. I've never seen so many different shades of one color—so many variations. And pink—I've never seen a pink flower. It looks like they've all been painted."

She walked over to a row of flowers and touched them. They were real. and each had its own shade of pink, purple, or blue—some bright, some pastel. Together, they reminded Angela of the convent chorus, from soprano to baritone, all members dependent on each other to make music.

"My family is looking forward to meeting you," said Franco. He hoped Angela was as anxious to meet his family. "My brother works hard. I'm sure you'll like him. He's very young, and I hope he'll get a college education someday. I'd like to help him."

"And your sister?" asked Angela.

"She's only nine years old. She will appreciate having a young woman like you in the family. My mother tends to be old-fashioned when it comes to raising girls." Franco imagined them all together, celebrating their marriage. He saw his family all joyous, all giving.

"Tomorrow we leave for Genoa to get the boat to New York," said Franco. "Would you like to have an early dinner and go to bed early?"

"No, I would like to spend some time this evening in some of the piazzas, if you don't mind, Franco. I know you must be tired."

"No, I was concerned only for you. If you would like to spend your last night in Italy in the piazzas, then that's what we'll do."

~ ~ ~ ~ ~

Angela unfolded the white linen napkin and placed it on her lap. She felt stylish dressed in the blue suit Franco had given her. She watched the waiter as he went from table to table filling wine glasses. She closed her eyes and sensed the boat sway in what felt like slow motion—side to side, up and down. Angela imagined she was floating across the Atlantic Ocean toward the new world in a huge bassinet. The band began to play a slow melody as passengers entered the dining room. Three empty seats were at their table, and she wondered which passengers would join them for dinner.

A Roman Catholic priest approached their table.

"Hello, folks," said the priest in English. "I'll be dining with you tonight."

"Good evening, Father," said Franco, extending his hand. "It's a pleasure to meet you. Please be seated." Franco pulled the chair next to him away from the table and motioned for the man to sit.

"This is my wife, Angela. We're just married, and she speaks no English." He touched his wife's arm. "Angela, this is Father....ah Father...."

"Harris," said the priest with a grin. "I've just come from an audience with His Holiness."

"This is Father Harris, who has just come from Rome and applauded the Pope. I'm assuming he was the audience and the Pope was the entertainment," Franco translated into Italian.

Angela looked down and put her hand to her lips to muffle a giggle.

"A pleasure to meet you, Father," she said.

"My wife says it's nice to know you," Franco translated.

"A pleasure, Madame, a pleasure."

People filled the great dining room. The brilliant colors of the women's gowns, the gleaming burnt-umber wood, and the glaring white napkins and tablecloths impressed Angela. She realized what a black and white world she had lived in: the nuns' habits, the Princess's villa, her school uniform. She focused on a tall couple. They looked over the heads of the other people in the room. She knew they couldn't be Europeans. One of the waiters pointed the couple in Angela's direction.

"Hello," said the tall woman, "I believe we'll be sharing our table with you tonight."

Franco and the priest stood up.

"I'm Mrs. Sandra Knolls, and this is my husband, William."

"How do you do, gentlemen?" said the man as he bowed slightly.

Franco and the woman shook hands. The priest extended his toward the woman, but she put her hands on the back of her dress to smooth the material and sat down.

Angela stared at the woman. She knew she shouldn't, but it was as if her eyes were frozen in their sockets. She had never seen a deep rose-colored gown before. The gown was covered with shiny small stones, creating darks and lights throughout the design. The sleeves were off the woman's shoulders, and the yoke was cut low. The woman wore rouge, lipstick, and had long red nails the color of her gown. How could she do any work with those nails? Maybe she has servants, thought Angela.

"I'm Father Harris," announced the priest, "and this is Mr. and Mrs. Bellini. They're just married."

The waiter poured the wine.

"Well, Mrs. Bellini, what do you plan to do when you arrive in our great country?" asked the woman as she lifted her wine glass to her lips.

"My wife doesn't speak English, Mrs. Knolls. She speaks Sicilian and has never traveled before."

"Oh, what a pity. I had hoped to speak to a real Sicilian woman. I've heard so much about them. I hear they're so strong and talented. I also hear they're excellent cooks. I've never been good at such things."

"I can vouch for that," said her husband as he chuckled.

Angela listened to the laughter; it echoed inside her head. She knew that the joke was at her expense. Even though she couldn't understand the words, she could not mistake the feeling. She noticed the priest's face turn the color of the American woman's dress.

As soon as the priest's glass was half-empty, Franco attentively filled it again.

"Yes," said Mr. Knolls, "I think Italy is on the verge of ruin. The worker unrest has devastated this country—and with the rumblings of war in Europe, people will not travel here. It is a good thing you are escaping this mess."

"We didn't escape," said Franco, "I am an American citizen who chose to marry an Italian. She left of her own choosing. That doesn't make us refugees, does it, Father?"

"Oh, definitely not. Say, folks, what kind of wine was that? I really like the taste." He picked up his napkin and shook it. Angela suddenly found his napkin on her shoulder. Father Harris looked at his empty hand.

Angela quickly took the napkin off her shoulder and pretended that she had dropped it. She bent down and handed it to the priest under the table. Franco and the two Americans seemed to have a lot to say to each other; even the woman entered into the conversation. Franco was not able to translate quickly enough to draw Angela into their banter.

The priest slumped back in his seat and stared. Too much wine, thought Angela. It looked like he was not present—as if he had gotten up and left his body. She wished for someone to talk to.

~ ~ ~ ~ ~

The steamship crept into New York Harbor, and Angela saw the Statue of Liberty come into view. She felt the statue was strong but gentle and thought the huge sculpture would be a place for her to run to if she were ever in trouble.

"Have you enjoyed the trip?" asked Franco.

"Yes, Franco, it was very nice. I had a nice time," said Angela as she lowered her head.

Franco put his finger under her chin, lifted it, and looked into her eyes. He remembered Sister Regina and her visit after the wedding and thought that maybe she wished she were back at the convent.

"Angela, what's the matter? You look so sad. I'm trying to please you and make you happy."

"It's my sister, Franco. I'm not sure she was killed in the earthquake."

"What are you talking about?"

"Her body was never found. I don't know if she's dead or alive."

"Why didn't you tell me before we left Sicily? We could have stayed and looked for her."

"No, I couldn't have said anything. You were so happy. I didn't want to spoil anything. Besides, it was time for me to leave."

"Well, that gives us good reason to return someday."

A foghorn blast startled the newlyweds. As land approached, Angela took in the view of New York. The people waiting on the pier appeared to be specks compared to the size of the buildings. She felt the light of her unseen friends as she greeted her new life.

Chapter 3
America, 1913

Franco blindfolded Angela and led her into his family's building on Goerich Street.

"Where are we going?"

"It's a surprise, Angela, now don't spoil it," said Franco.

"But I don't like the idea of not being able to see."

"That's the idea—so you'll be surprised. Now turn left and down the stairs. Be careful now."

"Franco, I don't like this." She reached out and grabbed his arm.

"Shh. Move to the right, there's a door here. Let's see what's behind it."

Angela heard the door open and a crowd cry out "Surprise!" She took off her blindfold and saw her husband's family and friends.

"Welcome to America, Angela," said one man.

"Good fortune in your marriage," said another guest.

"This is a combination wedding and welcome party for us," said Franco.

Angela thought that the guests' faces were reminiscent of the Sicilians on deck to watch the sunrise. The women in this group would be her only connection in her new world. Franco told her some of them had been in America for many years and still couldn't speak English. Their husbands kept long hours at work and when they returned home, it was easy for them to speak Italian and not bother with English. She felt a tug at her skirt.

"Angela, I'm so glad you're in America now," said a young girl said in Italian. "We'll go out and have such fun together."

Angela knew who this was.

"Oh, Speranza, I'm afraid I don't speak English well enough yet to go out." She hugged her sister-in-law.

"I will help you learn English. I'll take the train up to Nelsonville every weekend and bring my schoolbooks. You'll learn."

Angela saw a large figure in her peripheral vision.

"Angela, I am Franco's mother—and now you are my daughter," said Franco's mother, folding her arms across her chest.

Angela kissed her mother-in-law on both cheeks.

"I am so happy to be a part of this family and America," said Angela.

"Come and meet the other guests," said Franco's mother.

"Yes, Ma. I'm coming," said Angela.

Angela remembered Sister Priscilla's wisdom regarding in-laws; she must appear to be obedient.

"Speranza, go play with the other children," said Franco's mother.

"But I want to talk with Angela. She and Franco will only be in the city for a few days, and then they will move to their house in the country."

"You'll see her; she's not gone yet. Now run along so Angela can attend to things."

Angela smiled and greeted her guests; they kissed her cheeks and wished her well. All the women had cooked and made exotic-looking dishes. Angela had never cooked before. At the convent, they had a nun who cooked all the meals for the students. Cooking was something a girl learned when she left school and was out in the world; creativity and learning were what was important.

"Angela, I'm so glad you're part of the family now," said Alessio, "I've never seen my brother so happy, and I can see why."

"I hope you don't mind that we stay here for a few days. I look forward to getting to know the family, but I know that the apartment is small."

"It's worth it just to see you two happy."

There was a knock at the door. Alessio opened it.

"Alessio, I haven't seen you in a long time," said a short man.

"Salvatore, it's been a while. How's everything?"

"Not too bad. I haven't met Franco's pretty wife."

"Angela, this is Salvatore Cino. He works with Franco at St. Mary's Convent. They were roommates together."

"Nice to meet you." Angela remembered Franco saying that there was a worker at the convent who wasn't strong in body or mind. The other men thought he was slow mentally, since it took him double the time to do a job. Franco had said that it was because of his infantile paralysis. Salvatore was also looking for a wife and couldn't find one.

"We will see each other many times once you move to Nelsonville," said Salvatore as he took Angela's hand.

Angela watched him throw his right leg out in front of him and limp as he walked away. She understood why he wasn't married; no woman would marry such a man, because her children would be born with the same deformity. Salvatore went over to Franco's mother, who embraced him. As they talked, she put her arm around him and motioned Speranza over to them. Salvatore fingered the little girl's long, dark hair and patted her head.

Angela disliked a disheveled look on a little girl. Speranza's hair needs to be braided, she thought. She made a mental note to do that tomorrow morning. She would also tell her about her wedding, the Princess of Palermo, and how she came to marry her brother. Angela also noticed the unraveled hemline on Speranza's dress. No one is looking after this child, thought Angela. She would make sure from this day forward to look after Speranza and make sure that her personal appearance was valued. There would be no more unraveled hemlines.

The next morning, Angela braided Speranza's hair and told her about her wedding and the Princess of Palermo. Speranza sat and listened without a sound, even when Angela combed the knots out of her hair. When Angela sewed up the unraveled hem on Speranza's dress, her mother-in-law asked why she would bother doing that; the girl was just going to school. Who would look at her? Franco's mother told Speranza to do the dishes before she left for school. Angela said that she would do them, but the large woman said no, it was the little girl's job.

"Besides, she will be married in a few years. She needs to learn to be a wife," said Franco's mother.

Angela hadn't washed a dish or boiled water in many years. The nuns strongly believed creating beautiful linens was more than just sewing; it was a highly regarded art form. It did not seem that Franco's mother highly regarded anything. Angela would have to find a way to help Speranza.

~ ~ ~ ~ ~

Angela carefully folded the linen tablecloth and put it on a chair. She spread a piece of red material over the oak table and began to arrange a dress pattern. The doorbell rang. She had been in Nelsonville for five months, and the doorbell had never rung in the afternoon. Angela listened to the hall clock and practiced in English: "Hello, my husband is not here. Please go away." The doorbell rang again. She walked slowly to the window and looked out. A man in a uniform stood at the door tapping his finger on a large box that stood on legs with wheels.

His uniform didn't look like a regular police uniform. Angela wondered if he was some sort of local police who was coming to tell her that her husband had committed a crime. What would she do without him? The man began to pace. As he turned his back, she saw that there were three words written on the back of his jacket: two starting with S and the other with M. He knocked on the door. She had never seen a police uniform with words on the back.

"Singer Sewing Machine," Angela heard him shout. She couldn't translate his words. Maybe he wanted to give something important to her husband? What if he should break down the door and the neighbors should see?

Angela opened the lock and stood for a moment. She opened the door but then ran back into the house like a frightened cat.

"Hello, hello. Anybody home?" called the man as he wheeled the package into the hall.

"Yes, yes," said Angela as she slowly came out from the other room.

"Are you Mrs. Bellini?" asked the man.

"Please, husband not here."

"But you're Mrs. Bellini?"

Angela nodded.

"Well, Mrs. Bellini, this is for you. Could you sign this?" He held out a piece of paper and pen. She backed away from him.

"See your name is on this tag." He held it up to Angela. "Oh that's no problem, lady. We can get your husband's signature another time." He pushed the package toward her and left the house.

Angela approached the box on wheels, gave it a small push, and shook it back and forth. There was a small metal bar attached just above the wheels, which she lifted. Beneath was a wooden cabinet. The top of the cabinet was a dark walnut and was so shiny that Angela could see her reflection. There was a small door on top of the cabinet that had an indentation for someone to put in a finger and pull up. She placed her finger in the indentation, then stopped. Should she wait for Franco to come home? It was clearly addressed to her. She pulled up on the door and uncovered a sewing machine lying on its side. She released the machine from its cocoon and stood it upright. There was an electric cord wrapped around it. An electric sewing machine! Her husband must have saved for a long time to buy her this!

She would be able to turn out dresses more quickly—and maybe even quit her job at St. Mary's School as one of the seamstresses for the students. The machine could be her independence in the future. Franco really wanted her to be happy.

Minutes later, she heard, "Angela, where are you?" Franco closed the front door.

He walked through the hall and into the dining room, where he stopped to admire the tapestry of St. Peter's Cathedral in Rome. He had bought it in Rome from a street peddler who said it was modeled after a famous eighteenth-century French painting. When Franco asked who the artist was and where the painting hung, the man gave him the name of a nineteenth-century Italian portrait painter Franco had heard his cousin Roberto mention. The peddler gave such an intriguing speech about the life of the artist that Franco bought the tapestry.

"Franco, you're home already!" said Angela, emerging from the kitchen. "I was so scared to open the door." She hugged Franco. "You've made me so happy. The electric machine is beautiful."

"I know you get pleasure from your sewing, and I wanted to help you," he said.

"We can't afford it," said Angela.

"We can afford it. Now you can sew whatever you want, whenever you want."

When Angela was with the nuns, she had to sew what they wanted: covers for the altar, vestments for the priests. Her husband got her a job making dresses for the well-to-do students at St. Mary's School shortly after her arrival in Nelsonville. But with this sewing machine, she could be more independent and make Speranza new school clothes and make dresses for the neighborhood women. She could also occupy her time until she had a baby.

"Come outside and look in the driveway," Franco said.

Angela noticed he had the same triumphant look that he had at their wedding reception. As she looked over the side of the porch, she saw a black, shiny automobile. Two large headlights sat perched on the front of the vehicle like an owl's eyes. To Angela, it looked like a carriage with a motor.

"Who owns this automobile?" said Angela.

"We do," said Franco. "I did work on a rich customer's house, and we made a fair exchange."

Franco guided her to the car.

"Get in. I need to show you more."

"I hope this is safe," said Angela. She did not like anything that moved uncontrollably. Angela preferred sure footing.

Franco cranked the car, and the motor started to run.

"Where are we going?" Angela asked over the engine.

"We are riding around town. I want to show you a few houses."

Angela wondered if he was thinking about buying another home. How could they afford it?

As Franco backed out of the driveway Angela gripped his arm.

"My God, this goes fast," Angela said.

"Relax, it will be fine."

Franco drove up the hill that led to St. Mary's School, but he made a left turn onto a side road. He stopped in front of a small but well-kept house surrounded by flowers and trees. There was a stone walkway that led to the front door. The design reminded Angela of the walkway Franco had created in their backyard.

"Why are we stopping here?" asked Angela.

"I own this house and two others like it. We both own them."

"You own it? When did you buy it? I was not aware." Angela suddenly feared that she had married a spendthrift with high ideas.

"I bought this a year ago, and the other two just before we were married."

"Did you rob a bank?" asked Angela.

"No, I worked and saved every penny. I exchanged room and board for work. All three of the houses are income properties. I have hard-working Italian tenants, and I do all of the repairs myself."

"Do I have to do anything?" Angela asked.

"No," laughed Franco. No one knows I own them—just you and me. This is our security. If we need money, we sell one of the houses. We work for ourselves. We make as much or as little as we want so that no matter what happens, we are safe. Our skills will always be in demand. Our children will have security."

"Why did you take so long to tell me?"

"Because I felt it might have interfered with our marriage. I did not want the nuns to go poking around my business. And also, my family might want to live in these houses. I only want paying tenants."

Angela had thought Franco smart when she first met him, but she had no idea he had a business head. The risk she had taken in coming to America had turned in her favor. As long as she did not have to clean another house, she was delighted about his ambition.

"Do you want to see the others today?"

"I would like to go home and work with my sewing machine," said Angela. Now she could start making dresses for people. A good seamstress is needed in this town, she thought.

~ ~ ~ ~ ~

"Come and see what your brother has bought," said Angela to Speranza as she opened the front door.

"Oh, I heard about it, Angela. I'm dying to see it," said Speranza. She put her schoolbooks down on the hall table. "Oh, Angela, it's beautiful. I've seen these in shop windows."

"Now you'll have proper clothes for a schoolgirl."

"Oh, I'd love that! I'm not such a girl, Angela. I'll be 11 in a few weeks."

"Who told you you're not a girl? Of course you're a girl. Don't let your brother hear you talk like that. You're a child, and I'll make dresses for a girl your age. It will be my way of paying you back for English lessons."

"Oh, Angela, you don't need to pay me back. I love coming up here on weekends to be with you and Franco. You're so good to me. It's so nice not to do dishes for a few days." She embraced her sister-in-law.

Angela remembered how good it felt when she and her sister had strolled hand in hand down Messina's streets. Now God had sent her Speranza to take care of. It was a sign that she was to lavish all the love she felt for her sister on the little girl.

~ ~ ~ ~ ~

Angela had been in America for over a year. She now felt confident in holding conversations in English when she went shopping or talked to neighbors, but she vacillated between Italian and Sicilian when expressing deep feeling or communication with her unseen friends. The sewing machine worked wonders; she had some of the affluent ladies in town as steady customers. They would ask Angela about Italian fashion and what they were wearing in Europe this year. She would giggle to herself and give serious suggestions about the lengths of hemlines and the arrangement of darts. Angela had never even seen a fashion magazine until she came to America.

Angela moved the chalk dispenser around the skirt, marking where the hemline would be.

"Mrs. Bellini, do you think the skirt will be too short?" asked Mrs. Woldman.

"No, Mrs. Woldman, I think it is just right. Besides, they are wearing the skirts a bit shorter this year. At least that is what I hear from my cousin in Rome." Angela had made up an alter ego in the form of a cousin who was a dressmaker in Rome. It made her customers feel that they had a direct link to fashionable Europe. She squeezed the bulb that left a small white mark on the bottom of the skirt.

"Oh, I'm so glad. I'm trying to get George to go abroad after the war, but he said it is premature to make plans. What do you think, Mrs. Bellini?"

Angela thought about the nuns living through the war. Italy had not joined the war, but there was talk that it was only a matter of time before Italy would have no choice but to fight. Sometimes she dreamed that the Austrians took over the convent and killed all the orphans and nuns. Then her sister would find her way to the convent and find everyone dead, then roam the desolate streets alone. Angela thought of her sister as a vagabond in some remote part of Sicily, starving and suffering.

"Mrs. Bellini, did you hear me?" asked Mrs. Woldman.

"After the war, Mrs. Woldman? I cannot say."

"What does your cousin say? She must have an opinion."

"She does not mention politics much. My cousin is a simple girl who comments on fashion and people on the street."

"Well, I don't know how one can live in Europe and not comment on all the destruction going on."

"My cousin is a simple girl, Mrs. Woldman. I am finished. You may take off the suit."

Angela opened the sliding oak doors that led to the bedroom. Mrs. Woldman went into undress, and Angela walked into the dining room to make out a receipt for her customer. A pad of paper was open on her husband's smoking table. She reached over to put it away and saw that he was writing to his cousin Roberto.

Franco and Angela had heard from recent immigrants that Sicilian life had become unbearable for the common citizen, and they had begun to speak out against the war that was ravaging European villages and killing women and children. The immigrants saw the peasants flock to the Mafia chief for protection against the war and starvation.

It had been months since they had heard from Roberto, but Franco wrote him faithfully every two weeks. Every day, when Franco came home from work, the first thing he did was look at the mail. She knew he worried about the war and his family. It was a relief for Angela to talk about fashion. She needed simple talk.

"Well, Mrs. Bellini, I'll pick up the suit next week. Thank you so much."

"Thank you, Mrs. Woldman. I like your company very much," said Angela as she walked her customer to the door.

Angela thought about Mrs. Woldman's interest in the war. Her sons were far too young to be drafted, and her husband was a doctor who made plenty of money. They would never be hungry, and she had no relatives in Europe to worry about. Angela imagined most Americans' situations to be similar; no real interest in stopping or speeding up the war, just talk about a Europe they did not understand.

Maybe she shouldn't have told Mrs. Woldman about a cousin who didn't exist. Through her customers' imaginations, the stories grew—and her cousin in Rome became a well-known character. When the women came to fit their dresses, they would all wait anxiously to hear about the girl's adventures. Angela gave them the Europe they wanted: dramatic and sweet, but most of all, simple.

In Angela's mind, her imaginary cousin looked like her sister. She projected a life for her sister filled with creativity, adventure, and love. If her sister was dead, then Angela would create the life she should have had through the stories she told her customers. Angela knew what people needed to hear for peace of mind.

Patriotism was foreign to Angela. Her customers talked about America and how strong and exceptional the country was. She couldn't imagine anyone making statements like that about Sicily, except maybe Roberto. She admired his strength and courage in speaking out against the war and the Mafia. He had been married only two years, and his wife was already expecting their second baby.

Then Angela wondered why she was not in the family way. After all, she had been married for over a year. She busied herself with her sewing at St. Mary's and at home, but she had planned to have a family. That was her future. Maybe God was waiting before He blessed them with children because there were other things she had to do first. Maybe He had not taken her sister away. It could be that Angela had to search for her. A child would prevent her from traveling.

~ ~ ~ ~ ~

Angela and Franco stepped off the train in Grand Central Station. She stayed close to her husband, as the size of the train station was still overwhelming to her. Even the Central Station in Rome, said to be the largest and busiest in the world, didn't seem as intimidating. Americans moved fast and would stop at nothing to get to their destination.

"Let's get a taxi to the hospital," said Franco.

They rushed down the long ramp that led to the front doors on 42nd Street. The sun had been shining before they left Westchester, but now it was overcast. Franco lifted his arm and a taxi pulled up to the curb.

"St. Luke's Hospital, please," said Franco.

"Franco, are you all right? You didn't eat anything this morning," said Angela.

A few months earlier, when they were in the city to visit Franco's family, Angela had noticed that Alessio was losing a large amount of weight and coughed a lot. She and Franco urged him to see a doctor, but he said he felt fine and that they shouldn't worry. The night before, Franco's mother called to say that Alessio had collapsed at the stockyard where he worked and was rushed to St. Luke's Hospital.

"I'm all right. I hope Alessio will be all right. He's never been in a hospital before," said Franco.

"Has your mother talked to the doctor at all?"

"She told me Alessio had some kind of chest problem, that's all."

Angela touched his hand and held it there. She loved Alessio. He had tried to lift her spirits when she first came to America by telling jokes.

"My brother is a good man. Maybe he had to work too hard in this country to make a living," said Franco.

"I'm sure that since he is in a hospital, he'll get better soon. When my brother died, he was at an orphanage. In America, Alessio will have good medical care and will get better," Angela said. In America, anything is possible, she thought.

As they entered the hospital, the smell of rubbing alcohol seeped from every crevice. They walked down the long hallway and stopped at the nurses' desk.

"Nurse, excuse me. Sorry to bother you. We are looking for Alessio Bellini," Franco said.

"Over there," said the nurse, pointing to the corner of a large room with about fifteen beds. "He's one of our favorite patients. He keeps everyone's spirits up."

The stench of the ward was familiar to Angela; it reeked of decomposing human innards. After the earthquake, it had taken several days for rescue teams to be formed. Bodies were left to bake in the hot Sicilian sun for days and weeks. Angela saw one body that had melted into the stone it was lying on. Members of the rescue team had to peel the flesh off the stone.

Death has taken up residence here, Angela thought as she glanced around. Large plastic tents enclosed patients to help them breathe. Some patients coughed and spat up phlegm. A nurse bent over a patient and gave him a sip of water. Another nurse put up a white screen around a bed. She snapped the screen into position so that death was concealed. Angela knew better.

They came to Alessio's bed. He was even thinner than Angela remembered. His eyes were like two grey pools of water surrounded by dark sunken circles. The skin sagged over his high cheekbones.

"Alessio, Alessio," said Franco as he kissed his brother's forehead. Alessio took his brother's hand. "I have been waiting all my life for us to work together on some project," said Franco. "When you get better, I promise—we will design a great house and build it with our own hands."

Angela often heard the brothers speak of building houses and what had to be done with electric wires and plumbing. It made them so happy to talk about what they would do. Alessio understood how Franco worked, but most Americans found it difficult to work with Franco because he was so fussy. Alessio understood that. Angela knew how important it was for the brothers to be independent when they worked.

"I will look forward to building your house," said Alessio as he wheezed and tried to stifle a cough. "We will someday build a house together."

Angela saw Franco squeeze his brother's hand tighter. Franco lowered his head as his tears dripped on the sheet. She put her hand on Franco's shoulder. To watch someone, you love suffer was the ultimate grief.

"Angela, please take this guy home," said Alessio with a wink. Franco reached in his vest pocket and took out a white linen handkerchief to wipe his eyes.

Angela heard the rattle in Alessio's chest as he attempted to take a deep breath. The fluid was drowning the Alessio they knew.

~ ~ ~ ~ ~

The pallbearers carried the coffin into the small church on Fourth Street. Franco leaned on Angela as she supported his arm. His head rested on his wife's shoulder. How could his beautiful brother have died? Tuberculosis was what the doctor said killed him. He must have had it for some time, said the doctor. Alessio was skinny as a boy, but healthy. Franco remembered chasing him home for lunch because he never wanted to eat. He would chase him around the piazzas and around to their house. He remembered his mother as a young woman, hanging out her kitchen window, calling for her sons. Life never remains simple—never.

Angela led him into the first pew beside his mother, stepfather, and Speranza. They all kneeled and bowed their heads as the priest prayed over the coffin. Franco asked God why He would waste a young life like this? Why? He listened for an answer but heard the altar bells instead. It was a sign for the congregation to stand up. The Catholic mass began to make no sense to him. Franco had never been particularly religious, but he used to find some comfort in attending mass. The incense and solemn mass helped him go into himself. Now, he wondered why he was here if he could get no answers.

The priest took the incense burner that hung from a long chain and circled the coffin, waving the burner. He muttered words in Latin that Franco could not understand.

"In the name of the Father and of the son and the Holy Spirit," said the priest as he made the sign of the cross.

Franco blessed himself and tried to pray. He told God that he accepted his brother's death as his Holy Will and that whatever He had in store for him in the future, he would accept. It was no use. His life in God's hands? It didn't feel right. He could no longer find God or comfort in church or with the ritual of the Holy Mass. But if not in church, where else would God be? Where else could he or anyone else find God?

The priest stood in front of the altar. The mass was over. The mourners followed the coffin down the main aisle and out to the street. Franco's stepfather opened the door to a car for the immediate family.

"Father should have said a high mass for my boy," said Franco's mother, wiping away her tears.

"It's best this way," said her husband. "It's over quicker. I don't believe in stretching these things out, especially death. Soon we will be at the cemetery, and it will be all over."

Franco did not tell his mother that when he went to discuss the funeral arrangements that the priest wanted more money for a high mass and Franco refused to pay him. It didn't seem right. His family had been a part of the parish since they came to this country. Everyone in America seemed money-hungry.

"Angela, are you feeling all right?" asked Speranza as she huddled between Franco and Angela. "You keep touching your stomach."

"My stomach feels a bit uneasy, that's all," said Angela as she pulled the little girl closer.

Speranza put her arms around Angela's waist, and Franco embraced them both. He felt as if he held two parts of a whole as the image of Palermo came to his mind. The same connection and energy flowed through his body: the city streets, people arguing, children running and the sun, the warmth of the Sicilian sun. He could feel it penetrate his limbs and face. It would never shine on his brother again.

~ ~ ~ ~ ~

Angela felt privileged to work for the nuns at St. Mary's School and Convent in Nelsonville just 45 minutes from New York City, as she saw many immigrant women in New York who were forced to work in garment factories. When she and Speranza shopped in the Italian grocery store, Angela listened intently to the women's conversations. The conditions at the factories were hazardous and over-crowded, and the women worked long hours for little pay. But the women needed jobs, and all they knew was sewing. Angela prayed that she would not end up in such a place. When Franco said the nuns needed another seamstress at the convent, she was relieved.

St. Mary's was an Episcopalian order of nuns, not Catholic. Angela's first impression of the Mother Superior was that of an efficient and intelligent leader. She was certainly as kind as the Mother Superior in Sicily, and both were wise—but it was in the type of wisdom that they differed.

Angela felt the Mother Superior at St. Mary's kept an arm's distance between her and the other sisters. The nuns had to make an appointment to discuss anything personal or professional. In Sicily, all a nun or student had to do was knock on the Reverend Mother's door. The sisters at St. Mary's elected their head by democratic vote, which meant the office of Mother Superior was earth-bound. At the convent in Sicily, the Reverend Mother was chosen by the present nun in office. She was usually given a sign by God or the Blessed Virgin as to which nun should assume the position.

Angela's adjustment to the convent and the work was easy. The more formal aspects of convent life in America agreed with her; she felt detached from the nuns, yet there was a familiarity that transcended country or custom. The detachment allowed her to grow in different directions.

"Good morning, Angela," said the Mother Superior, intertwining her fingers and resting them on her stomach. "Are things going well?"

"Yes, well, Moth-a," said Angela, covering her mouth with her slender fingers. Her comprehension of English was total, but she knew her pronunciation needed work.

"I'm glad to hear it. You've learned to use the electric sewing machines quite well in a short period. Many of the other seamstresses were surprised, but I expected you to do well, knowing Franco Bellini the way I do. He would have to have a wife who was as capable as himself."

"Capable," Angela repeated to herself. She never heard the word before. It sounded like a compliment about the work she did as a dressmaker. She disliked the English word seamstress because she felt it didn't accurately represent the kind of work she did. She didn't just sew seams, she made an entire garment. She always referred to herself in English as a dressmaker.

"Have a good day at work," said the nun.

"The same to you, Moth-a," Angela said. Same mistake, she thought. Angela hurried to the sewing room to start her day.

"Good-a day everyone," said Angela. She sat at her sewing machine. The women were standing in a semi-circle and talked softly.

Angela looked up and found everyone staring at her as if they were waiting for someone to speak.

"Angela, um, we've all been talking, and we thought it would be best to bring the matter up now," said a tall thin woman.

"Yes, Angela," said another young woman who wore bifocals. "We have all been sewing all our lives and have stable jobs. The problem is that since you've come here, the sisters have been complaining about our work."

"Complain! No, no. I talk with Moth-a Superiore. She like what we do!"

"No, you don't understand, Angela." The woman looked over her bifocals at Angela. "Mother Superior likes your work, not ours. She feels we should sew like you, and quite frankly, we don't have the time."

"No time?" Angela asked. "Sew like me?"

"Listen," said the thin woman. "Do you see this gray hair?" She grabbed a section of her hair. "I'm only thirty years old. I'm all gray from working hard and raising my family. We have to produce a certain amount of sewing each day or Mother Superior says we're slacking off. If we were to sew like you, we'd be here all hours!"

"I donna understand," Angela said. She tried to grab every word as the women spat them in the air, but the words faded as quickly as they were spoken.

"Those double hems you put on the altar linen," said the gray-haired woman. "That's not necessary. One hem is enough. And the designs you embroider on the dining hall tablecloths for the students. They're too fancy. How can we possibly do that, especially for the amount we're being paid?"

"And I usually make the girls' graduation dresses," said the woman with bifocals. "But Mother Superior told me you were making them this year. I depend on that extra money for my children. It's not fair. You have no children, and you and your husband live in a big house!"

When Mother Superior had asked Angela to make the graduation dresses a few weeks ago, she almost declined. The thought of making twenty dresses from the same pattern and material was not attractive to her. Besides, she could make more money with her private customers at home. But Angela held sincere affection for all the students. She always greeted them with a bright smile, especially during exam time when brightness was needed. She decided to make the dresses because she could find out more about their lives and learn more about America. She wanted to know about the students' plans for the future. She wanted to know if any of the girls would choose marriage, like she had, at such a young age.

"No, we no hav-a baby," said Angela. She stared at the women. She understood that they wanted her to sew like them and be like them. She had not come to America to be like everyone else. She came to make a home and work the way she always had, with a harmony of design. The nuns liked her work because it was different. It wasn't her fault that she had no children. God hadn't seen fit to give her any just yet.

"I work-a good," Angela said as she winced—another mistake in pronunciation. She was determined to find the English words to express herself. "I work-a for nobody but-a me. If-a Moth-a Superiore like it, good. I am-a happy. But I work-a this-a way for me."

Angela turned her attention to her work. The other women stared at her. A bell tolled, and they all took their places to begin work.

"We've wasted our breath. She doesn't understand," said the tall, thin woman.

91

"She understands," said the gray-haired woman. "She just told you that she understands."

Angela missed the girls at the convent in Sicily. Work was a joy then. Everyone did her best. It wasn't a question of how much could be done within a certain time frame. America was a strange place when it came to producing quality items. She would make the girls' graduation dresses, and when she did, she would pay attention to every single detail. Each buttonhole and hem would be done with such accuracy that they would seem machine made.

~ ~ ~ ~ ~

Angela bent down to shorten the hem on one of the student's dresses. It was graduation time at St. Mary's, and she had several more dresses to alter. A pain pierced her abdomen, and she fell on her hands and knees. She had experienced dull aches in the area below her navel for a few months, but she thought it was either her body longing to be pregnant or preparing to become pregnant. For a time, she thought there was something growing inside her— but there was no sign that she was expecting a baby. Her stomach hadn't become big at all. What was happening to her?

"Are you all right, Mrs. Bellini?" asked a student.

"I have terrible pain. Please-a get the Moth-a Superiore." The girl helped Angela to a chair and then ran to get the nun.

She couldn't get sick now. She had to work so they could afford their home. Maybe she had been working too hard by taking on new customers at home for extra money. Franco had paid for Alessio's funeral, which had depleted a lot of their savings. God wouldn't take her now and leave Franco all alone, without children. To die now, like this, after she had survived the earthquake, seemed too mean to be God's doing. She thought of the Blessed Virgin and how she felt protected by her. If she prayed to the Virgin Mary, no fatal harm would come to her.

The pain slowly dulled, and her thoughts scattered like frightened geese. She couldn't tell if the pain was subsiding or if her mind simply turned away from it. There was so much to think about, so many thoughts floating in her mind. Things appeared to wave at her as they somersaulted, danced, and bounced through her consciousness. She saw herself run after one, fall and run after another. Angela heard their laughter and knew they were playing with her. Finally she caught one. It was her unseen friends. Their light lifted her, and together they traveled somewhere in space. She was sure the Virgin Mary sent them to guide her. They finally stopped, and Angela felt her awareness become focused.

Her mother stood over the kitchen table and kneaded bread. Angela saw her as an old woman, even though her mother had been young when Mt. Etna erupted. The old woman was tall and slim with her hair pulled tightly in a bun. She turned and smiled at her daughter.

"You have grown up exactly the way I've pictured you," said her mother.

"But Mama, you're old. How can that be?"

"I've aged the way you've grown up," said the old woman, picking the sticky dough off her fingers.

"Why are you here now?" asked Angela as she walked toward her mother.

"Because you called for me."

"But you died young. You can't be old."

"I am the way you want and need me to be. Now, you have some problem?"

"Well, I'm getting sick and I'm afraid I'll die."

"And if you die, what will happen?"

"My husband Franco would be alone, and I would never find my sister. You remember my sister, don't you, Mama?"

"It is important for you to look for her, isn't it?" asked the old woman, putting the dough in a pan and placing a towel over it so the dough would rise.

"Yes! She may still be alive. I left Sicily and didn't even look for her! I have to see if she's still alive. I have to do that!" Light flashed around her mother's body. Suddenly, her mother's form separated and shifted into those of her unseen friends.

"Is it time for me to go back?" asked Angela.

Angela heard voices coming from outside her mind. She could see a man in a white coat hovering over her, even though her eyes were closed.

"Mrs. Bellini, Mrs. Bellini," echoed a voice.

She raised her eyelids, and the room began to spin.

"You've had an operation. We're taking you to your room," said the man.

She felt her body sail along corridors and down ramps. An antiseptic smell filled her nostrils, and she heard wheels squeaking. How could she have had an operation while she was busy chasing her thoughts and talking with her mother? There was no longer any pain, although she did feel sick to her stomach. Her body stopped, and she felt herself ascend for a while and then abruptly stop. She heard doors open and the clanging of beds and doctors and nurses whispering. Her husband's voice was in the distance. He called to her.

"Over here," she mumbled, "I'm over here."

~ ~ ~ ~ ~

Franco had hammered the last nail for the day. He had asked the Mother Superior for extra work and was laying a new floor in one of the convent's rooms that overlooked the Hudson River. When she told him that he could do the project alone, he was glad. The view from the window was the most breathtaking in the school. In the mornings, the river had a thin mist hovering over it. When the small steamships blew their foghorns, the mist parted and they seemed to be floating above the water.

In the late afternoons, activity on the river stopped, letting the last ray of sunlight shine undisturbed upon the water.

He heard an ambulance siren in the distance.

"Franco! Franco Bellini! Are you still here?" yelled a woman's voice from the staircase.

"Yes, I'm here. Who is it?" He rushed toward the doorway. The Mother Superior bounded toward him, her dark habit waving behind her.

"I ran from the main building at the bottom of the hill. They've just taken Angela to the hospital. I'll have my driver take you there."

"What happened?"

"I don't know. She fell ill with a pain in her stomach. Come collect your things, and my driver will be here in five minutes."

At the hospital, Franco stood by the large desk and waited for one of the nurses. He was reminded of the hospital in which his brother had died a few months earlier. It held the smell of illnesses with a sense of doom.

The doctor told him Angela had fibroid tumors that had burst inside her uterus. They had to operate and remove her uterus. Peritonitis had set in, and she was having difficulty overcoming the high fever.

Franco reached into his pocket, pulled out his wallet, and flipped through the pictures of his family. Angela, dressed in her convent uniform, looked healthy and content. He would not pray for her recovery, because he had given up prayer after Alessio's death. If God were just, He would let his wife live. If something should happen to Angela, then he would deny God's existence for the rest of his days.

Franco had imagined his house filled with children, but there would none now—at least not his own. He held a genuine affection for kids and disliked people who pretended to like them. Some people got married just to have children and not for companionship. Children were important, but Angela came first. He felt she was the kind of person who held the earth together; she was the glue the earth needed.

"Mr. Bellini, I'm glad you're here," said a nurse as she approached the desk. "Your wife's fever is high, and it doesn't seem to be going down. The doctor ordered alcohol baths, so we'll have to start them right away."

"I can bathe her," said Franco. "I know you nurses are busy."

"I'll prepare the solution for you," said the nurse. "I'll bring it to her bedside."

Franco went to Angela and put his hand to her cheek, but he pulled it away quickly as if he would be singed from the heat that radiated from her body. Every pore of her skin was drenched with water. Her skin reminded him of smooth marble.

"Here's the solution, Mr. Bellini," said the nurse. She put the basin and towels on a bedside table. "Nurse Carrington will be on duty here if you have any problems. Be careful of the dressing on her stomach. The wound is still draining." The nurse encircled the bed with white screens.

Franco took off his jacket, unbuttoned his cuffs, and rolled up his sleeves. His hands were still stained with grease from work that day, but some stains were impossible to remove. He put his hand on Angela's chest and felt her heart beat against it—not too rapid but slow and definite.

"Angela, Angela? Can you hear me? I have to bathe you with alcohol." Her eyes didn't open, and she let out a moan.

He slipped her arm out of the hospital gown, careful not to remove the top sheet and expose her to the cool air. Reaching over, he slipped her other arm out of the gown and pulled it out from under the sheet. A large brown spot on the gown emitted a pungent stench. Franco picked up the sheet and saw that the dressing on her stomach was soaked with brownish-green drainage. The poison flowed out of her; her body was being cleansed.

Franco picked up a towel and submerged it in the alcohol solution. He squeezed out the towel and gently laid it across her chest, tucking it in at her sides. He repeated the procedure with her limbs and head. Impurities in the body had to be drawn out slowly.

Some time later, the nurse looked in on them.

"Her temperature still hasn't gone down, Mr. Bellini," said the nurse as she shook the thermometer. "Why don't you go to get some coffee? I'll take over. Besides, I have to change the dressing."

Franco couldn't understand what was happening. He had surrounded Angela's body with ice and soaked her in alcohol. With rounded shoulders, he put on his jacket and made his way to the hospital cafeteria. As he walked down the corridor, he could feel his chest sink inward. He felt he could no longer stand up straight. He came to several hallways and looked up at the signs on the wall: left was the cafeteria, right was the hallway to the chapel, and straight ahead was an exit.

He knew of his wife's affection for the Blessed Mother and that she placed great trust in Her. If she could, he knew that she would pray to the Virgin Mary— but the thought of going into a church made his shoulders slump even more. He did not want to give in, not even to God. But he didn't have to pray to God the Father. He could pray to Mary, His Mother, whom Angela loved.

The simplicity of the chapel put him at ease. He had never seen a church so unadorned. There were no gold candleholders or dramatic holy paintings of saints being slain. A wooden cross hung on the wall behind a small altar covered with a white cloth. Several pews faced the altar. A row of small white candles could be lit for the families of the sick to speed recovery. The atmosphere suggested he could pray to whomever he wanted. For the first time in his life, he intentionally sat in the front row.

Franco didn't bow his head, kneel, or fold his hands in prayer. He simply began to pray to the Virgin Mary. In his mind, he conjured up an image of a Botticelli painting of the Madonna. He spoke to the woman in the flowing royal blue robes and delicate features and begged her to please help his wife heal. He asked that when he returned to the hospital the next day, Angela would be sitting up in bed waiting to greet him.

Franco put his hand on his heart and not only promised that if this should come true, he would light candles in his home every Friday—but that he would offer up to the Madonna all of his work. When he fixed a water pipe or painted a room, he would do it in the Blessed Mother's name. Then he got up, lit a candle, and pulled back his shoulders as he left the chapel.

~ ~ ~ ~ ~

The next day, Franco returned to the hospital. He thought about his experience in the chapel the day before. He considered himself a modern man not given over to superstition or easily swayed by organized religion. It was for Angela that he had gone to the chapel and asked the Madonna to intervene. Franco saw himself as a medium between his wife and Mary, the Mother of Jesus.

"Mr. Bellini, I'm glad you're here. Your wife's fever began to break after you left last night," said Nurse Carrington.

He went to Angela's bedside, where a nurse was just raising the head of the bed. Angela's face had lost its fullness, but her skin was fresh and her eyes clear.

"You're up! I'm glad, I'm so glad." He embraced Angela, careful not to hold her too tight because of her wound. "You were unconscious for a week. I thought I would lose you."

"All that time, I wasn't really unconscious. I was doing something else. I was somewhere else," said Angela.

"And I wasn't invited," said Franco with a smile. "You're back with me. That's what matters, my dearest. Speranza has called many times. She's been afraid you were going to die."

Reaching down into his bag, Franco said, "I've brought you some broth. Every day, I brought it in case you were able to eat. Today you can." He called for the nurse to help his wife.

"But where are you going?" asked Angela, her voice hoarse.

"I have to go to the chapel for a few minutes. I'll be back."

~ ~ ~ ~ ~

Franco took Angela home two months later. She still needed help bathing and changing her dressings, but these needs were met by a visiting nurse. When he left for work every day, he would make Angela's breakfast and put her in the easy chair in the dining room. He came home at lunchtime and carried Angela out to the front porch, put her in the recliner, and covered her with blankets. It was June, and the doctor recommended plenty of sunshine.

One day, Angela lifted the blanket and uncovered her left arm. Her wedding band had become too big for her finger. When she left the hospital, she weighed eighty pounds. She had gained ten pounds since coming home. She felt sorry for Franco, who had so much on his mind, especially his brother's death, and the fact that he had not heard from Roberto since the onset of the war.

People said it was to be a long war but that it couldn't last forever. Angela knew that any catastrophe could last forever in the minds and hearts of the people who experienced it. She heard quick footsteps on the porch stairs.

"Angela, it's me," said Speranza. She skipped over to Angela.

"What are you doing here? You have school today!"

"No, today there's a teachers' conference and there's no school. So I came to keep you company."

"Does your mother know you're here?"

"Sure, she put me on the train, and I walked from the station."

"That station is a terrible place for a little girl to be alone. Don't do it again. Call, and someone will meet you."

Speranza was dressed in a jumper and blouse that Angela had made. The jumper was red with a pleated skirt and two small silver buttons at the waist. The blouse was made from white Italian wool Angela had brought with her from Sicily. The wool was light and could be worn in winter or spring. When Angela saw Speranza dressed so nicely, it made her feel happy.

"Angela, I will cook supper for both you and Franco," declared Speranza, hands on hips.

"You can't do that. You'll burn yourself on the stove. Just the other day, I heard of a little girl who burned herself."

"I use the stove at Mama's all the time. I cook for everyone," said Speranza. "Besides, Franco is so tired when he comes home from work. He shouldn't have to cook."

Angela looked down at the hem of Speranza's jumper. She certainly didn't make the hem that short; it was almost to the girl's knee. Angela was about to scold her for shortening the hem when she looked at Speranza's waist and saw how long and slim it had become. The little girl was growing, and soon they would be the same height.

"All right, go in and prepare the chicken. The sauce is in the icebox. There are string beans in the garden, and the pasta is in the cupboard over the sink. Don't light the stove oven until I explain it to you."

"I'll make you a meal that really tastes good," said Speranza, letting the screen door slam behind her.

"And don't slam doors! You'll break them." Some parts of her were grown up, some are still a child's, thought Angela.

Angela reached over to the table beside her chair and picked up the writing tablet. For the past few days, she had attempted to write to Mother Superior in Sicily and explain what happened to her, but she never seemed to find the words.

It frightened her to think that God punished her by taking away her ability to give birth. She remembered the nuns teaching about the wrath of God and what could happen if He was displeased with an individual, city, or country. The Mother Superior would think Angela had done something that had angered God, but Angela felt that God had taken away her ability to bear children because she was to make sure that Speranza grew up properly. She picked up her pen:

Nelsonville
June 1915

Dear Mother Superior,
I have been home sick for a few months. I had an operation and now cannot have children. I am recovering with the help of my family...

Angela sat back and stared at the words she had written. A few weeks ago, she would have never written them. It was still disturbing to write those words: I cannot have children. Her inability to have children was part of her experience now. She no longer knew who she was or how she could find out.

Angela also longed to ask the nuns to inquire about her sister, but the war was on and she felt this would be an imposition. People were dying, and she was only worried about her sister, who might have died years before.

How could she ask anyone to search for her sister when she should have looked herself before she left Sicily? She needed to return to Messina and search for her sister. She needed confirmation that her sister was no longer among the living.

Angela heard the rattle of pots and pans and then a crash.

"Speranza! If you destroy my kitchen, that will be the last time I let you cook on your own."

Angela noticed her strength was returning.

~ ~ ~ ~ ~

Franco finished his work on the new floor. He thought of his brother as he smiled at the vista from the convent window. The tranquility of the water as the sun began its descent toward the earth would have sparked Alessio's imagination. Franco imagined Alessio saying something like, "The sun descended slowly so that when it reached Mother Earth, they experienced a slow, lingering, passionate kiss. Not a slap like a wave breaking on shore or a tree pushing its energy against the earth to protrude through its crust, but the illusion of the earth and sun's silent embrace at the same hour every day was the most perfect union of God's visible gifts to people."

Franco felt his face flush. How could he think of such an idea? When Alessio was alive, he was used to such romantic sentiments coming from his brother's lips, but not from his own mind. It was so unlike his own thinking that for a moment he entertained the idea that Alessio had planted those thoughts. Franco looked around to make sure he was alone. He didn't want anyone to see him blush.

Since Alessio's death, he thought of Roberto often. He hadn't heard from Roberto since Italy entered the war, and he wondered if he would ever see his cousin again. Before, Franco had written to his cousin every two months, but now he only wrote on holidays. His last link to Sicily was slipping away. The last man on earth he could call brother had maybe been murdered by either a political group or the Mafia. Franco wondered if it was Roberto who kept him writing or if it was the island of Sicily. He wanted to stay connected to Sicily, but Roberto was the link. Franco picked up his tools and left the room.

~ ~ ~ ~ ~

"I'll get it," said Franco. He got up from his smoking chair and picked up the receiver.

His mother talked excitedly about her husband not waking up, even when she put cold water on his face. Franco told her to call an ambulance and that he would catch the next train to the city.

"Angela, Angela I have to go to New York. Ma's husband is sick." He hurriedly put on his coat.

"What happened?" Angela asked. She wiped her hands on a dishtowel.

"I don't know. She can't wake him up."

The doctor said he was gone by the time Franco got to the hospital. He'd gone into a diabetic coma and they couldn't bring him back. Franco's mother's moans shot right to his stomach. Franco had never been close to his stepfather, but he did support his mother and Speranza. He would now bear the burden of supporting them both. There would have to be changes, but first he had to concentrate on the funeral.

~ ~ ~ ~ ~

Franco tossed his black fedora onto the dining room table. It had been a simple funeral with no frills. Most of his stepfather's family was still in Sicily. Franco was glad it was over, but now he had to worry about his mother. She could not afford to live in New York, and her failing health prevented her from working. He would have to find a place for her and Speranza in Nelsonville. In addition, his mother and sister would now depend on him financially. Any money he had saved for a trip to Europe had gone to bury his stepfather.

He picked up the mail on his smoking table and perused it. Nothing from Roberto. Should he bother to keep writing? Maybe they had hung the poet from a tree months ago, his body left there for hungry birds. After a few weeks, no one would be able to identify the body. And even if they could, who would they try for the murder? The Mafia? The Austrians? The situation was hopeless. He went into the kitchen.

"Angela, what do you think about my mother and Speranza moving to Nelsonville?"

"Do you want them to live with us?" Angela asked.

"Well, Salvatore said that his sister, Paolina, was looking for Italian tenants for the first floor of her house on Orchid Street. The rent won't be too bad for me to carry until Mama can get some kind of work. Then, maybe, I'll just have to pay half the rent."

"Salvatore?"

"You remember. I told you about him. He was my roommate at St. Mary's with infantile paralysis. Paolina is his sister."

"Oh, yes, I remember now," she said and picked up a dishtowel. The image of Salvatore touching Speranza's hair came to mind. She thought about how easy it would be for Salvatore to have contact with Speranza. There was something unhealthy about that.

"I don't know. Maybe they could stay with us for a while. Your mother is not used to being alone." She dried a plate and put it on the table.

"But the apartment is available now. It's much nicer than where she lives at this time, and it will be cheaper. Besides, it would be more work for you, having two more people in the house, and I want you to rest. I'll call Paolina in the morning."

~ ~ ~ ~ ~

Angela moved the pasta dish to make room for the veal plate on the dining room table. Sundays were a hectic day: early morning mass, visiting whoever was sick in the community, and cooking for family and friends.

"Does anyone want more wine?" asked Angela as she reached over and put a piece of veal on Speranza's plate.

"That's too big a piece," Speranza said.

"It's not too big," Angela said. She leaned over and filled her husband's raised wine glass.

"Ma, would you like a glass of wine? It would calm your nerves."

"Don't worry about my nerves. It's more important to eat than drink wine," said Franco's mother. She filled her plate with pasta and made the sign of the cross.

Angela thought her mother-in-law felt out of place, even at the family dinner table. The American way of life was something to live around and not in. Angela had felt that sensation the day she became ill. She remembered floating into an odd frame of mind where she felt on the outside of what was going on. She was aware of her mind, but she felt like a stranger in her own experience. It must be what this woman in black felt all the time; they were her family, but she was a foreigner where she lived.

"*Buon appetito*," said Angela as she lifted her wine glass.

"*Buon appetito*," said everyone.

"This veal is delicious, Angela," said Paolina, who was a short, stout woman.

"Thank you, Paolina," said Angela. "Please eat. There's more in the kitchen.

"Can I leave the table?" asked Speranza. "I'm finished."

"Oh, Speranza, you must eat everything on your plate. You want to grow up big and strong and have healthy babies," said Paolina. She wiped her mouth. The pierced holes in her ears were so stretched that her dangling earrings nearly touched her shoulders.

"It's too soon to be thinking about that," said Angela. "There's plenty of time for that."

"It's never too soon to think about it for a girl," said Franco's mother.

Angela said nothing. She looked over at her husband, who ignored the conversation. To him, it was just female chatter—but Angela did not like such talk, especially about Speranza. Her mother-in-law and Paolina were conspiring. She didn't like it.

"Speranza, you can leave the table if you like. You've eaten enough," Angela said.

"That's not enough," said Franco's mother.

"In a few hours, she'll be hungry again and she'll eat some more," Angela said. "It's better for digestion if she eats a little at a time." Angela got up and moved Speranza's chair away from the table.

"I promise I'll eat more later," Speranza said. "I want to look at the garden."

The doorbell rang. "I'll get it," the girl chirped and ran off.

Angela heard a heavy step in the hallway and Speranza's giggles.

"Good afternoon, everyone," said Salvatore. He stood at the dining room door, holding Speranza's hand.

"It's my brother," said Paolina, as she got up and kissed him on the cheek. "I told him to come by if he was in the neighborhood."

Angela saw her mother-in-law and Paolina exchange approving smiles.

"Salvatore, sit down and have some wine," said Franco.

"I didn't mean to intrude on your meal," said Salvatore.

"Oh, it's no intrusion," said Angela. "Sit in Speranza's seat. Speranza, you can go out now."

The day before, Paolina had hinted at extending an invitation to Salvatore for Sunday lunch. Angela ignored her hints. Angela wondered what made Paolina think she could invite people to her house. What made her say that about babies? How often did Salvatore visit his sister? Angela felt the incision line on her abdomen pulsate with the churn of her insides.

"Salvatore, come with me out on the swing," said Speranza, swinging his arm.

"No, Speranza. Don't bother Salvatore," Angela said. "You go out and look at the garden." Angela motioned for him to sit down in Speranza's chair.

"No, please finish your lunch. I'll go outside and keep Speranza company."

Before Angela could say another word, Speranza ran to the back door, calling out for Salvatore to hurry.

"It's wonderful to have children," said Paolina. "Mine are all grown now and married. Having Speranza in the house is like having my daughter back. Salvatore, well, he's still my baby brother."

"Ma, please pass the veal," Franco said. His mother passed him a plate. "The veal, Ma—not the eggplant. When was the last time you saw the eye doctor? I think your eyesight is getting worse."

"Doctors, what do they know?" His mother wiped her plate with a piece of bread.

~ ~ ~ ~ ~

"I want my next dress to be black," said Speranza. She turned so Angela could pin up the waist to her dress.

"Black! Why do you want to dress in black?" Angela asked. "You'll look like you're going to a funeral." Angela didn't understand Speranza's desire to grow up so quickly.

"But all the ladies dress in black and are called Signora. I want to be called Signora." She jumped down from the stool and began to twirl in her white ruffled dress. She grasped Angela's hands and began to spin.

"Stop it. You'll make me dizzy, and I'll vomit. Get back up on the stool so I can fit this dress. You are too young to be a Signora, Speranza." She wanted to keep Speranza as young as she could for as long as she could. She was slipping away too fast.

"Angela, do you hear yourself?" Speranza asked.

"Of course I hear myself. I get tired of hearing myself. Now get back up on the stool so I can finish."

"No, I mean your language. You hardly hesitate any more or have to think about what you're saying in English."

Without realizing it, Angela had held the entire conversation in English. Even when she spoke with the more Americanized immigrants, they had lapsed into Italian for some of the words or images.

"You sound so different," said Speranza.

"I sound different?"

"Yes, I can hear you better."

"Really? Well, hear me now. Get back on the stool."

Speranza was right—her English flowed better, but Angela felt it was because she felt different inside. She wasn't sure why, but ever since her body recuperated from the operation, she seemed to instinctively know what she wanted to say and easily found the suitable English words.

Angela recalled when she would go with Speranza to the A&P grocery store. It was there that Speranza gave the most valuable language lessons.

Speranza would hold up an item and ask for the English word. She would lift up a zucchini squash or an apple.

"Zucchini," Angela said.

"Zucchini what?"

Angela would stare at the bent Italian vegetable, and say with a nod of her head, "Sqausha."

It wasn't just her English that had improved; even her Italian flowed better. She spoke her Sicilian dialect more beautifully than she had ever done before. Franco had remarked that her Sicilian was better than his. She found this strange, since she had not been allowed to speak her dialect at the convent.

"All right," said Angela, "I'm finished." She stepped back and observed Speranza in her birthday dress, with row after row of white ruffles. She tied a soft pink satin bow around Speranza's waist. The doorbell rang.

"Now who is that?" asked Angela. "Stay right there. I'm not finished."

Speranza jumped off the stool and followed her to the front door. It was Franco, who had steadied a heavy package on his right knee to ring the bell. He couldn't wait for Angela to see his new purchase.

"Look, Angela, Franco's got a present!" said Speranza.

"Franco, what do you have?" asked Angela. Franco came in the house and set the package on the dining room table.

"It's a surprise. I got it cheap at the convent." He lifted it out of the box.

"Oh, it's a clock! A beautiful clock," said Angela, "and it looks like a bell."

"Well, Angela, what do you think?" Franco smiled.

Angela knew that her husband wanted her to have nice things—things they couldn't afford without the generosity of the convent.

"It's beautiful, but awfully heavy. It will have to go on the hall mantle. I've never seen anything like it." She stepped back from the clock to look at it from a different angle. Angela had begun to tire of the heavy antique furniture they had. She hadn't said anything to Franco, not only because they couldn't afford new furniture because of their extra expenses, but because he had refinished every chair and table by hand. The clock seemed like another piece of heavy, immovable furniture. Angela heard the mailbox open and close.

"Speranza, the post has come. Will you get it please?"

The young girl ran to get the mail.

"I don't know, Franco. It's so heavy looking."

"Yes, but listen to the chimes. They're so sweet and light," said Franco. He moved the hands of the clock around until the chimes rang out. She was surprised to hear how delicate and faint the chimes were.

Angela recalled a man who played a tiny triangle in a band on the streets of Messina. The man was also one of the city's wrestlers and bulged with muscles. Angela though it was funny that the smaller men played the heavier instruments like the trombone. The large man held the small triangle between his thumb and forefinger with such grace and dignity that people never noticed the strangeness of the scene. But the man's reputation as the fiercest and most celebrated wrestler in the city never conflicted with his musical aspirations. Perhaps she could find a place for this clock after all.

"Here's the mail. You got something from Europe," said Speranza. She hid the letter behind her back. Franco grabbed Speranza and tickled her until she gave up the letter.

"Franco, don't do that. It's bad for her digestion," said Angela, but she realized that somehow the old wives' tales didn't ring true anymore. She laughed along with Speranza, who was now on the floor giggling and grabbing at her stomach.

"That's enough. Get off the floor with that dress. Go in and take it off, and wash up for supper."

Angela noticed her husband staring at an envelope. She looked at the name on the envelope. There was no return address.

"Roberto. It's from Roberto," Franco said. "He's alive. This is his handwriting." He thought his cousin had been lost forever. Franco opened the envelope and unfolded the letter. He read out loud as Angela listened intently.

Paris, May 1917

Dear Cousin,

It is only now that I am able to write you. After Italy entered the war, I was forced to leave Sicily because of the anti-war speeches I gave in piazzas and churches. During an especially heated speech one night, a good friend of mine brought a carriage to the church where I was speaking. There were government officials who were waiting to take me to Rome to be tried for my anti-war activities, but I slipped out of the church and into the carriage along with my family. My friend drove us to the train station, where we boarded a train to Paris.

I have been in Paris for a year now, writing for an anti-war newsletter. I could not write sooner for fear that I would be discovered and hunted down. The French do not understand Sicilian problems and are too intellectual in their approach to life. My wife and children long to be home, but it is not safe yet to return. I am sorry to have left Sicily.

Every day, I dream of sitting on my veranda and staring out over the sea. You remember the sparkling reflection of our sun on the water? I often thought of the Mediterranean Sea as a crystal; the colors reflected the history of Sicily and its people. I have yet to see properties of this sort in any other body of water. I have yet to see nature so expressive in any other form. Nature is so easy to understand because she loves so freely. Man is the difficult one.

If I have kept you worried by not writing, I am sorry. The war is near its end, and I hope we can meet again at my villa. You will always be connected with our small island; part of you remains there. I have written a special poem for you and Angela.

A Time Again

There's a time again
Always another chance
I call my two selves together
And ask: where can we be whole?
Whole? Look inward to be whole

Do not look to outer God
Or to someone else
If I am torn from my brother
I carry his memory in myself:

My limbs are his limbs
My chest houses his heart
And in myself I am whole.
There's always a time again
Always another chance
I call my two selves together
And ask: shall we be whole?

I will write again as soon as I return to Sicily.
Your Cousin,
Roberto

Franco pulled out a dining room chair and sat. His cousin didn't mention any of the letters he had written. If Roberto never received any of the letters, then he didn't know about Alessio's death. And yet the poem spoke to Franco so clearly. He had lost his brother but not completely; he still had his memories of his brother, and he still had Roberto. Franco had always planned to one day return to Sicily, and reading Roberto's letter made that desire stronger.

"Franco, it's wonderful. Roberto is alive and returning to his villa soon," said Angela. She put her arms around her husband's shoulders.

"Let's make a trip back," said Franco as he patted her arm.

"Back to Sicily? But it would take us such a long time to save the money," said Angela.

"We'll both take on extra work until we have the money for the tickets," said Franco. "We can save more money from the income properties by raising the rents a bit. I have been very good to my tenants; a few dollars a month would be reasonable. Besides, you still think about your sister, don't you?"

"I know you," Angela said. "You'll take on so much work you'll get sick. I don't like to see you work so hard. You don't rest enough."

"I rest when I'm tired. You want to go back, don't you?"

"Remember we have your mother and Speranza to care for now," Angela said. She straightened the tablecloth and brushed off some crumbs.

"Don't worry, I will take care of my family. I don't understand what you're so nervous about." Franco said.

"I'm thinking about our responsibilities." What if she went back, looked for her sister and found that she was dead? Her sister being gone forever was too much to think about. If she were gone, what would take her place in

Angela's heart and mind? What would she hope for then? What would propel her through life?

"Don't worry. We'll take care of our responsibilities." Franco put his cousin's letter back in the envelope.

~ ~ ~ ~ ~

Angela opened the front door and carried a plant out onto the porch. Today was Columbus Day, and she had a lot to do. She would take her mother-in-law and Speranza downtown to see the parade, and then she would cook a large afternoon meal for friends and family. That evening, there would be a dance at Columbus Hall, and she would have to make sure everyone was ready to leave on time. Angela arranged the plants on a small white table and went in the house. The war was over, and it appeared that everything was back to normal.

Speranza, who spent lots of time with Angela now that she and Franco's mother lived close by, was somewhere in the house. "Speranza, where are you?" Angela went into the kitchen and set up the ironing board. She heard her closet door shut in the bedroom. "Speranza, what are you doing in my bedroom? Come out here right now!"

Speranza jumped out of the bedroom and into the kitchen.

Angela turned around.

"My good clothes! You had to put on my best dress and shoes?"

"How do you like it on me, Angela?" She leaned against the doorway with hands on hips and peered over her raised right shoulder. The waist of the dress hit Speranza's hips. The oval yoke of the dress hung over her flat chest.

"Speranza, go take it off. You're too young for a style like that."

"When am I gonna look good in something like this?" asked Speranza. She clopped across the kitchen floor in Angela's shoes.

"You have plenty of time to dress like that."

"But the dance is tonight," Speranza said.

"I made you a dress for tonight."

"I wanna wear something like this. I don't wanna wear little-girl dresses anymore." She flopped in a chair.

Angela did feel that Speranza was too skinny for the age of fourteen. She and Franco both told his mother to take Speranza to a doctor, but she never did. Speranza seemed to eat enough, but she never developed like the other girls— and Angela began to see it more and more.

"Am I ever gonna look like you, Angela?"

"Don't worry, you'll fill out."

"When? My mother is ashamed of the way I look."

"Did she say that?"

"No, but I can tell. She always tells my girlfriends' mothers how much the other girls are starting to look like women. She never tells me that. And the boys never look at me in school."

Angela put down her iron and sat down next to Speranza.

"Listen," Angela said, taking her sister-in-law's hands. "There's plenty of time to grow up. If I hadn't been alone in the world, I would never have married at eighteen. But I wouldn't have had any future if I didn't."

"Don't you love Franco?"

"Of course I love him. I thank God every day for my good luck. But what I'm saying is that there weren't many things I could have done. I would have become a nun if he hadn't come along. If I had both my parents, my sister and brother, and we lived together as a family, I wouldn't have married so young. You have your mother, Franco, and me. Don't be in such a hurry." Angela thought about the old nun who told her about being a wife and how inadequate the advice was. Someday she would tell Speranza the truth about what it was like to be married, but right now she just wanted her to stay young. There was time enough for truth telling.

"Angela, you're a second mother to me. You've always been so nice. God sent you here so you could be with us." Speranza hugged Angela and kissed her forehead.

Angela was sure that God had sent her here to care for Speranza—and that He had taken away Angela's ability to have children so she could help raise her. This was God's joy for her, but Speranza was not her child, and she was limited in her say about how she would grow up. The truth was, she longed to have a child of her own. Without children and with the probability that her sister was dead, her history would no longer be significant. The earthquake wiped out her history.

~ ~ ~ ~ ~

Angela filled a glass with the last of the punch as the band played a slow waltz for the remaining couples on the dance floor. It was a wonderful evening, full of laughter and fun. She and Franco danced most of the evening, which brought a renewed youthfulness to both of them. Some of the women had to have their husbands carried home from drinking too much wine, but Franco never drank more than three glasses in an evening. He wasn't the sort of man to leave his wife at home while he went out with his friends. Her only complaint about Franco was that he constantly worked: at St Mary's, at someone's new home, or downstairs in the cellar. Even at the end of this evening, he was helping the custodians fold chairs and clear away tables.

Angela went outside for some fresh air. On the terrace she saw Speranza and Salvatore; Speranza was balancing herself on a wall while Salvatore held her hand and guided her along. Her mother-in-law and Paolina sat on a bench and encouraged Salvatore to hold onto Speranza. The two women nodded their heads in approval. Angela watched as Paolina spread the skirt of her dress on the bench. She felt that the bright floral pattern was too youthful for a woman of her age.

"Ma! Look at me! Look at me!" Speranza said.

"Brava! Brava! Let Salvatore hold you. I don't want you to fall," her mother said.

"She is safe with my brother," Paolina said.

Speranza is too old for these antics, thought Angela. Her behavior is inappropriate for a young lady.

Speranza jumped down at the end of the wall and ran to her mother. Angela saw her soak up her mother's approval like a sponge. Speranza leaned against her mother while Paolina stroked her head.

"You're such a good little companion for my brother," said Paolina. "It's no nice that we're like family." Franco's mother nodded.

Angela had worked so hard to protect Speranza. She made a point of teaching her manners, how to dress, and right from wrong. But Speranza wasn't her daughter, and she looked to her real mother for approval and love. No one can take a mother's place, thought Angela. It seemed the only time Speranza would get any encouragement and love from her mother was when Salvatore was around.

Angela looked up at the full moon. It felt right that Speranza would feel gay. Before dusk, the moon took in all the energy from the sun and stars. When night fell, it gave the energy to the earth so plants and flowers would grow. The moonlight gently molded itself around Speranza's body. With each breath, she took in whatever the moon had to offer. Maybe that's what Angela had to learn to do: have trust in the light of the moon.

~ ~ ~ ~ ~

Angela undid the clasp on her necklace. Franco took off his suspenders and lay down on the bed. He'd begun to light a cigar when Angela turned and looked at him. He put out the match.

"I don't like what's going on between Speranza and Salvatore," Angela said. She unpinned her hair and brushed it.

"What do you mean?" He took off his pants and got under the covers.

"He touches her too much."

"Touches her? What? When?"

"Tonight he was holding her hand while she balanced on a wall."

"He was just playing. You know how playful Speranza is. She was having fun."

"It was more than fun. I saw it in his eyes and in your mother's and Paolina's."

"Sometimes I think you see what you want to see. It's your imagination."

She began to counter her husband's statement, but something stopped her. A voice in her head told her to say nothing. The voice told her to let it play out and not to try to convince her husband she's right. You expressed your perceptions, and now it is beyond your control. Angela thought how she didn't have control over the earthquake that destroyed Messina—it was inevitable—but she had avoided death through listening to her inner voice. Angela finished brushing her hair and went to bed.

~ ~ ~ ~ ~

Franco picked up a large plank and loaded it on the truck. He pulled out a handkerchief and wiped his brow. There was a lot of work to be done at St. Mary's before the winter set in: rooms to be painted, plumbing to be fixed. It was a struggle to save money for the trip to Sicily, but he was sure that in a few years' time, he would have it. Franco saw Salvatore coming down a path that led from the flower garden.

"Hello, Franco," Salvatore said as he limped toward Franco.

"Salvatore, how are you?"

"Good. How's your family?"

"They're well," Franco said. He had never known Salvatore to start small talk unless he had something else to say.

"Franco, your sister is certainly growing up. Soon she'll be ready to leave home," Salvatore said with a grin.

"My sister? My sister is only fourteen years old. Look, Salvatore, she's not ready to get married. When she's ready, I want her to marry someone with a trade."

"With a trade? It should only matter that the man can support her. A trade shouldn't matter," Salvatore said.

"I want my sister to have a good home and be supported the right way. If someone has a trade, he is guaranteed work."

"Well, Franco, I hope she chooses someone to your liking. But she has to choose, not you. I will speak to your mother." Salvatore turned and limped back toward the garden.

Franco never took his sister's playfulness around Salvatore seriously, because he assumed that Speranza felt sorry for him because of his affliction. Salvatore was his own age, so it never occurred to him that there could be an attraction between them.

Franco had felt sorry for Salvatore. When jobs came up at the convent that required physical labor and paid well, Salvatore was passed over. A few times, Franco had asked the Mother Superior if he could hire a helper so Salvatore could make extra money. He found Salvatore to be a slow worker and unskilled. There was no future for his sister in a marriage to this man. He would have to do something.

~ ~ ~ ~ ~

"Angela. Angela. Where are you?" Franco called.

"Here. I was in the bedroom." She came into the dining room.

"Do you know who I saw today?" Before Angela could respond, he blurted out, "Salvatore. And he said that Speranza would be ready to marry soon. He means to marry her."

"Well, where have you been? This has been going on since I have been in America! I told you what he had on his mind."

"But not so seriously," Franco said. He folded his arms over his chest.

"Oh, yes, seriously," Angela said. "And right in your house."

"In this house? No, I would have seen it." Franco lifted his chin so he could feel slightly taller than his wife.

"You were there, but, no—you didn't see," Angela said.

"But she was a little girl having a good time," said Franco, raising his voice. "She felt sorry for him because of his infantile paralysis. There was nothing wrong with letting her cheer him. He is too old for her." His voice began to crack.

"You saw her cheering him, and I saw something else."

"But why didn't you say anything?"

"I did, the night of the dance, but you dismissed it. Your mother and Paolina decided long ago that Speranza should marry Salvatore. They have made a match."

"No, this is not going to happen. I've told him that I want my sister to marry a man with a trade. I'll call my mother tonight."

Franco thought about the past. There were times that he sensed Salvatore was anxious to be around Speranza, but he hadn't thought it meant anything. Why couldn't he see what was going on? Maybe he didn't want to. Franco thought about God and how He had taken Franco's brother but had spared his wife. He felt on the outside of events that happened around him. He had no control over what happened to himself or the people closest to him. He wondered if he had seen what was developing if he could have done or said anything to change it.

Chapter 4
Speranza, 1920

Angela bent down on one knee and tugged at the hem of Speranza's wedding gown. It had taken six months to make, and now it was finished: layers of silk with a wide train and white beads interwoven throughout the gown. At sixteen, Speranza was very slim and taller than most in the family. Angela remembered the little girl clothes she made for Speranza. Now that she thought about it, they had never really seemed to fit Speranza— not that they didn't fit her physically—they did. It was that the clothes were not who she was inside. She did not wear them well.

"Are the flowers here yet?" asked Speranza. The bridesmaids came into the room and gathered around the bride. Franco's mother stood in the doorway.

"Well, Angela," said her mother-in-law, "soon there will be grandchildren. It will be nice to have grandchildren around in my old age. The apartment will be fine for a while, but then we'll need a bigger place."

"What are you talking about?" asked Angela.

"The one Speranza, Salvatore, and I are moving into after the wedding." Franco's mother looked away. "You can't expect me to live alone, can you? I can't live with Paolina and her husband. They're strangers—not family."

"Ma, Speranza and Salvatore need time to adjust to each other. Please come and stay at our house for a while. You don't have to be alone."

"But I want to be near my daughter." Tears filled her eyes.

"But there is only one bedroom in Salvatore's apartment. Where would you sleep?" Angela put her hand on her mother-in-law's shoulder.

"I've brought over my pull-out couch and put it in the living room." She took out a white handkerchief and blew her nose.

Angela knew the layout of Salvatore's apartment. The only space available for a pull-out couch was against the wall that separated the living room from the bedroom.

"Ma, after the ceremony, I want you to tell Speranza that you won't be living with her."

Angela reached into her black purse and handed Franco's mother another handkerchief. She felt her mother-in-law's loneliness and fear, knowing there was nothing worse than the feeling of being thrown away. Franco's mother had done everything to manipulate the marriage and make sure she would have a place in her daughter's home—a home that would soon house the laughter of children. Now she stood before her daughter-in-law and hung her head, embarrassed.

"All right," she said, "I'll live with you and Franco for a while. Just until Speranza and Salvatore get settled."

~ ~ ~ ~ ~

Angela knocked on Speranza's door. She didn't see her sister-in-law as much as she would have liked. Speranza and Salvatore had been married for a year, and at the age of seventeen, she had a three-month-old baby and another on the way. Angela hoped that after this second baby, there wouldn't be any more for a while. Speranza remained thin, and Angela feared for her health.

"Angela, I'm so glad to see you," Speranza said. She took Angela's hands and led her into the house. A baby cried, and trucks could be heard delivering goods to the corner store. "I hope it's not too hot in here for you, Angela. It's so hot outside. The ventilation is no good in these first-floor apartments."

Speranza wiped the sweat from her neck and face with a cloth. She pushed back the loose hair around her forehead.

"Speranza, are you feeling all right?" Angela took her arm and guided her to a chair.

"I'm a little tired, I guess," said Speranza as she touched her cheek. "It's hard to take care of a baby and a household."

Angela looked around. Most of the furniture was secondhand, bought by Salvatore before the wedding. In the corner was a chair with a front leg wrapped with tape. To make matters worse, her mother-in-law had insisted on living with Speranza and Salvatore.

"Speranza, where are the two chairs Franco made for your apartment?"

"I'm ashamed to say," said Speranza. "We didn't have any money to pay a doctor's bill, so Salvatore sold them. And now, with Ma's eyesight so bad, I must take care of her, too."

"Don't worry about the chairs. And if you need money, ask Franco or me. There's no need for you to live this way."

Angela felt furious with Salvatore. He had offered to pay for the wedding pictures, but he never picked them up. He didn't have the money. Franco told Angela that it was becoming more and more difficult for him to have Salvatore as a helper for jobs at the convent because the nuns were cutting costs.

"Please don't tell Franco about the chairs," begged Speranza. She put her elbow on the arm of the couch and supported her head with her hand. The baby's cries grew louder.

"There's no need to tell him," said Angela.

"I have to go check on the baby," Speranza said.

Angela had never liked Salvatore, but not to the extent she felt now. She looked around the room; it was as if someone just set a lit match to her heart. How could anyone allow their family to live like this? Her heart burned until there was nothing left but a fierce and steady irritating anger. Franco's mother was to blame for all this. She made the match.

"Angela, isn't she beautiful?" asked Speranza as she returned with the baby.

"She's so tiny and delicate," Angela said. She had missed the baby's birth by minutes. Speranza had very little labor and delivered quickly." Where is Ma now?"

"At Paolina's," said Speranza.

"Don't worry. I'll go home and call Paolina. I'll talk to her about Ma moving in with us. This Sunday I want you to come to dinner."

"Thank you, Angela." Speranza kissed her sister-in-law's hand. Angela folded her arms around Speranza and the baby. Angela wondered why God didn't protect people from the harshness in the world. Why didn't He protect the people she loved most? She prayed for Speranza many times so that she would have a happy life. Angela wondered about God and His "goodness."

~ ~ ~ ~ ~

"Angela! Angela!" shouted a woman as she ran up Angela's steps in the thick snow. "Speranza is about to deliver her baby, and the doctor isn't there. He's in the country on another delivery!"

"Who's with her? You haven't left her alone!" Angela knew the woman as a neighbor of Speranza's who sometimes helped her with the baby.

"No, the visiting nurse is there—but Speranza asked for you. I've come to get you."

Angela grabbed her coat, and without a word, both women began to walk quickly toward Speranza's house.

Speranza lay in a pool of water.

"How long has she been in labor?" Angela asked the nurse.

"Just one hour. She'll deliver soon, though." The nurse rung out a wet cloth and placed it on Speranza's forehead.

"She had the last baby too quick, too," said Angela as she took off her coat.

"Here's the head," said the nurse. "Push, Speranza! Push!"

Speranza gripped either side of the bed, grunted, and pushed. The veins popped out on her forehead, and little red spots appeared on her nose and cheeks.

"One more. One more push. Angela, put your hands here." The nurse motioned between Speranza's legs while she applied pressure on her abdomen. Blood oozed from the birth canal as the head protruded out into the light of day. The nurse and Angela guided the baby's shoulders through and then the entire body. With one long "Ahhhh," Speranza gave birth.

"It's a boy," said the nurse, triumphant.

"A brother to the baby girl," Angela said. "Isn't that wonderful?" Angela held the baby still while the nurse cut the umbilical cord. The newborn squealed.

"Such a weak cry for a boy," said Speranza as she looked down between her legs. "He sounds like a baby chick."

"You can't expect Caruso right away," Angela said. "What will you name him?"

"I don't know. I have to ask Salvatore. Has anyone called him?"

"I haven't," said Angela. "I came over as soon as your neighbor got me. He'll have a nice surprise when he gets home." Angela did not want to go out of her way to locate Salvatore. He could be anywhere in the convent. She wanted to spend time with Speranza uninterrupted.

"You already had the baby," said the doctor arriving in a rush. "You're so quick."

"Yes Doctor," said Speranza, "and you're so slow."

Angela wrapped the baby in a white cloth as the doctor and nurse attended to Speranza.

~ ~ ~ ~ ~

For the next few years, Angela had the same daily routine. She walked up three flights of stairs to bathe her mother-in-law. Franco's mother was not only blind now from diabetes, but she was also a cardiac invalid and spent most of the day in bed. She had gained weight, and Angela had to lift her onto a portable toilet or up in bed. Angela cooked all her meals and brought them to her mother-in-law's room.

Each time Angela ascended the stairs, she thought about the old nun who counseled her about a wife's duties and caring for her husband's family. One day, as she ascended the stairs, it occurred to her that the old nun had never done what Angela had to do. The nun lived out her life peacefully and comfortably in the convent without worry.

Angela had meant to instruct Speranza about marriage, but she never had. The marriage was a mistake in Angela's mind, and she did not want to encourage Speranza to be obedient to people who didn't appreciate her, so she said nothing. Once, Speranza had brought a tray of food up to Franco's mother, who had refused to eat. Angela tried next, and for whatever reason she ate. Angela continued to feed her every day after that.

One morning, Angela opened her mother-in-law's door to feed her breakfast and found the old woman with her mouth drooped to one side. She touched her. Her skin felt like rubber, and her lips were blue and swollen. No more suffering, thought Angela. It is all over.

~ ~ ~ ~ ~

January 1925
Palermo, Sicily

Dear Cousin,

At this time, I am settled at my villa in Sicily. The first evening, I sat overlooking the sea. I cannot adequately express my joy at such a simple pleasure. My sadness at the changes in Sicily I am able to turn into rage. People are poorer and more despondent than before the war.

As you know, Mussolini is now in power. The demobilization of two-and-one-half million soldiers has increased unemployment, and the soldiers turned to Mussolini for help. He not only promised them employment but higher wages. Il Duce has yet to fulfill any of his promises. We are worse off than before.

But I stand by Sicily, as does my family. I know this is hard for you to under-stand, as you are just an American, but I want my little children to grow up here and know their heritage. I believe that my writing will have a hand in Mussolini's downfall. Sicily is a great island, and its people are precious to me. I will do every-thing I can to ensure its independence from invaders. My family has bread on the table while other people starve. This is the world we live in:

This is the World
With all the inconsistencies
And all the doubts
I stand out
This is the world

The doubts of brothers are hidden
With each new age
Each generation and houses
The inconsistencies
With guilt, jealousy, and rage

I stand out
To say this is me
I am guilt and jealousy
I embrace the doubts and inconsistencies

When doubt and inconsistency battle
War seems to be natural
When these warring concepts merge
My serenity is preserved

I stand out
With my inconsistencies and doubts
My brother is out for the world to see
Every creature on earth has the same inconsistencies

I look forward to your letter.
Your Cousin,
Roberto

"Roberto is safe at his villa," said Angela. She took off her reading glasses.

"We can go to Sicily in a few years," Franco said. "Roberto is back in Sicily, and we have been saving money regularly."

"But we have enough money," said Angela. We can go now." With each year that passed, it was less likely that they would find out her sister's fate.

"I want to make sure we can travel well and take an entire month. I don't want to rush." It disturbed him that Angela could take Roberto's letter so lightly. She seemed so relaxed when she read the poem. It was as if she read it for the tenth time. Maybe she knew Roberto better than he did.

"Angela, do you understand the poem? You read it so well."

"Well, I suppose he means that men war within themselves, so they make war with each other. I don't know. I don't know much about poetry."

Angela thought about when she first met Roberto at the convent and how young and forward he was, proud of his blue eyes and fine stature. She knew there was something different about him. In her heart, she felt she would be connected to him somehow. Beyond his forwardness, he possessed a tremendous compassion for people and a passion for living that she had never seen before. Angela sensed that Franco was slightly jealous of who Roberto was and his ability to create. It would be good if they could meet again. She needed to prepare for this trip, no matter how long it took.

Chapter 5
Sicily, 1929

Franco and Angela had saved more than enough money for a month abroad. They sailed from New York that spring, as the stock market crash had little effect on their lives. They worked independently, and the income properties still proved financially sound. They were on their way to a changed Europe.

~ ~ ~ ~ ~

The train eased past another seaside village.

"Is there any place or anything as sweet as Italy in the spring?" Franco asked. Villas tucked into hillsides half hidden by lush green foliage dotted the landscape. Every villa was situated differently on the hillside: some had front doors facing the railroad tracks and others had fronts facing toward the beach, but each had its own unique view of the Mediterranean.

"It's a sign that God is giving the world a second chance," Angela said.

The compartment door swung open, and a gust of wind swept through the cubicle.

"Passports," said the conductor. The conductor's eyes scanned Franco from the top of his head to his torso. When his eyes rested on Franco's feet, his face turned ashen.

"Signore, your toe is touching the upholstery on the opposite seat," said the conductor. He tapped the tip of Franco's shoe with his pen. "You're destroying government property. Uncross your legs."

Franco uncrossed his legs and handed the conductor the U.S. passports. The conductor's uniform was gray with brass buttons. Franco imagined army medals hanging from the man's shoulders.

"I should have known. Americans. Huh!" said the conductor. He handed back the passports.

The conductor wrote in his notebook and left, leaving the compartment door open. Several people were lined up in the corridors. They smoked cigarettes and blew smoke rings out the open windows.

"What did he mean by all that?" Angela asked.

"I don't know. I don't know what's going on."

Franco looked at the landscape rolling by. Appearances were often deceiving, and he started to feel that the picturesque villages seemed to cover something up. The view is sweet, but the people have turned as sour as the lemons they grow, he thought. He was glad he left Italy as a boy. He was content to be an outsider peering into a bad situation. As an American citizen, he was detached and free to express his opinion.

"Angela, did you notice the conductor's uniform? It looked military." Franco got up and closed the compartment door.

"If it's like this in the North, what will we find in Rome and Sicily?" asked Angela.

"I don't know. Maybe we'll just stay overnight in Rome and go straight to Palermo. Roberto will know what's going on."

~ ~ ~ ~ ~

"Via Sabella, please," said Franco to the taxi driver.

The driver remained silent and pulled away from the curb. The taxi circled Piazza della Republica. Bernini's fountain stood in the center of the piazza: a sculptured angel prayed to heaven while Romans sat around the fountain and sunned themselves.

As they drove down Via Nationale, policemen could be seen on every street corner. Franco remembered on his last visit to Rome that he could walk around the city and not see a policeman for blocks. Posters of Il Duce stared at Franco from building walls with his square jaw jutting out and his hand held high over the city. Franco tried not to look at the image. Mussolini's stance unnerved him. How could the proud Romans allow their beautiful ancient churches and buildings to be desecrated by such an image?

The taxi pulled up in front of their pensione just outside of Piazza di Spagna. The meter registered five thousand lire, but the driver pressed the meter again and the amount changed to ten thousand lire.

"That will be ten thousand lire, sir," the driver said.

"I will pay what was on the meter the first time," said Franco.

"Ten thousand lire is the right price. There are taxes now in Italy," said the driver.

Angela and Franco looked at one another.

"I'm sorry, but I am a stranger here and don't understand your taxes. Why must I pay ten thousand lire when the meter displayed five thousand lire?"

"How should I know? I don't make the tax laws. Even I don't understand them," said the driver. He held out his hand. "Pay me the right amount."

Franco hesitated. What would be the sense in arguing over five thousand lire?

"Sir, since you obviously feel I am doing you a disservice, you can speak to one of Il Duce's confidants," said the driver as he pointed to a policeman walking on the other side of the street. "You can take your complaint to him."

"Just pay him, Franco," Angela said. She turned to the taxi driver. "As my husband has said, we're strangers here. These new taxes are unfamiliar to us."

Franco looked over at the policeman, who now faced in the taxi's direction. Franco pulled out his wallet and paid the driver.

"Let's go in and register for our room and rest for a while. Then we'll take a walk and stretch our legs," said Franco.

Angela waited for Franco to deposit their room key at the pensione desk. It was 1 p.m. riposo time, which meant time for relaxation and gathering one's energy for the rest of the day. The idea of walking the Roman streets and seeing a sculpture when one least expected it excited her. She especially liked the fountains because they served a practical purpose—they offered water to the thirsty tourist and the Roman citizen.

"I want a cup of coffee," said Franco as he opened the pensione door. "Let's go to Piazza di Spagna."

They walked up the narrow street toward the open square. Angela saw people in the expensive shops touching fine leathers and furs. They dressed in tailored dark suits and spoke English with a British accent. This was the English section of Rome she had heard about from some of her dressmaking customers. She couldn't understand why they were in Italy when such strange things were going on.

The fountain in Piazza di Spagna was surrounded by tourists, local shopkeepers and policemen. Everyone was taking turns drinking from the fountain, and some had brought bottles to be filled up for later use while sightseeing. The fountain was an antique boat with water draining out from the mouth of sculptured faces on either side of the vessel. It looked like it had been abandoned on shore due to a storm or other act of God. Whatever it was, the boat survived intact and whole.

"Wait here, Angela. I'll go look at the prices of the cafe over there." He pointed down the street. "The one with the different colored umbrellas." The umbrellas reminded Angela of a flower garden.

"Why would anyone do a sculpture of a sinking ship?" asked Franco as he turned toward the cafe.

Sinking? thought Angela. Was the boat really sinking? It didn't feel to her that the boat was descending to the bottom of the ocean. The vessel seemed weary and battered, but triumphant. No, the boat had survived some awful storm and came to rest on the shore. It had survived something.

Angela remembered that the fountains in Messina had been covered with black soot and were chipped everywhere. One was an angel whose wings were broken. Next to it was a cupid with his arm drawn back, ready to shoot some unsuspecting person with the arrow of love, and no longer had an arrow to fire. Angela was surprised that she remembered the ancient fountain so vividly.

Angela's eyes closed; she tilted her head toward the sun and drew in the warm energy. In her mind, she saw a deserted street with abandoned buildings. Two little girls held hands as they skipped along. Angela decided to follow them. One ran ahead and giggled. The taller one was frightened to walk alone and ran after her. They stopped at the little fountain with the angels. Angela looked deeper to see the children's faces. She saw the little one clearly now.

"Felicita," said Angela aloud.

"What? What did you say?" asked a male voice.

Angela opened her eyes.

"Franco, I didn't see you coming."

"No, you were talking to the sun. Did you fall asleep on your feet and have a dream?" Franco asked.

"I guess I might have."

"Listen," said Franco, "let's get some coffee. That cafe is a bit expensive, but it doesn't matter. We both need to sit and rest."

~ ~ ~ ~ ~

Franco felt Angela slip her arm into his as they sauntered along the Via del Corso. He watched lovers and friends take their evening walk. You can always recognize the Romans, thought Franco. He noted that their gestures were loud but their speaking voices were soft and deep. Foreigners, who felt uncomfortable linking arms or hands like the affectionate Romans, touched each other with shy smiles.

"Let's walk over by the Colosseum," said Franco.

"But why? It's almost dark. It will be closing soon."

"I've heard it's beautiful to see in the moonlight," said Franco. "Besides, we leave for Sicily tomorrow. I'd like to walk around some more."

They walked down Via del Corso to Piazza Venezia and up Via Cavour. Franco saw two dark men in turbans and long flowing robes gesturing wildly to a local street merchant, while several Romans looked on and sometimes participated in the conversation. If something was happening in their vicinity, the Romans had to be part of it.

"It doesn't look like much of a moon tonight," Franco said. A sliver of moon appeared in the clear sky. They turned right off a side street. At the end of the street, the Roman Colosseum was in view. It stood by itself while multitudes of cars and trolleys circled the large amphitheater. Twilight settled above the circular structure while the burning floodlights illuminated it against the dark background. The thin moon was fixed over it.

"I don't think it's open," said Angela.

"Let's go over to it anyway," Franco said. "The lights are so bright around it, it looks like day time."

They went into the underground tunnel and came out at the Colosseum. A young woman was assembling paintbrushes and paints at the entrance of the tunnel.

"Good evening, Signorini," said the woman. "Are you here to sightsee? The Colosseum is closed."

"I know, Signorina, but my wife and I heard how beautiful it is in the evening." Franco watched as the woman dotted her palette with the paints. "Are you going to paint now? Here?"

"Yes, the Colosseum is being renovated inside, and I am an advanced student at the painting academy here in Rome. I am also restoring some ancient paintings on the walls."

"But at night time," said Angela, "how can you see?"

"During the day, there are too many tourists," said the woman as she covered the palette with a cloth, "and the sun is so hot I cannot concentrate on my work. Besides, my paintings require a subdued light." The young woman pulled out several large lights from her bag. "And when it's a full moon, then only some artificial light is necessary."

"What kind of ancient paintings are there?" asked Franco. "I've never heard of wall paintings at the Colosseum."

"Would you like to see what I've restored?"

"Are we allowed?" Angela asked.

"I'd be flattered if you would," said the woman. "It would give me a chance to try my work out on the public. It's this way." She picked up her equipment and walked into the circular structure. Angela held Franco's arm as they followed.

The young woman led them down a dark tunnel, stopped, took out her lights, and placed them on wooden shelves. The lights illuminated the paintings on the wall.

"Look at the colors," said Franco. "I've never seen such colors."

There was a picture of a meek, round dinosaur surrounded with vegetation. The painting below it was a detailed view of the insect world: little creatures with round heads and protruding noses leaned against leaves. Some had bright smiles, others slept peacefully. Miniature snakes wound themselves around leaf stems; some kissed while others played.

"I've never seen paintings like these," Angela said.

"That's why the Italian government wants them restored," said the young woman. "They seem to think these pictures tell something of the Italian past. Look at this one." She took a flashlight and focused it to the left of the insect painting.

Six monks sat around a table that had the alphabet and the numbers 0-9 written on it. Two of the men rested their fingertips on a white piece of porcelain with a glass piece in the middle; the number six was visible through the glass. The four other monks concentrated on the table and what was taking place. There was a transparent figure of an older monk behind the table pointing at the piece of porcelain. He seemed to be presiding over the entire affair.

"What are they doing?" asked Franco.

"Apparently, back in the twelfth century, there was an order of monks who consulted their version of a Ouija board for guidance. Especially in economic affairs and matters of health."

"Well, I suppose everyone has their own way of praying and asking for things," said Franco.

"But if they are monks, shouldn't they be in church praying?" Angela asked.

"That's right, Signora—at least that's what the church thought. Once the Catholic Church found out about the monks' attraction for the mystical oracle, the order was disbanded and all the monks were excommunicated. Experts think that the six monks sitting at the table were actually biological brothers."

Franco thought that sounded like the church. Wasn't lighting candles for someone's health mystical? Praying was mystical, whether you used a Ouija board or just made the sign of the cross. He looked closely at the faces of the men. They seemed to favor each other physically.

"Thank you for showing us your work, Signorina," Franco said, "but we have to go back to our pensione. We leave for Sicily tomorrow."

"Thank you for being my guests. Will you return to Rome after your time in Sicily?"

"I think we'll stop overnight. It's quite a journey from Sicily to Genoa at one time."

"Excellent!" said the young woman. "Stop by here, and you can see the end result of the paintings."

"I don't see why not," Franco said.

"I'd like to see them finished," said Angela.

"It's a date then," said the young woman. "I will show you out."

~ ~ ~ ~ ~

Franco and Angela stood in the train station in Bagheria, the suburb of Palermo, with their suitcases at their feet. The station was deserted except for a few pigeons that landed on top of the station cafe.

"Did you tell them the time our train was to arrive?" asked Angela.

"Yes. Maybe they're just a few minutes late. Don't get nervous," said Franco as he paced.

A man walked through the outer gates of the station.

"Roberto!" said Franco, "Roberto, I'm so glad to see you alive and healthy!"

The cousins hugged, then broke apart as if they were two magnets with positive charges repelling one another.

"You have some gray in your mustache, Cousin," said Franco.

"Ah, yes. It's from the struggle one has to experience in this rustic landscape."

"You remember Angela," said Franco. He took his wife's arm and moved her forward.

"Angela, you are beautiful." The poet kissed Angela twice on each cheek with sounds that reminded her of someone calling a cat.

"It's so good to see you, Roberto," said Angela. She found his enthusiasm inspiring.

"Let's go to my parents' house first. Giulietta is already there, waiting for us."

Franco and Angela got in the back seat.

Roberto drove along a narrow mountain road, swaying the car from one side to the other. Angela dug her fingers into Franco's thigh as Roberto turned a corner.

"How long have you been driving?" asked Franco.

"Oh, a few weeks," said Roberto. "I gave up my driver because I could no longer afford him. Driving is not hard. How was the train ride?"

"We had a little trouble," said Franco, "Rome is a completely different city."

"Ah," said Roberto, "things are not good. I'm afraid they'll get worse. You in America are not aware of what's brewing here. Tomorrow, Franco, I will take you to Palermo and show you a few things. Angela can spend time with Giulietta."

He made a sharp right turn, and the car went down a steep incline. Franco and Angela held onto each other. Angela thought that she had survived an earthquake and a journey to America, but she might not survive Roberto's driving. They came to an abrupt stop.

"Well, we're here," said Roberto. He pushed the car door open with his foot.

The Buttita house had not changed since Franco's last visit. Roberto's parents had been up north the last time he was here, so he looked forward to reacquainting himself with his aunt and uncle.

"Ma, Papa, they're here," called Giulietta as she came down the front steps. She stood between Franco and Angela, held their hands, and kissed them on each cheek.

A small slender woman appeared on the porch, followed by a graying man with a pipe.

"Aunt Rosa, Uncle Antonio," said Franco. He took Angela's hand. "This is my wife, Angela."

"I'm so sorry I missed your wedding," said Rosa.

"Let's all go inside," said Uncle Antonio." He put his arm around Franco.

~ ~ ~ ~ ~

Giulietta moved the salt and pepper shakers and placed a steaming platter in the center of the table. She picked up two large serving spoons.

"I hope you like fish," she said. "Franco, lift your plate so I can fill it." She scooped up several layers of fish covered with lemon and oil. "This fish is special. Yesterday, I went out with some local women and caught three."

"You caught three fish?" Angela asked.

"Imagine that," said Roberto, lifting his plate. "A schoolteacher and a poet's wife out fishing."

"Why not?" said Giuletta. "Next week, I'll teach my students how to fish. If they're hungry someday, they will at least know how to get food. Angela, tomorrow while the men are out we will do some fishing."

"What kind of work do you do now, Franco?" asked Antonio.

"I work with my hands, mostly. I'm an electrician, plumber, and painter." Franco thought that next to Roberto, who was so learned and smart, he must seem a mediocre person—an uneducated man.

"Well, Roberto can't do any of those things," said Giulietta, "and he doesn't have time to learn because he's too busy running from the Fascists and the Mafia and dragging his family along with him."

"We've been trying to get Roberto to take a job with my husband's wine and cheese business," said Rosa quietly.

"Trying!" said her husband. "I demand that you take a job, Roberto. You have three children to support."

"My children," Roberto said, "where are my children? I don't hear them."

"I was wondering how long it would take you to notice their absence," said Giulietta. "I've sent them to my sister's in Gela for a week."

"But I didn't kiss them goodbye," said Roberto.

"They'll be gone for a week, not a year," said Antonio.

The houseboy began to clear the table.

"Ah, Federico, my longtime house servant. You believe in my poetry, don't you? He reads it with fever!" Roberto threw his hands in the air.

"Please stop, Roberto," said Rosa, "you'll spill something, as usual. Tiziana is tired of mopping up your spills. She said she didn't mind when you were a child, but now…"

Franco was confused at his aunt and uncle's attitude. Their son was becoming one of Sicily's most celebrated poets. One newspaper article that Roberto had sent him declared his cousin as "a keeper of the Sicilian tongue." Was this the same man who had sent him such powerful poems? The townspeople honored him. Apparently his family didn't.

~ ~ ~ ~ ~

The houseboy unlocked the iron padlock and opened the gates to the poet's villa. The once green and fruit-bearing hills were now brown and burnt. The grapevines had not started to bear fruit, even though it was the season. To Franco, everything seemed in need of repair. Franco, Roberto, Giulietta, and Angela walked up the driveway to the villa.

"Come, Franco," Roberto said as he unlocked the door to the main room of the villa, "I would like to show you the books I've published since you were last here."

"You're not going to start that already. They've had a long trip and need to rest, not look at books!" said Giulietta, her hands on hips. "You'll have to excuse my husband. He thinks everyone is as interested in what he says as he is. Roberto, you'll have to remember that sometimes that just isn't true." Giulietta pulled the lounge chair away from the wall and motioned for Angela to sit.

"As you can tell, Franco," said the poet, "my wife complains that my poetry doesn't bring in money for food. But why should I worry about money for food when I have a fisherman for a wife?"

"I do not," said Giulietta. "I complain because you're against everyone so you can write poetry. That's all."

"I'm against fascism and the Mafia because they oppress people!"

"So you say," said Giulietta. She pulled out a handkerchief from her dress pocket and patted her neck. "I know you're sympathetic to our people, but it's the way you do it. Pick one side and stay there."

"It's no use talking," said Roberto. "Franco, are you ready to see my study now?"

"Oh, go on," said Giulietta waving her hands as if to shoo them away. "Angela, you and I will relax here." She took Angela's hand and pulled her to her seat.

Roberto opened the French doors to the main room. There were photographs displayed on the walls of the poet shaking hands and embracing men and women.

"Who are these people?" Franco asked.

"Fellow artists and writers," said the poet. "Some Italian, some not."

Roberto's poetry books were arranged on a table along with magazine and newspaper articles about the poet and his work. The titles ranged from "The Poor People, Rebirth" to "In Opposition to Fascism." Franco picked up several articles about the poet: "Roberto Mineo: Poet of the People," "The Poet in the Piazza," "The Anti-Mafia Poet."

"Roberto, you are lucky to be alive, when the newspapers call you a rebel." Franco held an article up to his cousin.

"I've had some close calls," said the poet. He opened a small oak box, pulled out two cigars, and handed one to Franco.

"That's why Giulietta is so upset," said Franco as Roberto lit his cigar.

"No, she's upset because she feels I'm friendly with anyone who will read my poetry. Sometimes the locals will drop by to discuss one of my poems they have read. They're not the best mannered people and they always stay late, but these are the people I write for and about."

Franco wondered if his brother, Alessio, had lived in Sicily, how would Roberto write about him? Would he call him a poor, unfortunate creature whose life was cut short by disease, and the great country he lived in could not, with all its money, cure him? Franco did not know of anyone in America who wrote about the everyday man. It just seemed that when a person died, especially if you were poor, it was as if you had never stepped foot on the earth. Even though Alessio had been dead for fifteen years, Franco still felt as though he had abandoned his brother. Alessio had not been in his thoughts lately.

"Giulietta has to realize that we have to survive," said Roberto. "I could never leave Sicily. There is too much inspiration for me here." He searched Franco's face. "Do you ever think about living in America—whether it's right for you?"

"I wonder about my brother and if his health would have failed had we stayed in Sicily," said Franco.

Roberto walked toward the table where he displayed his books. He picked one up.

"I'd like to read you something." He flipped through the pages. "The Figure 8," began Roberto.

The figure 8 can be dissembled
Here straighten, there stretched
When coiled many snakes appear
When flattened the head of the snake is dominant

The head is the source
The eyes are the windows
It opens its mouth and swallows its tail
Now the circular form prevails

The figure 8 has no source or beginning
And like the human spirit it is never ending
Through the main source other sources are born
But remember

The head is the origin
The eyes are the windows
The snake opens its mouth and swallows its tail
Now the circular form prevails
The head of the snake gives birth to the figure 8
The eyes slant away from one another
Its body thickens when stretched out
Where is the end? Look.

The head is the source
The eyes are the windows

"I think we're all running around like figure 8s," said Roberto, "looking for the beginning and the end when there probably is none. Maybe that's what I was doing in Paris."

"Well, I haven't thought of myself as someone who runs in circles," said Franco. "In America, people are free to do what they want. But you know sometimes I wonder how free I really am," said Franco.

He scratched his head and wondered where all this was leading. He had never read poems before and certainly didn't understand Roberto's. Franco had never told anyone about his doubts. He was grateful for America but always wondered about what his life would have been like had he never left Sicily. Franco knew that when his father immigrated, like many of his countrymen, he never intended to stay in America. It was supposed to be a temporary situation, but each passing year made it more difficult to return. News from Sicily was not encouraging. Sicilian life was not improving, and the Italian government continued to exploit Sicilians by levying heavy taxes on the worker.

Franco's father had been a small farmer, but there had been a sharp drop in the grain and citrus market and he could no longer make a living. The government taxed Sicilians so heavily that many small farmers had to leave Sicily. They migrated to American cities to work labor jobs that paid well. Laying roots in a foreign country was not their intent, so they did not farm.

Roberto put his arm around Franco.

"Tomorrow we'll go into Palermo, just you and me. I have a few things to do, and I'd like you to meet someone."

~ ~ ~ ~ ~

Angela closed the door to the bedroom and sat on the edge of the bed. The room was spacious and airy. An L-shaped drafting table was in the far corner. There were no screens on the window, so Franco lit some incense and placed it on the window ledge.

"That ought to keep the bugs away," said Franco.

"Giulietta seems annoyed with Roberto," said Angela. She got under the covers.

"No," said Franco, "I don't think so. That's how their relationship is. Besides, poets are hard to live with. I remember Roberto when he was a kid. He would sing the praises of Garibaldi, who was for the common man. He was always a smart kid."

"I admire him for what he does," said Angela.

"I do too, but I can't understand his poetry, at least not the poems I've read."

"I'm going fishing tomorrow. Franco, I don't know how to fish."

"Oh, it's just a bunch of local women. They probably don't know anything about fishing either. Stop worrying and go to sleep. I'll sleep like a lamb tonight after that long trip." He turned out the light.

Later, Franco turned over on his back and looked at the clock on the night table: 3 a.m. He only had a few hours more to sleep, because Roberto wanted to go into the city early. The ticking of the clock resounded in his head as he closed his eyes and sank into the pillow. He breathed the sea air and relaxed. His mind drifted. The past few days began to run backward: Roberto in his study, Giulietta's fishing, and the experience at the Colosseum. As he moved into sleep, the ancient structure formed clearly in his mind.

Franco saw the young woman point out the painting of the six monks. He focused on the painting. It gradually increased in size, and the monks began to move. The monk with his hands on the porcelain oracle began to move it across the numbers on the table. Each time he reached a number, it would come to life and form the figure 8. The zero overlapped itself and formed an 8, and the number 2 twisted itself to form an 8 as it hopped off the table. The monks smiled and enjoyed the scene.

The monk with his hands on the oracle cautioned everyone to step back while the numbers 6 and 8 began to rise. The figure 8 grew as large as the monks and stood erect, obviously proud of its great stature. The number 6 sprang up with a gust of energy. The monks' robes flapped in its wake. The 8 wobbled a bit next to the mighty 6, which grew larger and larger, emitting a white light.

The 6 encouraged all the numbers to straighten their lines and form a circle. The numbers complied and began to spin. After several turns, many figure 8s sprang out of the circle.

"Franco, come on, it's five o'clock," a voice called from the door.

"I'll be right there, Roberto," Franco threw off his sheets and dressed hurriedly.

Franco and Roberto stepped off the train in downtown Palermo into the morning light.

"It's only six a.m.," said Franco. "Why did you want to come into the city at this hour?"

"Because it is good to wake up with the city," said the poet as he stretched his arms up and drew in a deep breath. "We'll have some bread and cheese for breakfast."

Roberto led Franco across the wide main street into the old city. The morning sun disappeared as the streets narrowed and the buildings leaned in toward each other.

"Where are all the police?" asked Franco. He remembered the police in Rome and the changes in the city.

"Police? The police are here," said Roberto.

"In Rome, the Fascists have policemen on every street corner," said Franco, "but I do not see them here."

Roberto stopped and pulled his cousin close.

"When Mussolini came to visit Palermo, he was escorted by a Mafia chieftain, who was chosen by a member of the Fascist government. Do you know why?"

Franco shook his head.

"It was because the Fascists know they cannot wipe out or control the Mafia. They know the Mafia controls Sicily and that it has been that way for a hundred years. If the Fascists put policemen on street corners here, they would disappear faster than they could be replaced. Palermo has its own police, and they watch from the shadows."

They turned on a side street. Franco pulled out his white handkerchief and placed it over his nose and mouth; Palermo was slow in picking up garbage. Franco thought how the stench had not changed since he was a kid. It hadn't bothered him as much then.

"Roberto, where are we going? There were some cheese shops on the main street. Why take us here? The smell is disgusting."

"I have a cheese shop I frequent because I like the people. Don't worry, we'll eat our breakfast in a piazza far from this section of the city."

Five or six shops stood side by side, small buildings huddling together for protection against the rodents and thieves. Franco's nostrils filled with the aroma of Provolone and Romano cheeses.

"Remove your handkerchief," said Roberto. "Signore Bertuccio will think you don't like the smell of his cheese. We do not want to offend him."

Roberto lifted the blanket that covered the entrance to the shop.

"Signore Bertuccio! It is good to see you." Roberto kissed the shopkeeper on both cheeks.

"Il Poeta! It is always a fine day when you come to my shop. How is your family? How goes it?" asked the bald shopkeeper.

Franco watched Signore Bertuccio's fat stomach reverberate like a jellyfish with the sound of his voice and the gestures of his thick body.

"Good. Everyone is good," said Roberto as he put his arm around Franco. "This is my cousin Franco Bellini, from America. He was born here and spent his early years on our island."

"Welcome," said Bertuccio. "But you have come at a bad time. Things are not so good, eh?"

"It seems that things are bad throughout Europe," said Franco. On the walls were pictures of Bertuccio's family. On the wall behind the counter, children were depicted in every stage of growing up, from christenings to weddings. In one picture, Bertuccio stood smiling as he held a baby in his enormous arms. On the side wall were pictures of funerals: people crying, caskets being carried on men's shoulders out into the countryside. It reminded Franco of Roberto's room at the villa. Instead of displaying books, Bertuccio shared what meant most to him: his family.

"Bertuccio, my friend, how is business?" Roberto asked as he took the package of cheese.

"Mine is surviving," Bertuccio said. "Today I have had a big order from some of the politicians in town. They always order the best cheese while many people starve. What can I do? I need to make a living."

"Ah, I do not envy your position," said Roberto. He opened the package and bit off a piece of cheese. "Delicious! We must be leaving. I want to show my cousin around while the city is still quiet."

"Il Poeta, I'll keep you up on what happens in the city. I'll send messages to your villa if anything important should come up."

Franco saw his cousin's photograph hanging on the wall beside the doorway. The enthusiasm in Roberto's eyes could not escape the camera's lens. When people left Bertuccio's shop, they got more than cheese and bread.

"Let's go and sit in a piazza near the market," said Roberto. "I have other people I want you to meet today."

A frantic beep startled Franco. He ran to the side of a building. A man in a monk's robe sped by on a bicycle with a motor attached to it.

"Who invented bicycles with motors?" asked Franco as he wiped the sweat from his forehead. His cousin calmly walked on.

"People do not seem to be free here," Franco said. He could not imagine the conversation between Roberto, Bertuccio, and himself taking place in America.

"People are free in America, and we are enslaved here?" asked Roberto.

"I don't mean to say everyone is enslaved, but it just seems that people are struggling against outside forces that invade private lives."

"The commitment of my poetry is to struggle against negative outside forces, and I feel I have freedom in what I write."

"Yes, but if this struggle did not exist, then you would write about something else," said Franco. "Something less disturbing, more pleasant."

The two men came to a piazza and sat by a fountain. People were setting up stands to sell their goods. Roberto broke off a piece of cheese and gave it to Franco.

"Roberto, why don't you come to America? There would be less struggle for freedom," said Franco.

"You Americans are strange. Money seems to be your God. You think that money equals freedom. Well, your freedom could be easily taken away by someone as simple as say, Bertuccio, because your noses would be buried in how much money you made that week. Americans have lost their awareness." The poet waved his arm and broke off a piece of bread with his teeth.

Franco felt that Roberto did possess more awareness than most Americans. There were many situations his cousin could see clearly by tuning into not only human nature but the nature of the individual involved. He certainly knew his own nature well. Maybe this allowed him to reach out and tune into others.

"Good morning, gentlemen," said a small, old man as he guided his bicycle loaded with packages. Franco recognized him as the man who had sped by them.

"I am sorry for being so impatient before," said the old man, "but there was a sale on, and I wanted to be the first person there. My name is Fra Giovanni. I am the abbot of the monastery of San Pietro della Roba in Mondreale. Please excuse my rudeness before." The old man smiled; he had several front teeth missing.

"No harm done, Fra Giovanni," said Roberto. "My cousin here is from America and is not familiar with our way of driving."

"I see, I see. Tell me, what part of America are you from?"

"I am from New York, but I was born in Palermo and lived here for twelve years."

"Isn't that wonderful, wonderful. You have both worlds in your character. Fortunate, extremely fortunate. Ummmmm." He turned his attention back to Roberto. "And yourself, paisane. What is your work?"

"I am Roberto Mineo, the poet." Roberto inhaled and raised his chest. "And this is Franco Bellini."

"Oh, oh, it's our own sage! Yes, yes, I have read your work. You have talent, my son. There is no doubt that you have talent." The abbot shook and shook Roberto's hand. "We are both writers, you and I."

"Really, Fra Giovanni? What do you write?" asked Roberto as he nudged Franco. "Are you still writing romantic novels at your age?"

"Why, how perceptive of you!" said the monk, clapping his hands. "Yes, yes, I saw your potential for perceptiveness in your second book. No doubt it can be developed."

"Potential? What do you mean?" asked Roberto.

"Not to overly concern yourself, my young friend. Everything in time."

"And what does a monk, who has spent most of his life in a monastery, know about love and romance if there is no woman around for inspiration?" asked Roberto.

"A very good question—an obvious question, indeed. But it is not necessary to experience some things in the physical world. My inspiration comes from the universe at large. You see, my boy, how you need to work on your perception."

"Fra Giovanni," said the poet as he stood and pulled his shoulders back, "my poetry does lack in spirituality, but there is much going on in the world today that must be dealt with in clear and precise language. The flowery writings of a romance novelist have their place, but there are more important issues to explore at this time." Roberto did not want to hurt the old man's feelings, but he felt he must stand his ground.

"Oh, no. On the contrary, dear boy, your poetry is drenched in spirituality. You have misunderstood me." The old monk put his finger to his lips. "You praise the individual soul in your work, and that is praising God. I suppose a better word is intuition." The monk looked up and raised his finger. "Yes, that is it, intuition. I would like to show you two young men my writing studio at San Pietro della Roba. I am sure you would find it interesting, and your cousin could see Mondreale. It is only fifteen minutes by bus."

"I am sorry, Fra Giovanni, but my cousin and I have plans for the day. I have many things to show him because he may never return to Sicily," said the poet.

"Yes, yes, I could see you were in deep conversation. I am sorry if I disturbed you, but you both looked interesting, and I get to meet so few people outside of the monastery that I thought...."

"Not at all," said Franco, " I have enjoyed meeting you." Franco felt there was something special about this old man. "I would like to accompany you back to the monastery for a visit."

"But we don't have time," said Roberto, looking at his watch.

"It's nine in the morning. We'll be back in town for lunch. Besides, I am a free man—free to go where I choose, remember?"

"And so you are, so you are," said the monk. "All the brothers will be excited to meet you both." The monk clapped his hands and quickly bent down and picked up his bicycle. "We are located near the duomo, the cathedral. Ask anyone for directions. I will see you both in an hour." Fra Giovanni beeped his horn and rode away.

~ ~ ~ ~ ~

Roberto and Franco stood in front of the cathedral in Mondreale.
"Wait here," said Roberto. "I'll go ask directions to the monastery."

Franco scanned the outside of the edifice; statues of the saints lined the building on the second floor, and thick, white pillars supported the entrance of the church. The cathedral bells tolled and he looked up at the huge structure, stretching his chin toward the heavens searching for the belfry. Suddenly, he started to imagine that he was staring down at himself from the top of the cathedral. He saw how insignificant he appeared on the ground. He shielded his eyes from the sun with his hand and from the top of the building, he imagined not only seeing San Pietro but sensed he was able to project himself beyond the confines of the city.

"I've got the address," said Roberto. "The monastery of San Pietro della Roba is two streets over."

Franco's two bodies merged quickly. He couldn't decide if he had been daydreaming or had actually been someplace else.

"Anything wrong? You look a little confused," said Roberto.

"I was just daydreaming," said Franco as he rubbed his eyes.

"Well, prepare yourself. These monasteries are loaded with history and valuable objects. It can be a mystical experience. Where in America would this happen? In Sicily there are wise men on every corner." He patted Franco's back as they walked to find the monastery.

Roberto pulled on a long cord that hung outside the door of what looked like an ordinary building.

"This is no monastery," said Roberto.

"Maybe they can't afford to live in a big monastery anymore," said Franco. "Are you sure you have the right address?"

"Of course, I wrote it down." He showed the piece of paper to Franco.

The sound of someone dragging furniture came from behind the door, then silence. A small square piece of wood in the center of the door slid sideways, and two brown eyes looked at the men, They then heard the sound of the clang of bolts disengaging.

"Well, it's our sage and his cousin! Welcome." The old monk stepped aside and let the two men in. He pushed a chair back against the wall. "As you can see, my height does not allow me to reach the peep hole without some help. It is so good of you to come. The brothers have been so excited to meet a national poet and an American—and all in the same day! I am always thankful when such miracles happen."

"We're not miracles, Fra Giovanni," said Franco.

"To us, everything is a miracle. Especially people such as yourselves." The monk rubbed his hands together. "First I will take you to my studio."

"Fra Giovanni, my cousin and I were wondering what happened to your monastery," said Roberto as he looked around him. "Your monastery is being renovated, no doubt."

"Oh, my, I didn't tell you. Well we have lost our monastery—the building—to the church. His Holiness in Rome is using our monastery for other things. Since there were only twenty-four of us left, they moved us here. Yes, we were quite sad to leave our home, but we're happy to be here." The old monk bowed his head as if in prayer. "Well, let's move on. No sense in burdening you with our troubles. Up the staircase we go."

They followed the monk down a long corridor with white walls. Franco could see over the monk's head; the hallway gradually narrowed and he could see a door ahead. When they reached the door, Franco and Roberto could just about fit through it without stooping.

"Oh, this is fun!" said the monk. "I enjoy company."

"Fra Giovanni," said Roberto, "I hope you have saved your valuable possessions."

"Possessions? What possessions, my friend?"

"Well, your gold chalices and crucifixes, of course."

The monk's face saddened.

As you know, Il Poeta, Il Duce's first political program called for confiscation of church property. Unfortunately, our gold stayed behind. Let us continue up the stairs."

"But in February of this year, there was a reconciliation between church and state, and church property has been returned. The Citta del Vaticano has been returned to the Holy See, and Mussolini has declared the Vatican an independent state. The church now recognizes the Fascist government."

"Oh, you are aware, my sage, but my monks and I have found that it is unnecessary to live on church property."

The monk opened a door at the top of the stairs. The aroma of freshly cut wood saturated the air. Fra Giovanni picked up his robes, climbed the last step and jumped into the room.

"Well, gentlemen, how do you like it?" asked the abbot, rubbing his hands together. "The good brothers and I just built it."

Franco had never seen such a spacious room. A globe sat on a tall wooden stand next to a window. A large table with a leather top stood in the middle of the room under a window in the ceiling. The monk obviously worked there. A large telescope stood in front of the north window.

"Fra Giovanni, do you use the telescope?" asked Franco.

"Oh, of course. The stars tell me many things."

"As a man of the cloth, you use the stars for mystical purposes?" asked Roberto.

"Mystical? Well, let me see… I know when to plant certain vegetables and when it would be a good time to publish my manuscripts. I suppose you could call that mystical. I am very interested in the sciences, especially astronomy. You seem to be disappointed in the way we live, Mr. Buttita."

"Not at all," said Roberto. "You must be terrorized at times by the Fascists. The struggle must be tremendous. My cousin here is ignorant of such a struggle."

"My dear poet, we are a small, self-sufficient order and live a peaceful existence. We grow our vegetables and maintain our own house. Not only does the government not bother us, but my feeling is they do not even know we exist."

"I'm not disappointed," said Franco. "This room was done by expert craftsmen. I build houses myself, and I know excellent work when I see it."

"Oh, nothing makes me feel better than a colleague praising my work. I accept your praise graciously," said the monk as he put his hands together and looked up toward the window in the ceiling.

"What are you working on now?" asked Franco as he looked down at a writing tablet on the table.

"Yes, yes, now here is something the poet here will be interested in. I am experiencing a writer's challenge."

"What is the book about?" asked Franco.

"I think the story might intrigue you. It is about an earthquake in Messina that took place at the beginning of this century. My father was an archaeologist and was in the city on excavation when the earth moved. He was killed, along with my mother and brother."

"My wife lost her family in that earthquake," said Franco.

"Really?" asked the old monk. "Oh, how I know she has suffered. You see, in my book, I'm imagining what my father would have done had he lived through the disaster—what he would have felt. Many people could not find their families' bodies. Your wife is a survivor, which is not an easy thing to be. I am at a difficult part now in the novel where my father cannot find my brother's or my mother's remains. He knows they were swallowed by the earth but cannot actually believe they're dead until he sees their bodies. And so he digs and digs."

"Does he ever find them?" asked Franco.

"No. He never does. To lose a loved one and never bury the person properly is devastating."

"Why does God permit such things to happen?" asked Franco.

"God? Oh no, my boy, we humans are responsible. We put so much hate and negative energy into the world that it blows up on us. Let me read you a paragraph." The monk reached into a desk drawer, pulled out a thick manuscript, and began to read.

"The city of Messina was so full of poverty and filth that the earth could no longer support such an atmosphere. One day, when Giovanni and his wife and son were walking down the street, the earth began to shake with such a force that could only be described as outside the known universe. But yet, the energy came from inside the earth and pushed its way to the surface. In an instant, Giovanni saw his wife and son disappear into the gaping hole that the energy had forced open. For the next few days, Giovanni, the archaeologist, dug for his wife and son."

"Excuse me, Fra Giovanni. I am sorry to disturb you...," said a young monk as he tapped on the doorframe.

"Oh, Brother Marizio," said the abbot, "come in, come in. Don't be shy. My friends, this is our talented illustrator. He illustrates all my novels. Brother, these are the two men I spoke about this morning. This is our sage and poet, Roberto Mineo, and Franco Buttita from America."

The young monk acknowledged the visitors with a nod as he put his hands inside the sleeves of his robe.

"It's a pleasure to meet you," said Brother Marizio. His long nose came to a point and hid his thin lips as he looked down.

"I was just telling them about my latest book. Why don't you bring the illustrations so we can all see them?"

The monk quickly left the room.

"I hope you don't mind if I show you Marizio's work. He really is an extraordinary artist."

"Illustrate a novel! People will never go for it," said Roberto. "It's too medieval."

The monk returned with several rolls of paper. Franco was drawn to the movement of the composition; the brown earth opening, spitting bits of rock and dirt. People screaming and praying to God for help. In the corner of one painting was a man with tools doing an excavation—the abbot's father, no doubt. Franco thought about Angela and how she must have felt to experience such a terror.

"In the corner of the painting is my father digging for my mother and brother. It is my way of expressing loss. That is how I see him to this day. He later died in an aftershock; an archeological team came in and dug for him, but his body was never found."

Franco wondered how Angela expressed her loss. She rarely spoke about the tragedy. It didn't seem that she could. He now realized how important it was that she return to Messina.

"It embodies your writing, Fra Giovanni," said Roberto, forcing a smile. Why would anyone be interested in an old monk's writing? thought Roberto.

"Oh," said the abbot as he rubbed his hands together, "a great compliment coming from you, Il Poeta. Yes, two wonderful compliments today. I thank God for my good fortune. Franco, I hope my work was illuminating for you?"

"It was," said Franco. "We should be getting back. Thank you so much for your time, Fra Giovanni." He held out his hand.

"Oh, look at this American," said the abbot. The monk embraced Franco. Fra Giovanni turned to Roberto.

"You have helped me a great deal today, Il Poeta. You have been of service to an old man by showing him another part of the world through this American. I'm sorry if I have disappointed you. Maybe I was not what you had expected."

Roberto had wanted to show Franco what Sicily was all about. How there was a sage on every street corner; how difficult it was to live a happy life, what misery the people lived in because of the government. He wanted to show him pain and degradation. But instead, he showed Franco how alive and passionate one old man could be if his spirit were kept alive. All Roberto felt he got from the abbot was a clear picture of his inconsistencies. Why had he come away with so little?

"Well," said the abbot, "I don't like goodbyes, but I'm afraid they are part of life. Brother Marizio will show you out."

The young monk walked to the door while Franco and Roberto followed. The poet turned before he descended the stairs.

"I wasn't disappointed," said Roberto. "When new ideas are presented, one's mind is always put at odds." The poet left the freshness of the newly constructed room, taking the scent of pine with him.

~ ~ ~ ~ ~

Angela had never been in a small boat, and the feel of it made her unsteady.

"Nothing to be afraid of, Angela," said Giulietta as she pushed off the shore and jumped in. "Now put the oar deep in the water and push. Like so." As Giulietta rowed, Angela could see the muscles of her upper arms bulge and disappear with each stroke.

"I don't know anything about fishing," said Angela. She wiped the sweat from her cheek and unbuttoned the sleeves on her white blouse.

"I told you to wear something lighter," said Giulietta. She wore a sleeveless cotton dress with multicolored polka dots. Giulietta pinned the skirt of the dress between her legs. "We don't have to go far from shore to fish." As they rowed a bit farther, Giulietta spotted two women with straw hats in a boat fishing. "It is Annunziata and her sister, Graziella. They knew I was coming today. They came early so they would catch the biggest fish."

"Buon giorno, Giulietta," shouted Annunziata.

"Good morning, ladies," said Giulietta. "It is a fine morning. Tell me, are the fish biting?"

"Oh, not so good this morning," said Annunziata.

"I bet they've caught five or six already," whispered Giulietta.

Angela held on to the sides of the boat.

"We wish you luck," shouted one of the sisters as they rowed toward shore. Giulietta nodded her head and waved.

"Well, let's get started." Giulietta picked up a fishing pole and opened the can of worms. She took out a long, thin worm, wrapped it around the fishing line several times, and stuck its end through the hook. With a splash, she threw the line in the water.

"Roberto tells me you are here to look for your sister." Giulietta stared out over the water.

"Yes, I am. This trip isn't so much for pleasure. I know I have to go back to Messina and look for my sister."

"You must have missed her all these years," said Giulietta.

"I feel like I raised my sister-in-law, Speranza," said Angela. "I gave all my love to her. She helped with my adjustment to America. But now she is grown and has her own children. I think of them often."

"I wish you luck, Angela. I wish you luck." Giulietta swatted a fly that landed on her arm.

"You and Roberto do not get along?" Angela asked softly, unsure if she should ask the question.

"Of course we get along. He just needs to be put in his place sometimes, and at times forcefully. He thinks he's so grand. Those peasants who come to see him are all lazy good-for-nothings, but Roberto says they are the salt of the earth. I ask him which earth he is talking about. I always tell Roberto," continued Giulietta as she reeled in the line, "I tell him that he has to think of his family first. Our children have been exiled to Paris and up north to Turin. They think Papa's job is to run from the government and the police."

"It must be a hard life," said Angela.

"Hard? You have no idea. At least you know where you'll be next year or next week. Another war could be declared in Europe next week, and we would have to leave because my husband would be speaking out against it." Giulietta looked at the hook with the worm still on it. "Well, let's go on shore and have our lunch. Now dig the oar deep in the water and row."

~ ~ ~ ~ ~

Angela looked out over the sea in the direction of Messina. She decided it was far beyond the palm trees in the distance. Soon she would be in her city again to search for her sister. In her mind, she saw herself and her sister dancing around the small fountain. They twirled and twirled each other until they fell, laughing. Angela had kept her sister's laughter close to her, but now the giggles were more clear. She thought of Speranza; maybe her sister-in-law's laughter kept it alive for her.

"Angela, where is your mind?" asked Giulietta. "I don't think you've heard a word I have said."

She stretched out a long chain of knitting and pushed the yarn down the knitting needles. "What are you looking at? It is almost dark. The time to look at our sea is in the morning just after sunrise. Roberto says that the morning air is so clear you can see the fish swimming."

Angela hardly noticed that darkness had descended. When she thought about her sister, the sun shone down around her. Even if she were in a cave with no light, all she would have to do is think about the fountain in Messina to feel the sun's warmth.

"I am listening, Giulietta. I don't get to look at such a beautiful ocean every day where I live. How can you see to knit? Don't you make mistakes without a light?"

"No mistakes can be made here. I do not know what I'm making. This keeps my hands busy. It's always a surprise when I finish. Sometimes it is a blanket, other times a shawl or a centerpiece for a table."

"Good evening," said Roberto.

"Oh, Roberto, has the houseboy finished cleaning the kitchen?" asked Giulietta.

"I did not know he was here."

"He came when you were in your study. If I don't keep after him, nothing gets done properly." She darted toward the door.

"While you're at it, check on Franco," said Roberto. "He went to wash up some time ago." He turned to Angela. "Tomorrow I will take you both to the train station in Palermo."

"Thank you, Roberto. I am going to Messina to look for my sister," said Angela. She looked intently at the poet's face as if it were a map revealing her sister's whereabouts.

"If you are sincere in your intentions, then by all means look for her. No matter what anyone says, you search for your sister if you must."

Angela smiled. She was comforted by Roberto's assurance. She feared people would think her silly to even think about searching—but now, it was of no consequence.

~ ~ ~ ~ ~

A ngela steadied herself on Franco's arm as they stood on the train platform.

"I wish you both luck," said Roberto.

"Thank you, Roberto," said Franco. "We will see each other again." The two men embraced. "Wait here. I'll see that our luggage is loaded into the right compartment."

"Angela," said the poet, "you have been quiet the past few days. What it is?"

Angela dreamed of the day she would return to Messina, but she was frightened of what she would find. She never told anyone about the dark energies that resided there. The experiences she had as a child remained in her mind and heart. She did not want to be labeled as a heretic or witch, as so many had been. It was time to board, but all she wanted to do was run back to New York—where she could live with the hope that her sister could still be alive, and where the dark energies were now in hell where they belonged. Angela had to accept the possibility of her sister's death.

"It has been so long since I was in Messina that I'm afraid of the memories..." Angela could not complete her sentence. She could not reveal her real concerns, not even to Roberto.

"Memories cannot do or be anything but what they are: shadows of the past. It's the present that has power, not the past. If unpleasant memories should arise, look at them straight in the eye, then let them fade. Recognize them for what they are."

Angela noticed that Roberto rarely showed this side of himself to others, and she was infinitely grateful that she was the recipient of his best qualities. She felt he had something to gain by the success of her journey.

"Well, the luggage is on the train," said Franco as he rushed toward them. "We'd better get onboard."

"Good luck to you both," said Roberto. He put his arms around them both and walked them toward the train. "Angela, don't forget what I said. Look them in the eye!"

Chapter 6
Palermo, 1929

Franco and Angela stood at the convent's main door, and Angela heard muffled voices on the other side. They were talking in normal tones, from the outside of the great door they sounded like whispers, vague utterances from another time.

"Mother," said Angela as the door opened. The nun had not changed. She was exactly as Angela remembered her from sixteen years before: ivory skin without lines and clear, wide eyes. "You look the same," said Angela. "You look the same. I'm so glad you are as I remembered you."

"Glad that I am still the same, or glad that I am still on God's good earth," said the nun. She smiled at Angela.

"Mother, I am so glad to see you," While Angela lived at the convent, she thought of Mother Superior as made of granite. She would never change. Even if she made a yearly pilgrimage to the convent, the nun would not grow old—at least not to Angela.

"Come in. Come in," said the nun as she opened the door wide and stepped aside.

"I have thought of you often," said Angela. She waited for the Mother Superior to signal that a show of affection was permitted. No one ever showed physical affection toward the Reverend Mother unless she held out her arms first.

"Angela, if I had a lira for every time my mind shifted to you without warning, I would be running a rich convent." The nun opened her long arms, and the sleeves of her habit hung from them.

Angela rested her head on the Mother Superior's shoulder. She felt the nun's arms close around her and the black habit sleeves drape her back. Not even on her wedding day had the Mother Superior embraced her like this. Angela had feared she had been forgotten. That was not the case.

"Franco, you are as handsome as ever," said the nun as Angela stepped back. She took hold of his hand and said, "Good to see you. It was good of you to bring Angela back to us."

"Mother, we would never make a trip to Italy without coming to the convent," said Franco.

The nun's confident, diplomatic approach to situations disturbed Franco. The linen situation at the beginning of his courtship with Angela was still disconcerting to him. This was a woman who was clear about her motives only to herself.

"Lunch is prepared for us in the dining hall. I hope you are hungry." The Mother Superior led them down the corridor.

To Angela, the air felt like mist—just as she had remembered it. When she lived at the convent, she felt she was living in a dream—every room was clean, and she had clean clothes and all the food she needed.

"Have there been many changes here, Sister?" asked Franco. He sat at the lunch table.

"Some. The government has given back church property to the religious orders."

"Did they take the convent?" asked Angela.

The space was empty, and as they talked their voices echoed off the wall. The last time Angela ate in the dining hall was with fifty other girls before her wedding. No echoes could be heard above all the chatter. Now it was just the three of them, their voices mixing with the echoes of the past.

"Some religious orders were not affected. The land our convent is on belongs to the Princess of Palermo, so we are safe. They took many monasteries up north."

"We heard that the Princess was up north in her villa," said Angela. "I hoped to see her." The Princess had shown Angela a world of possibilities. When she visited her that day in her villa, the mists of the convent lifted and she saw the outside world for the first time. She was sure this influenced her decision to marry Franco, although she never told anyone why she chose to marry and leave Sicily. It was not even clear to Angela why she chose a life away from what she knew to be her only life.

"Everything seems the same, Mother," said Angela.

A young novice came in and served chicken. Angela thought she looked no more than sixteen.

"We run the convent the same way. Most of the sisters are still here. We just have different students."

"Sister Priscilla," said Angela, "the old nun who talked to me before the wedding. I assume she died."

"Oh, yes, it wasn't long after you left," said the nun. "A delightful woman in her day."

"What about the other girls?" asked Angela. "What about Filomina?"

"She married a local man and moved to Naples."

"Mother, I would like to see the dormitory, if I may," said Angela. "I'll just be a few minutes."

"Of course, if you like. The girls are still in class, and I can take Franco to the chapel. Franco, if you don't mind, we are having construction done and I would like your opinion on a few things."

"I will meet you in the chapel," said Angela.

The windowless corridor leading to the dormitory seemed darker than Angela remembered. She opened the door to the large room, and a shot of sunlight showered over her. There were three huge windows that were always kept open to warm the room during the day because there was no central heating.

Angela walked to the bed where she had once slept. She thought of the recurring dream she had in that bed. There was a time she thought the bed itself gave her that dream of the earth opening and swallowing people. She had pleaded with the other girls to swap beds, but when she did sleep in another bed, she still had the dream.

She had not had the recurring dream since she moved to America. When she left Sicily, did she leave everything that was hers behind—even her dreams? No matter how bad they were, she still owned them. When she lived here, it was like living in a dream. Perhaps the dreams she had were generated by the convent.

Angela looked around the room at the beds standing neatly next to each other.

She walked out into the hall, pulled the door shut and closed in the sunshine.

~ ~ ~ ~ ~

The courtyard was the same, and the olive trees were in full bloom. Angela stood outside the chapel and smiled. The day the Princess chatted with her after mass flooded her memory. She remembered her as refreshing. There was a crispness to her manner—a clarity to her voice that dissipated the haze of the convent.

Angela went to the chapel, stood in the vestibule, and listened.

"Do you think, in your expert opinion, that I should remove that beam?" asked the Mother Superior.

"No, it is one of the major supporting beams in the chapel. If you remove it, you will weaken the entire structure."

Angela entered the chapel.

"There you are, Angela. Your husband is telling me that I should not remove this beam, but I had hoped to put a statue of a saint here. He said the building would be weakened. We certainly cannot have a house of God weakened, especially in these times."

"I agree with you, Mother," said Angela.

"Remember the day you were married here?" asked the nun. "It was a lovely ceremony—not a dry eye in the chapel."

Angela remembered her wedding day. She had felt hazy most of that day: her veil, the incense and candles all added to an already established uncertainty. She wondered if she would do it all again.

"Mother, I was thinking," said Franco as he scratched his head. "Is there any way I can get upstairs to see where this beam goes? I would like to make sure I'm right."

"Of course. Go through the door next to the altar and up the stairs. There is an attic for storage."

Angela and the nun faced the altar and sauntered toward it.

"So, Angela, you are happy with your choice?"

"Yes, Mother. Things have happened as they should."

"You sound resolved."

"I suppose. Franco is a good man."

"Yes. I know that." They walked a few steps without speaking. "Have you found what you came back for?"

"We are on our way to Messina to look for my sister," said Angela. She turned to the nun. "I want to know if my sister is dead or alive."

"Can you go back satisfied if there is no record of her at all?" asked the nun. "Many victims have not been found."

"I want to leave nothing undone. I will accept whatever God has decided about my sister." Angela secretly harbored the hope that her sister was still alive and that God would not be so cruel as to condemn her to a kind of purgatory, never knowing of her fate. They embraced as Franco came downstairs.

"Well, Mother, I was right." Franco dusted off his pants. "Leave the beam where it is."

"I guess a radical change in decor would not service us very well if the building will fall down around our heads," said the nun. They walked toward the vestibule. "Where do you go from Messina?"

"We get the early morning ferry to Rome and stay a few days," said Franco. "Then onto Genoa and New York."

"World travel," said the nun, "it is truly amazing. Do you have time for a walk around the garden?"

"I would love to walk there again," said Angela.

The Mother Superior opened the main entrance, and a clear light penetrated the haze.

~ ~ ~ ~ ~

Angela and Franco walked hand in hand along the streets of Palermo. "Let's go left here," said Angela.

"Why? Our hotel is straight ahead, on the main street," said Franco.

"I want to see something." Angela held Franco's hand tightly as she walked in front of him. "Pick up your step, Franco. I feel as if I'm dragging you."

"Tell me where we are going, and you won't have to drag me."

"You do not have to know everything right away."

They came to a wide cobblestone street, where there was a sidewalk elevated higher than usual above the road. An outdoor cafe stood on the sidewalk as waiters busily attended customers. A row of shops lined the opposite side of the street.

"What are we doing here?" We should be at our hotel, packing," said Franco.

"Look across the street," said Angela.

"Yes, so it is a cheese shop..." Franco saw himself sitting at the cafe many years ago. "God, I had forgotten. I sat at that cafe!"

"You sat there waiting for me," said Angela.

He was so nervous that day. The Mother Superior had told him how beautiful both girls were, but coming from a nun, that did not mean much. Franco sensed that the Mother Superior wanted to rid her convent of girls who would become a financial drain. Both girls were past sixteen and would become a burden if marriages or other positions were not found.

The moment Franco saw Angela, he knew. It was not love at first sight the way people said; it was a deeper understanding of life situations that compelled him to choose her. He felt an urgency about meeting Angela. If the Mother Superior had permitted, he would have married Angela in a week without reservation.

"Well, the Mother Superior said there were two beautiful girls she wanted me to see. She suggested I sit leisurely at the cafe across the street from the cheese shop and make my choice. It was a difficult one. I could not make up my mind at first."

"Oh? I had no idea you could not make up your mind," said Angela. "It must have been difficult for you." She patted his arm and they smiled at each other. Angela had felt his gaze on her that day; it was warm and assuring. He desired her, not her companion.

"I knew right away," said Angela. She looked around at her surroundings.

"You did?" asked Franco, speaking a little too quickly. "I did not know that. I thought you wanted to be a nun and you couldn't decide."

"Yes, I did, and if I had not met you I never would have married. I would have gone into the order. But when I met you I knew right away—that is why I had such confusion. If it had been anyone else, I would have declined."

"You don't wish that you had stayed at the convent?" asked Franco.

"No, I made the right choice." She put her arms around her husband's neck. She had finally left the haze behind. Angela had felt secure in her choice to leave the convent and build a life in the new world. There would have been no point in choosing convent life, even though her decision took her away from her homeland.

Angela was about to embark on the last part of her journey. Her sister could have been living in Messina all these years, but maybe Felicita was too ill to try to contact her. Her memory may have been affected from the trauma of the disaster. Any number of things could have prevented her from contacting Angela. Whatever what was ahead of her in Messina, she was determined to remain hopeful.

Franco ran his hand down Angela's spine. Franco felt how straight and erect she stood. Angela was five foot three inches, but she appeared taller. They had lived together for sixteen years, but he could never really express himself with words. He thought it was because he didn't have the gift of talking. He hadn't realized he feared that Angela secretly wished she had stayed at the convent. Something about being at the place they first saw each other made him think he should tell her. Should I? No, he thought. She knows.

Tomorrow they would leave for Messina and then home. All the past would be behind them.

Chapter 7
Messina, 1929

Angela walked slowly up the steps of the building that housed the records of deaths and survivors of the earthquake. Franco had wanted to accompany her but she wanted to go alone, it was her quest. Many of the survivors were relocated to other cities in Italy, and many had immigrated to America. What if her sister was somewhere in America? How would she find her?

She took a deep breath and climbed another step. She just had to find out if they had a record of her death or survival. She considered how she would feel if it was confirmed her sister was dead. That would end her connection to the past and her childhood, and she would have no blood relatives—only her imagined cousin to entertain her clients. What would she do if her sister were alive? Her heart jumped for joy at the thought. She would take her back to America to live with her and Franco.

As long as Angela stayed on the steps, there was the possibility that her sister could come back to her. No, she thought, I have to find out.

She stood in front of a large desk. A man with grey, wavy hair and bifocals asked if he could assist her. Angela explained about her sister and that she needed to know what happened to her. The man took all the information that Angela provided and told her it would take a few days, as he would have to research all the documents in Sicily and elsewhere in Italy. He promised her that his findings would be waiting for her when she arrived in America but that she should try and find her old home and see if she could find neighbors.

"Thank you so much, Signore," said Angela.

"You are very welcome, Signora," said the man. "I lost my brother in that earthquake. I know many families who never recovered bodies of their loved ones. They had to assume their family members were dead."

"How many have found their family members?" asked Angela.

"To be honest, very few," said the man. "Signora, it has been many years since the disaster, so the possibility of finding out what happened to your sister is slim. If your sister were still alive, she would have tried to get in touch with the authorities and we would have looked for you."

Angela's heart shook. Slowly, any hope she harbored inside began to drain from her head to her feet. Her weariness returned without warning as she forced a smile and thanked the man for his trouble.

~ ~ ~ ~ ~

Angela walked down the long, narrow street that led to the little fountain. She thought how small the cobblestones seemed, now that she had matured. The buildings were in the same dilapidated condition. Women still hung their laundry out like flags across the narrow streets. Angela spoke to several citizens, but they had no memory of her family. She learned that her neighborhood had been demolished in the earthquake and many of her neighbors died or moved away. She was hoping for a confirmation of Felicita's death or survival, but that was not to be.

She found comfort in being where her sister played and imagined. Her sister's imprint was still here; her feet danced on these cobblestones, and her laughter made an impression in the air. A human being's energy could not be ironed out like wrinkles on a shirt, or washed away like stains on a sheet; it was there forever. How long was forever? Angela could not imagine. Maybe the last time she saw her sister to the present moment was a blink of an eye within the space of forever.

The fountain was barren and alone. Angela stared at the angels in the center: the only sign of life was the mildew growing on their legs and groins. It was dusk, and the moon peeked out from behind clouds as the sun gave a final thrust of fiery energy. Angela noticed her shadow on the ground. It seemed minute and insignificant.

What was the purpose of coming here? It did not change anything. She knew she would never be reunited with Felicita, but she came to Messina anyway—a waste of both time and money. Heavy tears dripped down her face as if someone had turned on a rusted faucet that was abandoned years ago. She tried to push the weariness away, but it engulfed her like a tidal wave. She sat at the base of the fountain, leaning against it; she could no longer hold herself upright. Angela closed her eyes and allowed herself to drift.

Out of the darkness, human shapes began to form. These forms rushed toward Angela, as if she had something they wanted. She wondered if her sister was among them. They were faceless, but Angela felt they were staring at her. She wanted to be invisible but knew that they were aware of her presence.

The shapes encircled Angela, and she started to hear their voices. They were some of the energies dislodged by the earthquake that were still trying to find their way home. Others sometimes heard these voices too, and these forms sometimes overtook people and made them do things that they would ordinarily not do. The forms were usually hidden from view, trapped between the buildings.

Angela desperately tried to reach out to the forms. Maybe they knew something. "Is my sister here? Do you know where she is?"

Suddenly there was silence. There is nothing to be gained here, thought Angela. It is the same hard life with little hope. Everyone here is lost, and her sister was gone. She would always miss her, never forgetting her for one day. Once Angela had these thoughts, the shapes disappeared and she opened her eyes.

The fountain felt old and vacant. Roberto was right about the past. It was time to go home, but she had one more stop on her journey. She knew in her heart that her sister was gone.

Chapter 8
Returning to America, 1929

The 4:30 a.m. ferry to Rome was never full, because most people preferred to travel at night. Angela and Franco had decided it was best to leave early to arrive in Rome by early evening.

"It is a good hour to cross the Strait of Messina," said Franco. "We can see our last sunrise from the boat."

"I don't think I would want to see another sunrise from the boat. The sun rises and sets everywhere, so there is no need to say good-bye to it. I will nap."

Franco looked at Angela as she slept. The train was loaded on the boat to cross to the mainland. He silently went up to the ship's deck.

There were a few men talking and drinking wine, while several policemen sat at a table and played cards.

"Signore, what are you doing?" asked one of the policemen.

"I am here to watch the sunrise," said Franco. The men spoke Italian but with an accent. Franco suspected they were Germans.

"All right," said the first officer as he shuffled the deck of cards, "but don't be long."

Franco walked to the bow of the ship and looked out into the rising sun. As the sun ascended, the face of the moon gradually faded. The sun's burning light became brighter, and the moon gave back whatever energy it had stored during the night. In Franco's mind, the moon was always there, and as the sun rose, it slowly absorbed the moon's glow. As the moon became transparent, it gave the illusion that it had gone on some journey.

Franco lifted his face to absorb the drops of water the wind carried from the ocean. If the sun could absorb the moon's energy, then when darkness fell, the moon could reabsorb the sun's glow. He imagined that the drops were energized by the dawn when the sun and moon were exchanging their light.

He thought about the old monk and his book. The disasters of the earth that people survived were more numerous than he thought. Angela never talked about her ordeal very much. He assumed it was all behind her, or she simply did not remember. He realized that something as violent as an earthquake could never be forgotten once experienced. If a man did harm to you, then you could direct your anger toward that man. If the earth was the culprit, how could one seek retribution? Curse God? Fra Giovanni had said, "It was the mass negative thoughts of all mankind that caused the earth to separate." Who could the earth hate? The entire human race?

The moon was completely invisible now, and the sun beamed. Franco turned, nodded at the policemen, and went back down into the ship.

Franco and Angela arrived at the Rome train station at dusk when the city was just about to awaken for the evening. Waiters were setting up tables, and streetlights began to spring on. Franco checked their luggage until the next evening when they would leave for Genoa. Angela carried an overnight bag.

"We are free of our luggage," said Franco as they walked out into the dry evening air. "We can walk to our pensione."

Angela liked Rome. She had been undecided on their earlier visit because of the taxi charges, but stepping into Rome just before dark gave it a different feeling. It felt less ominous, much softer. The idea of strolling to the pensione without the weight of luggage delighted her.

"Can we have dinner before we check into the pensione?" asked Angela.

"We should check in first. I told the manager we would be there before half past-eight."

"Phone him and tell him we're here," she said. "We've stayed at his establishment before. He knows we are responsible people. Besides, it is getting late and most of the restaurants will be crowded if we wait."

"I suppose," said Franco. "Piazza della Republica is just to our left, and there are many restaurants there."

At the piazza, a band was just setting up to play. Angela and Franco sat at an outdoor restaurant.

"I will go make the phone call," said Franco.

A group of Americans was led to a nearby table, and Angela strained to hear what they were saying. She wondered what Americans really thought about Italy and the Italians. Her customers used to ask her if this or that was true about life in Italy. Were Italian men as grabby as people said? Were people desperately poor, and were there actually blond Italians? Angela tilted her head toward the Americans' table.

"Well, I can't wait to see the restored paintings," said a middle-aged man as he raised his pipe to his lips.

"I don't know about going to the Colosseum at night," said an older woman. "It seems a bit unseemly."

"Please, Mrs. Hawkins, you know these paintings are best viewed in the evening," said the man.

The paintings at the Colosseum! Angela suddenly remembered that the young woman who was restoring them encouraged them to return and see them finished.

"It is all set," said Franco. "The manager said that we can check in until eleven..."

"Franco, listen to the people at that table," whispered Angela as she gripped his arm.

"What?"

"Listen to those Americans." She leaned toward Franco and put her hand to her mouth. "They are talking about the paintings we saw at the Colosseum when we arrived."

"What paintings...oh, I remember. Are you sure they are talking about the paintings we saw?"

"Listen to their conversation."

"Angela, that's impolite."

"Shh..."

"I hear there are paintings that are out of this world," said the man. "I hear they hold some metaphysical significance." He tapped his pipe on the side of the table.

"Did you hear that?" whispered Angela.

"Angela, we saw no paintings like that," said Franco. He handed her the menu. "Here, busy yourself with selecting food, and let's mind our own business."

"What time are we supposed to meet our guide at the Colosseum?" asked the woman.

"We have about an hour and fifteen minutes," said a man in a multicolored shirt. "You know, I heard one woman is restoring those paintings all by herself."

Angela saw her husband straighten up.

"You see, they are talking about the woman who invited us back," said Angela.

"Shh," said Franco, "let me listen."

"Well, I don't know about that," said the woman. "It still seems unseemly to go around that pagan structure at night."

"Franco, we have to go with them. They mentioned they have a guide who will take them on a tour. Please go over and ask them if we can accompany them. We will never see the paintings otherwise."

"Angela, it has been a long day. Let's just go back to the *pensione*." Franco thought that it would be worthwhile to see the paintings again, but approaching a group of strangers who had special permission to see the artwork made him uneasy.

"Don't you want to see the paintings? It was nice of the young woman to share them with us. She really wanted us to come back."

That was true, thought Franco. After all, he and Angela had seen them in the early stages of restoration and were asked back by the artist herself. They had as much right to see the paintings as the American group did. He got up and slowly approached the Americans.

"Excuse me," said Franco, "I could not help but overhear that you are going to the Colosseum tonight to see restored paintings."

"Yes," said the middle-aged man. He put on wire-rimmed glasses and stared up at Franco. "That is correct. We're curators from a museum in America. I'm a curator from a small museum outside of Boston."

An art expert, thought Franco. He must seem ignorant to the curator.

"My wife and I saw the paintings in progress before we went to Sicily to visit our family," said Franco. "The artist invited us back, and we would very much like to see them again. Would there be a chance that we could come along with your group?"

"You speak very good English," said the curator. He looked Franco up and down.

"That is because I'm an American, too. My wife and I are from New York." If they met Angela, they would take them. He waved Angela over.

"Angela, these men are curators of a museum in America."

"Pleased to meet you," said Angela.

"Well," said the curator, "I don't see what harm it would do. Is Italy your native land?"

"Yes," said Franco, "for both of us."

"Well, then, you certainly want to see them finished," said the curator. "Just follow us into the Colosseum when the guide comes. I'll explain the paintings to you. We're viewing the paintings in the evening, because it's best to see certain colors without sunlight. Do you know anything about art?" The curator raised his eyebrows.

Angela and Franco looked at each other.

"Signore," said Franco, "I know how to put things together. I know about art."

"Well, after we've eaten, we will leave for the Colosseum."

"Thank you so much for your kindness," said Franco. A frail-looking assembly of people, thought Franco.

Angela and Franco went back to their table.

~ ~ ~ ~ ~

The group entered the Colosseum and walked along the circular corridor. The guide stopped and turned on several flashlights.

"Our first selection of paintings we believe were done by an astronomer during the Roman empire." He focused the beam of the flashlights on the wall. "These paintings are unique in that they seem to give us different views of the sun and the nine planets in our solar system."

Franco clutched Angela's hand, and they moved forward in the group. In the first painting, the artist gave the view of the planets from the sun. Blazing yellow and red rays extended beyond the sun's surface. The planets rotated swiftly around the sun, some were blue and others were purple. The purples, reds and oranges radiating from the plane melded into one another.

"I find it hard to believe that there are no paintings of the Madonna here or Christ on the cross," whispered Angela.

"I cannot imagine how the painter did that," Franco said. "I know he did not have to visit the sun."

"The next painting is even more extraordinary," said the guide. "Its view is from outside our solar system looking in."

Franco found the colors were the same as the last painting; there was a vastness pulsating from the artist's angle. Franco felt the painting was not about the nine planets in the solar system but about something beyond.

"And here we have a most charming painting," said the guide. "It is of a group of sixth-century monks using a Ouija board. Why and who created these, no one knows."

Franco looked at the painting with fresh eyes. It was a different way to view spirituality and religion. In the monks' painting, men of the church were depicted almost as witches, using mystical means to tell the future. It was obvious that traditional religion was not enough—that there was something more in the universe for human beings to know about.

"These are extraordinary," said the middle-aged curator. "Nowhere in art history do you see such an unusual perspective and skill at depicting the known universe."

"You have absolutely no record of the artist?" asked one of the curators.

"None," said the guide. "These were discovered in the Santa Croce Monastery in Rome. Since the themes are pagan, the church wanted them here."

Franco thought all the paintings had one thing in common: they all taught the viewer to see life from many perspectives.

"Ladies and gentlemen, thank you for your cooperation and interest," said the guide as he pointed the way out of the Colosseum.

~ ~ ~ ~ ~

Angela and Franco walked silently and arm-in-arm along Via Cavour, stopping occasionally to look in a shop window.

"Anxious to get home?" asked Franco.

She stared ahead. "She should have showed the monks' painting first."

"What?"

"The guide showed us the wrong painting first," said Angela.

"Why do you say that?" asked Franco.

"The monks with the Ouija board seemed like a beginning to me—and then the paintings of the planets and universe. But first I would want to see human beings who were preparing to explore like the monks."

"You know, I felt that they were all about the same thing," said Franco. "They were all about seeing things differently."

"Or seeing things at different levels," said Angela. "Maybe things are in the world that we do not see."

"The Ouija board painting reminded me of the old monk Roberto and I visited. The feel of the artwork made me think of him. Even the house Fra Giovanni lived in seemed like the paintings, because its shape was different. It was unlike any house I have ever seen. It was built by someone who knew how to put something together, like the artists we just saw."

Angela knew this night was their last sight of Rome and Italy. She did not like all the police and talk of fascism. Her place was in America. When they reached the top of Via Cavour, she looked back toward the Colosseum and thought of it as an oasis in the middle of despair. The full moon hovered over the round structure, and the sky was so clear that it looked like a painting. Angela imagined the moon protected the Colosseum, shedding its light on every visitor who passed through.

The night she had seen Speranza and Salvatore on the porch under the full moon, she felt the solid bond between them. Maybe moonlight solidified relationships that had to run their course regardless of outcome. Angela felt her life could be viewed from within the moonlight, not under it. The haze in the convent could have been accumulated moonlight, and whoever walked past the convent's great doors had to fulfill their destiny because that is where the moon's mist would lead them. When she was a young girl, she could not see the mist in the convent—but now she did and could make that a part of her. She was of the moon now.

"Angela, is your mind at ease about your sister? You have not said..."

"I do not know if I will ever have an easy mind about my sister, but I am resolved that she is not here. I decided this at the fountain."

"What do you mean?"

"I realized in my heart that there was nothing for me here. Like the paintings, I gained another perspective. I saw what there was to see: the fountain, the old buildings. It all felt different, and my whole feeling about what I expected changed."

Franco sensed something had changed about Angela—or no—not changed, but was missing. There was a somber side to his wife that he often saw. Now, he found it gone. He thought that he made her somber at times, but now he saw that he had nothing to do with it.

"Are you ready to leave Italy?" asked Franco. He put his arm around his wife.

"I do not think there's anything else for me to do, so I must be ready."

They sauntered arm-in-arm down Via Nazionale toward the *pensione*.

Chapter 9
New York, 1929

A ngela stepped off the gangplank and saw Speranza and the children. They were all dressed up, all frills and smiles, waving their hands. Angela took in the scene; passengers and greeters ran toward one another, and once they touched, they hung off each other as if time had frozen their embrace. Angela wanted to imprint in her memory the way Speranza and the children appeared today. Angela thought if she could stop a moment in time, this would be it.

"Angela, you are back safe!" said Speranza as she rushed toward her. The children jumped up and down and hugged their aunt. "So much is happening in Europe that I was afraid you would have problems getting home to us."

"Speranza, it is good to be home. It is so good to be home."

"Where is my brother?"

"He is getting our luggage," said Angela. She hugged her little girl. "Alicia has grown so much in a month."

"Here comes Franco," said Speranza. She rushed toward her brother.

Angela watched as Franco grinned and Speranza cupped her hands around his cheeks. When they embraced, Angela felt as if she were in between them receiving their warmth and energy. Since their trip, both she and Franco suddenly had more to give—to each other and to others. It was not that they saw many new things but that they saw the familiar with widened vision.

~ ~ ~ ~ ~

"Tell me about your trip, Angela," said Speranza. They walked through Nelsonville's public park. "You have not said much the past few weeks."

"You would not know any of the people we visited. It was meaningful to Franco and myself."

"Oh, come on, if it's important to you and Franco, I'm interested," said Speranza, holding Angela's arm. "Did you find out if your sister was killed in the earthquake?"

"I doubt very much if we will ever find out what happened."

"I'm so sorry to hear that."

"I went back to the fountain where my sister and I played as children."

"Oh, and what did you find there?" Speranza searched her sister-in-law's face.

"I thought to myself that Speranza would have liked to have played at that fountain when she was a little girl. If you were brought up in Sicily, I would have taken you there to play."

Speranza put her arm around Angela.

"I have something to tell you," said Speranza.

"Oh and what's that?"

"I'm going to have another baby."

"Speranza, congratulations," said Angela as she held Speranza's hands. "But remember to take care of your health. Maybe you and the children should move in with us for a while. This way I can take care of you better. Remember what happened the last time—the doctor did not come in time."

"No, Angela, I can't leave Salvatore. He would be furious."

"Well maybe, but the kids can stay with me anytime you want a rest." Angela squeezed Speranza's hand. She had hoped for the best for Speranza since the first day they met. She did not want her to marry so young or to marry Salvatore. This was not the life she wanted for someone she felt was both her sister and daughter.

"Angela, I've never seen you so peaceful. What happened when you went away?"

"We saw some old things that were familiar and some new, but we saw them with different eyes."

"Franco doesn't talk to me about how he feels and what happened when you went away. I asked him the other day and he said, 'Ask Angela. She can say it better than I can. Whatever she says is correct.'"

Angela smiled. Little was said between them about the trip since they returned. Angela felt she had become more distant since their journey, but Franco had been easier about things. The events of the trip were irrelevant; the outcome was what was important.

"The wind this fall is fierce," said Angela. Trees flapped in the gust of wind that came out of no- where.

"Fall is my favorite season," said Speranza. "Everything becomes so quiet. It feels secure to me. I like wearing sweaters and seeing children walk past my house on their way to school. I love the first morning you can blow smoke with your breath…" Speranza paused and looked into the distance. "Funny, that's the first time I said that. I didn't know I enjoyed fall so much."

"I am glad I reminded you." Angela remembered Speranza running in the fall leaves when she was a little girl. It was her favorite season even then.

"Angela, come to my house for a cup of coffee. You have time."

"All right, but I can't be long."

Angela and Speranza made their way down the path and out into the street.

~ ~ ~ ~ ~

Speranza opened the door to her apartment. The two women walked in.

"It's so nice to have the kids in school," said Speranza as she took off her sweater.

"Speranza," said a male voice from the kitchen.

"Salvatore, what are you doing home?" asked Speranza. He appeared in the doorway. Speranza stepped back.

"Why are you home? Are you sick?" she asked.

"It looks like the nuns have no use for me anymore. They have decided to hire other people to work in the garden who can do the work quicker and cost them less money."

"You mean they fired you?" asked Angela.

"Not in so many words. They said they would call me if they needed me. Those damned nuns, they are cheap."

"Salvatore, do not say that," said Speranza.

"They are!" He swung his hand past Speranza's face. "Do not tell me what to say!" Speranza went into the living room.

"Salvatore," said Angela, "there are many florist shops in Nelsonville. It would be easy for you to get a job."

"The nuns still should not have treated me like that."

"I think you are right, but the only thing left to do is get another job. Your cousin owns a flower shop. I am sure he will help you."

Angela wanted to say that he had two children and one on the way to support, but she knew it would anger him. Angela knew Salvatore as a mild man, and his behavior worried her.

"Why don't the two of you come to our house for dinner?" asked Angela. "The kids would enjoy the night out."

"No, we will stay home for dinner," said Salvatore. He went into the kitchen, picked up a glass, and turned on the faucet.

"There is cold water in the refrigerator," said Speranza softly.

"I do not want cold water," Salvatore growled.

Angela felt like someone had put ice cubes on her spine. She did not want to leave Speranza alone with an angry man. When Speranza was a little girl, Angela made a point of telling Franco not to raise his voice in anger when his sister was present. Speranza was a frail girl, and Angela disliked the idea of three pregnancies in a row. Having children weakened the body; because Salvatore was born with a feeble body, it was if he wanted to destroy Speranza's.

"Angela, I will come by the house tomorrow," said Speranza.

"Are you sure you won't have supper with us tonight?" asked Angela.

"I think we'd better stay here tonight," said Speranza. "I will drop by tomorrow."

Angela listened for a response or movement from Salvatore in the kitchen.

"All right, but walk me to the door," said Angela. She took Speranza's hand and led her to the front door.

"Do not worry, Speranza. Franco and I will help you and the children." Angela wanted to say that she could pack her bag and come live with her, but that would not solve anything. Angela could not imagine the little girl she practically raised in a situation where she had to be afraid. She examined her conscience and asked herself if there was anything she could have done to prevent Speranza's situation. She kissed her sister-in-law on the cheek, then walked home.

~ ~ ~ ~ ~

Franco looked at the hedges in front of his house. They need to be cut, he thought. He put his fingers into the greenery and slowly pulled up to estimate how much he would take off. He told himself he was a hedge barber and smiled.

"Hello," called Angela. She came out on the porch carrying water for the plants.

"I have to cut these hedges soon," said Franco. "They are far too tall."

"Did you have a busy day?" asked Angela.

"Yes, as always." He came up the stairs.

"Speranza has bad news," said Angela. "I was over there today."

"Everything all right with the kids?" asked Franco.

"They are fine. It is Salvatore. The nuns have laid him off. Do you know anything about it?"

"I have heard the convent is bringing in union workers because they are cheaper than the independent worker who asked for a specific wage to do a certain job." Franco had not mentioned to Angela that some of the jobs he thought he might be offered went to other men. He knew about the stock market crash and the panic that was happening in America, but he was not tied to the stock market or any other outside source. He was always able to find work. The day before, he had quoted a price to the Mother Superior about painting several rooms in the convent. She told him she would let him know about the job. It had been this way since he returned from Italy. He told himself that he kept this from Angela because he did not want to worry her, but he could not stand to think of himself as dispensable. He could not say it, even now.

"I am sure they will be calling him back," said Franco.

"But what if they do not?" asked Angela, "and she has another baby on the way. Poor Speranza..."

"Do not worry about Speranza and the kids. I will take care of them."

"I told Salvatore that he should call his cousin to see if he can work at the florist shop."

It struck Franco that one day he could be reduced to working for some mediocre carpenter.

"Will you stop interfering with their business? Please stick to your own house."

"Why should I not be concerned? We practically raised her."

Franco knew she was right, but he could not express what he felt. He saw too much of himself in Salvatore's position.

"I will go wash up for supper," said Franco.

~ ~ ~ ~ ~

Franco knocked on the Mother Superior's door.

"Good morning, Mother," said Franco. He removed his hat. "I wanted to know when you wanted the two rooms painted."

"I am sorry, Franco, but I have hired someone else," said the Mother Superior, folding her arms. Her hands disappeared into the loose sleeves of her habit. "Times are difficult, and I had to hire a man who charges less for the same job."

"Sister, with all due respect, I have done top quality work for you over the years, and I feel that it is unfair for you to hire someone else."

"The convent has to conserve money, Franco," said the nun. She peered over her wire-rimmed glasses.

"Well, I do not feel I can work here if the large jobs will go to someone else," said Franco.

"We are going into a depression, and I must hire the less expensive worker. By law, the union men work shorter hours, and they get more work done in less time."

"Mother, I respect your decision, but I cannot work here any longer."

As Franco walked down the winding hill from the convent, he wondered why he had wasted his time working there. He received no pension and no benefits except that he could collect unemployment, however meager. Franco thought he should have gone into construction like many other Italians. Construction workers take better care of their families, he told himself. But he loved the soft smoothness of a paintbrush against a naked wall. He preferred the feel of wood to steel, and most of all he liked working near water and trees. Construction would not have been for him.

He thought of Roberto the poet. What would he have said about the situation? The individual artisan was being pushed out. There was no personal touch, no sign that a certain man painted that room or that he also laid that floor. One could always tell whose work they were looking at. It was like a signature on a painting. Roberto would have told him to go out on his own. But where?

~ ~ ~ ~ ~

Franco clutched his newspaper under his arm and walked quickly through the shopping area of Nelsonville. He had found an ad in the morning paper that asked for skilled plumbers, electricians, and carpenters. Someone was building a mansion in an undeveloped area of Garrison, about twenty-five miles north of Nelsonville. He was rushing to speak to the foreman of the project.

Franco thought about the dream he and his brother Alessio shared so many years ago: they wanted to build a home together. They would design it, purchase the materials, and construct it. Maybe raise their families in it. Passersby would look at their home and say that they had never seen a house like it in America. Franco slowed his stride. Alessio was gone, and there would be no house of his dreams. Even the nuns could do without his abilities. Franco arrived at the foreman's office and stood outside the door.

The structure of Fra Giovanni's study took shape in Franco's mind. If he could only build something like that: clean lines, the best wood, light streaming in. If he could do something like that, he would impress everyone and be offered work. Franco shook his head; the truth was that all he had for a reference was the nuns. He opened the door and went into the office.

There were several men sitting in straight-back kitchen chairs with papers resting on their laps.

"Is Mr. Hacks here?" asked Franco.

"Yeah, but he is interviewing someone," said a man. "We're all waiting to be interviewed."

Franco sat down. He wondered why these men carried papers. Was there something he should have brought?

"Where have you worked?" asked the man as he lit a cigarette. Franco was not sure if he should disclose that information.

"I say, where have you worked?"

"I worked at St. Mary's School," said Franco.

"Where else?" asked the man. He took a long, slow drag on his cigarette.

Franco thought about lying, but he had no idea what other places he could have worked.

"That's all," said Franco. "Just St Mary's."

"And you're applying for this job. That's brave of you."

"What do you mean, brave?"

"Mr. Hacks requires at least three references. The man who's having the mansion built is European and only wants the best American workers on this job. No American could afford to build a mansion in these times. Mr. Hacks will also hire union men. He's a union man, Mr. Hacks." The man took out a match and rubbed it against his front teeth.

"I worked at St. Mary's because I could be my own boss and work at my own pace. I have done quality work for the nuns. I stayed there because I could be independent."

Franco thought that he had been less than brave to think he could have a chance at this job; maybe he had been stupid. No, that was not true. These men qualified for the job with references and union cards, but he could build a more beautiful staircase or vestibule than any of them.

Franco looked at his watch; two hours had passed. He would be interviewed next. Franco could not understand the applicants' nervousness when they went into the interview. They certainly had all the papers necessary for the job.

Franco had never been interviewed for work before. He had gotten the job at St. Mary's through a friend who had an excellent reputation with the nuns. Franco's first job had been to provide a new banister for a small stairway in the rectory. When he showed it to the nuns, they were dazzled. It was made out of solid oak, and in the center of the banister Franco carved the initials of St. Mary's Convent. He liked to see the nuns surprised and happy with his work. Each building project he did, he tried to personalize it for the convent.

The last man came out of Mr. Hack's office, and none of them looked happy as they left. Franco thought about leaving, but he had waited this long. Besides, he was proud of his work and enjoyed talking about it.

"Next," said a deep voice.

"Name," said the foreman hovering over his desk, pen in hand.

"Bellini. Franco Bellini."

"Worked?"

"St. Mary's Convent."

The foreman hesitated.

"Where else?"

"That is it," said Franco.

The foreman looked up from his desk.

"You mean you have no other reference? I am sorry Mr. Bernini, you..."

"Bellini."

"Bellini, you haven't had much experience, and it's been a long day."

"I have had plenty of experience. I can build anything from staircases to roofs."

"Do you have a union card?" Mr. Hacks asked as he leaned forward.

"No, I do not," said Franco. It was not enough to say he would join the union to get the job. The foreman wanted men committed to union beliefs.

"Mr. Bernini, what I have to build is no ordinary house. It is a mansion designed by a Frenchman. He wants union workers so he knows exactly what it will cost and how long it will take. Since you have no card, then our interview is through."

Franco wanted to talk about his work and what an asset it would be on this project, but the words would not come. He might have to join the union after all to get even the most menial work. At least he would be protected. But from what? He needed no protection. He charged exactly what he felt a job was worth and never had a problem collecting payment. His work was his self-expression, and he did not want to build a room like everyone else or paint a wall a certain way to save time. If he had to take something below his capabilities for now, that is what he would do.

~ ~ ~ ~ ~

Franco looked in the hall mirror and straightened his tie; little gray hairs peppered his mustache. His father had not lived long enough to develop gray hair.

"Franco, you will be late for the meeting," said Angela. She brought a dress over to the sewing machine.

"I am getting tired of the Knights of Columbus meetings. We never get anything done." Franco pulled on his tie and began again.

"Last year, they raised money for St. Joseph's orphanage," said Angela. "They do good work." She went over to Franco and pulled up his starched collar.

"Angela, I can tie my own tie," said Franco. He stared at the mirror, hands at his side.

"Yes, when you have time. You are late as it is, and I have a woman coming for a fitting."

He had told Angela about quitting the convent. She told him she was sure he would get other work because he worked hard and could fix and build anything. Franco wondered what everyone at the Knights of Columbus thought about his unemployment. They all felt sorry for him, no doubt, but he did not want their pity. Even his lame brother-in-law was working at a flower shop.

Tomorrow he had an interview at a small electrical repair shop. It was a job that would not require him to be a part of any union.

Angela smoothed down his collar and brought over his fedora. She still did sewing for the nuns, and he knew how close she felt to them because she was raised by sisters. His quarrel was with the nuns at St. Mary's and did not involve Angela, so if she wanted to continue her association with them, that was her business.

"Goodbye, Angela," said Franco.

"Goodbye." She cupped his chin and kissed him several times on the same cheek. Franco saw his smile reflected in the mirror. His teeth had tuned yellow because of cigar smoking. He saw the delight on his face but wondered what kind of image he projected when he smiled in public. Angela went to her sewing machine, and Franco left the house.

~ ~ ~ ~ ~

The Knights of Columbus hall was filling with members. Everyone stood around and chatted before the opening toast.

"Franco! It is good to see you," said a husky voice.

"Gino, how are you doing?" asked Franco. Gino was a boxer who never made it to the big time. Franco heard that he now spent his time beating up people for the local small-time Mafia.

"I heard you got some bad times," said the boxer. "That's too bad. You should speak to my boss. He'd help ya out." Gino smiled, exposing a gold front tooth.

"No, thank you, Gino. Something will come up for me soon." Gino's boss helped people by obligating them to him for life. No, if he would not join a union, he would certainly not involve himself with Gino's boss.

"Ciao, Franco," said a tall, dark man. Franco did not recognize the young man.

"Don't you know me?" asked the stranger.

"Oh, Emilio Luci! The last time I saw you, you were small enough to sit on my knee." Franco embraced the young man.

"I am now a member. How is your family?"

Emilio felt older than his years to Franco.

"Everyone is well. You should drop by and see us sometime. Angela would like to see you. What are you doing now?"

"I am being trained to head the local electricians' union. I apprenticed as an electrician with my father. Now I would like to get involved with the other end. Have you joined a union, Franco? It will be hard to get a job if you do not." To Franco, the young man showed white straight teeth and a condescending smile. These young people had so sense of being an individual. They were only interested in not getting their hands dirty.

"I have no need of a union," said Franco, waving his hand. "With my skills there will be no problem in finding a job."

"But the union will protect your rights. My father has joined and does well."

"I will work as I have always worked," said Franco as he walked away from Emilio.

Franco had worked with Emilio's father on odd jobs, and he would sometimes bring the boy—who would laugh and cry for more as his father blew smoke rings with his cigar. Franco had looked forward to working with Emilio's father because his son would be there. At the time, there was still the possibility that he and Angela could have children. He recalled telling Emilio that he hoped his first son would be just like him.

A loud voice came over the speaker system and asked everyone to take their places at a table.

Franco sat next to Gianni Galucci, a tailor by profession, who had sent Angela business by referring his customers' wives to her.

"Gianni, it is so good to see you," said Franco. They embraced.

"Good to see you. You are looking well. How is Angela?" Gianni was a tall, heavyset man who always wore a suit, even at backyard gatherings. Franco wished he could advertise his talents as Galucci did. Invariably, someone would ask the tailor where he got his suit.

"Franco, I heard a rumor that you no longer work at St. Mary's."

"No, I no longer work there," looking away from Galucci. Did everyone in the Italian community know that he had no job? Is this how people looked at him; the poor man with no job and no ability to get one? Well, what did they know—any of the men in this room were only laborers, so it was easy for them to find work.

"Times are hard now, Franco. We're in a depression, that is for sure. I hope you do not mind my suggestion, but I know of a job at Camp Smith. It is an army base that ships ammunition. It is not what you are used to, I know, but it could turn into something. Maybe they could use your carpentry skills."

Franco stiffened. He needed no help in finding a job, and certainly not from a man who called making clothes like a woman satisfying work. A man his size should work outdoors and build things. Franco looked at Galucci's soft face and felt ashamed; all work was good, and all construction was good, whether it was landscaping or sewing.

"Thank you for your suggestion, Gianni, but I have an interview tomorrow. It is just a matter of time before I get work. Thank you anyway."

"Give me a call if it falls through. Christmas is a few weeks away, and I know you like to treat your family well."

"I am sure things will be fine, and I will have no need of loading trucks," said Franco as he picked up his wine glass for the opening toast. Franco imagined if he took such an unskilled job, people would say, "Look at Franco, poor man. He had to take something beneath him to make ends meet, poor soul." No, that would not happen. Tomorrow he would accept the electrical shop job and then look for something better.

~ ~ ~ ~ ~

Franco looked at the electrical repair shop from across the street. It was a small, dingy place with broken appliances scattered in the window like an abstract sculpture. The unemployment office sent him on a job interview here. He wanted to tell the man at the unemployment office that he wired houses, not irons and toasters, but he needed work. He went across the street and opened the door. A bell rang.

"My God, I cannot believe this," whispered Franco. He blinked his eyes to bring all the electrical appliances into focus. There was a long desk littered with household items: irons, electric coffee pots and toasters. The appliance cords were wrapped around one another as if engaged in charging each other's currents. Electric saws and large items hung on the walls. Was this a repair shop or dumping ground? A thump came from behind a grey curtain in the corner of the shop.

"I'll be right there," called a man. A red-faced man pulled back the curtain. "What can I do for ya? Harry Stone," said the man and held out his hand.

Franco felt a pulsing generate from the man's hand like an electrical current.

"I am Franco Bellini. The unemployment office sent me for an interview."

"I'm in need of a helper," said Harry as he spread his arms, "as you can see."

"Yes, I see." Franco thought the windows looked like they had not been cleaned since World War I. It was no wonder he could not see into the shop from across the street.

"There's a back room where I work. I'll show you." He opened the gray curtain and motioned for Franco to go through.

The room had no windows, and a pile of appliances rested on work tables like ancient ruins.

"Well, what do you think?" asked Harry.

It was impossible for Franco to take the job. All his life he had worked in large open spaces, and oftentimes he worked outdoors—summer or winter. He loved St. Mary's because of the grounds and the views of the Hudson River. The elements were important to his work. He would just fade away in a shop like this. He also could never be another man's "helper."

"Thank you, Mr. Stone, but I do not think I could work here."

"But we didn't talk about salary."

"I am used to working outdoors, so I do not think I would be happy here."

"Oh, I'm not surprised. It's been hard for me to get help. That's why I'm so backed up."

"I am sure you will find someone." Franco walked toward the door.

"If you have a friend who needs a job, just send them in. They don't have to know anything about appliances—I'll train 'em," called Harry as Franco left.

Franco sauntered down the street and cringed at what he would have to do. He needed a job before winter set in. He had to call Galucci and accept the job at Camp Smith. At least he would be outdoors and moving around, not cooped up in a dingy shop. It would be temporary, something to tide him over. Once spring came, he would begin to look for work again.

As he walked along, he came upon two young men around nineteen digging a ditch in front of a house.

"What are you boys doing?" asked Franco.

"We're replacing water pipes," said one youth as he wiped his brow.

"Take my advice, boys," said Franco as he peered into the ditch. "Get yourselves an education. You will not always be young, and you cannot do this kind of work forever."

The young men continued to silently dig.

"You will become tired of digging ditches for other people," said Franco.

"We're already tired," said the other young man, "but we've got to get done so we've got no time to talk."

Franco was ready to call Galluci because he was weary of looking for work. He was tired of searching for something that was not there. Maybe he had judged Emilio Luci unfairly. Franco thought that if he had a son, he would want him to be in Emilio's position.

He walked up the steps of his home and decided to call Galluci and get it over with.

~ ~ ~ ~ ~

Franco accepted the job at Camp Smith. He had been there for six months and kept looking for other work, but to no avail. There used to be many opportunities and demand for his skills, but the fallout from the stock market crash had seeped into everyone's pockets.

He walked up the steps of his home and into the kitchen, where he found Angela frying veal.

"You are home late again, Franco. I think Camp Smith is working you too hard. Maybe you should say something."

"I am doing my job the right way, so I have to stay late," said Franco, raising his voice.

"You do not have to yell. I was just thinking of you," said Angela.

"We have to maintain the house, so I have to work a lot."

"Not if it costs you your health. It is not worth it."

"I bought this house for you. What do you mean it is not worth it?"

"For me?" asked Angela as she turned off the gas. "You made that decision, not me. I would have been happy anywhere."

"This house is important. It is important that we keep it."

Franco walked past Angela and opened the cellar door.

"Where are you going? It is time to eat."

"I am not hungry."

"You will get sick if you do not eat."

"Angela, leave me alone."

Franco went down the cellar and walked over to his tool shelf. When he worked at St. Mary's, he would bring his own tools because he did not find the convent's tools satisfactory. He had no need for them now. People were hiring union men, not independent contractors. Even if he did get a carpenter's job, he would be bothered by the union. He had been loading trucks at Camp Smith and had offered to do some carpentry around the camp for a small wage so they could see what kind of work he did, but they always had their own men to do the job.

Franco did not want to join any union. He did not need anyone to tell him how much to charge a customer or how to do a certain job. He knew his capabilities and what each job would cost. Franco took a hammer off the rack and grabbed a nail and an old piece of wood from the floor. He raised his hammer and pounded the nail into the rotting wood. With each blow, the hammer came down with more force. Even when the nail was far into the wood, Franco continued to hammer—until finally, with one fierce blow, the wood split in two.

The next day, Franco went to the main office to sign in for work.

"Bellini," said the sergeant. He put his feet on the desk. "I heard you're a carpenter by trade."

"Yes, sir," said Franco. "I would like to do some work around here. I also do plumbing, electrical work, and can put a house together."

"I might have a few jobs for you. Report back to me at lunch."

"I will," said Franco. My luck is turning around, he thought.

He greeted his co-workers with a smile and climbed up on a truck.

"Franco, you're sure happy this morning," said one of the privates as he strained to lift a large, heavy box up to Franco.

"Why not? It is a bright, sunny day," said Franco. He moved to the edge of the truck, grabbed the box, and lifted it to a co-worker on the truck. Franco lost his footing and fell backward onto the ground.

"Franco, are you all right?" asked the private, helping him to his feet.

"I am all right," said Franco, rubbing his head.

"Did you hit your head?"

"I do not know. I do not think I did."

"You should see a doctor. Take the rest of the day off."

"No, I am fine. I did not fall very far."

"Let's go tell the sergeant," said the private.

~ ~ ~ ~ ~

"Angela, I am home," said Franco.

"You are home already? What happened?" Angela got up from her sewing machine.

"I fell off the truck, and they told me to take the rest of the day off."

"Have you seen a doctor?"

"No, I do not need a doctor. I just need to rest."

"Where did you hit yourself?"

"I fell off a truck, not the Empire State Building," said Franco.

"You should see a doctor anyway."

"When I need a doctor, I will go to a doctor." Franco picked up the newspaper, went out on the porch, and sat on the recliner.

Angela finished setting the table and went out to call Franco for lunch.

"Franco, Franco, wake up, it is time to eat," said Angela as she touched his shoulder. There was no response. Franco was a light sleeper.

"Franco, are you all right?" She shook his shoulders.

"Uh, what time is it?" said Franco, shielding his eyes from the sun.

"It is time for lunch. Come inside. You were sleeping so heavily."

Franco stood up and felt a weakness on his right side. His right leg moved ahead of him reluctantly. He shook his leg; it seemed to be revived. He assumed his leg had been in a deeper sleep than his mind. Franco limped into the house.

"You know, Angela, I have been thinking," said Franco as he sipped his soup. "Maybe I should start a small business."

"What kind of business?"

"Contracting. People know me around here as someone who does quality work. If I could get some money together, I would be all set."

"Talk to a lawyer and find out what you have to do," said Angela.

Franco felt his right hand freeze. His soup spoon fell in the bowl.

"What happened?" asked Angela.

"My hand is numb," said Franco. He touched the fingers on his right hand.

"Oh, my God. I will call the doctor."

"Wait. Help me up. I want to see if I can walk."

Angela pushed his chair away from the table, put her arms around Franco's waist and pulled him up to a standing position.

"Stand back. I will walk toward you."

Franco willed his right leg forward but had to wait a few seconds for it to respond to his command. After a few steps it was clear—he had to drag his right leg with him.

"There is no life in my right leg."

"Sit down, Franco. I will call the doctor and he will come right over."

~ ~ ~ ~ ~

Angela sat in the hospital waiting room. The image of Salvatore throwing his leg out in front of him flooded her mind. Franco was a proud and active man; he could never live with an affliction like that.

"Angela, please come in," said the doctor.

She saw Franco sitting on a stretcher with just his underclothes on—a small, worried man. She went over, picked up a blanket, and put it around Franco's shoulders.

"Franco, I want Angela to hear what I have to say. You need an operation right away, Franco. You have a blood clot at the base of your skull, and it has to be surgically removed. If you do not have it taken out, you will be paralyzed in a few weeks."

"Will he be completely cured after the operation?" asked Angela.

"I cannot promise anything, but he should only have to have therapy to walk properly again. If the surgery is done immediately, he should have no deficits that therapy cannot heal—but again, I cannot promise anything."

Angela touched Franco's right hand. She had depended on his firm grasps, such as his firm grasp of a hammer and paintbrush, When he picked up Speranza's children and threw them in the air, she knew they were safe. Now he could not pick up a spoon. She sat up on the stretcher and touched his hand to her cheek.

The nurse finished giving Franco an injection; he was ready to go to the operating room. He stared at the ceiling and thought about his trip to Italy and how nothing seemed the same since his return: not work, and not his relationship with Angela. Things were both better and worse. Not having steady work freed him to think about himself and what he wanted, but there was a feeling of uselessness that came with being unemployed. Angela had become stronger since their trip. She was no longer the girl he married but someone who was capable and had opinions. There was more tension between them now, but he knew who she was and respected her more.

A shadow passed over his white sheets. Franco looked to his side, and a priest stood beside his bed. Franco never liked priests. What they preached at church had absolutely nothing to do with the real world.

"Would you like to receive communion before you go into surgery, Mr. Bellini?" asked the priest.

"I have no need of prayers, Father. I am going to the operating room, not to my death." Franco was about to turn away when he thought of Fra Giovanni and how much he liked the old man. The monk would not have thought much of him for speaking such harsh words to a priest when he was trying to offer comfort.

"Excuse me, Father. It must be the medication. I will not take communion, but I will take your blessing."

Franco felt his body being lifted off the bed and onto a stretcher. The injection had taken effect. His mind was active, but he did not feel he needed his flesh. The body he inhabited felt like the ship he sailed on so many times to Italy; he needed to be in it until he reached his destination. What his destination was, he had no idea.

~ ~ ~ ~ ~

Franco felt someone touching his right hand as he came out of the anesthesia. With blurred vision, he looked at his hand. Angela intertwined her fingers around his so it was difficult to discern which fingers were his own. He lifted his thumb up with his other fingers and closed them tightly around Angela's hand. He had no trouble moving his fingers. Angela took her other hand and rested it on their hands. Angela pulled down the white sheet and put Franco's hand on his chest, near his heart, then covered him to his chin. Franco could feel himself wander in and out of consciousness. He decided to count his heartbeats to keep himself alert.

He heard Angela speaking to someone but could not see who it was. His mother? No, she had been dead for a while, although he could not remember for how long. Was she dead at this time? He had to keep counting his heartbeats to stay awake in the present. Two figures moved closer to his bed.

"Everything went well," said the doctor. "Although you will have some trouble with your speech. Therapy will fix it."

How could his speech be affected, when his words were clear in his mind? But then he had not tried to speak out loud. What would he say? He formulated a sentence in his mind: I love you Angela, and you, Speranza, and the children. He had never said it before. At least not in words. It was certainly time to say it. He opened his mouth.

"Bring it over here," said Franco.

That was not what he wanted or had intended to say. What happened? He would try again. "Where are the kids?" That wasn't it. His mouth would not obey him. Was this the speech problem? His mind was crystal clear, but his voice box was not his own. Would he have to reclaim it?

Franco thought that he was being punished for something. He had taken care of his family. God took his brother, and Franco had not reproached Him for it. He had lost his job at St. Mary's through no fault of his own, and he had roamed the streets searching for work. He had done his best. Would God punish him for that? Franco moved his hand away from his heart and fell into a dreamless sleep.

~ ~ ~ ~ ~

"How are you?" asked the speech therapist. "Try and answer the question, Mr. Bellini. Try and answer appropriately."

Franco heard his mind scream, "Awful! Awful! I feel awful inside this body." But as much as his mind rebelled against cooperating with the therapist, his brain worked on a response. His brain told him to say "Fine." He was "Fine."

"Good," said Franco. "No, no good." He shook his head and put his hand to his forehead.

"Was that what you wanted to say, Mr. Bellini?" asked the therapist.

"Bene!" Franco's fist slammed on the table. He could verbalize responses in Italian but not in English. It was as if the two languages could not be separated. How could he have stored them in his head all these years and not mix them up as he did now?

"Did you mean to say 'good'?" asked the therapist excitedly.

Franco nodded his head in exhausted agreement. It was close but not what he wanted to say. The therapist obviously thought they had taken a big step. Let her think that, thought Franco. Tomorrow there was a possibility he would be discharged from the hospital. If they saw him making progress in his speech, maybe they would let him go.

"Mr. Bellini, we are making such progress. I think that you may be able to go home, and soon. You can come to the clinic once a week for speech therapy."

Is this how he would live out his days—going to speech therapy and physical therapy? What difference did it make if he said "good" instead of "fine"?

Would anybody really care? Franco lowered his head. He cared. He had learned to speak English well, and now he could not express himself. It was not long ago when he was young and vital. When he was a boy, he would run into the sea just after a thunderstorm and the waves would tower over him. The waves would spit him out on the beach, daring him to try again. He told himself in those days that he was strong enough to swim against the tide.

"That's enough for today, Mr. Bellini," said the therapist.

Franco picked up his cane and limped toward the door.

"Shall I call a nurse to escort you back to your room?"

Franco shook his head and waved his arm. If he could jump into an agitated ocean after a storm, he could certainly find his way around the hospital.

He made his way down a long corridor and pressed the elevator button. An arrow that said "Pediatrics" written over it was on the elevator door. Franco felt sorry for sick kids. It was unfair that they should have to suffer illness when they ought to be outside playing. He had been in the hospital for a month now and missed his niece and nephew; he felt well enough to have a child on his lap. The elevator door opened, but Franco turned in the direction of the arrow.

Pediatrics looked no different than any other medical department except that everything was in miniature. It is a large dollhouse, thought Franco. The little wheelchairs and stretchers could have been toys for children who played with big dolls. The sweet scent of baby powder filled the air.

"Beep! Beep! Watch it, mister."

Franco turned and saw a boy of about five lying on his stomach on a small stretcher. The boy held onto two large wheels in the front of the vehicle.

"You have to watch it, mister, there's a lot of traffic here and I'm late for class."

The boy's hair was so thinly cropped that his skull was visible. His ears stuck out like antlers on a fawn.

Franco saw that the boy had both legs in casts. The child saw him staring.

"They covered my legs with white stuff to fix them." The boy turned on his side, propped his head up with his arm, and smiled.

Franco turned away from the boy's impish face. It was obviously a conversation that the boy had many times, and he felt foolish.

"Why are you in the hospital?" asked the boy.

"I fell down from the operation.... Ah, no. I hit my head and..." Franco mimicked a fall. Franco stared down at the floor to hide his frustration.

"Oh, ya can't talk right yet. Well, ya gotta work at it. I had an accident, too, in the factory where my mom works, and as soon as my cast comes off I gotta learn to walk all over again. I will, and you'll talk right again."

The impish smile disappeared, and the look of an old wise man crept over the boy's face. Franco thought that this child knew about his struggle, and he had given him a dose of encouragement. How could the boy not be afraid of what was ahead for him? He did not know that the world would look down on him if he walked with a limp after his casts came off.

"My name is Jerry," said the child. "What's yours?"

"Fran... Francis... Frank..." He hit his fist against the wall.

"All those names, huh? Well, I'll call you Fran because it's the shortest."

Franco had not tried to speak to anyone but Angela and the speech therapist until now.

"No, no, no," said Franco firmly.

"Frank. Your name is Frank."

"Yeah, yeah," said Franco.

"Christmas is coming, Frank, and I'm so excited. All the presents. My mom said that she'll take me home by then. It's just another month."

Franco had not thought much about Christmas. He could not buy much of anything for his family, and he was not looking forward to facing them in his condition. A baby cried in the background.

"Oh no, that's one of the babies," said Jerry. "She probably needs a refill on her bottle. I'm supposed to go to class. We have school every day, but that can wait." He wheeled himself into one of the rooms.

"I see you've met our resident old man," said a nurse.

"Yeah," said Franco. He had meant to be more polite and say "yes," but the word did not come.

"He loves the younger children," said the nurse. "He's a sad case, though."

"Legs?" asked Franco, grateful that the right words came.

"I'm referring to his living situation. His mother dropped him here a few months ago, and we haven't heard from her since."

Franco looked concerned.

"Unfortunately, she's living on the street. Destitute. We don't even know if she's still alive."

"But..." said Franco, pointing to the room Jerry had just entered.

"Did he tell you his mother is taking him home and that he hurt his legs at her job?"

Franco nodded.

"He tells everyone that. It's his way of reassuring himself that everything will be all right. His legs were bowed at birth, but he never got the medical attention."

"Family?" asked Franco. Surely the boy must have other family.

"No, not that we know of," said the nurse. "He was taken away from his mother by a social worker who made sure his legs got corrected. Every Sunday, he sits in front of the elevator and waits for his mother's return, but she never comes. He still loves his mother, but it's just as well she doesn't come. He wouldn't be permitted to live with her anymore." She went on to tell Franco that two couples were interested in adopting him. In fact, she was taking him to meet with a couple now.

"Jerry, come on," called the nurse. "You're keeping the Malones waiting."

Franco saw a couple standing at the nurses' station. The man wore a dark blue suit, and the woman had fur around her collar.

"Who's here?" asked Jerry as he came out of the room.

"The Malones," said the nurse.

Franco felt the boy's embarrassment. He was caught in a lie. Franco reached over and touched Jerry's head. His thin, fine hairs were like bristles on a sable paintbrush. Jerry looked up and smiled.

"They're my aunt and uncle. My mother comes on Sundays," said the boy.

"Go, go. Visit," smiled Franco. He was glad that he could leave Jerry with his hopes and fantasies intact.

"I wish I had met ya when ya first came to the hospital. We'da been good friends," the boy said.

"Jerry!" called the nurse, standing with the Malones.

"Well, good luck, Frank." He offered Franco his small hand.

Franco patted the boy's hand.

Gerry turned his stretcher around and wheeled himself toward the nurses' station.

The world felt turned upside down to Franco. How could a child like that go unloved? Illness was one thing, but complete abandonment was another. He loved children, and if he had a son like Jerry he would keep him close. Franco thought he would never forgive his mother if she had abandoned him to such a degrading life, but Jerry waited faithfully for his mother every Sunday—even after she had deserted him. Franco looked down at his leg. He and Jerry were kindred spirits; both had physical problems and both had no voice or say in their lives.

Franco watched as the couple was introduced to Jerry. If the two couples decided not to adopt him, why couldn't he and Angela do so? Franco was impaired now, but he was making steady progress in his therapy. They had a home to offer the boy, and he would bring Angela to the pediatric ward tomorrow. He was sure Angela would like the boy, and they both wanted children. Besides, most couples wanted babies. It would be best for him and Angela to adopt an older child.

~ ~ ~ ~ ~

Franco handed Angela a set of pajamas. He was going home. The doctor said that his progress was good and there was no need for him to remain hospitalized. He could come back for speech and physical therapy on a weekly basis.

"Speranza and the children are so excited that you are coming home, Franco. They are all waiting for you at the house," said Angela. She placed his clothes in an open suitcase.

Franco had woken up that morning drowning in dread. The thought of feeling useless and helpless in his own home terrified him. He was no companion for Angela. All she had for company was Speranza, her children, and an afflicted husband who had no job and slim prospects for getting one. It would be nice for Angela to have a child.

"Angela," said Franco. "Sit."

"What?"

"Sit," said Franco. He motioned for Angela to sit on the bed. "There is a son... no, a boy here to take home... No, no." Franco waved his hand as his body swayed.

"Be careful, Franco," said Angela. "You are getting excited over nothing."

Franco conveyed that there was an orphan boy that he wanted her to meet.

"Are you ready, Mr. Bellini?" asked a nurse, bringing in a wheelchair.

"We are ready, nurse," said Angela. "My husband is telling me about an orphan boy. He wants me to meet him."

"Are you talking about Jerry?" asked the nurse. Everyone knows him. He tells everyone he has a mother but she abandoned him. Now he's up for adoption. He's in the lobby this morning."

"Adoption?" Angela turned to her husband. "Franco, do you think we can adopt him?"

Franco nodded his head and smiled; this was the child they had waited for.

A few years earlier, if Angela had answered for Franco, he would have been furious—but now it was a relief. He did not have to worry about using the correct word; he could let her be his voice for a time. Franco could see how capable she was and how she had developed a social personality that he did not have. Now he could pay her back with Jerry. The boy would be his present to Angela. She had taken care of his family, and now she could take care of him. Also, Jerry could take care of Angela after Franco was gone.

Franco sat in the wheelchair while Angela walked alongside him carrying the suitcase and his cane.

As the elevator descended to the ground floor, Franco felt his little finger. He touched Angela's coat sleeve and pointed at his finger.

"Here you are," said Angela as she took his ring out of her purse. The red garnet stone seemed brighter than usual as he placed it on his finger. Franco imagined the glow from the stone was an approving smile because he had survived his ordeal. His father had told him that the ring would protect him whenever he needed it and would keep an eye on him through life when his father was gone and could no longer watch over him. Franco had interpreted that as, "This is my eye, and I can see how you are doing in life and make sure you are doing the right thing." But now Franco had more of an idea of what his father had meant: use it as a focal point when you need to, and it will remind you of me.

The elevator doors parted on the ground floor. Franco looked up and saw Jerry lying on his stretcher with his head resting on his hands. It was Sunday—Jerry's day to sit by the elevator and wait for his mother.

"Hi, Frank," said Jerry. "You're goin' home today?"

"Yeah," said Franco. The nurse wheeled him out of the elevator.

"Well, it was really nice to know ya. I know we could'a been good friends."

"Is this the boy?" asked Angela.

"Yeah, yeah," said Franco, his voice straining.

"I met Frank yesterday," said Jerry. "I know he'll talk soon."

"You are a smart boy to encourage someone older than you," said Angela. "But what are you doing in the lobby by yourself?"

"I'm waiting for my mother. She comes on Sundays."

Angela hesitated. "She is a lucky mother to have a son like you."

"I'm goin' home in a few days, too," said Jerry.

Angela and Franco looked at one another.

"My aunt and uncle, the Malones, are taking me home for a while. My mother has to work, and she wants someone there all the time to take care of me. She'll visit a lot, though."

It was too late, thought Franco. He almost had him—for a short time he almost had him. He could relate to how Jerry felt, waiting for his mother every Sunday. Franco had waited for a child to come along, only now that one had, he did not belong to him. It seemed they were brought together to say goodbye. It was God again giving him crumbs when he asked for a loaf of bread.

"Work hard at your speech," Jerry said.

Even if Jerry had to stay in the hospital for another year, thought Franco, he would still wait by the elevator every Sunday for his mother. And if the Malones adopted him, he would still wait for his mother, regardless of where he was. Franco looked down at ring. He did not need it any more.

"Jerry," said Franco as he took the ring off his finger, "this jewel—no, gem—it was my mother's... No." Franco shook his and looked up at Angela. She hesitated for a moment, surprised that he wanted to give such a special ring away. After she searched Franco's face, she put her hand on his shoulder.

"My husband means to say that he would like to give you a ring that his father gave him," said Angela. "It has special meaning to my husband, and we have no children to pass it on to. He would like to give it to you because you are special." She looked down at Franco as he patted her hand approvingly.

"It won't cost me any money?" asked Jerry.

"Money?" asked Angela. "No. It is yours as a gift."

Franco reached over and put the ring in the boy's hand.

"You're giving this to me?" His eyes widened. "I never had anything like this. I don't think anybody ever gave me anything." Jerry held the ring close to his chest.

"It is probably too big for you now," said Angela, "but you will grow into it soon."

"Thank you, Frank. Thank you for the present," said Jerry, rubbing his eyes with his fists.

"You have it," said Franco. He reached over and kissed Jerry a few times on the cheek.

"We had better go," said Angela, blinking to dissolve the tears. "The hospital car is waiting. Have a good visit with your mother, Jerry, and I hope Santa Claus brings you everything you want."

"Thank you, Frank. Thank you and Merry Christmas," Jerry called out as the nurse wheeled Franco down the hallway toward the exit. Franco pulled his coat collar up around his ears as he was wheeled into the crisp, late fall air. The cool air dried the tears that stained his cheeks.

~ ~ ~ ~ ~

Angela put a crystal bulb on top of the tree. It was Christmas Eve, and she prepared the traditional Italian fish dinner: mussels, squid, and dried fish. Franco still walked with a cane, but in a few months he would no longer need it. The speech therapy was going well, although he still had difficulty with sentence structure.

The front door opened, and in came Speranza, Salvatore and the children. Both children wore outfits Angela had made.

"Merry Christmas, Aunt Angela," said Joseph, the oldest. He wore a blue suit with a white shirt and red tie.

"Merry Christmas, bello," said Angela. She embraced and kissed him.

"Not in front of everyone," said Joseph. He wiped his cheeks.

"Oh, look at little Princess Alicia," Angela said. She hugged and kissed the girl on each cheek. She had light hair and large, brown eyes. "Hurry, Franco, and dress," she called. "They are here!"

"Hello, everyone," said Salvatore, with Paolina supporting him.

"It was nice of you to invite me, Angela," said Paolina, "since I will not celebrate Christmas with my children and grandchildren until tomorrow. How is Franco?"

"He is recovering slowly," Angela said. She had invited Paolina because Speranza had mentioned she would be home alone on Christmas Eve. Angela thought of her as a gossip and meddler, but no one should be alone on Christmas Eve. She had heard that Paolina had told her neighborhood that Franco Bellini thought himself superior to Salvatore and that now he knew what it was like to be crippled. Angela was informed about Paolina's attitude through one of her dressmaking clients.

"Angela, the children look wonderful in their new clothes," Speranza said. "Thank you so much."

"It is a joy for me to do that. You do not have to thank me. I wish I could do more."

The two women looked at Speranza's protruding belly.

"I hope you do not have this baby tonight," laughed Angela. She patted Speranza's abdomen.

She helped Speranza off with her coat and noticed that she wore the bright green maternity dress Angela had made for her first pregnancy—but it seemed far too big for her this time.

"Speranza, did you let that dress out? It seems so big. It fit you well at this stage during your last two pregnancies."

"I think I might have lost some weight," said Speranza. She sniffed, "I have had a cold."

Angela could see the outline of Speranza's shoulder blades, and her arms appeared lost inside the sleeves of the dress. She could see the green dress and a prominent belly, not the person inside it. Her sister-in-law's flesh seemed to be dissolving underneath the weight of a new life and an old dress.

"She does not eat anything," Paolina said. "I try to get her to eat, but she does not." Paolina sat at the table.

How does she know what Speranza ate or did not eat? thought Angela. She knew Salvatore would not know if or what Speranza ate either, because if he did not like what Speranza cooked, he ate at Paolina's.

"Have you been to the doctor lately, Speranza?" Angela asked.

"A few weeks ago. I told him I get short of breath easily, but he said that is because the baby's so high up."

"We can go see Dr. Greenberger together." Angela led her sister-in-law to a chair. Her lips looked blue to Angela.

Franco walked into the room slowly, leaning on his cane.

The children ran to him, wanting him to swoop them up in his arms the way he always had.

Franco lowered himself into his easy chair. The children sat on either knee.

"Look, look, Uncle Franco, I got a Christmas coloring book," said the little boy. "I got a chemistry set. I'll be able to do experiments." Joseph held up a beaker.

"Ulk!" his little sister said. "He'll probably blow us all up."

"So what?" shouted Joseph. "If I want to blow stuff up, I will!"

"Stop, stop. Enough," Franco said. He motioned to Angela.

"Children, come away from your uncle. Everyone sit at the table," said Angela, clapping her hands. "Dinner will be ready in a few minutes." She walked over to help Franco up from the chair.

"I can do it," Franco said. He pulled his arm away from Angela, pushed his weight forward, and balanced himself on his feet. Angela handed him his cane, and he shuffled over to his seat at the head of the table. Everyone was silent until Franco was seated. Angela went into the kitchen.

"When do we open our presents?" asked Alicia.

"When we have finished eating," Speranza said. "Now sit in your seat."

"Speranza, too thin," said Franco.

"I keep telling her to eat," said Paolina, "but she is a grown woman and has her own mind." She took a piece of bread from the center of the table and took a bite.

"I wish everyone would stop talking about my weight," Speranza said.

"You look bad," said Salvatore.

Franco banged his fist on the table.

"Salvatore, you bring her to the office... uh, doctor," Franco said. He wanted his brother-in-law to know that he was serious when he spoke, but with his verbal difficulty he wondered if Salvatore would understand.

"All she has to do is eat," said Salvatore. "Why spend money?"

Franco stared at Salvatore, his voice ready to fire, but the words were no longer adequate ammunition. His sentences would have been ramblings. Franco had spent enough time with Salvatore to know that his brother-in-law was ignorant of many things, and one of them was human feelings. There would be no sense in arguing with him.

"Angela!" called Franco." Angela!"

"What is it? Supper is coming," Angela said. She dried her hands on a towel.

"Look here," Franco said, pointing to Speranza.

"Yes, I know. Tomorrow, when I bring Dr. Greenberger the Christmas bread, I will make an appointment for Speranza after the new year. Please, do not worry."

"Most of the time doctors do not know what ails you anyway," Paolina said. "Franco, how is your leg coming along? I see you still walk with a cane."

"Ok," Franco said. He could not change the subject even if he wanted to; now he was forced to listen to conversations that he did not want to hear. Why had Angela invited all these people?"

"When the body is hurt like that, I do not know if anyone can be the same," Paolina said. "Look at Salvatore with his leg; he never got better."

"Salvatore was born with a physical problem," Angela said. She put a hot dish of steaming fish on the table. "Franco is different. He has to learn to walk again."

Franco wondered if he actually was any different. Who would hire him now? If he went out in the world and presented himself as he was at this moment, who would want him as an employee? Franco had a sense of what Salvatore had been up against all his life—people staring as if you were sub-human, not being able to keep up with everyone else.

"I say we must accept the fate God has given us as best we can," Paolina said. "My poor husband died before his time. I had to accept it."

"Paolina, do not talk about such things on Christmas," said Salvatore. "It is a holiday of birth."

"What would birth mean if we did not have death?" Paolina asked.

"Let us eat before the food gets cold," Angela said. She put the last dish in the center of the table.

Chapter 10
Nelsonville, 1930

Angela sat in Dr. Greenberger's waiting room and leafed through a magazine. She looked around at the patients waiting to see the doctor. Most of them appeared old but thriving, with red cheeks from the freezing weather. If these old people were hardy, she thought, then Speranza had to be healthy.

Angela thought about her own illness. She had been a young girl of nineteen when she became ill—a greenhorn from another country. There was no reason for her illness; it just happened. God did not take her life but left her barren instead. She supposed it was because she would have to take care for Franco and Speranza.

"Mrs. Bellini, could you come in? The doctor would like to speak with you," said the nurse.

The smell of a medicine cabinet stung Angela's nostrils as she walked into the treatment room. It reminded her of when Franco's mother was an invalid and Angela had to feed her and administer medication. Angela smiled to hide a wave of nausea.

"Hello, Doctor, how are you?" Angela asked.

"Angela, it is good to see you," said the doctor. "How is Franco?"

"He is doing much better," Angela said. "But how is Speranza's health?"

He motioned for Angela to sit on a low stool.

"She is in the bathroom. I have found her heartbeat to be irregular. There is a good chance her heart valve is opening too quickly. After the baby is born, I will put her on digitalis and do further testing. The high heart rate is what has caused her shortness of breath."

"My mother-in-law was on digitalis," Angela said. "I used to give it to her." She used to turn her head away when Angela tried to put the liquid in her mouth. As the doctor spoke, Angela could not dispel the mental image of her mother-in-law turning away from her in disgust. Was the old woman turning away because the medication was revolting, or was it Angela herself that left her disgusted?

"Will the medicine cure her?" Angela asked.

"It will not cure her. It will normalize her heartbeat, but I cannot start the medication until the baby is born. She is not due until the beginning of April, so we must watch her closely. The baby seems fine, but it will be a good idea if she goes to the hospital for this birth."

Angela thought about Salvatore and how he did not feel his wife needed a doctor. Stupid man. He did not think of anyone but himself. He could not see beyond his nose. If he could, Speranza would not be pregnant again. It was all wrong, all wrong.

"I have explained everything to Speranza," said the doctor, "but I wanted you to know."

"How can this be, doctor? Speranza was a thin child but always healthy." She was a skinny ten-year-old aching for a mother who would teach her things. Angela had set out to be the kind of mother Speranza needed, but what she was able to give was not enough.

"Maybe because of the pregnancies. I really cannot say, but she needs to eat properly and rest."

"That will not be a problem. I will see to that."

Speranza came out of the bathroom wearing a black coat that Angela had given her. It was much too big for her now.

"Are we finished, Doctor?" asked Speranza.

"Yes, I have explained everything to Angela. You can go home and rest. I will see you next week. I will have the results of your blood tests then."

Angela and Speranza walked out of the office and sauntered arm in arm down the street in silence. Angela touched her sister-in-law's hand; the loose flesh around her bones was like the flesh of a chicken. Speranza seemed to be fading away.

"It is a good thing we came to see Dr. Greenberger," said Angela.

"I do not think anything good will come of this," Speranza said.

"What do you mean? Dr. Greenberger will help you. He said he could," Angela said emphatically.

"I had a dream about this," Speranza said quietly.

"A dream? What kind of dream?" Angela put her arm around Speranza.

Speranza told Angela that she dreamed a doctor took out her heart because it was damaged and unhealthy. She was awake on the operating room table, and the doctor told her that she did not deserve it because she did not make a proper marriage. He told her that it was not a union of the heart, so it was no longer of use to her. Speranza said she remembered screaming for Angela.

Angela thought that Speranza would be frightened by a dream like that, but she went on as if she were telling her children a bedtime story.

"And then you came," Speranza said. "I asked you if you would save my life, and you said that you would preserve me. I remember feeling grateful to you for everything."

"Speranza, stop thinking about sickness and dreams. God is the only one who can save and preserve. You will have a healthy baby. It is a new year. Think only good thoughts."

When Speranza was a little girl, Angela would tell her to pay attention to her dreams, for they could tell her things. She shared with her sister-in-law stories about her time in Sicily and how she depended on the information in her dreams. Since she had been in this country, Angela either discounted or could not remember her dreams. She did not like Speranza's dream; it reeked of danger. She put her arm around Speranza's waist and imagined she could ground her sister-in-law to the earth and keep her body dense and whole.

~ ~ ~ ~ ~

"What happened?" Franco asked as he sat back in his dining room easy chair and lit a cigar.

"You should not smoke," Angela said. She took off her hat and opened the closet to hang her coat. She had not thought about how the news of Speranza's illness would affect Franco. She was so busy thinking about how to help her that Franco had slipped her mind.

"When the spring comes, I will smear...ah, paint the house," said Franco as he blew smoke. Would he ever learn to speak again? "Speranza and the doctor?"

Angela could tell by the sound of his voice that he sensed something was wrong. Angela hesitated.

"Speranza!" shouted Franco. He pushed himself up from the chair, lost his balance and fell back on the chair.

"Be careful," Angela said. "We have to take care of Speranza and the children now. We will need to work together. Please do not get so excited. You are not that well, either."

"Where is my mother...I mean...sister?" asked Franco. He ground the cigar into the ashtray.

"She is at home. I fixed supper and made sure the children were washed and in bed. I told her to call us later."

"No. More," Franco said.

"Nothing has happened," Angela said, raising her voice. She conveyed the doctor's findings and that Speranza would need medicine.

"Tell him to come here and live…I mean her." Franco waved his hand.

"Franco, we cannot make her come and live here. She has her own home and Salvatore is there…"

"Salvatore! Him! You let it happen!"

"I am not God. I do not have power over people. If anyone let it happen, it was your mother and Paolina. Do you think I like watching Speranza live the way she does? I told you what was going on before they thought of marriage." Angela slammed the closet door and went into the bedroom.

Angela sat on her bed and stared at the statue of the Blessed Mother on her dresser. She wondered if Mary heard her prayers anymore. When she lived at the convent, the Blessed Virgin was more alive to her. Angela felt that she answered her prayers quickly. Now she did not hear answers, if there were any. Her unseen companions were also a distant memory, even though she sometimes thought of and dreamed about them. She needed to reconnect with them so that she could help Speranza.

~ ~ ~ ~ ~

Angela lifted the lid to the mailbox and pulled out some letters and bills. She flipped through the mail and saw a blue air-mail envelope. It was from Franco's cousin, Roberto.

She and Franco had not been talking much. There was a wall between them. Franco drew more and more into himself. Maybe she should leave the letter on the smoking table. No, she knew how much this letter would mean to Franco.

She went into the kitchen, opened the cellar door, and called for Franco to come upstairs. During the past few weeks, he had spent more and more time working alone in the cellar. He would hold the railing and place one foot on a step and then the other, pausing in between to gain his balance. She hoped that when spring came, he would get outside work. Fortunately, his speech was improving daily. He never missed his appointment with the speech therapist.

She heard the grinding of the saw stop and a shuffle on the floor as Franco walked to the bottom of the stairs.

"What?"

"There is a letter from Roberto here," Angela said.

Franco slowly climbed the stairs. He stepped into the kitchen and sat at the table, and Angela handed him his reading glasses. He opened the envelope and unfolded the letter.

"Dear Franco and Angela," Franco read as he held the letter out in front of him. "I am writing the...this..." Franco held the letter closer and squinted. "It is the glasses." He handed it to Angela.

The accident had affected his ability to read. Angela felt the therapist assumed that Franco was an immigrant who did not read English very well, so she focused only on his speech and balance. She sat next to Franco as she read.

February 1930

Dear Franco and Angela,

I am writing to wish you a happy and prosperous New Year. I hope your journey home was a safe one and that your family found you content and happy as you arrived in New York. I know that your country is in economic decay, and I hope this has not affected your lives too much. It is winter now, and the cool breeze from the sea sweeps over my villa. The colder weather cleanses and calms the air after a hot summer.

I hope, Franco, that you went away with a clearer view of your mother country. I am sure you have a sense of our struggle here through the people we encountered during your stay. Unfortunately, I heard that Fra Giovanni has died. I met the young monk, Marizio, who did the drawings for the abbot, at a church meeting where several well-known speakers were expressing their views. Fra Giovanni was supposed to have attended the meeting but had died the week before. It seems that Marizio will succeed him as abbot. I was sorry to hear about the old man's death, but he was old and not active in the struggle.

My family is well, and Giulietta sends her love. The situation is the same here, and we do not expect any improvement. In fact, the atmosphere where we live will most likely worsen in the years to come. I will continue to correspond until we are able to meet again.

With Affection,
Roberto

What struggle? thought Angela. What did Roberto know about struggle? He did not have to worry about money or feeling useless. The people whose lives he touched treated him with respect. He had his health, a beautiful villa, and lovely children. Angela failed to see the struggle.

"This man, Fra Giovanni, certainly affected the two of you," Angela said.

Franco shrugged.

"Franco, half of this letter talks about Fra Giovanni. You were taken with him."

Franco motioned for Angela to get a pen and paper.

"Dear Roberto and family," said Franco loudly. He cleared his throat. "I talk...no, I am...ah...Angela, I can't. You know...you write. Dear Roberto, I am not well...I suffer...I suffered...ah..."

"An accident," Angela said impatiently.

"Yeah, and I now feel better. Um, now..." He looked at Angela and shook his head. "Angela...you know. You write."

He has nerve to ask me to be his voice after he accused me of creating Speranza's situation in life, Angela thought. She looked at Franco's pleading face. She once thought that he would always protect her, and now it seemed it was the other way around. Angela remembered how he cared for her when she was seriously ill.

"I will write it, but let me know if I am saying what you want."

He nodded his head.

"My cousin Roberto," said Angela as she wrote. "I was glad to receive your letter. It brought back many pleasant and happy memories about our return to Sicily." She looked at Franco.

"The villa...beautiful."

"Your beautiful villa helped Angela and me to feel welcomed and safe in a country that we once called home."

Franco nodded again.

Angela thought about the sound of the waves caressing the rocks below the villa in the night. The salt air seemed to rise from the sea and rush over the villa at dark, while in the daylight it was hardly noticeable. The villa felt like a fortress to her then. It gave her a superhuman feeling—and the strength to go back to Messina and search for her sister. The villa played a part in calming her fears about the outcome of her quest.

"Struggle," Franco said.

"Struggle? With whom?" Angela asked.

"The people..." said Franco spreading his arms wide.

"Oh, the Sicilian people?"

"Yeah, yeah."

"But what about struggle?" asked Angela.

"Me," said Franco, pointing to himself. "Me and the people."

Angela started to write again.

"No, wait," said Franco. What about his struggle? How could Angela put it into words when he could not? Roberto would laugh at him. Franco's struggles were not so blatantly political. He and Angela did not live in poverty like the peasants in Palermo or so many immigrant families in America. Ever since he started working in America, he had saved every penny he could. He had enough saved to last for several years, and Angela continued to work and pay their weekly bills. What was the point?

"No, stop," said Franco.

"Why?"

"Stupid, put it back," he said, motioning at the writing paper.

"No, it is not stupid. Let's finish the letter. You wanted to write it. Did you want to tell Roberto that you sympathize with what he is doing?"

"Yeah, yeah," said Franco. He put his right hand on the table and relaxed back in his chair. Angela knew what he wanted to say. She picked up the pen and began to write.

"I sympathize with your struggle and the struggle of the Sicilian people to be free. Through the people we met, it became clear to me what an important man you are to everyone."

"Good, good. Me...my struggle. No job." He gestured for Angela to write.

"I can now understand better," recited Angela as she wrote, "how the citizen of Palermo feels when there is no work. When I returned from Sicily, I lost my job and could not find another." She looked to Franco for more thoughts.

"Feel...no good here." Franco pointed to his head. "And...there is no use." He shrugged his shoulders.

"I had nothing to do for the longest time. The days became long, and I felt..." She stopped.

"By myself..." said Franco.

Angela had felt this kind of frustrated loneliness after the earthquake. She remembered wandering among the dead and talking to them; begging them to tell her the whereabouts of her sister. She ran from corpse to corpse. It must be the same with Franco; only he was unable to talk to people and express himself.

"I felt alone and useless," said Angela, aloud, "being unable to support my family. I got an odd job and had an accident, where I hit my head. I have spent the past few months recovering from my misfortune..."

"Struggle to get strong," said Franco as he leaned forward. "Like a boy...kid..."

"Baby," said Angela softly. She remembered feeding him in the hospital after surgery. Her focus was not on how Franco felt, but on getting the necessary nutrition into him for recovery.

"Yeah, yeah." He had never admitted that before, not to anyone. He would have been too ashamed.

"I have struggled to learn to walk and talk again. It is like being a baby again. I wish I could do more, but it will take time to become completely well."

Franco thought about the way Angela said, "it is like being a baby again." It did not make him feel embarrassed or ashamed. It was exactly the way he felt while he learned to walk and talk again. He saw now that he had to experience being a baby again to get to where he was.

Becoming "completely well," meant the way he used to be, and this did not feel right to Franco. He had a strong body and would survive, but things would not be as before. It was as if he had had different beginnings, since he had experienced the early years of childhood again. He would now live with this new experience for the rest of his life. His new body was not as sturdy as the old one. Angela had helped him arrive at this stage of recuperation and development.

"I am sorry...about..."

"I am sorry to hear about Giovanni's death," said Angela before Franco finished expressing himself. "He had a great influence on both of us."

Franco wanted to say he was sorry for blaming Angela about Speranza's marriage. She had wanted the best for his sister, and he blamed her out of anger.

"No, no," said Franco, smiling. He thought about what Roberto would say after reading those lines. It was not that Roberto disliked the old man personally, but his cousin clearly resented the effect Giovanni had on people. Or was it jealously? No, how could a man like Roberto feel jealous?

"Franco, you both were impressed with him. Why would Roberto mention him if he did not want you to comment on the abbot?"

For the first time, Angela saw her husband blush. She had seen him happy, joyful, and sad, but never shy.

"All right, all right," said Franco. He turned his head.

"When I was sick and in the hospital," continued Angela as she wrote, "I met a little boy that Angela and I very much wanted to adopt." She stopped and waited for Franco to urge her on; he did. Angela cleared her throat and went on.

"Unfortunately, another couple adopted him, and I realize now that it was not meant to be. I had always hoped we would have children, but it is not to be."

"Enough...enough, rest," said Franco.

Angela put down her pen, took out a tissue, and wiped her eyes.

What was the point in talking about what could have been? thought Franco. Jerry was in the past. Why mention him to Roberto Mineo, the great Sicilian poet? He only met the child twice. Franco felt he would never understand life or how people's minds worked. His own mind was a puzzle, but since his accident the speech in his mind seemed sharper—or was it that he just noticed more? Before the accident, he had been unaware of what he was going to say—but now he caught every thought that passed through his mind, no matter how faint. Even though his speech would never be what it was, his mind was clearer; after many years he had befriended it.

He had not understood Roberto's poem The Figure 8 and could not remember any of the lines. But the dreams he had had the night Roberto read the poem to him began to take on new meaning. His mind used the painting in Rome with the monks consulting a Ouija board to highlight the number 8. Franco felt that to his cousin, the figure 8 represented something negative; it symbolized Italy and how it swallowed its own tail and was doomed if it did not struggle against an evil force called fascism. Now Franco felt the 8 showed him something different. It did not represent a country or an individual, but it came to him in a dream to illustrate that life flowed within that form; two pulsating circles together, always connected.

"Go on," Angela said.

"No...not today," said Franco. "Tired."

"We can finish it tomorrow if you want."

Franco reached over and touched Angela's hand. He felt that it was just the two of them in the world. He had no fears left.

"All right," said Angela. "We will finish it tomorrow."

~ ~ ~ ~ ~

Angela spread gold material over the dining room table, carefully pinning a dress pattern on the cloth. Gold was one of her favorite colors to work with; it radiated life. If any of her customers were undecided on material for their patterns, she would suggest a fine, light golden wool that she purchased from the local sewing shop.

She thought about last night and the letter to Roberto. With all that had happened in the past few months, she had not thought much about the trip to Sicily. Since her visit to Messina, she had not even thought much about her sister. Her search was over.

Angela picked up the scissors and began to cut the pattern. What if they made another trip to Sicily next year? She wondered if she could save enough for two tickets. She lost some clients because of the depression, but she always seemed to be able to save a few dollars every week. The nuns at St. Mary's gave her as much work as they could. They would only had to save for the ship's tickets because they would stay with Roberto. That would cure Franco and give him his strength back.

Franco had always loved the Sicilian sun; it healed anyone who stood under it. No, it could not be next year. With the depression, she could not afford to put her work on hold and leave the country. As she cut around the pattern, her mind searched for something she could do to help Franco become himself again. The bronze clock in the hallway chimed twelve. Angela remembered the day Franco brought the clock home and announced that they would be making the trip to Europe. They were two completely different people now.

Angela heard a bang at the door and a muffled voice calling her name. She rushed over and looked out the window. Paolina stood at the door and frantically looked around her. Everything was a crisis to Paolina, and Angela was not in the mood. She opened the door.

"Angela! Speranza is going to have the baby!" She stood in the doorway wringing her hands.

"Did you call the ambulance?"

"No, I do not have a phone," puffed Paolina. "I came here as soon as she had the feeling."

"Why did you not use a neighbor's phone?"

"Because I wanted to talk to you. You delivered the last baby, and I am not as strong as you. You know what to do." Paolina's hands moved so fast that Angela could not discern her right from her left.

"Wait on the porch," said Angela. She went in and called the doctor.

"Come on," said Angela as she took Paolina by the arm and pulled her up the street. "Why could you not have called the doctor, or at least called me from a neighbor's?"

"Oh, no! I was too frightened!" said Paolina, panting. "Besides, Salvatore is with her."

Salvatore! That useless man! She wanted to tell Paolina what she thought about her brother from the day they met, but she felt it was not the time or place. She pulled Paolina harder and harder until they could see Speranza's house in the distance. An ambulance was parked outside.

They brought Speranza out in a stretcher. Angela went over and clutched Speranza's hand as they climbed into the ambulance.

"My contractions are not that close together."

"Good luck," said Paolina as she waved from the sidewalk.

"What do you think you are doing?" said Angela. "Come up here."

"In the ambulance?" Paolina backed away more until she reached the front door of Speranza's house. Angela tried to step out of the ambulance to get Paolina, but the driver started to move away with the siren blowing. Angela stepped back in. Where was Salvatore in all this?

"Speranza, where is Salvatore?"

"He is in the house. He said he would be coming along," Speranza said. "He has the children. Angela, what do you think it will be, a boy or a girl?"

Angela looked out the ambulance window so Speranza would not see the anger on her face. She had never met two people so ignorant in all her life. Paolina and Salvatore were aware that Speranza was ill, and yet they completely refused to take any responsibility. It did not appear that they were even interested in the baby. She knew Paolina was a fearful person, but Salvatore? She could not understand it. If Franco were well, he would be right there with Speranza and herself.

"Angela, what do you think it will be?" Speranza repeated. "You are good at predicting these things."

Angela went over and knelt by the stretcher.

"I think it will be a girl," Angela said.

"A girl, really? Why do you say that?"

"Oh, just a feeling. But do not tell your brother. He does not believe in premonitions."

Speranza giggled.

It was the first time in years she had ever heard that kind of laugh. Angela was glad this pregnancy was coming to a close. Speranza's ankles were always swollen, and she could not climb stairs without panting and some slight chest pain. It was also difficult to take care of Speranza and her own husband at the same time; she was helping Speranza clean and cook and then came home to did the same. Now Dr. Greenberger could put her on the needed medication and things would get back to normal.

Angela held her sister-in-law's hand; the skin slid easily over the bones. It felt like the pie dough she would spread over apples or some other ingredients. Her skin was becoming even thinner.

The ambulance drove up to the emergency entrance, and as the door swung open Angela saw Franco stepping out of a taxi. He shuffled toward the ambulance.

"Franco, you are here," said Speranza as she held her belly with one hand and the other held on to Angela's. "I am glad you have come."

"Yeah," Franco said. He had never been near a woman in labor before and did not know what he should say. It was difficult for him to think of his young sister as actually having labor and bearing children.

"Angela said it will be a girl."

"Listen to your sister," said Franco. He blinked. Did he really say that sentence without hesitation, or was it someone else? The surprise on Angela's face confirmed his thoughts; it was the first straightforward spontaneous sentiment he had uttered in months. Angela reached over and grabbed his hand. They escorted Speranza into the hospital.

~ ~ ~ ~ ~

"Salvatore?" asked Franco. They sat in the hospital waiting room. "He is at home with the children," Angela said.

"What! Stupid…bastard," said Franco loudly.

"Shhhh. You are in a hospital. We can talk about it later."

Why doesn't she want to talk about it? thought Franco. Maybe she did have a hand in this marriage. Who knows, anything was possible. Speranza would come home with them and live with the kids. What was the point of his sister having a husband when he was never there?

"Salvatore...no good," said Franco. He tapped the bottom of his cane on the floor. Sooner or later, she would have to answer him.

"Franco, do you have to do this now? Can't you think of your sister? I do not want to think about Salvatore."

Think about Speranza! What did she think he was doing? He could have stayed home and waited for a phone call.

"I do think...of my mother...sister." He slammed his cane on a chair.

"I know you do, but you cannot act like this here. It will do no good to complain about Salvatore. I am only thinking of Speranza now. You know she is not well."

Franco wished he could forget about Salvatore. How could such an afflicted man have so much in life and not appreciate it? Salvatore had a steady job, even though he had lost his job at St. Mary's. He had two beautiful children and a lovely wife. Franco had been born able-bodied but now he could not utter a sentence, and he had no children and no job. Angela was right, he admitted to himself. He had not thought of Speranza; he was angry that he had not achieved in life what he felt he should have.

"Sorry...sorry," Franco said.

Angela put her arms around Franco and thought about their last trip to Sicily. Their visit to the place where they first saw each other had renewed everything for them. They saw each other as if for the first time. Since their return from Sicily, so much had happened that it was time for renewal again.

"When you are better and Speranza has recovered from her illness, we can take another trip together," said Angela. "We can even take the children." She knew that this was beyond their means, but it gave Franco hope.

"Yeah, yeah," said Franco. Maybe she was right that he would recover.

The nurse came into the waiting room

"Congratulations, it's a girl. The mother is doing fine."

"Oh, wonderful—a girl, Franco," Angela said.

"Nice, nice," said Franco.

"Can we hold her?" asked Angela. "You know, I delivered her last child."

"Well, just for a few minutes. It's almost time for the babies to go out to the mothers."

Angela helped Franco out of the chair. For the first time since the accident, Angela saw him muster energy to reach the doorway before she did.

Angela gently cuddled the baby in her arms while Franco touched the newborn's forehead.

"Sit down so you can hold her," Angela said.

"No, no. Not now," said Franco.

"Sit over here." Angela motioned to a chair with her chin. Franco sat down.

Angela laid the baby in his lap and sat down beside them. Franco looked at Angela and then down at the baby. Her small face reflected the entire family. Franco could see her grandmother when the baby yawned and Speranza when she looked up at him with steady eyes. And when the baby stared at her moving fingers, Alessio appeared. They were all there in one tiny being. He and Angela had been parents all along and were again with the birth of this baby. Roberto's poem was correct; the cycle continued like the energy of the figure 8.

"Angela, Franco," said Dr. Greenberger, "I see you have met your new niece."

"Yes, Doctor, we are so happy," Angela said.

"Well, I have just come from Speranza's room. She is doing fine, but she is extremely tired. I will start her on the digitalis tomorrow. We will keep her for a few extra days for testing."

"Thank you, Doctor," said Angela. "When can we see her?"

"In a few minutes. The nurse will bring you in. I will see you both in a few days."

The baby twisted her fingers around her toes. Franco put his finger in the child's hand. She stopped moving and seemed to listen for a moment. Franco and Angela were silent and waited until the baby moved again to bring her back to the nursery.

~ ~ ~ ~ ~

"Mr. and Mrs. Bellini, you can go in and see Speranza for a little while," said the nurse.

"You go," Franco said. The maternity ward was no place for a man. He had been a patient on a ward and had been a visitor, but the thought of walking into a maternity ward made him nauseated. Only fathers should be allowed in.

"What, without you? Come on. You are her brother."

"I don't know..." said Franco. Why was it easy for him to show anger toward Salvatore, but to express how much he loved his sister was beyond his grasp? He had discharged Speranza's upbringing to Angela and when she tried to tell him about Salvatore he dismissed it as a woman's babble. He had viewed

Paolina and his mother as harmless creatures, never dreaming they could have an impact on anyone's life. Now he saw the results of his blindness.

Angela held Franco by the arm. They entered the maternity ward and moved toward Speranza's bed. Angela could see her eyes before she reached her, glistening between dark circles like the guiding rays to a lighthouse for ships lost at sea. Angela saw how thin her sister-in-law was now that she had delivered the baby. Her cheeks were sunken, accentuating her nose.

"Did you see the baby?" asked Speranza.

"Yes, she is beautiful," said Angela. She leaned over and kissed her sister-in-law. Speranza's skin was cool and loose. Angela focused on the rise and fall of her chest; it was as if she could not take in enough air. Angela hoped that the digitalis the doctor prescribed would clear up any problem, but it appeared the pregnancy had taken its toll. Any good health that was Speranza's was now lying in the nursery fast asleep.

Angela wanted to blame Salvatore but knew that it was not just him—it was everyone. They all created this situation. It would have been easier to point a finger at one person, but life was not like that. Angela scolded herself for thinking this way. She must think positive thoughts for Speranza and Franco. The medication could help Speranza, and Franco could regain his powers of speech. When she was a girl and communicated with her unseen friends, it was always positive and insightful. She tried to maintain this mindset with her dealings with family. She still felt the sensibilities of unseen friends; her connection with them matured and her feeling and points of view seemed to have melded with theirs. They had guided her through the dark energies of Messina and continued to guide her.

"Franco, did you see the baby?" asked Speranza.

"Yeah, yeah," said Franco. He looked down at the floor.

"You need your rest, Speranza," said Angela, "We will be back later today. I will bring you some broth to eat."

They both kissed Speranza and walked away from the bed. Angela looked back at Speranza and imagined her as the little girl she once was strong and healthy.

~ ~ ~ ~ ~

It had been a few weeks since the baby's birth, and Franco and Angela settled into life that centered around Speranza and the children.

"Franco, I am going over to Speranza's," called Angela out of the window. "Are you all right to stay alone?"

Franco waved his hand without turning around. He leaned on his cane as he stood in his freshly planted garden. It had taken him several weeks to overturn the earth this year, but it was well worth the time and effort. He bent down and touched the soil, rubbing the earth between his fingers. Dry. He would have to water it later. Franco moved the soil away from the tiny green buds that pushed against the ground to give them more room to grow.

He thought about his new niece. Babies should always be born in spring. There was another cycle coming; another generation. Even though he had no children, he was still a part of it all. The baby's birth gave Franco new hope. Physically he had stayed the same, but he felt at his peak mentally. Franco felt a slight tightness in his right arm. He rubbed it, thinking he had been working too hard in the garden.

Franco felt the right side of his face go numb and then rigid. Saliva began to ooze from his mouth, and he could not speak. He slowly let his weight take him to the ground, where he felt the sun penetrate his back. All he could do was moan. He tried to scream for his wife, but his mouth was pushed against the soil. He tried to kick his legs; the right leg was completely paralyzed and the other one was stiff. How could he die like this, face down in the dirt? Speranza's face came to him as she lay in the maternity ward, serene and accepting. With this image, Franco lost all sense of organized time and place.

~ ~ ~ ~ ~

Angela finished feeding Speranza and the children. She watched Speranza sip her broth as she dried the dishes. The medication had worked some, but Speranza still became out of breath whenever she did housework or walked up the stairs. She also had a chronic cold that never seemed to get better. The new baby had to be bottle-fed, because her milk had dried up due to the medication.

"When is your next doctor's appointment?" asked Angela.

"Next week, I think."

"I will go with you. Let me know so I can schedule my customers."

"Salvatore can come," said Speranza. "You are doing too much for me."

"Salvatore works during the weekdays. I am not doing too much."

Angela did feel spent. It was difficult to take care of two houses at once. She kept waiting for Franco to get better. There was hope, as every morning when she got up, the space beside her was empty and she would hear the saw vibrating from the cellar. Franco's clothes would be hung neatly on the bedroom chair where she had laid them the night before. He would not get dressed in the morning until she called him for breakfast. She longed for the days when he was up and out by seven a.m., full of energy and vitality.

She could not give up thinking that those days would return. When the new baby was born, Franco seemed to be more outside of himself, but that dissipated as the days went by. Angela saw him as caught between two worlds. He lived in the outer world as everyone did, but there was a spot in him that Angela could not penetrate. Sometimes she would watch him smoking a cigar while he sat in his chair. His face would be completely relaxed, as his eyes seemed to dance.

Although Franco had planted the garden this year, Angela watched as he completed tasks that used to take him fifteen minutes take forty-five. She saw him pound the earth when he had misplaced seeds he wanted to plant or he lost a trowel. But she saw how proud he was when he had finished the job. Angela's hope now was that he would work out in the garden rather than spend his time in the cellar. The soil was alive, and it would be good for Franco to dig in the earth. It could possibly draw him out.

Angela looked at the clock. "I have to go, Speranza. I do not want to leave Franco alone too long,"

"Thank you, Angela. I appreciate everything you do.

Angela cupped her hands around Speranza's face. "I remember how you helped me when I first came to this country. You made me feel welcome."

"I was only a kid. I always wanted a big sister, and I liked the way you treated me."

Angela knew she was going to care for Speranza the second she saw her. She needed someone to take care of while she adjusted to American life. Speranza accepted her in a way that no one else did or could have. It was a perfect situation: Angela was looking for her sister, and Speranza needed both a mother and sister.

"I will see you tomorrow," Angela said. "I cooked enough so Salvatore will have dinner when he comes home. Goodbye, kids."

~ ~ ~ ~ ~

As Angela drew closer to the house, an image of Franco in the garden came to mind. The image produced an uncomfortable sensation. Angela quickened her step until she reached the driveway. The back gate was open. She closed the gate and began to walk up the side staircases when she heard a moan. She thought it might be a cat and took a few steps. There was another moan. This time it sounded human, and it came from the backyard. She opened the gate and saw Franco lying face down in the garden.

"Franco! Franco! What happened!"

She turned him over. His face drooped on one side, and his eyes were shut. Angela was immediately fearful that she would now be alone in the world. Alone in a foreign country! No, how could she say that America was a foreign country? Sicily also felt like a foreign land. She would not only be alone but she would have no place to call home. What had she done to deserve this? What had they both done but take care of their family? Now it was all over.

Angela felt something shake loose from her. What was it? Her hope—it was her hope. It began to fall, and when it did it felt like a lead weight hitting cement. She heard the cement crack and give way. She imagined the earth opening up like in her earthquake dream.

"You cannot have him!" shouted Angela. "You cannot have him."

She dragged Franco out of the garden.

"Mrs. Bellini," called a neighbor. "Do you need help?"

"Please! Please call an ambulance!" Angela looked back at the garden and saw the imprint of Franco's body in the earth.

Chapter 11
Retrieval, 1930

A ngela sat in the dining room in Franco's chair, where a faint smell of cigar smoke still hung in the air. She had always told Franco that smoking cigars was not good for his health. Two cigar butts lay in the ashtray.

The doctor said that Franco had suffered a major stroke and that he may never walk again. In her mind's eye, Angela could see another long road that extended far into the future. There was no end in sight—only twists and turns, steep hills and sharp drops. What if Franco never walked again? How could she manage alone? She had no children to help her, and Speranza and the children depended on her.

Even now, she had no one she could depend on. There was no one for her to talk to. She did not understand how she could be so completely alone. Angela thought of her sister, Felicita, and how they used to meet by the fountain in Messina. They were there for each other as friends and sisters, as were her unseen friends; she missed her sister all over again.

She settled back in her chair and looked down at the smoking table. The unfinished letter to Roberto rested on the side table. She would need to tell Roberto what happened to his cousin. Roberto was insightful about her life and had encouraged her to look for her sister. He would have words of reassurance when he learned of Franco's misfortune.

Angela decided to write her own letter to Roberto. She picked up the writing tablet and sat at the dining room table. Should she write it in Sicilian or Italian? Sicilian would be a better choice for a man who wrote poetry in the southern dialect.

May 1930

Dear Cousin Roberto,

A few weeks ago, Franco wanted to respond to your letter. We never finished the letter because he has now had a major stroke and might not recover.

Angela stopped writing. Franco had abandoned her; he was only in this world in body. Why should she have to turn to Franco's cousin for consolation? Why not write to the nuns with her troubles? They were her family. She had nothing left of her own. No, Roberto had deeply understood the necessity for her quest for her sister and never judged her. Angela picked up her pen.

When I was in Sicily, you encouraged me to search for my sister. I had been so discouraged over the years about not knowing if she was dead or alive. She weighed so strongly on me that I could not fully live my life. You told me to look, and that the answers would be there for me.

And they were. I know that you have no answers for my husband's illness, but I would ask that you write some words of encouragement to Franco so that I can read them to him. I will keep you informed about Franco's progress. Please pray for his recovery.

With Affection,
Angela Bellini

Angela reread the letter. Why had the Blessed Mother not intervened on her husband's behalf? All her life, Angela had placed her faith and trust in the Virgin. She worshiped her like most people paid homage to God.

The bronze clock struck twelve midnight. Angela rubbed her eyes and decided to go to bed. She wanted to be at the hospital at seven in the morning to feed Franco his breakfast.

Angela went to the bedroom and took her hair out of the bun. She separated it at the back and draped it over her shoulders. She thought about the possibility that God was punishing Franco for doubting Him. And, if God punished Franco, then she was also being punished. It was unfair. He should have considered that she was an innocent bystander.

Angela looked around the bedroom. If she had stayed at the convent and become a nun, she never would have been left alone like this. If something should happen to Franco, she would return to Sicily and live at the convent. A small voice spoke from behind a crevice of her mind. Who would take care of Speranza? Angela loved her as much as she loved her sister.

She still communicated with her sister, Felicita, in her dreams. Some of the dreams were joyful, and others carried a heavier energy. Her unseen friends also continued to connect with her in her dreams. She wished that they were all real—that her sister was with her once again and her unseen friends were flesh and blood so they could touch one another. Angela rubbed her eyes; she was determined not to let her mind wander. Of course they would only be present in her dreams. Felicita was dead, and her unseen friends were never in physical bodies.

Angela walked over to the dresser and picked up a hairbrush. She placed the brush at her scalp and brought it down her dark hair. Again and again in fluid strokes, she brushed her hair. The click of the brush when she reached the end of her hair reminded Angela of a metronome one of the nuns used when she played piano. Even at night, the nun would play. Sometimes Angela would leave the dormitory, pretending to go to the bathroom, and sneak downstairs to hear the nun play. One night, just before she got married, she walked into the room where the nun played. She stopped and looked at Angela.

"Why have you shown yourself to me now?" asked the nun. "After all these months of hiding?"

"You knew, sister?"

"Yes."

"Why didn't you scold me and tell me to go back to bed?"

"Because I knew you were the girl who was engaged to be married. It hardly seemed worth the trouble. After all, you are a grown woman. So, why so bold now?"

"I am getting married on Saturday, and I wanted to tell you how lovely your playing has been...how I have enjoyed it."

Angela did not know how she mustered the courage to reveal herself. She had wanted to ask why she still used the metronome. The nun had played for years; she certainly must have developed an inner rhythm. Angela was also attracted to the tick of the metronome. She could hear it in her head for hours afterward; its regularity soothed any fears.

Angela stared in the mirror and thought she saw Felicita's reflection peering out from underneath hers. She blinked her eyes. Being tired and alone was making her see things. The hallway clock struck the hour as Angela turned on the small night-light. She turned on her side and saw the room's reflection in the dresser mirror. The room expanded and then contracted into a circle surrounded by darkness. The rhythm reminded Angela of the metronome; expand, contract, expand, contract. She closed her eyes and heard the ticking in her head.

The ticking grew louder and louder until Angela thought she had awakened. She sat up and looked at the clock on the night table; it was one o'clock. She had heard the hall clock toll one o'clock hours ago. Angela saw the hairbrush on the night table and got out of bed to put it back on the dresser. She caught her reflection in the mirror; it was vague and out of focus. She leaned over the dresser and squinted.

The image of Felicita began to form as her own face became translucent. Angela reached out and touched the mirror. Even though her sister had never grown to full womanhood, Angela saw her sister as a young woman. She smiled at Angela and pointed to the area between her eyes on her forehead and then to her heart. In her mind, Angela heard Felicita say, "Keep looking." Angela felt a deep peace spread throughout her mind and body. Her sister was still there, and they would always be connected. The entire room brightened—not like an electrical light had been turned on, but from a warm glow that came from everywhere and nowhere.

Angela sat on the bed and thought for a minute. She turned to the pillow and wondered why she was not sleeping. The clock still read one a.m. I am dreaming, thought Angela. She lay on the bed and closed her eyes. She thought about tomorrow and what she had to do. Like the metronome, the ebb and flow of her thoughts rocked her into a still sleep.

~ ~ ~ ~ ~

Angela pushed the button and waited for the hospital elevator to descend. The hospital now felt like her second home. It was strange; some people never entered a hospital, and others spent a lifetime there. She got on and went up to the fourth floor.

She nodded to the nurses and walked cautiously toward Franco's bed. His skin was glossy, and some of the lines had disappeared. He reminded Angela of a store window mannequin. She put the broth she had brought on the bedside table and took off her coat.

"Franco," she whispered in his ear. "It is Angela." She waited a few seconds. The doctor said that he might slip into a coma. Angela applied gentle pressure on his shoulder.

"Franco, Franco, it is morning. Wake up!" The patient next to Franco stirred. Franco took a deep breath and opened his eyelids halfway.

"Franco, I will feed you breakfast," Angela said. Franco widened his eyes but stared past Angela. He never blinked. Angela felt he was punishing her by not looking at her.

"Franco, please look at me," said Angela emphatically.

Angela took his head in her hands and turned it toward her. There was no eye movement. She felt he had abandoned his body. What was she supposed to do? Keep his body alive in case he decided to come back? I never had a free moment in my life, thought Angela. It has all been struggle and sadness. When Angela woke up that morning she had a feeling she had had an active dream, but she could not remember what it was about. Her first inclination when she woke was to look at the clock to make sure it was the correct time. I have no time for myself, she thought.

"Angela, we called you this morning," said Speranza as she rushed into the hospital room. Salvatore limped behind her.

"I wanted to get here early to feed him breakfast," said Angela.

"Has the doctor been here this morning?" asked Speranza. She turned her head and coughed.

"I am sorry to see him this way," said Salvatore. He looked around the ward.

"No, not yet...Speranza, I do not think he recognizes me," said Angela as she took her sister-in-law's hand. "You try. See if he knows you."

Speranza leaned over Franco, trying to get his attention. Angela felt that Speranza was an extension of herself. If Speranza showed affection to Franco, then he was getting double the love from the same source.

The clang of the meal trucks rang throughout the ward. A nurse brought Franco's breakfast.

"I will feed him, Angela," said Speranza. She covered her mouth as she coughed.

"You are not feeling well yourself," said Angela. "You might catch something."

"Angela, he has had a stroke. I cannot catch that."

Speranza bent down and cranked Franco's head up. She stopped and took several breaths.

"Please do not strain yourself," said Angela. "I will do that." She did not want Speranza to fall ill. She could not take care of everyone at once.

"She will not listen to you," said Salvatore.

Angela wished she had not brought Salvatore to the hospital; he was no help.

Angela and Salvatore sat near the bedside while Speranza fed Franco. Angela watched as she carefully inserted each spoonful into her husband's mouth.

"Chew, Franco," said Speranza. "Do not forget to chew."

Angela felt he could not tell the difference between his wife and his sister. She observed Speranza as she encouraged her brother to swallow the food in his mouth. Part of her was nourishing and touching Franco. She felt gratitude for Speranza. Her life would be unbearable without her.

"Well, he almost ate everything," said Speranza. "Franco, you get better soon if you keep eating like this."

Angela stood up and searched Franco's eyes. She could see a hint of expression in the lines around them. When she first saw him this morning, the skin had been smooth. He seemed to squint, desperately trying to look out from behind his frozen eyes.

"Angela, why don't we go to get some coffee," said Speranza. "We can have the nurses call us if the doctor comes."

"All right, but I want to come right back."

"It's a good idea," said Salvatore. He got up and went over to Franco, kissed him several times on the cheek. "You get better, Franco, you get better," said Salvatore.

Angela remembered the night of the Columbus Day dance before Speranza and Salvatore were married. She could see the moon shining its subtle light on them. She had felt bitterness toward her mother-in-law and Paolina for encouraging the relationship. Franco did not want to believe that his mother had anything to do with Speranza and Salvatore's marriage, so he blamed her. What did it matter now? Her mother-in-law was dead, and Paolina was a frightened and confused woman. Now Franco could accuse no one.

~ ~ ~ ~ ~

The homecare nurse wheeled Franco out onto the front porch, then sat and perused a magazine.

Franco felt the early summer breeze on his face. He knew he had been ill and had lost track of time until now. It had to be early summer. He could smell the honeysuckle, so they must be in full bloom. He could taste the honeysuckle on his tongue and lips; its sweetness, unlike any other in nature. It consoled him that he was aware of summer approaching.

His speech was gone. Even in his mind, he could not speak in words; they were always images. When people spoke to him, sometimes he could not understand them. All he could do at times was cry. His right side was completely dead, but the therapists continued to work with him. Sometimes he would drool and cough because he had trouble swallowing.

Often he did not recognize the person who cared for him, even though that caretaker had been with him many times before. At times he saw his mother's face on the person who lifted him into bed or his brother's face on the person who fed him. Maybe it was a cruel joke that God played on people who had displeased Him. He often wondered why he was alive.

He heard someone ascend the porch stairs. A woman kissed him on the cheek and said something about how he looked better when he was outside in the fresh air. Was it his mother? Franco kneaded his brow. No, it was his sister. Or was it his wife? He heard the front door open and shut. People did not stay around long enough for him to figure out who they were.

The nurse got up and wheeled Franco into the house. She placed him at the head of the dining room table and then left the room. What was this all about? The house felt familiar and strange at the same time.

"Thank you, nurse," said Angela. "See you tomorrow."

"I'll see you tomorrow, Franco," the nurse said. She patted his shoulder.

"Franco, I will make supper," Angela said.

Why was she bothering him? All he wanted was to be left alone with himself. What was she talking about? He shrugged his left shoulder.

"Eat, Franco." Angela mimicked eating with a fork and chewing.

He did not want to eat. He picked up his left hand and waved it over the table. If he did not want to eat, no one would force him.

"Uhhhhhh..." Franco slammed his fist on the table.

Angela left the room, returned with a plate of pasta, and placed it in front of Franco. He pushed it away. Who was this woman forcing him to do something against his will? His mother, sister, wife, nun? He could not walk out in the sunshine when he wanted or go for a walk, but he could certainly decide when—or if—he wanted to eat.

Franco grabbed the while linen tablecloth and flung it on the floor along with his dinner.

"Uhhhhhh...!" He waved his arm furiously and slammed it on the oak table. His entire body trembled.

The woman stared at him with disgust and anger. Who told her to bring him food? He watched as she bent down to pick up the mess. Images of her as a young woman flooded his mind. She wore a dark blue school uniform with ruffled sleeves. He must have known her from long ago when he was well. He saw her in a flowing white gown: this was his wife.

"Uhhhhhh," groaned Franco and reached for Angela.

"That is all right," said Angela, tears flowing down her face. "You can eat later if you want." She wiped her sleeve across her face.

He waved his hand at the dishes.

"I will clean it up," said Angela.

Franco continued to reach out to Angela, but she kept cleaning up the mess. When she stood up, he held out his hand. He could see that she was tired and worn. She hesitated, put down the plate, and touched his outstretched hand. Was this his wife? He had thought so before, but now her face morphed. Who was she now? One of the nurses at the hospital? He pulled his hand away and motioned for her to go.

The doorbell rang, and Angela heard the door open.

"Angela, it's me. Are you home?"

"Yes, Speranza. In the dining room." Angela heard more than one person's steps.

"You left the door open," said Paolina. She put her shopping bag on a chair.

"Oh, I must have forgotten to lock it." Angela touched her forehead.

"What happened here?" asked Speranza.

"Franco's mood changed all of a sudden. The doctor told us to expect it. What are you doing here?"

"Let me help you clean it up," said Paolina. She put her hand on her hip. "Franco, you should not do things like this. Angela works very hard."

Franco glared at the large, meddling woman. If he had the strength, he would have pushed her over. He quickly leaned toward Paolina.

"Well," said Paolina, as she backed away from Franco, "it is certainly hot today. Angela, maybe he did not like pasta on such a hot day."

"Salvatore is minding the kids, and the doctor told me to walk—so I came to help you," said Speranza.

"Of course I would not let her walk alone, so I came along...to help, of course." Paolina sniffed the air. "Angela, the air smells of smoke, and it is stuffy in here. I would be happy to clean this room."

Paolina was known to gather information for pieces of gossip that she shared with neighbors. She would tell all the women in the neighborhood that Franco was like a baby again, throwing temper tantrums, and that his house reeked of smoke.

"Franco, why did you throw the food on the floor?" Speranza pulled over a chair and sat next to him. "Angela was only trying to give you dinner." Speranza wiped the tomato sauce that had splattered on Franco's shirt. Franco felt his mind fade; bit by bit, the dining room and all the people in it felt transparent.

Angela noticed his eyes become transfixed. "Now he is in his own world. Every time he has an outburst, this is what happens. Sometimes I feel like giving up."

"No, Angela, things will get better. You'll see. He'll come back. I'll warm up more pasta, and then I'll try feeding him. Don't give up."

Speranza still coughed and was out of breath when she exerted herself, but there was a peacefulness about her now. Angela watched her sister-in-law love Franco; she wiped and straightened his shirt, pushed back his hair.

"If you want, I can stay here tonight," said Speranza.

"No, Speranza, you could not leave the children."

"I will mind the children," Paolina said. She wiped her neck with a handkerchief. "It is always wonderful for me to take care of the children and Salvatore."

"Speranza, I am so lucky to have a sister like you." Angela embraced her sister-in-law. When their bodies met, Angela felt the familiar warmth. The room pulsated with a burning glow. Even Franco's right hand that contracted from the stroke began to relax on the dining room table. The feeling reminded her of something she had experienced before, but she could not remember what it was.

Angela heard the tick of the hall clock. Sometimes, when she was sewing or ironing, she would focus on the sound of the clock. Time seemed to speed up when she did that, and the work went quicker. It reminded Angela of a heartbeat: quick but steady. When she thought of a heartbeat, she immediately thought of Speranza's heart condition.

"Do you have your digitalis with you?" asked Angela.

"No, I take it in the morning," Speranza said.

"You can stay if you promise to go home first thing in the morning and take it."

"Oh, no, no," said Paolina. "I can bring it over first thing tomorrow morning. That way I can start cleaning this room." She wiped her nose.

"Paolina, I do not need you to clean my house," said Angela, exasperated. "Please sit down and I will make some coffee."

"Angela, I'm fine," said Speranza. "I've never felt better. I promise tomorrow I'll go right home and take my medicine. It's still sunny outside. I'll bring Franco out on the porch." She backed Franco up and wheeled him toward the porch.

"Go slowly," Angela called after her. "Be careful not to strain yourself." Her voice softened and trailed off as she watched her sister-in-law walk down the hall. Speranza had not gained much weight, and Angela felt she was slowing fading away. Each day, Angela saw less and less of Speranza's form. Her energy level had improved, but her physical body was so light that a wisp of wind could knock her over.

"Angela', I can go make the coffee if you want," said Paolina.

"Uh? Oh, I am sorry, Paolina. I will make it. The last time you made coffee, it went all over the place."

"Your coffee machine was not working right. Besides, I am used to a certain espresso maker that has…"

"All right, all right," said Angela. "Forget it. Let's go into the kitchen and sit."

Paolina followed Angela into the kitchen. Angela wondered how long she would stay and be a pest.

~ ~ ~ ~ ~

Angela rolled down the bedspread, folded it, and placed it at the end of the bed. This was the time of day she hated. It was not helping Franco into bed that was terrible, but sleeping next to him. It was like sleeping next to a corpse. When she touched his paralyzed side at night, his cold skin woke her up. She would lean over to make sure he was breathing. He never moved from sleeping on his back.

Sometimes during the day, Franco would recognize her. Over the summer, he had begun to walk with a walker—but the summer was now over, and he would be indoors must of the day. She would have to get through the winter living with a stranger. All her life she had searched for connection, and now her own husband had become remote to her—as the English language had once been.

The phone rang. Angela put on her bathrobe and went out to the hallway to answer it.

"Hello?"

"Angela, Speranza is sick," said a shaken voice. "Please come over."

"Salvatore, what happened?"

"Angela, come over," said Paolina for her brother and hung up.

Speranza had a relapse! But she had been so healthy these past few months! She had to go.

"Franco, Speranza is sick and I have to go," said Angela. She put her coat over her nightclothes. I will be back as soon as I can."

"Uhhhhhh." He reached out to her.

"I cannot help it. You do not understand. Your sister is sick." She helped him into bed, grabbed the house keys, and rushed out the front door. As she hurried up the street, she told herself it was probably one of Paolina's false alarms. She always blew everything out of proportion. Angela ran toward Speranza's house. The front door was open.

"Paolina, Salvatore. I am here."

A priest came out of the bedroom. She heard whimpering.

"Where is the doctor?" asked Angela.

"I am sorry to say that Speranza has passed away," said the priest. "She went peacefully. The doctor is with her."

Angela rushed past the priest into the bedroom. This was enough punishment for several lifetimes. She thought about when she first came to this country. It was all so different then: the possibilities were endless. It had been a new beginning. She could not imagine this was happening.

The doctor closed his black bag and approached Angela.

"I am so sorry, but there was nothing that could be done," said the doctor. "She passed while sleeping."

"Thank you, Doctor," said Angela, looking passed him.

Paolina was kneeling next to Speranza's bed murmuring the rosary. Salvatore sat on the bed and stared at the body. Angela put her hand on Salvatore's shoulder. She looked at Speranza's hands and face. They still seemed alive to Angela. Her energy was still there.

"You sit here," said Salvatore. He motioned for Angela to take his place and wiped the tears that streamed down his face.

"No, Salvatore. Stay where you are."

"I am going to check on the kids," said Salvatore. "They are with a next-door neighbor." Angela put her arms around Salvatore as he wept. "You have been kind to us." He turned and dragged his foot across the room.

Angela sat on the bed. Speranza's body felt heavy and dense. For the past few years, she had appeared translucent and light.

"Hail Mary, full of grace," mumbled Paolina.

Angela had thought about kneeling and praying with Paolina, but she refused to be on her knees in the sight of death. She did not mind being in the presence of death, but she would not kneel in fear.

"The Lord is with thee," said Angela. She stayed seated next to Speranza while she and Paolina recited the prayer together.

~ ~ ~ ~ ~

Angela wrapped the black scarf around Franco's neck. Today they would bury Speranza. She told him about his sister's death over and over again, but she was still not sure if he understood; at the wake, he just sat there and looked confused. Over the past few days, Franco would look at Angela as if to ask about his sister—but she couldn't be sure.

"Franco," said Angela, "let's go out on the porch and wait for the hearse to take us to the funeral parlor." She wheeled him out on the porch into the light of a sparkling early fall day. It was one of those mornings that God created for all the hopeful people so they would feel his presence.

The hearse pulled up, and the funeral director got out to help Franco and Angela into the car. She thought of Speranza as the child she had met eighteen years ago. Angela felt she had found something nearly indestructible; a child so full of life that she would forever stay that way. When Angela learned that she would never bear a child, there was Speranza to love. Life now will be different, she thought. It will be hollow. She felt she had nothing to fill up that hollow space. Franco could not console her; he lived in some remote part of his mind accessed only by himself.

The hearse stopped in front of the funeral parlor. The priest who would say mass was in the front car. The long ritual that led to the burial had begun.

~ ~ ~ ~ ~

Angela wheeled Franco across the graveyard to the head of Speranza's coffin. His mind faded in and out, and he could not focus on what was happening. People sobbed and grieved over the solid box in front of him. It was so unbearably sad for some people to look at the box that they turned their faces away in fear and dejection.

The priest made the sign of the cross and ended the ceremony. The crowd began to depart. Franco saw a man with a great limp bend down and kiss the box. Salvatore. The man who wanted to marry his sister is here. He did not want him to marry his sister because he had no trade and could not make good money. But, oh yes—they did marry, he remembered. Angela would not like that.

Franco looked around. Where was Speranza? Two men pulled him away as the coffin descended into the open grave.

Franco remembered Speranza in the funeral parlor now. He had seen her lifeless body laid out for viewing. He stood up from his wheel chair. Angela held his arm. She motioned for someone else to take his other arm. They stepped to the edge of the grave, and Franco peered downward. Now the earth claimed his sister. The gape in the land reminded him of Angela and the earthquake. He turned and recognized his wife. He could tell that she knew he had recognized her.

"Franco," said Angela. Her face drenched with tears. "Franco, Speranza has died, and I do not know what to do."

"All right...all right," said Franco as they leaned on one another. The casket stopped at the bottom, and they slowly moved away from the gravesite so the space in the earth could be filled in.

~ ~ ~ ~ ~

Angela went through the motions of everyday life. She helped Franco dress in the morning, made breakfast, and made dresses for her clients. In the evening, she stopped at Paolina's and visited Speranza's children. She would then come home and make supper. Franco was slightly better now and walking with a cane, but he still could not speak in long sentences.

She did not have the heart to celebrate the holidays this year. She and Franco went to Paolina's on Christmas Day to eat and watch the children open their presents.

It was 1931. The years had passed quickly since she came to America. She feared the darkness of the impending winter without Speranza. The feeling was similar to the dark energy between the buildings in Messina; one could only stay away from the spaces between the buildings, but the darkness in the mind was a different matter.

~ ~ ~ ~ ~

On New Year's Eve Day, Angela decided to clean out Speranza's clothes closets. She did not think she could ever do such a task, but the time had come. Reluctantly, Angela put on her coat and scarf. She kissed Franco on the forehead.

"I am going over to see the children."

Franco stared ahead with an unlit cigar in his mouth. He pointed to the cigar for a light.

"After supper, Franco. You know you are not to smoke between meals."

She saw him blow imaginary smoke rings into the air as she left the room.

~ ~ ~ ~ ~

Angela walked up the street and into the hallway of the two-family house. She could hear the children's laughter coming from upstairs. Slowly she opened the door to Speranza and Salvatore's apartment. She walked through the house and into the bedroom. The bed had been stripped, but nothing else had been touched since the night Speranza died. She went over to the bureau; even the brush still had Speranza's hair between the bristles. Salvatore and the children had been sleeping at Paolina's since Speranza's death.

Angela opened the closet door and began taking out Speranza's dresses. One by one, she laid them on the bed. Angela had made almost all of them for the different stages of Speranza's life. Seeing them all together was like a story of one woman's life. She had made the pink lace dress when Speranza was in her late teens and had been going to parties. The navy blue jumper she made for Speranza's first pregnancy. She always told Speranza a pregnant woman should wear dark colors.

Angela reached up and pulled a few boxes off the closet shelf. One was filled with jumpers and skirts she had made for Speranza when she was a little girl. Angela thought she had given them away long ago. Maybe Speranza was saving them for her daughter to wear, or maybe it was Speranza's road map back to the past—and happier times.

A red wool jumper caught Angela's eye. She took out the frilly white blouse she had made to go with the jumper and spread them out on the bed. She recalled how Speranza looked in them. Red had suited Speranza more than any other color. She picked up the white blouse and brought it to her nose; Speranza's scent was still on it.

"Angela, you are here," said Paolina. She entered the room. "I thought I heard someone. You are cleaning out the closets. Let me help you."

"I will do it, Paolina. I am sorry I have not been much help with the children, but now they can spend as much time as they want at my house." She folded the jumper and put it into a box.

To Angela, Paolina seemed like a child in an adult's skin and clothing. Her wide eyes had a vague look, as if she were constantly in a daze, asking, "When are we going to get there?"

"I have some good news," said Paolina. "Salvatore has been thinking of marrying again."

"Marrying again? Who would…" Angela caught herself disclosing what she thought; who would marry him with his affliction? And with three children?"

"Yes," said Paolina lifting her chest. "Salvatore and I have a sister in Sicily with a sixteen-year-old daughter who is ready to get married. I have written to my sister to ask her if the girl would like to marry Salvatore."

Angela was stunned. She knew that Paolina lacked common sense, but this was beyond anything common; it was against God. This woman was suggesting that Salvatore marry his own sister's daughter. No, she must have misunderstood.

"Paolina, are you telling me that you are encouraging Salvatore to marry his sister's daughter? His own niece? Was this your idea?"

"My brother needs a wife," said Paolina, straightening her blouse and looking down at her breasts. "He cannot raise three children by himself. And why should they be brought up by strangers? It is better to have someone in the family raise the children."

"Paolina, my sister-in-law has been dead for only a few months. How could Salvatore even think about remarrying? If anyone should raise the children, it should be me and you."

"I did not say he was leaving tomorrow. I only said that I have written to my sister about it."

"Does Salvatore know what you have written to your sister?" Salvatore and Paolina think alike, thought Angela. Why would I even ask such a question?

"Yes, of course. I would not have done it without his permission." Paolina put her arms behind her back, and her chest protruded. She looked like a defiant adolescent.

Angela thought of Speranza and the senselessness of her death. To Salvatore, she had just been someone to clean his house and wash his clothes.

Now that she was gone, he would get someone else to take care of his needs. Paolina knew that her brother needed a wife because a man could not remain single—especially one with children. Angela thought they probably told the young girl that Salvatore was rich in America. Thank God Franco will not understand when I tell him about Salvatore's plans, thought Angela.

"The marriage would be too close in relation," said Angela, "even you should know that." She quickly stuffed the rest of the clothes into the box. Salvatore was even more ignorant than she had thought. "Your sister will not allow her daughter to come to America and marry."

"Of course not. Salvatore will go there," Paolina said.

Angela picked up the box of clothes and walked past Paolina, brushing her arm.

"The children need a mother, you know," shouted Paolina. The door slammed.

Angela walked up the street, breathing heavily. It was against God's law for close family members to marry. If Paolina's sister were an attentive mother, she would never permit her daughter to marry Salvatore.

Angela looked up and saw the moon beginning to show its face. She feared the moon's energy now. It had drawn Speranza to marry into that family, and now it was if she never existed. If Salvatore did go to Sicily and marry his niece, Angela could never look at the moon again with love and awe. She would no longer see moonbeams as a gentle force; she would view them as life taking.

Angela unlocked the front door. She decided not to tell Franco about Paolina's plans until she knew the marriage would take place.

~ ~ ~ ~ ~

What Angela had feared and thought improbable occurred during the spring; Salvatore married his niece in Sicily less than a year after Speranza's death. Angela told herself that she was obligated to welcome Salvatore's new wife to their community and family. After all, Salvatore was Franco's brother-in-law, and in Sicilian tradition that still counted. The truth was, she wanted to keep an eye on Speranza's children—so she'd have to develop a relationship with the new wife.

Angela told Franco that Salvatore had married his niece, but she was not sure if he understood what she meant. When she told him, he waved his hand and limped out into the yard. Angela thought that he did not want to understand. There was no point in worrying about it, things were as they were. Salvatore had committed a great sin by marrying his niece. She wondered if he realized that.

~ ~ ~ ~ ~

Alicia stood in front of the mirror as Angela fitted a dress on her. "Stay still, Alicia."

"But it's been too long! I want to go out and play." She stamped her foot.

"Alicia, if you want me to fix this jumper, stand still. Your mother was never like this." Angela had promised herself she would never compare them, but she couldn't help herself.

Every time she mentioned Speranza, Angela was reminded of what she had lost. Salvatore and his new wife had returned from Sicily a few days ago, and today Angela was to meet his new wife. She would need to befriend this woman so that she would have easy access to the children.

Angela looked at Alicia's pouting face in the mirror. She was only eight years old, and Angela should not expect her to take Speranza's place.

"What about Mommy?" asked Alicia.

"I just remember how she stood still while I fitted..." In her mind, Angela saw Speranza turning this way and that in the mirror, admiring her form. It was a celebration when Angela fitted her a new dress. Alicia retreated from her own image, not wanting to look. Speranza had loved to observe herself—not in a conceited manner, but in a way that that was joyful and happy. Since Speranza's death, it was difficult for Angela to look in a mirror and not remember her sister-in-law.

"Get down from the stool, Alicia," Angela said. "We will take a break, and you can have milk and cookies."

"Oh goody, cookies," said Alicia. "I know where they are. I'll get them." She ran into the kitchen.

"Do not make a mess," Angela said, "and do not disturb your uncle."

Angela looked in the mirror and wished she could see Speranza's reflection just one more time. She felt inspired to create when she fitted her for a new dress. She never used a pattern for Speranza; it was far more interesting to make her own design. Angela dealt in the world of human form, and each person had a different body type. But now, when she made garments for people, it had become a labor—not a joy. Angela touched the corner of the mirror, where the oak frame met the glass, and found dirt build-up in the crevice. She brushed her hand across the glass and found her image clearer where her hand had touched. Angela knew the mirror was filthy, but she did not see the point of seeing clearly anymore. Angela felt that her clear vision was buried with Speranza.

~ ~ ~ ~ ~

Franco opened the cellar door to the kitchen and saw Alicia sitting at the table drinking a glass of milk. He wished Angela would not invite children to the house. They did not have the responsibility of children, so he did not see why they should cater to other people's offspring. He watched as Alicia crossed her legs at the ankles and swung her legs back and forth.

"Hi, Uncle Franco," said Alicia, as she took a bite of a cookie and looked up at him. "You finished working?"

This was Salvatore's child, and anything associated with his brother-in-law he did not want around him. Salvatore had killed his sister by having many children, so the children were also responsible for her death.

"Up," said Franco.

"Up where?" asked Alicia.

Why did children ask so many questions? thought Franco. He could not bear to look at her; she reminded him of all he had lost.

"Up, up," Franco shouted.

"Up where?" laughed Alicia. She spread her arms open in a questioning gesture.

Franco saw that the child thought it was a game. She wouldn't understand if he disciplined her. She tilted her head and looked up, Franco lifted his hand over her face. He remembered Jerry in casts, with his impish face and cropped brown hair. He remembered how sad he was that he could not adopt him, but how right it was that Jerry should have healthy, young parents. If he had adopted Jerry, is this how he would behave toward him?

"Franco, what are you doing?" asked Angela from the doorway. "Were you going to hit this child?"

His hand still hovered over Alicia. He brought it down quickly.

"No...no," Franco said. He patted her on her head.

"How could you? She has done nothing wrong. She is just enjoying cookies."

"He didn't do anything," Alicia said. "He was just looking at me funny."

"I saw what he was doing," said Angela, "and I am tired of being quiet. Franco, go down to the cellar and stay there! My life would be easier."

"Aunt Angela, please don't yell like that," said Alicia. She tugged at her arm. "I think Uncle Franco is confused."

"Alicia, go wash your hands. Your step-mother and Aunt Paolina will be here any minute."

Franco glared at his wife. He wanted to tell her to mind her own goddamn business.

Franco opened the cellar door, leaving it half open. He could feel his mind give way. The image of Jerry was squelched. The lucidity he had experienced for those few minutes floated away from him like driftwood. His emotions dissipated as he descended the stairs, and he was left with a vague recollection of the past half hour.

"You are a selfish man, Franco Bellini," Angela called. "You should be ashamed."

She slammed the cellar door shut.

~ ~ ~ ~ ~

"Angela!" called Paolina from the front door. "I have Immacolatta with me."

Paolina turned to her new sister-in-law. "You will find Angela to be a very nice woman, although she can be a bit stern at times. But we all have our faults. Just be nice to her." Paolina's pocketbook hung from her arm as she folded her hands over her stomach.

Immacolatta stood with one arm clasping the other, shifting her weight from leg to leg.

"Stand still," said Paolina. "Angela will think you are nervous about something. Be confident about your place. Angela! Angela, we are here!"

Immacolatta's new life in America had not turned out the way her mother had explained. There were no beautiful rugs in Salvatore's house. In fact, there was no house—just an apartment he rented from Paolina. Salvatore was not as handsome as her mother had described, and she was not told his limp was so pronounced.

"Immacolatta, this is Franco's wife, Angela Bellini. Her sister-in-law was Salvatore's first wife."

The two women silently kissed each other lightly on each cheek.

"Thank you for looking after Immacolatta for a few hours while I am shopping," Paolina said.

"I thought we would take a walk around St. Mary's School grounds," Angela said.

"Oh, that sounds so nice," said Paolina. "I will be back in a few hours. Immacolatta, Salvatore likes fish on Friday. He likes it cooked a certain way, so I will make dinner tonight."

"Is your husband here?" asked the girl.

"He is busy in the backyard," Angela said.

"Oh, I like meeting women's husbands," said Immacolatta. She took out a fan and fanned herself in short quick movements. "It makes me feel that I am not the only one married."

Immacolatta wondered what this woman's husband looked like. Was he strong and healthy and able to provide for his family? She assumed so when she looked around Angela's house: the furniture was polished, and there were figurines and framed pictures all around. She did not have a husband like Angela.

"I will take you up to St. Mary's, and from the hill you will be able to see all along the Hudson River." Angela closed the front door and locked it behind her.

~ ~ ~ ~ ~

The two women climbed the hill to St. Mary's. Angela had walked the hill many times before,, but it was always invigorating to reach the top. The winding driveway up to the main house was lined with wildflowers. Angela pulled her sweater around her chest as the wind blew.

"The weather must affect you," said Angela, "Sicily is so warm."

"Not really. It is just damper here. Sometimes it can get very cold at night in Sicily."

"Yes, that is true," said Angela. Angela was uncomfortable making conversation with this young girl. She wanted to know what was happening in Sicily because there was talk of a war. Roberto had never responded to the letter she had sent, and she worried.

"Immacolatta, how is the situation in Sicily? Do people come and go as they please?"

"Come and go? Sure they do. Why do you ask that?"

"Because there is talk of war, and Mussolini has a bad reputation."

"Mussolini?" responded Immacolatta, her blue eyes brightening. "My mother says he is a wonderful man. She says he is just what Italy needs. A strong father to pull us through hard times. There are people who speak out against him, but they are punished."

Angela wondered if Roberto had become one of the punished. Now Roberto had abandoned her too. And if he were no longer available to her and Franco, what family did they have left?

"Here is the main house," said Angela. "If you go over to the patio, you can see along the Hudson River."

Immacolatta looked out over the river and shrugged her shoulders.

"This is not like our sea at home," said the girl, pouting. "At home, the water is truly blue. Here it is an ugly green. It is not beautiful."

"Sometimes you have to look a little deeper to see the beauty in something," said Angela sternly. She sensed that Immacolatta thought everything in America would be perfect and beautiful, but at the same time expected it to look and feel like home. She deserves to be disappointed, thought Angela. True, the girl was only sixteen—but she was certainly old enough to know better than to marry her own uncle. Someone had to be blamed for such a match. Angela felt that everyone was playing innocent.

She felt that she was the only one who viewed this marriage as unholy.

"I thought Salvatore would be more beautiful," blurted Immacolatta. "My father said he was handsome. And I am surprised about where we live. I thought it would be bigger."

"Oh?" said Angela, hoping Immacolatta would reveal more.

"Yes. My mother told me America was a rich place."

"She did not tell you about Salvatore's situation?"

"Well, not the way it is," Immacolatta said. "I knew he had three children, but I have taken care of children before. My mother said nothing about Salvatore's leg, or where he lived."

She waited for Angela to say something, but there was silence. She continued, "When I first met Salvatore, I thought there was some mistake—but soon I learned there was no error made. I cried to my mother, but she said that I would lead a privileged life in America. But that is not true, either."

Angela thought that Paolina's manipulations had gone too far. No one existed in her world but her brother, and he was a puppet. She had obviously told lies to her own sister about Salvatore's living situation and prospects for the future so that Immacolatta would agree to marry him.

Angela looked at the young girl; for a moment, she saw herself. Not that Angela was ever led to believe that Franco was rich before they were married, or that even life would be beautiful, but she had also been young in a strange country with only her husband to talk to.

"Mama also said that Aunt Paolina would be like a mother to me. But I do not think she wants to be." Immacolatta could sense Angela's annoyance. "I hope I have not made you angry. You have been so kind to me."

"No, I am not angry, just surprised that no one told you about Salvatore." Angela softened a little, seeing the disappointment in the girl's eyes.

~ ~ ~ ~ ~

Angela was next in line for confessional. Father Barbarino took a long time with people confessing sins, but he asked the right questions and gave the right answers. When Angela had arrived in this country, Father Barbarino had heard her first confession because he spoke Italian.

"Bless me, Father, for I have sinned," said Angela, making the sign of the cross. "I have sinned, Father, and it has come out of an even greater sin."

"What is it?" asked the priest. Angela saw a dark figure lean toward the screen that separated them. "What is the greater sin?" The priest bowed his head and put his ear to the screen.

"Father, you know my sister-in-law died less than a year ago, and Salvatore, her husband, has remarried."

"This is not a sin."

"No, Father, but he went to Sicily and married his...his sister's sixteen-year-old daughter." The impact of Angela's words in the small space of the confessional box reverberated to the core of her being. The priest was silent. Angela waited within the silence for a response. Then Father Barbarino stirred.

"Does the couple see that they have committed a sin?"

"No, Father, not that I know of. It is a sin against God and the church. They should atone for it."

"In the theology of the Catholic Church, a sin is committed only if the sinner knows that the act is a sin but does it anyway."

"But, Father, his sister's daughter," said Angela.

"No one can repent but the sinner. If they do not see themselves as sinners, then I cannot give penance for a sin that is not acknowledged. You cannot receive penance and forgiveness for them. Is there a sin you want to confess? I can forgive your sins."

"Father, if they came to you to ask God's forgiveness for their sin, would you forgive them?"

"If they were heartily sorry, then God would forgive them. Christ often said that if you are sincerely sorry, no matter the sin, it is forgiven. I only give the appropriate penance."

"It is unnatural to marry so close." Angela wanted the priest to say that their souls would burn in hell for all eternity and that there would not be forgiveness. Immacolatta was not guilty because she was so young, but Paolina was another matter. She was a meddling, selfish woman.

"It is not for us to say," said the priest. "You can only find comfort by forgiving yourself."

Even the church was unfair. There was no justice to be found. Salvatore and Paolina walked around as if Speranza had never existed. He married his niece as if they had a perfect right to be together. Angela felt she would never have peace. Maybe Franco had been right to doubt God and the church.

"What was the sin you wanted absolution from?" Father Barbarino asked.

"After listening to you, Father, I no longer feel it was a sin."

"Go in peace." The priest raised his hand to bless Angela, but she got up and left before he had finished.

~ ~ ~ ~ ~

Angela walked briskly away from the church. She tried to let go of her unrest, but it came back stronger every time she tried. Apparently it did not matter to God that this marriage had taken place. If it was of no consequence to God, then she decided that it should matter even less to her—but she would not accept that Speranza's name was hardly spoken. She would keep talking to the children about their mother so they would not forget.

In the distance, Angela saw a small, round figure that seemed to float toward her. As the figure drew closer, Angela could tell it was Paolina. Of course, thought Angela, who else would walk as if her feet never touched the ground? Paolina always looked as if she were going to a tea party. Angela remembered Paolina at Speranza's funeral: black dress, floral pocketbook, and a pink lace neckerchief.

"Good afternoon, Angela," Paolina said, resting her arms on her abdomen. "Where are you coming from?"

"I have come from confession, if you must know." She stared Paolina in the eyes. She had resolved not to lie.

"Someone like you would have very little to confess. You are a good woman. Everyone says so."

Angela felt her face become as fixed as cement. It was you who brought me to confession, thought Angela. I was confessing your sin.

"No, but you have plenty to confess. I told Father Barbarino about your hand in Salvatore's marriage."

"Why would you tell that in confession?" Paolina asked, her eyes blinking.

Angela could see that she did not understand. All that mattered to her was that Salvatore had a wife and that she had a sister-in-law who would not give her any trouble.

"Because they are blood relatives! It is a sin against God and against the Catholic Church. Sometimes I think you pretend to be as stupid as you are!"

Paolina adjusted the pink sweater that hung around her shoulders.

"I am sure I do not have to remind you that they were married by a Catholic priest in Sicily—so, you see, you are wrong. If it were against church law, they would not have been married. The church approved it, so God approves."

There was no law and order in Sicily, and anything was possible for a price; which included the church. Angela experienced this at the convent when the Reverend Mother wanted Franco to buy the linens produced by the girls.

"You made this match like you matched Speranza with Salvatore. She should never have married him! She is in her grave because of him. It was all his fault."

Paolina did not cower the way Angela had expected. If Salvatore and Immacolatta were married by the church, then Paolina's position was valid.

"You can believe what you want, Angela, but there is nothing that can change what has happened. You can go to confession and confess every day, but that will not change anything."

"You and my mother-in-law encouraged Speranza to marry Salvatore. That is why she married him. I do not believe she wanted to."

Nothing can change the past, thought Angela. She knew that if she continued to blame others for certain misfortunes, then it would only weigh on her. No one forced Speranza to marry Salvatore. Every time she thought of

Speranza, she felt angry, and the anger took the pleasure out of her memory. She wished she could pretend Speranza had never existed, like everyone else.

Paolina turned and headed downtown. Angela thought about calling after her but realized there was nothing more to say. Words were never going to change anything. When she thought of Speranza there was a void. She tried to hang onto any feeling she could muster around her sister-in-law, even if it was anger, resentment or unanswerable questions. Anything was better than nothing, and now it seemed she was left with nothing.

When Angela reached her house, she brought the full-length mirror outside and rested it against the side of the house. She turned on the garden hose and let the water flow down the glass. The mirror had not been cleaned in months, and she disliked using cleaners to do the job. Flowing water made mirrors sparkle. When it was clean, colors reflected in it were more vivid than real life. Whenever a customer came for a fitting, the dress seemed more vibrant reflected in her mirror.

Franco sat in the yard chair with his cane next to him. Angela had been in a dark mood since the day at St. Mary's Convent, and she was still was not sure if Franco understood that Salvatore had married his niece. If only she could talk to him about it. No, it was no use. He just sat there, sometimes in his body, sometimes not.

"Alicia is coming today," Angela said to Franco. "I am going to fit her into some of Speranza's dresses." She waited for a response. "It seemed a shame to throw away her clothes when they could be altered to fit her daughter."

Some of her words seemed to hang on the trees; others dissipated in the warm air. There was no one there to listen. She picked up a rag and began to wipe the mirror. She looked into the eyes of her reflection. All the years she had spent in front of this mirror fitting women for dresses, she had never really observed herself. She was sure she appeared older, but she could not swear to it because she had never looked at her face for any length of time. Even the few photographs she had of herself were taken too far away to see her face.

Angela hoped that with Alicia coming for a fitting, some of the old, tender feelings about Speranza would return. Lately, she felt that she only had a vague memory of her sister-in-law. Franco did not want to be reminded of his sister or of not having children—but what he wanted was not important to her now.

Angela went into the house to get another cloth for the mirror, and on her way in she heard the mailbox open and close with a squeak. Angela reminded herself to oil the mailbox as she went out to retrieve the mail.

"The mail has come," said Angela, putting the envelopes on the arm of Franco's chair.

~ ~ ~ ~ ~

Franco had learned to say a few words, but most of the time, he did not know what words were coming out of his mouth. When he did speak, it frustrated him and other people—so he said little. There was more silence in the house now.

He watched Angela as she washed the mirror. She paid more attention to the mirror than she did to him. He picked up his cane and slammed it on the arm of the chair next to him. The envelopes fell to the ground.

"What are you doing now! I cannot do anything around here without you making a fuss. I am sick of it." Angela yelled.

Franco leaned over and picked up the mail. One of the envelopes had a familiar name on the return address: Roberto Mineo. He knew the name was important to him, but could not remember why. He held the envelope up to Angela.

"What?" she asked as she walked over. She perused the envelope. The return address was from Paris. "Roberto! Franco, it is from your cousin, Roberto. I did not see it when I got the mail. I will read it."

"No, no, no," said Franco. He did not want to hear from anyone—even if he was a relative.

"Franco, it is from your cousin, the poet." She pointed to the name over the return address. "Roberto, your cousin."

He slapped the letter out of Angela's hand.

"Get out! Away!" yelled Franco. He raised his cane toward Angela. She grabbed the letter and ran inside the house. Who was she to tell him what he should listen to? And who was Roberto Mineo? Someone who lived in a world he had left long ago. He did not want that old world forced on him.

Franco picked up the small pillow at his side and placed it at the back of his neck. He pushed his cap over his eyes to shield himself from the sun's rays. There was no one there to bother him now. He could rest and be with himself. Franco shut his eyes and began to visualize people and places. He liked doing that when he was left on his own. His mind drifted from one landscape to another. He heard the birds singing in the background, but they gradually faded away. When he no longer heard the sounds from the outside world, Franco knew that he had entered deeply into himself. At these times he felt completely at peace.

Franco saw himself standing in the hallway of his house when the doorbell rang. He opened the inner door, stepped into the vestibule, and opened the outer door. There was no one on the porch.

"Franco, Franco. Here I am," said a woman's voice.

"Who is here?" Franco asked. There was still no one on the porch. He loved to hear his voice. It had not deserted him, but he could only hear it when he was inside himself. He went to close the front door when he saw a shadow of someone standing behind the door. As the door closed, Franco saw a woman standing in her wedding gown.

"I am here," said the young woman.

"Why are you standing here, in my house?"

"Franco, you have forgotten me. I feel so bad. How could you have neglected me?"

Franco looked at the young woman and thought that she did look familiar. Images of a young woman as a girl stepped out of her form. He saw her standing in front of a mirror, and Angela pinning a dress on her. Then the image changed, and he saw her sitting on his lap giggling as he blew smoke in her face. Was it his daughter, his child? Flashes of the girl growing up flooded his mind. He knew her now.

"Speranza, Speranza, I would never ignore you. I love you. I have always loved you. You are my sister."

"Why did Salvatore go off and marry his niece? I do not understand how that happened. How could you and Angela allow it?" asked Speranza.

Franco did not pay much attention to what happened to Salvatore or anyone else. He only wanted to be with himself, and now he was embarrassed.

"Angela has been very upset about it. I cannot look straight at anything anymore. Angela takes care of everything. You know she always took care of everything. I have not been well these past few months."

Franco felt his awareness broaden and the events of the past year became clear. He saw himself laying face down in the garden and being fed by Speranza in his hospital bed. Then Speranza's death and how he did not—no, how he refused to—understand when Angela, sobbing, explained it to him. And then the day when Angela had told him that Salvatore was to marry his own niece. He pretended not to understand that too. It was too painful. He knew that Angela would be very angry and grieve for both of them. There was no need for him to do anything for himself, not even feel his own emotions.

He watched as Speranza's form turned into Angela, but she still wore the wedding dress. She looked so youthful. He had forgotten how she had appeared to him years ago.

"Why did he marry his niece, Franco? I made Speranza such a beautiful gown. Look." Angela pointed to the waist on her dress. The material began to glow. His sister reappeared while a circle of white light began to grow and engulf her entire body. He shielded his eyes with his hand. When he removed his hand the little boy from the hospital was standing in front of him. Jerry.

"Hi, Frank," said Jerry. He tipped his baseball cap off his face.

"You are in a baseball uniform," said Franco. "You can play baseball?"

"I sure can. I carry the ring you gave me for good luck." Jerry reached into his pocket and showed Franco the ring.

"It is very shiny," said Franco.

"I polish it often," said Jerry. He rubbed it against his uniform.

"It is so good to see you," said Franco.

"I wanted to show you how well I am doing. You helped me a lot."

"No, I did not do enough. I should have kept up with you."

"You did what you were supposed to do," said Jerry. He put his hand behind his back and pitched a baseball to Franco. Franco threw it back, but Jerry had vanished and the ball disintegrated in midair.

Franco opened his eyes. He did not know how long he had been asleep. The sun was in the same position, so it was possible it had only been for a few minutes. Roberto. He remembered the letter from his cousin and how he had treated Angela. Franco grabbed his cane and went into the house.

He found Angela sitting in his smoking chair with the open letter in her lap. How could he make her understand that he was sorry for his behavior and that he wanted to hear from Roberto? She looked up at him and wiped her eyes.

Franco nodded his head as he pointed toward the letter. He felt he could understand now. Even if he could not comprehend all the words, the emotional content of a sentence was something that he could now translate.

"You want me to read this?" Angela asked, holding up the letter. He shook his head again.

"Sit here," said Angela. She began to get up.

"No, no. Sit." Franco said. He sat in a dining room chair.

Angela adjusted the overhead lamp and began to read, her voice trembling.

Dear Franco and Angela,

> *I am sorry that it has taken me so long to respond to your letter, but as you can tell from the return address I am no longer in Sicily. My reasons for leaving are, I am sure, obvious to you.*
>
> *It has distressed me greatly to hear about Franco, therefore I will write this letter as if he were recovering. Franco, I know that you are not someone who will just let your life slip away. All the help I can give is to tell you that every day I will think of you as alive and in the best of health. I will imagine you as I remember you on your trip to Sicily, standing on my veranda looking out over the sea. I will see you chatting with the old monk at the marketplace. I will think of you often this way. I send all the energy of my spirit to you to speed your recovery.*

Franco remembered the old monk; his zest and playfulness. He smiled. It seemed like a century ago now. He had felt so out in the world then. Now he cared little for the outside world, even though he was still alive. He thought of Speranza and how she told him he had ignored her. He had turned his face away from the world to protect himself, but he had hurt the people he wanted to keep safe. Angela continued to read.

> *Angela, these are the only words I can offer Franco. But to you I can say more. If you want to pray to God, by all means pray, but you must find your own strength and build on it. Any encouragement I can give will only have a temporary effect if you do not look to yourself. Whatever you found of your sister in Sicily, I am glad I was of assistance but that you took the journey yourself. I am sure you will proceed on your path with courage and persistence.*
>
> *I could tell that you had a certain light in your eyes. That kind of light is enviable, because it sees everything and can teach you much. It is something that men usually do without in a world of war, unemployment and social upheaval. Men do not develop such a light, and I believe it is the cause of much discomfort. And so, I can only tell you now to look to the light for guidance. It is your own, and it cannot mislead you.*

Affectionately Forever,
Roberto

Angela took off her glasses and let the letter fall to the floor. She put her head back against the chair. Franco thought about the light. He tried to find it, but he was walking in the dark for many years. Speranza showed him the light when she was alive. Angela had light. He had been attracted to it when he was a young man and met her in the convent.

Franco reached for his cane and tried to get up.

"Let me help you," said Angela.

His first reaction was to push her away, because she was treating him like a child again. Instead, he looked into her eyes and saw what Roberto meant: he saw Speranza and his mother. He put down his cane and rested his arm on Angela's waist. Franco leaned on his wife as they went out to the backyard.

~ ~ ~ ~ ~

Angela thought about Roberto's letter as she wiped the mirror and stood back to see if the glass was clean. She only had herself to rely on for comfort. When she thought of Speranza, she felt her sister's presence. To Angela, they were the same person. As long as she had Speranza, her sister was alive. They were both with her in her memory.

God created the world so that nothing was lost, thought Angela. The void she had felt since Speranza's death began to fill with understanding. Why had she always felt a loss if she had actually lost nothing? She thought about the paintings she had seen in Rome. They were centuries old, and they were never really lost. If objects could become present again, then people, who had souls, would certainly always be in the world. They would be part of the unseen world, like her unseen friends.

Angela saw Franco's reflection in the mirror. He sat in the chair with his head bowed. She felt he understood everything now, and she watched his chest rise and fall in the backdrop of the setting sun. The image of the painting in Rome of the setting sun and rising moon beside one another formed in Angela's mind. She remembered when she cursed the moon for bringing Salvatore and Speranza together and when Paolina told her that Salvatore was to marry his niece. She thought she could never enjoy the moon again. She watched in the mirror as the moon greeted the sun.

Slowly, the moon's face peeked out from behind a cloud as the sun changed from blazing red to a soft rose. The moon became more defined until both the sun and moon's energy were equal in the sky.

Angela looked back at Franco. Their eyes met, and at that moment she understood that nothing was lost.

About the Author

Carmela Cattuti started her writing career as a writer for the *Somerville News* in Boston, MA. She is a writer, painter, and yoga instructor in Boston, MA. After she finished her graduate work in English Literature at Boston College she began to write creatively. She was inspired by her great-aunt's experience of the eruption of MT. Etna in Messina Sicily in 1908. Carmela created *Between the Cracks* as a homage to her great-aunt. As she wrote *Between the Cracks*, she realized she could not convey her great-aunt's story in one book, so it became a trilogy. Her second novel, *The Ascent,* continues the story and we experience Angela's intimate experience with America. Carmela is currently writing the third book, *Transformation*.

To connect with Carmela, email her at cattutic@gmail.com or leave a comment at www.ccattuticreative.com/carmela-cattuti-books.

CPSIA information can be obtained
at www.ICGtesting.com
Printed in the USA
FSHW010703150321
79471FS

9 781595 982391